D0042036

SUN KEEP RISING

ALSO BY KRISTEN R. LEE

Required Reading for the Disenfranchised Freshman

KRISTEN R. LEE

SUN KEEP RISING

CROWN
NEW YORK

Text copyright © 2023 by Kristen R. Lee
Jacket art copyright © 2023 by Chisom Jacinta Mbewu

Visit us on the Web! GetUnderlined.com

Educators and librarians, for a variety of teaching tools, visit us at RHTeachersLibrarians.com

Library of Congress Cataloging-in-Publication Data is available upon request.
ISBN 978-0-593-30919-3 (hardcover) — ISBN 978-0-593-30920-9 (library binding) — ISBN 978-0-593-30921-6 (ebook)

The text of this book is set in 11.4-point Adobe Garamond Pro.
Interior design by Cathy Bobak

Printed in the United States of America
10 9 8 7 6 5 4 3 2 1
First Edition

Random House Children's Books supports the First Amendment and celebrates the right to read.

To my mama

If something isn't done, and done in a hurry, to bring the colored peoples of the world out of their long years of poverty, their long years of hurt and neglect, the whole world is doomed.

—Dr. Martin Luther King, Jr.

PART 1

CHAPTER 1

IT CAN'T HAPPEN *the first time.*

Don't believe that shit. That's why I got this baby in one hand while I'm trying to help hang up my high school graduation decorations with the other.

The banner hangs above the kitchen entryway. The missing *S* ain't noticeable to my country-ass family. My house is packed with aunties, cousins, and longtime neighbors. This many people didn't even show up to my baby shower. That's to be expected, though.

Babies common around here. College ain't.

To be honest, college hadn't ever been on my radar. Not until my girl Savannah got into the top school in the country, a whole year early at that. Then everyone began looking at me. If I was her right hand, that meant I could do it too, right? Wrong. High school ain't the same as college—everyone knows that. At my high school you can pass a class just by being quiet and pretending that you want to learn. That wasn't me, though. Being smart is my thing. I can play ball, too, but not good enough for an athletic scholarship. Nah, I have to use my brain. That's why people are always shocked whenever I get in trouble.

I heard these two lines my whole nine months with Mia:

You're too smart for that.

Too talented for that.

So, in order to please everyone, I worked my ass off my senior year. Big belly and all. I had to prove that Mia wasn't going to keep me behind. That I wasn't only a dummy that got pregnant.

Proved all they asses wrong, too. Worked hard and got into three whole universities.

But this ain't my dream. Can you believe that? All the hard work and I don't want to go to nan four-year college. On the real: my dream is to do hair in a shop, not just in my older sister Shana's kitchen when she isn't home. I've always been good at hair. Clipping my own ends turned into chopping my hair into bobs at seven and dyeing it bright yellow at twelve. I like making folks into different people. The only escape you can get around here. Having a salon would be dope. A real business. Something that's in my name that folks can't snatch from underneath me. That may never happen, though; a shop cost too much. Especially now, with folks moving to the neighborhood like they are missing something. Three years ago, you couldn't pay folks to come over here when the sun went down; now they bounce around like they own the place.

I haven't told my family that yet, though. That in September when everyone else is having trunk parties I won't be participating. I've already put one burden on their back in the form of this baby that's sleeping on my chest, and a few more months of lying won't hurt nobody.

My college acceptance letter to Hilbert University is blown up and placed on the one free wall in the house. Uncle and aunties laugh and curse each other all while screaming at the basketball game on our twenty-four-inch TV. Uncle LoLo is always talking about how he's going to get us a bigger one, but that'll be when hell freezes over.

"Give me that pretty baby." Auntie Nora holds out her hands for Mia, who's scrunched up in my arms. She can sleep through anything. You get used to the noises. The sounds of gunfire and car bass. Babies crying and mamas fussing.

"She's sleeping, TeTe." I pat Mia's back in quick hits. A technique that Shana taught me. She has kids too—but she only has custody of my niece Cyn—and we all live in this two-bedroom duplex. It's crowded, dusty, needs a repainting and an exterminator, but it's still one of the better ones on our dead-end street. We could live in the building next door, where people run in and out all day long doing every and any thing.

Shit about to change around here, though. I can feel it. The fancy people have a name for it: *gentrification.* A big word for a short process. White people come and push all the Black folks out. When you see a coffee shop pop up and a damn dog park, it's over with.

The dog park two blocks up will be finished next week.

Cops hound us every fucking day now. It used to be they only drove through Ridgecrest like they were keeping an eye on us. We are the last block in this neighborhood with a project still standing, and they are doing everything to make sure we know we ain't wanted no more. Now the police sit, waiting for us to leave one by one. If not by force, then by death. Our next-door neighbor, Miss Margaret, got bamboozled a few months back. White folk with monogrammed cuff links went inside her crib and came out with the deed to it. Now it's for sale, almost triple what she paid for it.

Once I start making some money, things will be different. I'ma move us out of this house somehow. Another reason I don't want to go to college. It takes too long. Four years from now I don't even wanna think of where we'd be. Probably bouncing from couch to couch or something. Shana doesn't say it, but feeding four people on one income got to be some form of magic. Sometimes she takes herself out of the equation. Skipping her serving of sugar rice for dinner just so we'll have more.

When I get my shop in a year or so (Savannah says I got to manifest), we won't have to worry about having our house snatched from us, 'cause we're gonna own it. Period. One day Mia is gonna have a house that she can pass along to her children. Them to theirs. I need to leave her with something. More than what my mama left me with. The only thing of value I have right now is Grandma's diamond necklace. One day that'll be Mia's, but you can't eat diamonds. Not unless I pawn it, which I'll never do.

I have to get there first. To being my own boss. Even though I technically graduated, I still have one class to finish during summer school. Mia came two months early. Guess my body couldn't take it anymore. Most teachers gave me a pass. They knew I could do the work, everyone except Mrs. Crenshaw. She made my life hell the entire pregnancy. "I'm pushing you to greatness," she'd say. "They won't coddle you in college."

That's why when I asked for an extension, she declined. I said fuck it and ended up with an F and a packet to summer school.

Being pregnant during senior year was a hot-ass mess. I missed everything. Homecoming, football games, and prom. Barely got to graduation, but I wasn't missing that. Hearing my family cheer me on was the highlight of my life.

Auntie Nora is still trying to get her hands on Mia, but I ain't letting her out of my arms. "If you never put her down, she's going to have a hard time later in life. You have to let other people take care of her."

It's funny that now they want to take care of her. When she was in my stomach, folks acted as if it was the end of the world.

The sun kept rising when my mama had my sister at fifteen. When my sister had my niece at sixteen, and when I had Mia three months after my seventeenth birthday.

"You're on your way, honey." Uncle LoLo slides a balled-up five-dollar bill into my hand. Old people act as if every money transaction is a drug deal. "What you majoring in?" he asks. "You know, I almost finished college. Had a semester left. Don't know why I never did."

Auntie Nora reminds him. "'Cause you dropped out like a fool. Thinking you were going to be a damn musician."

"I could have been. If Mama ain't hold me back."

Auntie Nora sucks her teeth. "Ask me, she did you a favor."

They still argue like me and Shana do, even at their big age.

"We don't have to declare until junior year, but I'm thinking about accounting."

That ain't a lie. Well, kinda. I don't want to be a boring accountant, but counting money is easy enough. Been doing it my whole life. I've been worried about money my whole life. Something we never seemed to have enough of, but somehow we got by.

I'm tired of only getting by, though. I want to thrive. One day I want to walk into the store and buy Mia a gift even if it isn't her birthday.

"Our baby gone be rich." Uncle LoLo, and everyone, cheers.

"Come on and eat, y'all." Shana doesn't have to shout too loud. Everyone rushes to the kitchen. "Don't be greedy, now. B'onca eats first since it's her party. Y'all act like y'all have no home training."

I squeeze through bodies and damn near feel like a celebrity. Everyone pats me on the shoulder and pinches Mia's cheek. They congratulate me and slide money into my hand on the low. I cradle Mia in one arm and fix my plate of catfish, spaghetti, and white bread.

Auntie Nora probably right. Mia might have issues being

apart from me, but having her close makes me feel safe. I know it's supposed to be the other way around, but to be honest, I think I need her more than she needs me.

Shana finally pries her from my arms. "I'm taking her upstairs. She doesn't need to be around all these people, no way."

"Put the baby-monitor camera on." A splurge that Shana said I didn't need, but Mia deserves the best of everything. I can't afford it all right now, but what I can, I get. Especially if it makes my baby's life a little easier.

My older cousin Jasmine sits down next to me. She's bouncing her own baby girl on her knee. "You think you can do my baby hair for me? I can slide you a twenty."

"I can. Mia don't have a lot of hair yet, so the only thing I really do for her is slick it back."

"I still can't believe you got a baby, girl," Jasmine says.

"I can't either," I say. "I mean, she's here, but it's like she ain't mine sometimes. As if I'm babysitting, waiting for her real mama to come back and get her, 'cause it can't be me."

No matter how close you are to it, you never think it'll happen to you. You make excuses why it won't. Always thinking how the other people must have done something wrong.

Then, when it does, you don't even know what to do.

In our family, pregnancy is discovered through fish dreams, usually by the women over fifty. Those fishes never were of me. Always a third cousin, a mama, a sister.

Never me until that day at CVS.

I googled once: What else fish dreams can mean? Abundance, personal growth, and accomplishing goals. If grandmas around the way told you anything about that, maybe them fishes wouldn't turn to babies.

Jasmine lets down her daughter, and she teeters over to the other small cousins. "I get it. Don't judge me, but if I had a choice in the matter, I wouldn't have kept Jade. I mean, I love her *now*, but I had dreams too, you know. You are still going through with yours, and I admire that."

"I have those thoughts sometimes, but I never let them linger too long." I scoop up my last bite of catfish. "She's here, she's mine, and I have to take care of her."

When my mama was still around, she asked me if I wanted to keep Mia.

The question made me pause. I didn't think I had a choice. Every girl I see push their li'l strollers down the street, prop their baby on their hip at the courts, push them on the swings at the park. They have their babies and go on. No one talks about wants and needs. All I knew was that there was a baby growing inside me and I loved it already.

Not that I was only seventeen and a kid myself.

That babies eat all the fucking time, and I don't have a real job.

Those things didn't matter for the girls at the courts, my sister, or my ma, but they made it work, and if they could, I could.

We are one and the same.

Back then I didn't see welfare. Scrimping and saving for strollers. I didn't see food-stamp cards or WIC vouchers. Putting the $5.50 pack of meat back for the $5.30 just to have something extra. I didn't see the people who won't give me a seat on the bus even when I have Mia with me. Their eyes that say everything they mouth won't. A way of punishing me, I guess.

All I saw was Mia on the ultrasound and how I swore she had my nose even when she was only the size of an avocado. Then, when I started showing, parents had their kids scoot on past me like pregnancy a deadly disease. For Black women, it can be. Doctors don't take shit we say seriously, and when they do, it's too late. Being young and Black, my fight was even harder. Shana wasn't going for none of that, though. She'd tell them to "check again" when I complained about the swelling in my feet, which sure enough turned out to be something serious. If she hadn't been there to advocate for me, I don't know if Mia would be here—hell, I don't know if I would be here.

Shana brings out a long sheet cake. A picture of a diploma decorates the front. She even got some Black girl normally used for wedding toppers on the side.

"For my little sister. You know I tell you this almost every day, but I'm really proud of you. You've never let anyone tell you what you can or cannot do. Lord knows I tried. You're going to do great in college."

Just when Shana is about to slice the best corner piece, the doorbell rings.

"Whoever that is, is boo coo late," I say. "There probably isn't even any fish left."

"Probably Auntie Sherri—you know she is always on CP time," Shana says. "Cyn, get the door for me, baby."

Cyn bounces to the door with her baby doll hanging out of one hand.

"Mama, it's a note," she yells. Shana licks the icing off her fingers and holds out her hand. Cyn drops it off and goes back to her own little world.

"It looks important," I say over Shana's shoulder.

Shana rips open the envelope and reads over the letter. Her face drops before she even makes it to the end. "We're getting evicted."

CHAPTER 2

Don't be late for your first day of summer school.
You're almost finished, boo.

The text from Savannah buzzes against my belly.
6:50 A.M.

Fuck. My alarm must've not gone off. I need to be out of the house by 7:30 a.m., which means I'm already late. Getting yourself and a baby ready takes a lot of time.

The phone buzzes again.

And send me a picture of my niece! I haven't seen
my baby in forever.

Mia is still knocked out, thank fuck. She finally started sleeping through the whole night a month ago. I guess she's catching up on missed z's, 'cause if she isn't milk drunk, she's dead to the world.

I unwrap the sheet from her and gently wake her. She's all sweaty even though the window is open. It's hot as hell, and my room doesn't make it any better. Everything touches in here. The foot of the bed touches my dresser. Mia's crib sandwiched between the wall and my bed. Our closet can't even close all the way because of all the shit in it. When Mama left we had to downsize to our current place that damn near costs the same as our old place, but Shana didn't have a choice. Shana's basically taking care of all of us on one income. Sometimes she gets money from Cyn's daddy, but like most men, he ain't reliable.

Things will be better. They have to get better. This is no way for us to live. For Cyn and Mia to grow up.

I have to tell myself that every day in order to keep going.

With little people looking up to you, there's no way you can fail.

Mia coos in my arm as I try to get her to latch on to my breast. People don't tell you how much it hurts, but I try anyway. Those parenting forums on Google say this is the best way for her to grow up and be smart. I can't afford those fancy development toys right now, but this I can work at.

Mia bites down *hard,* and that's the end of that.

I wish my own ma was here to teach me something, but I guess she didn't really know what to do herself. Shana tries her best, but she's still figuring out this mothering thing herself. We're all learning as we go, and so far it seems like I'm failing.

I throw plenty of clothes around before I find something that isn't too small or that doesn't have baby throw-up on it. My hair all right—it's in a week-old twist-out. For someone that knows how to do hair, I always look busted at the head. I put Mia in her elephant onesie, brush her hair into a tiny ponytail, and rub her down in baby lotion.

We snap a picture for Savannah and head to the kitchen.

My baby! 💙

You look cute too, friend. Have a good day.

She is lying, but I need that boost of confidence. Something I haven't had since Mia was born. During pregnancy I felt like a goddess. After pregnancy, it's like I'm a shell of my former self. I even had Shana take down old pictures of me. Each time I walked past them I damn near felt like crying.

Shana said I have the baby blues. Which is another thing I can't deal with right now.

This apartment is a maze of tiny shoes, bootleg American Girl dolls, and crumbs that lead to the kitchen.

"What are we going to do?" Shana and Cyn are already in the kitchen. I sit across from them with wide-eyed Mia. She sucks on the side of her hand like it's the tastiest chicken she's ever had. Yesterday, Shana put the letter away. We kept having a good time. *Tomorrow*, she said. We needed something to make us happy. One thing to keep our mood up.

"Get her hand out her mouth before she has buck teeth. The way we are going, we won't be able to afford braces until she's sixteen."

Shana thinks she's the damn mama guru. I mean, Cyn is well taken care of, and she always knows what to do when Mia starts crying, but dang. It's like she forgot what it's like to be a new mama. Sometimes you don't get everything right and that's okay.

I don't argue with her, though. She's tired, and I can tell by the frown on her face. Three kids (if you count me) in the house and she is barely twenty-five. Her dreams fell apart as soon as Cyn came. She had no one rooting for her to go to college, to do something different with her life, not like she's doing for me. Well, *was* doing for me. That bright eviction notice shifted everything.

She takes a deep breath and then another. Some type of technique she found from a YouTube video. I think it's bullshit, but whatever helps her get through the day. "I wasn't gone tell y'all this until I came up with a plan, but after yesterday I think it's something you need to know."

She pauses and feels along the edges of the eviction paper. "I lost my job a few weeks ago."

Anger rises inside me. "The fuck you mean you wasn't going to tell us?"

"No cursing, TeTe!" Cyn warns, and I get pulled back in. That little girl knows she can get me together.

"I'm sorry, Cyn. You weren't going to tell us, though? For real?"

"I ain't want to worry y'all for nothing. You know I usually find a new job quickly. I thought I had time to get myself

16

together. Then everything started coming so fast. Days turned into weeks. Now I don't know what I'ma do. Unemployment will barely keep our heads above water."

"Can Cyn daddy help us out?" I ask.

We can't move again. Where are we gonna go? I'm sick of moving. Another U-Haul truck. Another Section 8 house. Another reminder we don't have nothing to our name.

"Can Mia daddy?" Shana asks, and I get her point. Both of us pulled up the worst baby fathers out of the sea of men.

Far as Mia knows, she is a test-tube baby. An experiment made in a lab, because that's just what it was: a three-year experiment gone wrong. Scooter can provide, in his own way. He chooses not to. His fatherhood contingent on when I'm having sex with him.

Which is never again.

In the beginning it was cool. He'd spot me money every now and again. Take me out to eat, which is a luxury in my crib. *There's food at the house,* that was Mama's answer. Whenever we'd ask for the simplest thing like McDonald's.

Pretty much a Bible verse. The eleventh commandment. Thou shalt not ask for food when there's peanut butter and white bread at home.

With Scooter it was the same ole story.

I fell for the okey-doke. The fake promises. The pretty smile. The bad-boy persona.

The lie that he'd be there. He missed the baby shower and I let that slide. He missed the birth, and I got the message loud and clear. He doesn't want to be a father, and I won't make him.

His parents won't talk sense into him. They think Mia isn't

his, that I'm just looking for a handout, but that's a lie. I never asked him for anything; he gave it to me. I never asked them for anything either, just to be here to watch Mia grow up. That's too much asking, I guess.

"I can quit the pizza shop and start doing hair again," I say. "Closures are going for so much right now, and they have to come back every two weeks to get it tightened or they'll look busted. A quick YouTube session and I can start next week."

After I got fired from the grocery store, I started at the new pizza shop up the street. It pays fifty cents more, but that doesn't make up for the free deli food I sometimes got at the Shop-and-Save. Neither of them pays enough to keep us afloat.

"You know I don't like all them people in my house. Especially now. You mess up someone's hair and they can call the people on you. Fine you. There's more money we don't have right back in the government's hands."

"I'll get my license then and get in someone's shop. Start up my own, maybe? It takes half the amount of time and way *less* money than college. I even saw a braiding competition on social media. It's a fifteen-hundred-dollar prize. That'll help out a lot."

Judging by the page, I'd be the winner. Everyone's style was basic and boring.

"You're going to college, B'onca. *Real* college. Mama wants you to, and you're going. We didn't have that party for nothing."

Mama this and Mama that.

She ain't here helping us through this. What she wants shouldn't even matter anymore.

College got crazy hidden expenses. Shit you don't even think you need. Mandatory meal plans. Three hundred dollars for some technology fees. Mia has shots coming up, growing every day. I want to get her a new stroller. The kind she can grow with, not one of them foldable ones that break within weeks.

Things we deserve.

"You tripping, Shana," I say. "You didn't go to college."

She throws her hands up and looks around. "And look where we are now. Nowhere."

"How are we going to keep the lights on, then?" I say.

"Don't worry about that. I'll figure something out. You just worry about finishing summer school and going to Hilbert in the fall."

"You said that last time this happened," I mumble.

"And you didn't go hungry last time, did you? When you brought Mia home, everything was okay, and that was without your money."

"Can I at least apply to the hair show? It's in Nashville, so you'd have to watch Mia if I got in, but it's good money, Shan."

"I'll think about it," she says. "Cyn, hurry up with your cereal. Your great-auntie watching y'all today. Mama gotta go out for some interviews."

Cyn stares between us and pours herself a bowl of Frosted Flakes. She slides me a bowl and a jug of milk. I'm more of a Trix person, but I know better than to open two boxes of cereal at one time. One breakfast item per week. No opening two boxes of cereal, milk, or anything that can go bad quickly. A luxury if we can have bacon and eggs. Grits and sausage. Two things on the table are a signal that Shana got something extra in the mail from Cyn's daddy, or it's bad news like somebody dying.

Last time that person was my mama.

She ain't dead, but she might as well be. Left in the middle of the night. Didn't say a word. We haven't heard from her since. Sometimes I wonder if she's okay, but it's better to pretend she's dead. It hurts less that way.

Since that happened, I've grown comfortable with having Pop-Tarts for breakfast.

CHAPTER 3

> Crazy shit happened yesterday. FaceTime me later and catch you up about Mia. The doctor said she's gained a lot of weight.

I shoot the text to Savannah and duck out, taking in my surroundings. Tyrone pushes his cart of recyclables down the street; Miss Yolanda watches from the porch as her kids play in the front yard; a motorcycle backfiring makes everyone pause for just a second, praying it's not gunfire.

Cops sit on the corner. Waiting and watching. Every day it's the same shit. I hate it here sometimes. If it's not the guns, it's the cops.

Some days I want peace, but I don't know how that'll happen. All these apartments are going up in my neighborhood. They fixing shit after fifty years of folks telling them it was broken. Now that the others are moving in, they are getting done quick.

We getting eviction notices. They getting *welcome to the neighborhood* greetings.

My phone buzzes against my thigh.

> Can't wait to see those chubby cheeks. BTW, your bestie just moved into her first big girl apartment. Can't wait for you to see it.

Is it bad to be jealous of your best friend?

I know the answer, but it doesn't stop the feeling. Savannah got out. She ain't got no four-month-old hanging off her titty. Nothing holding her back. No eviction notices. In a few years she'll be taking care of her mother. Giving back.

Where will I be?

I can't even say *in my own shop* confidently anymore. Things like that cost money.

Money we ain't got right now.

"B'onca!" Deja yells from way down the damn street. Loud as hell, but that's my girl. Savannah my right hand but Deja definitely my left. She wraps me in a big hug, swinging me from side to side. We haven't seen each other since Dej got sent up north to her dad for a week to give her mama a break.

"Can I tell you something as friends?" Deja asks.

"Always."

"You looking raggedy as hell right now," she says, eyeing my white T-shirt that has a hole in it and leggings that have been worn so much they are see-through. "I know you're a new mama and everything, but whew."

Every piece of change I get goes toward Mia. I haven't had my hair done professionally in months. Forget new shoes or clothes. Everything I'm rocking now is handed down from Shana's post-pregnancy days.

"Let me see how you look if you are up every night changing shitty diapers and getting your nipples bitten."

She nods her head. "Points were made."

"How did our asses end up in summer school?" I ask.

"Well, you were pregnant as hell and I'm just lazy," she laughs. "Good thing my best friend is going to be a stylist all the girls want to go to. Then I can mooch off you. That's the career goal this year, right?"

"It was."

We follow a line of fresh fades, slick weaves, and braids, the sun beating down our necks and backs. "The landlord left a fat-ass eviction notice on our door. Shana is being a bitch and doesn't want me doing hair in the house."

Deja wraps her locs into a topknot. "Where is Scooter's ass at? I know he like to pretend he's on an episode of *Power*, but he got responsibilities now. Even if he doesn't want to be in her life, he can still send money to help. I mean, him being missing when you were pregnant was one thing, but now that you can see and touch Mia, that makes all the difference."

It does make a difference. I can see her cry, feel her sweat because there ain't no AC, hear her stomach rumble because breast-feeding hurts me and formula is expensive.

I have to deal with all these things, every night, while her daddy is God knows where. Shit ain't fair that everything falls on me all the time. Sometimes I wish that it was only me. That I'd been smarter. Surrendered her to a fire station back when she didn't know who I was.

Those are thoughts for only me.

Mamas aren't allowed to say that shit out loud. To say that raising a kid is a struggle. While daddies can pop in and out and are still praised for being a "good man."

"Don't worry, you got time before those eviction notices go into effect. Shana is gone take care of things. She always does."

This time I'm not sure.

The thirty-minute walk to school seems longer, and by the time we get there I'm sweating and out of breath. A mixture of hazel, brown, and black eyes stare down at us from already-full classrooms. Some chat with friends; others ignore their teachers barking to close the windows.

"Damn, how many people failed?" Deja and I climb the steps to Ida B. Wells High School.

"They gone pack us in here like sardines. Eventually we are all going to become sharks."

The halls are flooded with students. They lean against the lockers, catching up and ignoring the teachers who are trying to push them to class.

"At least there's a variety of fishes. You can definitely find Mia a daddy here. Maybe even one with money." She pulls her mouth to the side. "Mmm, but maybe after we get you some new clothes and your hair done."

I throw a finger sign at her. The only person Mia needs is me.

Deja and I walk the halls, eyeing everything they've changed in the two weeks we've been gone. Damn, even our school is trying to rebrand. On the concrete walls, Martin Luther King took the place of Malcolm X. John Lewis took the place of Fred Hampton. "Tamer" activists, folks that white people think didn't cause any trouble.

Joke's on them. Truth is, these folks were the most militant, and in the end they all equally important.

"Speaking of hair, I need mine retwisted. You got me?" Deja asks.

"Nah, do you got me? I can't do it for free right now," I reply.

"Now, you know I'm going to pay you. Don't even act like that."

"Bet. Stop by the house tomorrow and bring your own products. Big ole head ain't finna use mine up."

"Bet. I see your old junt Trent back in town." She nods toward the front of the building. He's taller, with a tan, but I'll never forget those bowlegs. Trent Dubois. I'd speed through my homework just to make it outside to watch him hoop. He left town before I got the chance to shoot my shot. If that was even possible. Even though Scooter didn't really want me, he put fear into any guy who tried to talk to me.

"He was never my man," I say. "We were friends. He was

a shoulder to lean on when I first found out I was pregnant. That's it."

"I'm surprised your friend showed his face around here again. All that snitching he used to do. He's bold."

I shrug. "Folks probably forgot all about that." I watch as Trent blends into the crowd, trying not to draw attention to himself. I want to say hello, catch up, but talking to Trent is a shot at your reputation.

Trent used to be Scooter's friend too, and I use the word *friend* loosely. Scooter sent him out to do all the shit he didn't want to do. At the time, Trent needed the money, and, well. Folks do a lot of wild things for bread around here. Nobody ever got into specifics, but when the leader of Scooter's crew got sent to the farm and Trent disappeared, people put two and two together.

"At least he grew into his ears." Deja fans herself. "And everything else."

I push her with my shoulder. "He was just a snitch, remember?"

Deja rolls up the sleeves of her hot-ass sweater. "Allegedly."

We stop at the wall with our class list. I find Deja's name but not mine.

Panic sets in. "Wait, you're supposed to be in the same class with me. You always are because of our last names."

"Maybe you're in something special," she says.

"This summer school. Ain't nothing special about summer school."

"You don't have to think the worst of everything, you know."

The worst is all I know.

We search all four sheets and finally find my room. Mrs. Crenshaw. Fuck me. She's like an annoying bug that I can't shake.

"Damn, I'm glad I ain't in that room. Go on before she starts running her mouth about you being late." She gestures to the end of the hallway. Mrs. Crenshaw stands at the door. Checking the time each second. "I'll catch up with you at lunch."

Deja walks into her class and throws her hands up. "What's up, my fellow dummies!"

She always got to be the class clown.

Mrs. Crenshaw stares right at me. Like she can't wait to say something about my being in summer school.

"I'm surprised to see you here. Where's your oops baby?" Whitney slides in front of me and swings her waist-length purple-and-pink box braids over her shoulder. Whitney got beef with me because of Scooter. No matter how many times I tell her that he's no prize and she can have him. Even left him clean in front of her one day. He is no use to me, or my baby. Always making excuses about how he can't be a daddy. Last time I checked, I'm only seventeen compared to his nineteen and making things happen. Far as Mia knows, I'm Mama and Daddy.

"Whitney, I already whooped your ass once. Don't try it a second time."

Before I could even announce my pregnancy, she had already spread it around the hood. That's my biggest regret: fighting with Mia still in my belly.

Whitney and her crew step together. "You know you sucker-punched me."

"This time you'll see me coming," I spit, spreading my arms. "I'm right here."

"Ladies, ladies. That's enough. Go upstairs." Mrs. Crenshaw eyes us like she is about to pull off her own belt. *"Now."*

Whitney rolls her eyes. Fighting not my style anymore, but if the opportunity ever came up to drag her by her old-ass braids, I wouldn't say no.

Mrs. Crenshaw makes sure Whitney and 'em are gone and then stops me before I can go into the classroom. "B'onca Johnson, that temper of yours is going to get you in a world of trouble one day."

"I ain't got a temper."

"That scene just proved otherwise."

Damn, she's on my ass already, and class hasn't even started yet.

"Why did you sign me up for your English class?" I ask. "You hate me."

"I don't hate you," she says. "And I wanted to keep an eye on you. Make sure you did the right thing. Look at you, already starting out on the wrong foot."

"She started with me first," I say.

"What did I tell you last year?" she says. "You can't let people get to you."

Mrs. Crenshaw might have been a big bitch last year, but she was the only one who treated me like a person. I guess it's because she was a teen mom herself. The baby wasn't the only thing she talked to me about. She listened to me, to my wants and dreams. That made me feel good about myself. Like I ain't fuck up my life all the way. Like I still could have a future outside of Mia. Seems like ages ago. All I think about now is Mia. It was silly of me to think I could separate being a mother from being a person with goals. The two bleed in together until you don't know where one stops and the other begins.

"Have you finalized your college plans yet?"

I can't even think about college when we barely have money for food. There's no college for me. Only surviving. But I can't tell Mrs. Crenshaw that. Last time I opened up about how I felt, a teacher sent me to the counselor. The counselor tried to say I was suffering from PTSD. Living in the hood is traumatic, but shit, everyone knows that. A fancy label on it ain't gone fix it. A white man in a three-hundred-dollar suit who volunteers to save the poor Black kids wasn't gone save me.

Instead, I tell Mrs. Crenshaw the usual.

"I'm getting my Hilbert fees together now, but I'm looking into cosmetology school, too."

I don't even have money to buy a piece of bubble gum.

"Mia is going to have a good life," I say.

Some nights, I cry myself to sleep because I birthed my daughter into a fucked-up world.

"That's great, B'onca. Life isn't over because you have Mia. You can keep going—don't let her stop you from reaching the stars."

Well, my stars aren't that bright; you can't reach for something you can't see.

If I don't get Mia in day care, that'll be another problem on my plate. Only so many times Shana will babysit before she starts screaming how she ain't the babysitter. Besides, when she gets on her feet again, Mia is going to need somewhere to go.

"Can I run by the main office real quick?"

Mrs. Crenshaw checks the clock that hangs on the wall above. "Be quick and don't make a habit of being late." She goes into the class and starts hollering about how summer school is only ten weeks, and everyone needs to take it seriously.

The main office is far as hell. This school is like a maze sometimes. Wild to think about how this my last month of being here. Freshman year is almost a distant memory. Backyard kickbacks and sneaking in late. Driving around with Scooter all hours of the night. I'd give anything to go back, even if only for a day.

The main office is empty for the most part. One girl sits in the green plastic chair, filling out a form. The assistant sits alert at her desk, typing away on her computer.

She glances up and then back to the screen. "How may I help you?"

"Can I speak to the childcare coordinator?"

She never looks up. "Who?"

There's usually two childcare coordinators. One that handles the paperwork and one that gets the babies registered.

"Who do I speak to about registering my baby for day care?" The girl sits her form beside me, and the assistant takes it and sends her off.

"Day care isn't available during summer school," she snickers. "Ask me, day care shouldn't be available to you at all. You are all babies yourself."

She is one of *those* people.

"I have a baby and she needs somewhere to go while I'm at school. Where is she gonna go?"

"Day care, I assume."

Deep breaths, B'onca. I put on my customer-service smile that I use when the folks at work get on my nerves. "Day care is supposed to be here. At school . . . where I am during the day."

"At summer school, we don't have enough students in your predicament to spend money to open the day care."

"My *predicament?* Lady, you don't know shit about my—"

She holds one hand in the air. *I know she ain't trying to dismiss me.* "Listen, I wish I could help. If anything changes, you'll be the first to know."

The only thing saving her right now is this five-foot barrier between us and the fact that Mia doesn't deserve to be raised without a mama.

She looks over me and to the door. "You're going to be late for first period."

I slam the door and let my head fall against it. Without day care, there's no school. College might be optional, but a high school diploma—damn, don't I at least deserve that? One foot forward to get knocked two steps back. I blend in with the crowd of kids before ducking into the bathroom. Everything is old here. Last year, they put in a free tampon dispenser. That lasted a shocking six months before the administration said fuck it. Now we have to pray that the nurse bought some for the month, and if not, it's a makeshift toilet-paper pad for the rest of the day.

I text Shana the news. Maybe I can have her watch Mia three times a week and I stay home with her two times. I won't be an honor summer-school student or anything, but I also won't fail.

I pull out my phone and a message from *him* sits on the screen.

Sperm Donor: I'm going to send Mia some dolls. Be on the lookout.

She doesn't need dolls she doesn't even play with. She doesn't need expensive clothes she's going to grow out of. She needs a father. An active father.

I close my phone. Ignoring his empty promises of this, that, and the third.

"You got this, Mama," I say to my ragged reflection.

CHAPTER 4

THE FIRST NIGHT Mia came home, I cried. Four months later and it seems that's all I do. Google says it's postpartum depression.

Take it easy.

What's the teen-mama version of that? I've never had nothing come to me easily. The shower the only time I get peace, and even then I have to step out every second because I think I hear Mia crying.

Like right now. I turn off the water and stick my head out. "Cyn, is the baby okay?"

"She's okay, TeTe," Cyn says outside the bathroom door. "We're watching TV. I think she's trying to sing along."

Doubt it. All she does now is make smacking sounds. Sometimes I think I hear her say *Mama*, but Shana says it's my imagination.

I might as well cut this shower short. Didn't even get to wash my hair. Sometimes I feel I can't admit I'm tired. I ain't nobody special. Shana went through the same thing, and she was even younger.

Steam flows out of the door. Cyn sits on the floor and Mia in her rocker.

The fresh smell of soap is cut short by the smell of shit. "That's you or the baby?"

Cyn pinches her nose and moves away from Mia. "Definitely the baby. Dang, what you feed her? Pork rinds?"

"I remember your sh—" I backtrack. "Your poop smelling worse than that."

We double-team Mia diaper. Cyn throws it away like it's hazardous material. A lullaby courtesy of Cyn and she's back asleep. Damn, I wish I could sleep like Mia. Only a day, that's all I need. I'll never take a nap for granted again.

Soon as I stretch across the bed, here comes Shana's loud ass. She opens the door so hard it bounces off the wall. Mia stirs in her sleep and opens her eyes for a second like she wants to know what's going on. Within a blink she's back in dreamland.

"Run by the store for me?" Shana says, more a demand than a question. Her hand extends with the food-stamp card in it.

"Shana, I was finna nap real quick," I say. "Why can't you go?"

"I got two job interviews today." She fluffs her hair as she uncurls it. "You need to be finding a *real* job that pays something, instead of napping."

"You know I have the pizza shop. I could drop that and start doing hair. That'll bring in way more than taking pizza orders."

"Hair," she groans. "Those eighty-dollar hairstyles ain't paying no bills around here. That eviction notice in there is for real."

I shoot up from the bed. "You think I don't know that?"

"Listen, I don't feel like arguing today." She writes down a list and texts it to me. "Nothing extra, you hear me?" She directs this to Cyn, who pretends she's not listening.

Shana gives all three of us a kiss on the cheek before walking out the door. "And, Cyn, clean that pot in the kitchen sink. It doesn't have to soak that long. I'll make some Ro-Tel when I get back home."

Cyn waits until she leaves to suck her teeth. "Always want me to do something."

Now I gotta get two kids ready for the store. Doodlebug mad 'cause I woke her up and decides to test out her lungs. She keeps sneezing, too. I check her forehead with the back of my hand. No fever, but I make a note to get baby aspirin.

"Come and let me do something to your head," I say to Cyn. She about to step outside with two undone twists like we don't take care of her.

She runs off with this bugged-out look on her face. Getting her tender-headed self in a ponytail is a full-time job that I don't have time for. I just hope we don't run into anyone we know.

Mia won't stop crying. Cyn wants one more episode of her show. It takes us a damn hour to leave and then another twenty minutes to walk to the store. Cyn points out houses she wants one day. It's slim pickings, but in some places we can see the diamond in the rough. Like people who are flipping these shotgun houses and selling them for three hundred thousand.

In my neighborhood there is only one market you can go to for prices that don't break the bank. It ain't quality or nothing, but you can afford it. At least a few months ago you could. Now everything's going up. The clerk doesn't even give things on credit anymore. Folks who moved in now don't need credit. They can pay for things outright, straight cash, whenever they want.

The market is empty. It's the middle of the day and everyone's at work or some summer activity. Summer school, if you aren't lucky. Where I should be, but Shana didn't tell me she was job hunting today. Mia testing out her lungs again. She's rubbing her eyes, and snot drips from her nose. She definitely has a cold.

Stares burn the side of my head as I try to calm her down.

"*Shhhhh,* I know you don't feel good, but we're almost done. I promise." I try to give her her favorite stuffed animal, Lamby, but she just wails louder.

"You know, if you pick her up and pat her back, she might be quiet," an older woman with a musky perfume says. She reaches out her arms for Mia, and I want to tell her about herself. People down South are too friendly.

I pick up two cans of diced tomatoes for the Ro-Tel. "You know, maybe if you had some business of your own, you wouldn't need to be in mine."

She pulls her shawl into her body and walks away, muttering under her breath. Mia is crying and embarrassing me in front of all these people in the canned-goods aisle. They already got enough reasons to judge me; *bad mother* isn't what I need added to my rap sheet. I want to cry, too.

"Put it back *now,*" I say between my teeth to Cyn, who found her way to the snack aisle.

"But, TeTe," she whines, clutching a box of Scooby-Doo fruit snacks. "It's only two dollars. I'll get it out of my piggy bank when we get home."

I feel bad for telling her no. She throws it in the cart when she sees my face relax.

"B, I got your regular right here," Apollo, my old classmate, says through a layer of plastic barrier.

A pound of catfish is usually two dollars, but they went up to four. Shana says that if it goes up again, we going back to canned tuna.

"Can you throw in a sour pickle?" I ask. "On the low?"

He looks over his shoulder for his boss. "This is the last time, B. You know the boss doesn't want me giving away things for free anymore. Even to you."

Back in the day, he didn't care about free pickles or small candies. Those things weren't breaking the bank. I can't blame him. The changes affecting this market too. You gotta do what you have to do to survive.

"I heard they giving out notices around your way," Apollo says.

"They got us," I reply. "We don't know what we gone do. If there is anything to do."

"I know a place." He slides a bright business card through the slot. "I stayed there a few months ago. It's nice."

A shelter. I've heard the stories. Nothing feels like yours. Damn near a job. A schedule to eat, sleep, and get fresh air. It's supposed to teach you discipline, but all it does is make you feel really low.

I ain't taking my baby there.

Cyn holds up her picture book. Black ballerinas dance from page to page.

"Read it to Doodlebug." I push them both in the cart, checking prices two times on everything we touch. Everything costs more than it's worth. Ain't no reason for a person not to be able to afford *real* food.

"TeTe, her pacifier fell." Cyn bends over the cart, trying to reach. "I can't get it."

I grab the pacifier, bumping into a big-belly girl on my way up.

"I'm sorry." She wraps her jacket as far as it can go around her body and shuffles to the next aisle. I eye her as she peeks around before pretending to accidentally drop cans of baby formula. She puts two back on the shelf and shoves two inside the stroller she pushes.

She's sloppy. Her technique, it's all off. Too loud, for one. Too noticeable. This isn't a big Kroger or a Piggly Wiggly. No one's going to miss the girl with the swollen belly who's stealing. She pushes her stroller around, pretending she's looking for something that can't be found. She shakes her head in frustration and then looks straight at the camera.

She notices me noticing her. Her grip on the handle tightens before she turns on her heel.

"I won't tell," I call out.

"Ain't nothing to tell," she hisses over her shoulder.

I nod and keep on pushing. You can throw a rock in my neighborhood and have it land on someone who stole something before. The stroller technique is the most popular one. Even Mama would take us in the stores sometimes and tell us to "hold" something. If we got caught, she'd say, "Oh, she must have picked it up on accident." It was fifty-fifty if the guard let us keep it or not.

Mia's lips begin to tremble, a sign that another tantrum is coming. I clean her nose, wipe her binky off, and shove it between her lips before the screeching begins. The cart bounces off sweatpants-covered legs. The red-and-white Jordans bring back memories I try hard to forget. "Long time no see. You don't answer the phone anymore?" His low voice got a bit more bass in it. He changes it depending on who he's around. You can't intimidate anyone if you still talk like you haven't hit puberty.

"You can't answer a phone that doesn't ring, Scooter." I reach around for a pack of hamburger meat—$5.99 for half a pound. Half a pound!

He slides his brush from his back pocket and brushes his waves forward. "Now, you know I texted you the other day about the doll. You left me on read."

"I remember texting you three times about your child needing diapers. Still haven't gotten a response. She got plenty of dolls and she's only four months old. Ain't like she plays with them."

He shifts his weight to one foot. "Whitney says she ain't mine. . . . I mean, she is kind of light-skinned, even though we're both brown."

I push my index finger deep in his chest. Trying to scoop out the place his heart is supposed to be. "You know I never had sex with anyone but you."

He backs away, leaving my finger hanging in the air. "How I

know? We were wild then. All them times you didn't hit me back, who knows what you were doing?"

"You were wild. I was lovesick."

When you are from darkness, any little shimmer of light can draw you in.

"You knew what you were doing." He cranes his neck around. "Listen, I heard they giving out them pink slips in your hood. I got a few people in need. If you want in on *it*."

It is boosting. The hood come-up. If you're good you can make a stack quick, and Scooter exceptional. Steal anything you need, and most times it isn't even him. He has a crew—they steal, split the profit, and in return Scooter gives them a place to stay and a sense of a family. He knows who to sniff out. The broken people who never heard their parents say, "I love you." He takes advantage of that.

Scooter grew up way different. With two parents, doing hobbies nobody heard of. (Fencing? Fuck out of here.) He's a chameleon. Changing his spots whenever he see fit. During the day, he's a rich boy on the hill; at night he comes down. Selling whatever he thinks will make him something he's not.

He pulls a stack out of his back pocket. That's all the child support he owes me and Mia right there.

"You're going to Hilbert, right? Them kids got money over there. I'm sure they don't mind getting a deal off stuff they already wear anyway."

I step in front of Cyn, shielding her eyes. "You know I ain't into that kind of shit. You shouldn't be either. You have a daughter to think of now."

He pops the rubber band against the stack. "Come on, you could be my best seller. You fine with a fat ass, and now you got the titties to match." He bites down on his knuckles. "No one gone fuck with you either. They know who'd they have to answer to."

"I *said* I don't do that."

"Maybe I need to get your boyfriend Trent in on it, then. I hear he crawled back into town. You seen him yet?"

"No, I haven't."

Scooter was always jealous of Trent. Which is funny, because Trent didn't have anything worth being jealous of. First time I met him he had on the most busted pair of shoes. His ma must have hit a lick or something, because he looks better now.

Anyway, Trent treated me like somebody. To Scooter I was only a pretty thing on his arm. Someone he could play house with when it was convenient for him. With Trent it was different. When Mia was still the size of a peach, he had me playing womb music for her. He said it'd help with her development. Scooter didn't care about things like that. He barely asked if I had eaten anything during the day.

"Keep it that way. I don't need that obsessed-ass nigga around my people."

"Can you leave now? I need to finish shopping. If you couldn't tell, your daughter has a cold," I say.

He slides a hundred-dollar bill into my shirt. "Think about what I said. Mia needs diapers, right?"

My mind says to shake it, let it fall to the floor, and walk away. That's Mia shoe money. Enough to buy two packs of hamburger, and fruit snacks.

"Just think about it. You can use something for yourself, too. Bye, 'Daddy' baby." He blows a kiss before walking down the frozen-food aisle.

Mia pulls at her tiny Afro and rubs her eyes. "We're almost done, Doodle."

We check out; Apollo has to spot me the fifty cent extra because I don't want to break the $100. That's for Mia. The walk home isn't bad. Cyn points at the tall red maple trees and butterflies. No matter how many times she's seen these things, they always excite her. Mia eyes wide open now, taking in everything on the block. Sometimes I want to know what she's thinking. How she sees things, how she sees me.

CHAPTER 5

KIDS SIT SCATTERED around the dining room as I clock in for my shift at the Pizza Junt. *Junt* is a Memphis word that the owner straight gentrified. He thought it'd get more young people in here, and he was right. It put Marco's right out of business.

Each evening when I clock in for my five-to-ten shift, the tables are packed. Most of these people used to go to my school. In here, though, we aren't classmates. We are customer and worker. They remind me of that each time they make my job difficult.

"Damn, B'onca, where you been?" My coworker Janae pulls me by the arm into a dim corner. Her shirt is already stained in pizza sauce, even though it's only the beginning of her shift. "You're late again. Joe is looking for you. He's mad because Stephanie called in and Khadijah had to leave early 'cause her baby sick."

"I had to run back home real quick and check on Mia." Shana said she'd been throwing a tantrum ever since the door shut behind me. When I walked in, she instantly stopped with those crocodile tears. I feel bad, leaving my baby, but we need my job; it doesn't bring in much, but it's enough for formula sometimes and an extra something on the water bill.

"Stay out of Joe's way for now," Janae says. "He has that wild look in his eyes."

I take my usual place at the register. Even though I don't actually cook the pizzas anymore, the smell always sticks to my skin after work. I have to scrub for at least an hour to get it off.

"Hey, B'onca." Whitney's voice causes me to have a stank attitude instantly.

I skip the pleasantries. "How may I help you?"

"Dang, ain't no customer service around here anymore." She taps her acrylics on the counter and pretends to read over the menu even though she gets the same thing every time. A vegan pizza with a side of wings.

"Whitney, there's a line behind you." I can tell they're getting impatient because of the eye rolls and *dang, mane*s that aren't even whispered.

"Let me get the vegan cheese pizza. Also, the spinach basil pesto pizza. You know Scooter loves that one. I'm trying to get him to eat better. We're expecting, so he needs to be around for a long time."

Whitney pokes her stomach out as far as it can go and gives it a rub. I bite the inside of my jaw to keep from screaming.

"We don't have the pesto pizza anymore." Which she knows. She just wants to get on my damn nerves.

"Y'all had it last week."

"It's a new week now."

"Where is your manager at? Dang, you can't do anything right. Can't even work this little job. All you do is press the buttons and get me my pizza."

"Bitch—"

"Go ahead. Get fired."

The people behind her already have their phones out ready to record whatever happens between us. *Think of Mia, B'onca.*

"Would you like something else?"

She flicks over the tip jar and pennies bounce to the floor. "Forget it. I'm taking my money somewhere else."

She says that like I own the place or give a damn.

"Have a nice day." I flip her off in my mind and take the next customer. After about ten complicated pizza orders (who doesn't want any sauce on their pizza?), the place is clear. I lean on the counter and scroll my timeline. Sure enough, Whitney is the first person that pops up. She's four months, according to her announcement. Her and Scooter rub an invisible baby bump. He's grinning like he doesn't already have a kid he doesn't take care of.

I want to comment that, but *bitter baby mama* is the first thing someone will reply.

"B'onca." Joe's hot breath warms the back of my neck. "Nice of you to *finally* show up. You're not on the register today."

I slip my phone into my pocket and fix my cap with the pizza logo on front. I'm not the best employee, I can admit that, but I normally show up on time and do my job. That's more than some people can say. The turnover rate here is wild. Most folks don't stay longer than three months. They don't have a reason to. Teenagers who only need to save money to get something expensive their parents refuse to buy. After that, they're gone. Free to return to their normal lives. I'm stuck here. Been stuck here for four months, since I had Mia.

"I'm always on the register, Joe." A perk of seniority. What my life has come to now. Being happy about doing this.

"Not today," Joe says. "Until you prove that you can show up to your job on time, you're going to be on cleanup duty. The bathrooms need a deep cleaning."

I whip my head around. "Those are disgusting. You know that!"

No one uses those bathrooms except people off the street. Team members sneak to use the one in the office, even though we aren't supposed to.

"That's why you're going to make them shine. You know where the cleaning supplies are. I want them done by the end of your shift, and I will check." He eyes the room. "Janae, come here. You're on the register today."

"But B usually—" she starts, but Joe holds up a hand to silence her.

"Well, today she's on bathroom duty, and you're on register." Joe's eyes narrow. "But maybe we can work something out."

"I promise I'll try my best to not be late again, Joe," I say. "With the baby, it's hard to keep track of time, but you know I'm a good worker. I never give you any real problems."

"I don't need you to try. I need you to do it." He scolds me like I'm his child. "Apologize to me."

Janae comes to my defense. "Joe, she said she'll try to be better."

"Do you want to be the one cleaning the bathrooms?" he asks.

She retreats and I can't blame her. Those bathrooms are that nasty.

"Go ahead," he says. "I'm waiting, or you can pack your things and not come back."

His words drip off his tongue like hot lava. He eyes me and smirks. Like hearing me bow down to him will make his entire day. Fuck that.

"You know what, Joe?" My lips tremble. *Bills. So many bills.* But I can't make it this way. There's got to be something else out there. "I quit."

I throw my hat on the ground and walk out. Janae runs behind me. "Wait up, B."

My breathing regulates as I pace beside the brick wall. "He thinks I'm going to kiss his ass over minimum wage. He's lost his damn mind."

"Think about this, girl. Don't you need the money?"

Of course I need the money. That's all I need now, but one thing I'm going to teach Mia is you never suck up to nobody who's hell-bent on making you feel less than them. I'll find a way. I always do.

Hearing Shana's mouth the last thing I want to deal with right now, Savannah is miles away, and Dej turned her location off, which means she doesn't want to be found. My feet lead me to the only other place that I know.

Trent's house.

It looks the same, plus a paint job and a garage extension. The biggest house on the block, passed down from Trent's great-grandma. Back then you could buy a house for two dollars and a smile. They practically gave them away, and folks like Trent's great-grandma flipped them and made this neighborhood into a community.

Shame all her hard work is going down the drain.

I don't even know what I'm doing here.

It's been too long since I've seen Trent. Talked to him. Known anything about him that wasn't from the mouths of other people. Trent Dubois was always a classy-ass name to me. He's Creole, Haitian or something. Folks used to clown him all the time for the food he ate. Once he had frog legs, which he told me was chicken. I ate three pieces before he finally confessed. I didn't stick my hand down my throat, though, only asked for more, because even weird food was better than the tragic potions that the cafeteria folks warmed up in the microwaves.

Fuck.

Life would have been different with Trent. I wouldn't have gotten pregnant, because he's not the type of guy that would pressure a girl. He would have actually dated me. Took me to meet his family during Sunday dinners, and not just his mama and daddy—uncles, aunties, cousins, and nieces. Everyone on the block would have known that I was with him. That we made each other whole.

Wouldn't have had to worry about girls coming to me as a woman.

Folks snickering behind my back because I'd be looking for Scooter and he'd be laid up somewhere else.

A real relationship.

I messed up.

Trent doesn't want to see me. He got other things to worry about. The whispers have started that he's in town, and now he has a big ole target on his back. I wish I could protect him, but there's nothing anyone can do. You can't run from shit like this forever, either. One day he's going to have to stand up and fight and pray that he's the one that comes out alive.

I'm about to turn and run when the door swings open.

"You been out here awhile—you coming in or what?" Trent's mama is a six-foot stallion. She looks like one of them early 2000s video vixens. Even the few times I met her last year she kept herself. She always said you didn't have to look like your situation. Now she's up, and honestly, money looks good on her.

I wish Mama could see how folks can turn their life around. Maybe then she'd try to get better.

Ms. Dubois golden bracelets jingle as she flips her braids. "Sugar, you okay?"

I tuck those memories back in that box, deep inside. "Yes, ma'am. I was looking for Trent. Is he home?"

"That boy hasn't made it home from the store yet." She checks her Apple Watch. "I'm getting nervous. You know, after what happened. I get scared when he's out in the streets."

The neighborhood got to Trent about six months before he left. He started to hang around Scooter's gang, and everyone knew it wasn't like him. He was scared to even hold a gun. After a shootout that ended with somebody real fucked-up, somebody snitched. Word on the street is it was Trent. Even though he swears till this day he didn't open his mouth.

"I'm sure he's fine. There's a game happening at the courts he probably stopped to play." I pull at my faded T-shirt.

"Well, you can come on in. I don't bite. Plus, I just made some dinner. Come eat with me." Ms. Dubois doesn't wait for me to answer. She just pulls me through the glass door. "Take off your shoes."

I yank off my flip-flops at the door. Everything is in perfect order. Three pairs of shoes are lined up against the wall, giving a picture of the folks who live here. Red bottoms, and *two* pairs of Jordans. A complete family. The one thing I wanted for my baby. A mother and father to line up shoes at the door. Give baths at night and read her to sleep. Another thing I failed at with Mia.

Ms. Dubois leads me through a living room with white furniture to get to the kitchen. Another space with a giant TV is right across from the dining room. Mia would have so much room to play, crawl, and walk here. Cyn could have a jungle gym in the back, and I could use a room as a shop.

This is making it.

Now I truly realize I'm barely surviving.

"Sit." Ms. Dubois pulls out a chair at the long dining table. Enough space for her family and then some. "You like rice dressing?"

"Never had it."

"You're going to love it." Ms. Dubois places a bowl in front of me and one directly across.

"Go on." That's all she has to say before I'm eating spicy-ass rice like it's my last meal. Shit, when *was* my last meal? A bowl of leftover ramen, a bag of fifty-cent chips, and school food. Nothing sustainable.

"Slow down—you can have more. Trent don't eat my food anymore. All he want is that Chipotle mess."

I fidget in my chair. "I'm sorry. Guess I was hungry."

"Don't apologize." Ms. Dubois takes a beat. "Are you getting enough to eat at home?"

Here we go. First adults lure you in with things they know you need. Then they start getting all in your business. Want to know your life and shit. I want to shout, *Stop trying to fix me!* This shit ain't as easy as supergluing a plate back together.

But I ain't stupid, and I want my second bowl because this rice bussing.

I just nod and take another scoop. Damn, Trent mama can cook.

She taps her Cardi B–length acrylics on the table. "You do hair, right? I remember seeing you when you were small and had your li'l porch business going on. Plaiting the kids' hair for a dollar. Even swooped their edges."

That seems like a lifetime ago. People saw a little girl making play money to buy candy. In reality, I gave Mama all that money. She said she was going to hold it for me until I was older. Now I know she used it to get high.

"I can still do hair, but I don't really get that many heads these days."

"Do you want to?" she asks.

My eyes leave my half-filled bowl. "Are you offering me a job?"

"Now, you won't be doing any braiding or weaving yet, because I run a legit business and you're not licensed, but you can come over in the evening during the week and mornings on weekends and wash heads and sweep up for me. Then we can work on getting you licensed. We all got to start somewhere. Lord knows if it wasn't for my mama leaving me this house, I'd be messed up myself."

"I have a baby. She's four months old and I'd have to find a babysitter."

The pizza place was only three days a week. Shana ain't going for seven whole days.

"Bring li'l mama with you. She can stay with the other kids. You ain't the only one with a baby, you know."

"Sometimes it feels that way."

"I had Trent young. I thought I fucked his life up and mine. Kids give you grace, you know? You don't have to be perfect. Trust me, I'm far from it. I know last year I was messed up, but I got myself together. You can do the same."

"Does this job pay?"

"How does fifteen for twenty-five hours a week sound?"

I try to disguise the emotion on my face, but I'm hype.

I do the math. Fifteen hundred a month. I made half of that working at the Pizza Junt. Numbers play around in my head. Rent is seven hundred and fifty dollars. Baby expenses are around five hundred. Utilities are a hundred and ninety.

We'd still be barely making it, but not as much, and like

Ms. Dubois said, it'll get me some experience and my foot in the door. One day I'll have my own clients, take home more than that per day, even. Mia will have a jungle gym, and I'll have a house with six dining chairs and a living room no one can sit in.

"When do I start?"

CHAPTER 6

MOVE. DANCE. TWO-STEP. Something. I'm like a saved auntie right now, holding up the wall in Deja's compact two-bedroom apartment, judging everyone else when I'm supposed to be in the middle, turning up, and celebrating my last night as an unemployed kid.

Tomorrow I start work. Nine to five or until the last head leaves. Ms. Dubois told me to get good standing shoes, but that'll have to come out of my first check. All the money we have now is for bills.

"Boo." Trent pokes one shoulder and then slides around me. "Long time no see. Thought you've been avoiding me."

"I have," I say.

"Dang. It's like that? We haven't seen each other in months."

"Exactly," I huff. "Months without a phone call. Text message. DM. Nothing but silence. I was worried about you, and then I had to stop, or I wasn't going to have any worry left for myself."

He grabs my shoulder and I want to pull him into a hug.

Squeeze him until his eyes bug out like those cartoons, but there's too many people here. They see me getting cozy with Trent and that's another hit at my reputation. Well, whatever is left of it. "I'm sorry I left without saying goodbye. Ma was being impulsive. She packed us up in the middle of the night and that was it."

"The phone still worked," I say.

"That's my bad. Really. With everything that happened and everything you had going on, I thought disappearing would be better."

Better for who? Definitely wasn't better for me. I answered every private phone call thinking it was him, only for it to be robocalls. That's how pressed I was.

"You missed a lot," I say.

"I see." He looks down at my pudge. I instinctively place my hand over my stomach. Losing the baby weight was easy until it came to the FUPA. I don't think that's ever going away.

"I had it. Uh, her. A girl. Her name is Mia. Thank you for helping me back then. You didn't have to listen to me bitch at two in the morning about Scooter ass and how we fucked up."

"No worries. Trust, I enjoyed spending time with you way more than I did with their toxic asses," he says. "You know back then I meant what I said. I would have pretended she was mine. If you wanted me to. No child should have to grow up with Scooter as a father."

"Good thing he made the decision for me. He isn't around, but that was to be expected."

"Speak of the de—" Before Trent can finish his statement, Scooter has him jacked up by the collar like Trent a badass kid.

"The fuck are you doing here?" Scooter tightens his grip. Trent's shirt halfway off his body.

"Let me go, man."

"What? You going to snitch on me, too?" Scooter drops Trent and pushes him back like five feet. "And don't be coming back trying to push up on my girl."

"I'm not your girl, fool."

"Baby mama, then. Stay from around her, or you're going to have to deal with me."

"Aye, B, I'll check on you later, aight?" Trent fixes his collar as much as he can before squeezing through a crowd of hyped teens. People film him, flash on, as he leaves the party.

"You always have to do the most," I say.

"Why you hanging around that clown? You don't need to be around him. His days are numbered."

"You better not hurt him," I say.

"Oh, it ain't gonna be me, but trust, somebody gonna get that fool."

His new girlfriend not even paying attention. She's snapping pictures on her phone. In her own little world. Whitney barely had her first ultrasound before he found a new girl to play with. I'm not surprised though, that's just the type of person Scooter is.

"Congratulations on your new job, though, for real. Fifteen an hour? You big time now."

"Get out of my face, Scooter," I say flatly, looking over his shoulder for Deja. No sign of her Bantu knots anywhere.

"It's like that now?" Scooter asks.

"Been like that." The last thing I need is more drama in my

life. Scooter can charm the birds out of trees. You'd be a fool to say yes. I wish I was a fool back then.

"Give me a minute," he says to his girl, not even turning to face her. I try to place a name to a face. Honey? Olive? Some kind of food that isn't fit for a child, but it works for her. She moves through life like she was meant to be consumed by the masses.

"I don't want to be out there alone." She raises her voice to compete with the bass of NBA YoungBoy. "You know I don't know nobody in this neighborhood."

"Chill. It'll only be a minute," he says. "Go in the kitchen and get us some chocolate cake." His wish is her command. Her sharp eyes pierce the side of my face as Scooter grabs my wrist and leads me through the crowd and out the front door.

I shake my arm loose. "Get off of me. You're not allowed to drag me out of parties anymore. I'm not your girl."

"I'm not dragging you out of the party. Besides, what are you doing here this late anyway? Where's the baby? You're here shaking your ass and she's home."

He got his nerve questioning me. I'm the one with Mia every day. I'm the one waking up in the middle of the night when she has a stomachache and up first thing in the morning to get her ready for the day. I'm there and he isn't.

"You don't have the right to ask me about my child," I say. "She can understand things, you know? That includes recognizing she has a sometime father. When you spend more than thirty minutes with her at a time, then you can ask me about Mia. Until then, fuck off."

"From what I hear, she only has a sometime mother," he spits.

"Working, going to school and then college. How are you going to take care of a baby? Shana can't be a mama to all three of y'all."

"Is that what this is about?" I ask. "What's not clicking, Scooter? You have no say in my daughter's life or my life."

I hate being that baby mama. Making a scene in the middle of a party, but he has all the nerve.

"You don't need me no more?" He pulls out a pack of Newports and slaps the back. Dej used to say that's him waking up the tobacco.

"I don't, but your kid does," I say. "You're going to give her a fucking complex. Walking in and out of her life. One day I might not let you back in, and then what? You cool with having your daughter in the world without a daddy?"

"Go on with all that dramatic shit. I'll be by to see her this weekend. My mama taking her to get ice cream."

"She can't eat ice cream yet," I say.

"We know that. It's just to get her out of the house."

"If I tell her you're coming, and you don't show up, that's it. Strike three. We're done. According to you, you don't even have a baby, remember?"

"You are so sensitive. I know Mia mine." He takes a smooth puff. "I'm going to do better. A girl needs her daddy or they end up fucked up in the head."

"Where did this change of heart come from?"

"I've been reading more lately. About childhood and how it affects you in the long run. Do you know you have this whole memory that you can't even remember if it's traumatic enough?

They gotta get doctors and shit to bring it to the front. But she's only four months old. She won't know the difference yet."

I trace the heart-shaped tattoo I got in honor of Mia. "She has a whole personality now. She knows you're not there."

"Like I said, I'll be there. Make sure she's ready."

I purse my lips. "Whatever, man. Now why you drag me out here? I know it wasn't to lie in my face about some funky ice cream."

"Do the baby need anything?" He pulls money from his back pocket and hands over another hundred-dollar bill. "That should cover whatever."

That won't even cover day care, but it can put food in her mouth for the week.

I fold the money in half and put it in my pocket. I'm no fool. "What the fuck do you want?"

His face curls into a smile. "You thought any more about what I said? Come work for me, baby. You'd be making more than fifteen an hour. You know I got you. You always been about your paper. You take a bad situation and you nip it in the bud. Don't let that shit get you down."

"You gotta do that when you have a baby looking up to you."

"Then come on."

"I'm not getting caught up with you."

He hushes his voice, even though with the normal sounds of the neighborhood, and the music from inside, no one will be able to hear us. "Y'all still ain't paid your back rent? Where y'all going? 'Cause I know you ain't trying to take my baby to a fucking shelter."

"You don't know anything about my business."

"I know that if you can't take care of Mia, my mama said I can go for full custody."

He's smug. They don't want Mia. Scooter just wants the satisfaction of me not having her.

"They are not giving my baby to you. You don't even know her. You can't cook, wash a bib; you're useless to me and her."

"The judge will know that I have a place to sleep that's not in the middle of the hood. We got money, and everything else Mia needs."

"You're not taking my baby," I say.

He stomps out the butt of his cigarette. Careful not to get any ash on his new retro Jordans, but no child support in months— you just have to laugh. "That all rests in your hands, baby girl. Good luck." He yells back into the house, "Olive! Come on, I'm ready to go."

She lurks in the back, near the door. She runs when called and slips her hand into his. "It was nice meeting you."

"He's not worth it."

She looks down at her stilettos.

"Let's roll." Scooter drags her along.

He's *not* getting my baby.

CHAPTER 7

"I'M LATE!" MIA perched on my hip as I fly down the stairs. Her little clip-on barrette that she finally has enough hair for hangs on for dear life. Today's my second day at the shop—being late to the Pizza Junt was one thing, but something like this? My dream? Nah, can't be late for those.

The first two days were slow. Only had to sweep once and washed half a head because the lady said I didn't massage her scalp the right way. Ms. Dubois said that she has some kids coming today, though, and I'll be able to wash them all the way through. Maybe even practice parting their hair for knotless braids.

"I'll watch Mia for you today," Shana says.

"Thank you!" I don't even question it. Extra money in my pocket for the day.

I unpack her baby bag. "Pampers, Lamby, her pacifier, and breast milk is in the fridge. I got a full pump last night. She should be good. Please don't let her nap all day, Shana. I have a paper due this week and I need to get it done. Can't do that if she's crying all night."

"B'onca, I gotta tell you something."

"There's an extra change of clothes, her books with the dancing ballerinas, and there are some *CoComelon* episodes queued up on YouTube."

"B'onca, sit down," she says again.

"No time." I make sure my own bag is packed with everything I need.

"B, Scooter died last night."

I still don't turn around to face her.

"You're tripping. I just saw Scooter. You must got him mixed up with his little brother. They look like twins. I'll call him later and check up on him."

Same face but couldn't be more different. Scooter's brother off at some fancy school up north. In his second year. Scooter was always jealous of how he was his parents' favorite, but who could blame them?

"It was on the news, baby. They said his name." This time, Shana comes to me. Tears fall from her face before they do mine. "I'm sorry. I'm so sorry."

My knees give out and I fall into the kitchen chair. Mia bounces in my lap. Questions. There are so many questions. Mia laughs in my arms, yanking at my cheap golden necklace. She doesn't have a clue what's going on. She doesn't know that she'll never see her daddy again. I pull her close to me and go over her face. My cheeks, Scooter's eyes. A mixture of us both. Grandma's face shape, Mama's smile. Now he'll only be stories in her life.

Stories that I have to tell her, but what do I tell a kid about a dead daddy who didn't want her? Do I make it up as I go along?

Hey, Google. What's the guide to that?

"You okay, B'onca?" Shana pulls me into a hug and kisses Mia forehead.

"How did it happen?" I need to cry, but tears won't fall.

"I called one of his aunties before you woke up. Someone stabbed him. Punctured some organs or something. Down at the park. A woman was jogging this morning and found him."

"Mama's park?"

Shana nods. "They are questioning people, but you know folks down there don't remember shit. They barely knew they were talking to cops; they were high as hell."

"Can you take her?" I say. "I need to get some air. I'll be right back. I promise."

"Don't worry. I already emailed Mrs. Crenshaw and told her you wouldn't be in for school next week. She saw the news and figured. I'll let Ms. Dubois know as well."

Mia won't let go of my thumb as Shana takes her from me. I slip on my tennis shoes and head out the door. The streets are empty. Quiet. Moving vans park along the street. Some neighbors are moving in. More people are moving out.

I walk the streets, retracing my life with Scooter.

The green box where we first met. I was fourteen and he'd just turned sixteen. Mama told me to stay away from him. That boys like him were bad for girls like me, but I ain't take Ma's advice. I mean, what kind of advice could a drug addict with two different baby daddies tell me?

Nothing but hot air being blown out. That's all Ma did. Talked but never took action. If I saw Mia running around with someone like Scooter, I'd snatch her up by the collar so quickly, her head would spin.

Not Ma, though. Especially when Scooter started leaving money and other things on the table. Fucked up.

Further down is the rib spot where we had our first date. Scooter was a show-off and rented it out for three hours. Must have cost a grip but he said I was worth it. He bought tons of food to sample. This was when money was tight for me and food was short. After a ramen and bologna sandwich diet, those ribs tasted like the finest cuisine.

We ate and laughed. He asked me things about myself that people never cared to know. He was the first person I ever told I wanted to go to cosmetology school.

He said he'd buy me a shop one day.

When we left, I was fully expecting him to tell me he wanted some. I mean, I ain't never met no one around this way who wouldn't ask, especially after a date like that.

We ain't doing nothing.

I said it with an attitude, but if he would have asked, I might have said yes.

Girl, I don't want nothing from you but to take you out again.

The next weekend he did. Weekend after that, too. Three months of weekends filled with dates to the zoo, dining on the river, money for nails and hair. Even Shana got jealous. And I can't lie. I liked the attention, liked feeling like someone cared about me for once.

That feeling is a drug that I got high off every time I was with Scooter.

At the end of the block is the first store I saw him steal from.

Only until things pick up again at work, Scooter said all sweet like. *You want to keep getting all these nice things?*

It's wrong, though.

You want to go back to being dirty? Not having shit? He held my hand up. *I'll pop these expensive-ass nails off right now and you can go back to the projects.*

Ma never asked Scooter where he got the income from. I guess she assumed his parents were funding his lifestyle. Shana caught on after a while. Threatened to tell Ma. Threatened to kick my ass. All the things you were supposed to do when your little sister rocking with someone like Scooter, especially as closely as I was.

By that point, Ma was too far gone to care. I hid it from everyone, even Savannah. I never told her that Mama was going through it. Everyone assumed she was on the up and up. In reality, she was too high to pay attention.

Too out of it to pay bills.

I never stole anything myself, but he taught me the ins and outs. How to time it properly to not get caught, what to do if you do get caught, and his most important lesson—see something, don't say nothing.

I never had to put my lessons to use. His way of protecting me, I guess.

The first time we had sex was when Mia was conceived. Ma had just left for her nightly get-high session. We had the apartment to ourselves that night, and he'd waited long enough, according to him.

There were other girls who'd give it up, according to him.

Other girls who'd be proud to call themselves his girl.

The first time wasn't bad. I'd never had sex before—shocker, I know.

But I hadn't. When you see up close what happens to girls who do, you chill out a bit.

Do you have a condom?

Nah, I don't use them. I can't feel anything.

Go get one.

It's late and all the stores are closed. It can't happen the first time.

We sat in silence after that. Listened to the music that blasted outside my bedroom window. He rubbed my leg, and then my back. Trying to loosen me up. It worked, I guess.

Go ahead.

There wasn't any excitement. No pain or pleasure. He bought me these fye earrings afterward, which I remember more than the act.

A few people are outside Scooter's apartment. I don't get too close because I don't want to talk to anyone. Whitney crying her eyes out on his stoop, rubbing her stomach like she's scrubbing a pot. She's giving people the show of a lifetime. He wasn't even with her anymore. I wonder where his other girlfriend is. Hopefully in the house like someone with common sense. I'm sure more women will come out on social media about how they were seeing him.

More kids. More lies. More fake tears.

But here Whitney crying like she the grieving wife.

She must spot me from across the street. She doesn't even look both ways before she crosses.

"I'm so sorry, B'onca." She grabs hold of me and won't let go, like we sister wives or something. Her tears soak my thin white tee.

"Whitney, go home. You shouldn't be here right now. All this stress isn't good for you or the baby."

"Why aren't *you* crying?"

There ain't nothing to cry about.

I say the socially acceptable thing. "I have to be strong for Mia. Like you have to be strong for your baby."

I hand her off to her two best friends and keep on my journey.

The grocery store where I took the pregnancy test with Deja in the small stall next to me. I took three of them—on each one the word PREGNANT turned up within five seconds.

Google what that means when it does that.

That your hCG levels are high.

What does that mean?

You're pregnant as hell.

Telling Scooter was a disaster. I didn't really even tell him, just sent a picture of the test. I still have that day screenshotted on my phone.

Read: 10:17

I didn't hear from him for three weeks after that. Waited. Only for him to tell me he didn't want it. That I should get rid of it. That we were too young and babies ruin things.

You just have to see it and you'll change your mind.

I won't.

I told you to use a condom.

I pulled out.

Google says that only works some of the time.

You probably were fucking around.

Fuck you, Scooter.

The park where he died is my last stop. Vials and other things lie strewn around. Even a touch of his blood that hasn't been washed away.

All the hell he put me through, and this is the last of him.

His blood on the sidewalk.

Passersby give me looks of sympathy as they place teddy bears and flowers, and light candles, at a nearby tree.

"I'm sorry for your loss, B'onca."

"Keep your head up, baby."

"Let me know if you need anything."

I need answers quickly.

What do you tell a child whose deadbeat father has died?

I could pretend that he died honorably. That he wasn't a liar, a manipulator, a criminal. Scooter might have been my hell, but he was heaven to some people.

But how do you tell a child that?

Even the few times Mia saw him, she knew he was her daddy. Didn't cry when he held her. Fell right asleep on his chest, as if she knew she was safe there.

Now I'm the only parent she has to keep her safe. To keep her healthy, protected, and fed.

I walk up to the memorial and look up at the dull gray sky.

"Rest in hell, Scooter."

CHAPTER 8

MIA IS NOT supposed to be here. She shouldn't have to see her daddy in a casket, but Scooter's parents insisted I bring her. The church is packed with people I barely know. His crew sits behind me in the second row. Whitney included, even though she acted an ass about wanting to sit with the family.

Mia sleeps in her grandma's arms. Shana and Cyn somewhere in the back. Cyn hates funerals. Mostly because she doesn't understand death yet. She's just a kid; the unknown is still scary to her. Everyone keeps asking me how I feel. Expecting me to break down in their arms. I don't have the energy to tell them I don't feel anything but stressed. I know it's stupid, but I had a little hope that Scooter would grow up. That one day he'd try to right his wrongs and be in his daughter's life.

I was looking forward to those Saturday ice-cream visits that never came.

Now he lies in a gold casket in front of me. His hands to his sides. A stillness that has the whole church in tears. Whitney the loudest. One of the ushers has to escort her out. I hear someone tell them that she's with child. His mama ain't even crying that much, and I'm not sure why. Maybe she'd already come to peace with it. That the way Scooter lived was never going to end well. Either in the grave or in prison.

A bunch of amens ring and I realize that I zoned out during the eulogy. The family stands and walks behind the casket. The burial ground is next, but I don't think I can handle that.

"She needs to be fed." Scooter's ma got Mia wrapped tight. The only thing in the world that's of him. Until Whitney's baby comes, of course.

"Are y'all coming to the burial?" She places Mia gently in my arms. "I know it's been a long day."

"She's tired. I think we should go home."

"At least come to the repast later. It's time for the family to meet Mia. I always told Scooter that he needed to do right by her while he still had time. Now look." She takes out a tissue as tears fall down her face.

I don't have the heart to tell her no.

I nod, say my goodbye, and find Shana. Cyn's face wet with tears.

"Let's go, y'all," I say.

We stop in front of the church and watch as Scooter's casket is loaded into a black hearse.

"B'onca, come take a walk with me." Mrs. Crenshaw pulls me to the side, guiding me through the hall of students before I can even respond.

"You don't have to come back to school," she says. "I'll keep emailing you your work. You've been doing an excellent job of turning everything in on time."

There was no point in sitting home and being sad. Scooter is buried six feet now. Under dirt, maggots, and worms. I'm sure wherever he is, he's paying for what he did on Earth.

"There's only a few weeks left of summer school," I say. "I need to make it count or I won't graduate for real."

She stops at the faculty mailbox, pulls out a stack of papers. "You're going to get your diploma. Trust me."

I can't help but wonder if it's because I deserve it or because my baby daddy just died.

"Is that all?" I ask.

She lays a stack of brochures in my hands. Hilbert open-house book. Black faces smiling in two-toned sweatshirts. AT HILBERT, WE ARE A FAMILY headlines the paper. Here we go again with college. Shana has been giving me a break since everything happened with Scooter. I can play the grief card for the rest of the summer if I want to.

"I'm not going to college. Not a four-year college anyway. We can't afford it, and now without Scooter, I have to think about providing for Mia."

"Then take these." She pulls a smaller brochure from the back of the pile. It's not full of happy Black people, but a picture of a smiling woman with a fresh perm looks back at me.

"You should check them out," Mrs. Crenshaw says, more like a command than a statement. "Trade school is just as good, and if you can do hair like you say you can, apply."

"I'm thinking I should get a job instead," I say. "College doesn't pay bills. Baby girl needs new things every day. I'd rather stack my money and then think of college down the road."

"That's what everyone says. They'll go back. It's not the right time. Before you know it, you're forty, and you have three more babies. College is the last thing on your mind."

"I'll think about forty when I get there."

"How about taking out an academic loan?" she asks.

"You have to pay those back, and you're not even guaranteed a job."

There's always a catch to the come-up. Go the academic route and you're stuck in debt for the rest of your life. Ain't no time to stop and enjoy your labor, because the thought that it can all come to an end is buzzing in the back of your head. Sometimes I want to give up. Collect some government money and call it a day. But Mia won't be a baby forever. She's going to look up at me one day, and I pray that she likes what she sees.

Mrs. Crenshaw presses the brochure into my hand. "Hilbert has an open house next weekend. Think about going. For me? There'll be some extra credit in it for you."

"I can't make any promises."

"Think about it." Mrs. Crenshaw pats my hand before disappearing into the principal's office. The clock hits twelve and the bell rings, clearing out the crowded hall.

College don't buy happiness. College spoils it. By trapping me in an environment that I won't be able to get into or out of. Savannah an exception to the rule. She has always been the exception. College working for her, but it's *not* for me.

Money is what I need.

CHAPTER 9

RIDGECREST IS FUNNY.

Folks trying to take over our part of the neighborhood, but three blocks up they won't touch. I guess they think Third Street's too rough. A street, but a neighborhood within a neighborhood. This is where Shana and I grew up. I can still taste the freeze cups and the hose water that got us through the summer days. When Ma bounced, Shana moved us to our current spot. Saved up every penny to give us a semblance of a better life. A yard to ourselves. Somewhere we ain't have to worry about bullets every night.

Seems like it's all in vain now.

In my new neighborhood, people can fight for our house, fight for our street. We have some sort of voice. The folks over here are silent, probably don't know they got rights because nobody ever told them that before. People nod at me as I enter the gates. Folks sit outside on their porches to give their AC a break during the day. They hang their clothes out on the lines, and voices float through the parking lot. There's always somebody selling something. Candy, socks, DVDs, fish plates. Any random thing you can think about, somebody got it. The sock man holds up his product and shouts through his hands, "Twenty packs for five dollars!" A steal, but it's summer, and I'm rocking cheap sandals until a strap breaks or a sole gets a hole in it.

"B'onca, it's good to see you," Savannah's ma, Ms. Howard, says between clipping her Sunday dresses on the clothesline. "You look good. Done lost all that baby weight, I see."

"Thank you! I'm trying to get to my old self again."

"That's good. What are you doing here? You know your sister doesn't like you over with us common folks."

Everyone in the projects is old-school. They believe that community helps keep the kids in line. It ain't work for their own kids, and it barely works for me.

"I wanted to come see old friends," I say.

She scrunches her face, checking the dryness of clothes on the line. "Them girls ain't no good, B'onca. You know that."

I try my hardest not to make a face or sigh too loud.

I yell over the bass of a Cutlass that rolls slowly down the street. "You know where Deja and 'em at?"

She crosses her arms over her chest. "They're in the back. Probably stirring up trouble."

I follow the sounds of music and laughter. There's a small area carved out for the kids to hang out. They got an unspoken pact with the older folks: if you gone do dirt, do it in secret, because no one wants to see that. Elders act like if they don't see something, then it doesn't exist. I ain't never got the logic of that.

Deja crouches down, rolls her dice, and snaps her fingers. "Damn, man! I told you not to take calls when I'm shooting. It distracts me."

A dude with tattoos covering his neck and head holds out his hand. "You ain't tell me a bitch-ass thing. Now give me my money. You wanna play with the big boys, you gotta pay like them too."

She kicks up dust and it lands on his new white Forces. Damn near a federal offense.

"Bet you gone clean them, too," he says.

"Man, I ain't cleaning nothing up." Deja steps, her five-foot-five frame tiny compared to his six-four. "You're trying to cheat me out of my money."

He turns to his partners, who all have yellow flags hanging out of their left pockets. "Man, somebody get this girl before I hurt her."

Deja not letting up. She never knows when to back down, even when her ops got the upper hand. Always relying on someone else for help.

"Dej, why you acting up?" I walk over, getting a closer look at the folks she's arguing with. All kids we went to school with at one point or another. Most of them dropped out. I think the tallest one is still trying, even though he is like nineteen in the eleventh grade.

"Oh shit." They all jump off the porch and to the gravel parking lot. "Look who's rejoined us hood rats. Sorry about Scooter, fam. He left us all fucked up out here."

"I ain't even get to cop the new Air Maxes," a guy with a half-done head says. "The boosters around here are all too scary."

Deja slides her wad of dollars into her pocket. No one notices but me and her.

"Cops are too hot nowadays," Deja says. "Nobody can barely get anything."

"I know Scooter taught you the game. Why don't you take over for him?" the ringleader says. He is fine as hell. Tall and a nice pair of teeth. Before Scooter, I wouldn't have hesitated to get his number, chill on the block with him until Shana started to worry, but now romance is the last thing on my mind.

Besides, I can't help but think my body belongs to Mia.

I shrug. "Y'all know I got a baby now. I can't be doing that."

Him and his crew flop around in unison. All dramatic and shit. "Aw, naw! Even B'onca got soft. There ain't no hope anymore."

"Buy your shoes full price," Deja says. "Since y'all got it like that."

"Whatever, girl." He packs up his dice and money. "Don't think I forgot you owe me, and I always collect."

"You need to stop playing with their money." I sit on the edge of Deja's car. "Shit like that catch up with you."

She jumps up next to me. "Ain't nobody studdin' his ass." We pass Skittles back and forth and watch a basketball game. The hoop is a milk crate, but it works the same.

"They tell y'all what's going to happen if they decide to tear this place down?" I ask.

"Nope, and to be honest, I ain't even tripping about it. They stopped doing anything for us a long time ago. The rats out of control now. The roaches. Everything is too much. If we can get a Section 8 voucher, I'd happily get me and Moms a crib. Maybe even over there by Davant with y'all."

"Shit, if we still be over there our damn self," I say. "Yesterday I saw a white man just sitting there. Watching us like a hawk, didn't move for a good two hours. I don't know what he was trying to see."

"How easy it's going to be to fuck us over," she says.

"They can have it." I shake my handful of Skittles. "It's too much trouble."

"Don't tell me you done gave up?"

"There's too much happening. I try not to think about Scooter, but sometimes the what-ifs pop in my head. Some days I can barely get out of bed. Ms. Dubois says my job there whenever I'm ready to come back, but sweeping hair for fifteen an hour doesn't seem like that much when I get down to it. After I'm done helping with bills, there's hardly anything left over for Mia. I need real money, but I can't think of a way."

Deja rolls her eyes. "That is chump change, to be honest. Maybe them boys were onto something when they said think about taking over Scooter's business. I mean, if his dumb ass didn't get caught, I know you could do it."

"I can't lose no time with my baby. She is the only good thing I got going for myself."

Deja passes a bottle of fruity liquor, and I take a swig. "You're right. It's the liquor," she says. "I'm talking crazy."

"I'll figure something out," I say. "Don't make any plans for next weekend. Mrs. Crenshaw wants me to go to some open house at Hilbert. She's going to give me extra credit if I do it."

"Bet." Deja helps me down from the car. The alcohol takes control of my body and I stumble over my feet.

"Damn, you can't hold your liquor anymore?"

"I've been sober for a year and a half." I hiccup and giggle at the same time. "Besides, I'm not that drunk."

"You gone be aight?" Deja asks. "You want me to walk you home? It's getting dark out."

I catch my balance, walk one foot at a time. "I got it. I told Shana I was going to the library to get her to watch the baby. If she sees me with you, she gone know that was a lie."

Deja bumps me with her shoulder, sending me damn near across the parking lot. "You tryna say I don't study?"

"You know the last book you cracked open was Goosebumps."

She laughs so hard she snorts. "All right, well, text me when you get home." She walks me to the gates and points me in the right direction. "You got this, B. Don't even trip."

"I hope so. I'll cya later, girl," I say before starting my walk. It's quiet. Too quiet for a summer night. It's making me anxious. Like anything can pop out at any moment. My house ain't far from here, four blocks and I'm home, but it seems to be taking forever. Everything's moving slow. Damn, what did Deja put in that drink?

Whistling starts behind me. I look over my shoulder at the shadow that fills the sidewalk. I can't tell if it's a boy or girl shadow. I just know I'm tipsy, and the whistling is making my hands tremble. I don't look both ways before crossing the street. The shadow follows.

You ain't no punk. "Damn, why you all up on me? Trent?" I blink twice, trying to take in his appearance. It's been a minute since I saw him at the party. Whenever I see him, it's like seeing something different.

"I saw you stumbling. I wanted to make sure you got home safe. I heard about Scooter, too. My condolences." He steps into the light, giving me a better view of him. He's dressed down in sweatpants and a cropped tee. His smart watch glows on his wrist.

"It's cool. You knew Scooter. It isn't such a tragic loss." Ugh, that sounds mean as hell. I blame the alcohol.

"Do you mind if I walk with you?" he asks.

"You going that way anyway," I say like I don't care, but we both know I do. Trent might have been the first boy I ever *liked* liked. Scooter was different. I don't think I liked him more than I liked what he did for me. With Trent it was different. Emotional. We did everything together from the time I was four months pregnant until he left. Sometimes I think about what could have happened if we'd continued to grow together, but there's no point in wouldas, couldas, and shouldas. Even when he was here, we'd already started to grow apart. He'd gotten more involved with Scooter and his crew, and I was too busy worrying about Mia.

"You never showed me a picture of the baby," he says, walking close enough for me to smell his signature jojoba-oil smell but far away enough for me not to think anything about it. "I know she has your entire face. Those Johnson genes are strong."

"She Ma's twin, to be honest." I steady my phone in my hands and flip through pictures of Mia.

"She's adorable. You couldn't deny her if you tried." He looks from the phone to me like he's trying to confirm his theory. "Got that big ole head."

"Boy, bye." I grin wider than I want to. "Each day she gets bigger and it's scary. Weird to think that one day she'll be our age and I'll be . . ."

"Thirty-four," he says.

"I don't even want to think about it," I say. "You glad to be back?"

"I mean, it's different. Being in a stable house and all. I'm sad Grandma moved away, but her giving Ma that house was the best thing that could have happened for us. Them shelters really messed me up. Then it's weird that all my friends from before—they haven't changed any. Still on the block watching time pass them by."

"I feel you," I say. "Sometimes I think that's what I'm doing."

We stop in front of the house. The porch light immediately comes on. Shana is nosy as hell—it doesn't make no sense.

"I'd invite you in, but Shana probably has on her night-clothes."

"That's cool. I'll drop by tomorrow. Mama wants me to bring by a dish Shana let us borrow. She came by today. I asked about you, must have been fate that we ran into each other."

"Must have been."

That damn alcohol again.

Shana opens the door in her housecoat with Mia in her arms and Cyn pasted to her side. Embarrassing as hell.

"That's my cue to get the hell in the house."

"I got a new number. Can I give it to you?" he asks. "We got a lot to catch up on. I'm sorry again about Scooter."

"It's cool. We weren't on the best of terms anyway. I'm sadder for Mia. It sucks growing up without a parent. I should know."

We exchange phones. He saves his number with a yellow heart emoji.

"B'onca, your daughter is asking for you," Shana yells from behind the screen door.

"I'm coming," I say over my shoulder. "Sorry about her. I'll call you later."

"I'll probably call you first." He waves to the door before disappearing into the dark.

CHAPTER 10

"**MANE, I HATE** coming here."

Shana looks side to side before whispering, "That's too bad. You know this is the only church in town that does things like this. We need the food. You want to be hungry?"

Shana closes her eyes, bows her head, and tunes me out with prayer.

I try to hide my face as more kids from my school come into the church. If we were here to praise God, then that'd be straight. God and I ain't technically on good terms right now, but I believe in giving higher powers second chances. Especially when they've given me my fair chance of repentance or whatever.

Anyway, we only come to the North Side Church of God in Christ for the food they serve in the fellowship hall after eleven o'clock service. Then we stick around until two o'clock for the food drive they do every first Sunday.

By then Mia is screaming because she is hungry, and Shana has to stop and talk to all her li'l friends. It's a whole mess.

We've been coming here for the food drive ever since Mama left. They always pity us and give us extra as long as nobody else complains about it. Sometimes our box is lit, but most times it's trash. Vienna sausages and saltines trash.

Mia bounces in my arms at the chanting, shouting, and loud drums that almost make my ears pop. After two hours of hymn lining, and another of preaching, it's communion time. Now, the only reason I ever got baptized was because Shana stood up when they called people to Christ. I popped up right beside her, not even knowing what baptism meant.

A few weeks later, we were both dipped in a pool and "renewed." I don't think they let me stay under long enough. If I never stepped foot in a church again, it'd be fine with me.

Like I said, God and I ain't on good terms right now.

Back in the day, Grandma kept us in church. Mondays, Wednesdays, and Sundays. Vacation Bible school during the summer and revivals in the fall. Sometimes I wonder: If she was around, would it have made a difference? If church could have kept us together. On the straight and narrow. Maybe Mia was Grandma's way of slowing me down.

I sit still as the ushers call us forward for our sacrament. Shana pops my thigh. "Come on, girl. We're next."

We stand in line for our Welch's grape juice and bland cracker. I wait for someone to notice that I don't have a ring on my finger. Pull me aside and ask if I've confessed before the Lord about the sin that's attached to my hip.

They don't, but I still feel judgment pouring over me.

Just as my stomach starts rumbling, it is time to hit the kitchen.

Shana has no trouble asking for an extra helping of green beans or the bigger piece of chicken from the buffet-style lineup. I, on the other hand, take what they give me. Two tiny chicken wings, a scoop of green beans, and a hard-ass dinner roll. Don't even have the decency to give us the Hawaiian kind.

We take our plates and sit with the other young people in the church. Girls with bright-colored hair and pierced noses. Tattoos on the sides of their faces. I'm the "normal" one, and that's saying something. I'm never the normal one. These the folks the church got to join through their outreach program. They wanted me to help recruit folks once upon a time. I guess they thought if they saw another heathen, they'd be more tempted to join in with us.

Mia sucks on a green bean, making a smacking noise as if it's the greatest thing she's set her lips around. She reaches out her hand for another.

"Slow down, Mama. The food ain't going nowhere."

"Told you not to start feeding her from the table so early. Now she's going to want everything you eat."

"The milk isn't cutting it anymore. Plus, I'm tired of her biting down on my nipples."

The other girls at the table look away, as if *nipple* is the dirtiest word they've ever heard before.

"I'm going to get our box and then we can get out of here," Shana says.

Praise God. I fix Mia up, her church dress stained with green beans now. I'm securing her into her sling when Scooter's parents pop up on me. I was supposed to bring Mia by a few days ago, but getting her ready is too much trouble.

I told them she had a cold.

"Come to Granny." Scooter's mama holds out her arms, and Mia acts like she's known her her whole life. "Where's your bib, huh? Got that pretty dress all dirty."

"Good afternoon, everyone." Scooter's dad doesn't look like the churchgoing type. He's iced out in gold jewelry, even a gold cap in his mouth. Scooter's mama probably drags him here to get his soul saved. Spending eternity alone isn't why people get married.

"When did you start coming to this church?" Scooter's mama asks.

"We come sometimes, not as much as we used to. This is my first time here since Mia was born."

"This is our first time at church in a while," he says. "Feels like old times, but unlike then, I actually pay attention to the word now."

I think back and I can't remember anything Pastor Jones was talking about. Something about Jesus never putting more on you than you can bear, *allegedly.*

"How are you two holding up?" I ask. I don't really care, but it seems like the respectable thing to say. My grieving for Scooter lasted all of three seconds. You can't really grieve someone you didn't know. I knew the *persona* Scooter, but I never knew the boy they named Christian. He kept that part of him shut away.

Maybe if he'd opened up more, done things differently, I could cry it out, but I can't.

But I pretend, because that's the right thing to do.

"We're trying to keep ourselves busy. It gets hard, but we're making it. You should bring Mia by more often. It'll be nice having a baby in the house."

That's not going to happen, but I smile and nod anyway.

"She looks just like Scooter when he was born." Scooter's dad almost seems in a trance as he rubs his thumb along her cheek. "Ain't no denying her, huh?"

"I guess not."

They damn sure tried, but this doesn't seem like the time or place to bring up how they tried to make me DNA test her before they'd even acknowledge Mia. I wonder if they are extending the same courtesy to Whitney. Although she probably volunteered to get a DNA test. Anything to stay in the good graces of folks with money.

Shana breaks the awkwardness between us. "They gave us a lot this week. Cold cuts, a whole chicken, and a bunch of canned goods." She stops going through our box and looks up. "Hey, Mr. and Mrs. Cane. Nice to see y'all again."

"Y'all don't have enough to eat at home?" Mrs. Cane asks. She looks between us, and now I feel self-conscious. This dress fits well, and I made sure to moisturize my skin. Everything can be bypassed if you have good skin. Even poverty.

"We've just fallen on hard times—eviction notices and all that—but we are making it. Ain't that right, B?"

I'm going to kick Shana's ass. Telling the pastor about our problems is one thing, but Scooter's parents, that's something I don't want to get into. They have it all. Enough to never have to even check their bank accounts if they don't want to.

"We're going to pay the bills soon," I clarify.

"I see." Mrs. Cane hands Mia to me, but not before checking her body as if she's searching for something. I know this bitch ain't trying to call me a bad mother. "We'll be talking soon, B'onca."

CHAPTER 11

SHANA SITS AT the kitchen table with bills on one side and a stack of money on the other. Her eyes narrow as she counts out four five-dollar bills. This is her new nightly routine. When she thinks Cyn is sleeping, she comes down and becomes a mathematician.

Somehow she's making it work, because the lights haven't been turned off yet. We still have food, even if it is Vienna sausages and saltines.

"Look who's home from work." Shana holds up Mia's arm and waves it. She's wide awake even though it's almost nine.

"Your tete has you awake this late?" I give Shana the death stare. "She must be staying up with you all night."

Google—that's my parenting book—says you should talk to your baby like anybody else. That *googoo, gaga* shit stunt their growth. Mia doesn't need any more strikes against her.

"She's the one that decided to nap all day." Shana hands Mia off to me. I smother her chunky jaws in kisses before putting her down on her tummy-time mat.

"I told you when she does that to wake her up anyway. She's the baby; you're the adult."

"I forgot, you're mother of the year." Shana stacks twenties, tens, and fives in little piles. No matter how many times she counts, those dollars won't turn into the fifteen hundred we need.

"Auntie cranky tonight." Mia chews on her fingers, not paying attention to anything we got going on. "She needs a nap herself, don't she?"

"You'll understand this adulthood shit one day," Shana says. "Real life hits after you get out on your own. How was work today?"

"It was straight. Took my mind off things for a little while."

"I still can't believe how dirty they are treating us," Shana says.

The late utility and rent bills spread across the table like a fungus. Shana hid the papers well. I never knew how deeply in trouble we were until it was too late to do anything about it.

"They can do whatever they want to us and get away with it. Rich people want to live here now, you know that."

I peek out the window at the river that divides us from them. Long ago, no one with toy dogs and suits crossed that river unless they were looking for things they had no business looking for. Until a few years ago, when things started to change. Small changes at first, like potholes we'd been complaining about for years were mysteriously filled. Actual stop signs were put up, and streetlights changed. Farmers markets showed up, and along with them came people who could afford shit like that. People who actually had Saturday mornings off to do shit like that. People took notice of us and decided we weren't worthy of the views, or the park that got the right amount of shade. The distance to downtown and midtown. No, we ain't take care of things. Scolded like hardheaded toddlers who took too many cookies from the jar.

Shana snaps a rubber band against a small stack of money. "The Canes left a message for you. They said they want to meet about Mia. I think they are looking for custody."

I grip the edge of the table to keep myself from falling out of the chair. "Fuck, no."

"Calm down," Shana says. "They can't walk in and take Mia out of your hands. I'm pretty sure that's not legal."

"You the one told them we were struggling!" I glare at her. She's counting out quarters and nickels now. "Now they are coming for my baby."

"It's not like that's something new. We have been struggling since forever. Don't blame me because you knew that and still made a bad decision."

"A bad decision? The fuck that mean? I don't regret having Mia."

"Not yet, but what about in a few years when you see your friends' lives and you realize that could have been you if you didn't have a baby attached to you? Regret creeps up on us all eventually."

"You want me to give up Mia?"

"I'm saying, it wouldn't be a decision that anyone would judge you for."

"When do they want to meet?" I ask.

"Monday."

The room goes quiet except for the clicking of change on the table. Shana doesn't look up from the pile of money.

"You need help with the bills? I have a little money saved up, and I get paid from the shop on Friday." The Folgers can labeled "rainy day" that hides on the very top shelf of my closet flashes through my mind. It's the last bit of money I have.

"Save that li'l money." She counts the dollar bills again, this time slowly, checking for stuck-together bills. "You might be needing it for a lawyer."

CHAPTER 12

THE TALL TAN building towers over all the others. It's generic. Nothing makes it stand out other than it's the place rich people come to take things from others.

Today, it's my baby.

The Canes didn't even have the decency to call me. To come see me face to face before they try and snatch Mia out of my arms. Talked through Shana as if she had any say. I'm the only living person with rights to Mia.

A man in a suit that makes him look like he's in a gangster movie holds the large door open for us. We step inside and Shana is stunned. Girl is almost straight drooling at the bustle of this fancy building. Folks swipe in and out to get in. Everything is basically made of glass. No privacy. Tall columns hold up the inside, and security arms the place. I guess when you take things from folks you gotta be careful that no one takes something in return.

"This is where you need to be working instead of Ms. Dubois

kitchen. That woman's purse and shoes are real leather. I can tell because she doesn't slouch when she walks."

"You work here, then," I say, searching the directory on the wall. There's law, accounting, and tax firms here. The floors go all the way up to a hundred. I've never been that high.

The Greg and Clayton law firm is on the thirty-fourth floor.

"It's too late for me to be thinking about working at places like this. Your life is just beginning." Shana smiles at everyone who waits at the elevator. Everyone is polite, but I know what they're thinking. *The fuck are these people doing here?* Our attire ain't exactly business, especially since our church clothes were dirty. At least we match, don't have visible stains, and smell good. That's all that matters.

"Shana, chill, you're still in your twenties."

"Miss, can I ask you a question?" Shana turns to a lady who has in AirPods, but Shana's yelling so loud that this woman can't help but acknowledge her.

"Of course." She pops one AirPod out and leans in, but I'm sure she's willing the elevator for the north side of the building to hurry the fuck up.

"How much do you make a year here?"

"Shana," I groan. "You can't be asking folks that, and besides, I do not care. No offense," I add.

"I care and you should too," Shana says. "My sister is going through that adolescent phase of not wanting to go to college."

Oh Lord, her code-switching voice is on.

"Well, I've been here for three years, and this year I'm projected to hit the six-figure mark with bonuses and everything. But trust me, it's not as much as it sounds after taxes."

The thing about rich people is that you can ask them what they make, and they'll say some exorbitant amount but then add some "it's not as much as it seems" shit. If I was banking a hundred stacks a year, there'd be no limit to the things I could accomplish. To her, a hundred stacks only the beginning. For me, I'ma have to work my whole life to make that, and maybe have ten years to enjoy it if I'm lucky.

The north-side elevator dings, and Ms. Six Figures slips Shana her business card and tells her to have a nice day.

"You see that, a tax accountant, and you talking about doing some hair."

I zone Shana out and focus on the beeping elevator as it reaches each floor. Shana got too many regrets. Her whole life story is full of things she wishes she could have done differently.

Am I being selfish by letting Mia stay with me? Will that be my big regret? Scooter's parents can give her more. A consistent roof over her head, for one. Organic baby food that they mix up themselves, not that jar shit that I don't even know what's in it. Toys not handed down from Cyn. But if they really wanted her to have those things, they could help me. Give me the resources to do better and not try and snatch her from me. My whole life, no one has ever tried to teach me nothing—they just expect that I know. With Mia it's no different: there's no handbook to parenting. We all make this shit up, but I guess the Canes forgot them days.

Mia takes up all the space in my heart. I can't have her out there thinking I abandoned her like Mama did me. That's a hurt that never goes away, even when you think you're over it.

Knowing your own ma isn't there to cheer you on makes every piece of attention you receive feel like Christmas.

Nah, Mia can't know that hurt.

The elevator finally stops at the lobby. People fly out before we step on. Shana is still running her mouth about all the things I can be, until we're on our floor. It's underwhelming compared to the lobby. Everything's tan and beige. I'd rather be in Ms. Dubois shop, where there are colorful walls and colorful people.

We find the reception desk and Shana does the talking. The older lady instructs us to keep straight and make a left.

"Listen to what they have to say and watch your mouth," Shana says.

"I don't need to listen to them. She's my baby, and I already know what I want to do," I say.

"You *think* you know."

Mr. and Mrs. Cane wave at us through the glass window, all casual, as if we're meeting for lunch.

"Good morning, you two." Mr. Cane holds the door open for us. The space is small on account of the long-ass oak desk that sits in the middle. They have an open file in front of them; Mia's picture is attached at the top. The lawyer's at the head of the table. Shana and I sit across from the Canes.

Them vs. Us
Us vs. Them?

Although Shana hasn't said it outright, I know she thinks I should give Mia to them. It'd be easier on her. One less child to worry about. It's hard enough on me taking care of Doodle. Three kids and I probably would have lost my mind a long time ago.

"Welcome, everyone. I'm Dominique Stone. Thank you for being on time for this important matter." Dominique is all of thirty-five, with a baby face. She's trying too hard to prove herself as someone to take seriously. Her whole outfit designer, but her heels barely lift her off the ground. To be honest, she looks like she belongs at summer school with me, and this is the person I'm supposed to take seriously? *Shit.* She passes out pens to us all. They really think I'm signing over my rights to my baby after a thirty-minute meeting?

"Can someone just hurry up and tell me why I'm here?"

"B'onca," Shana warns. "That mouth. Watch it."

Dominique returns to her place at the head of the table. "We are here today about the well-being of Mia Cane."

"Johnson. Mia's last name is Johnson, because Scooter wanted a paternity test before signing the birth certificate, even though he knew the baby was his."

"Is his name on the birth certificate?" Dominique asks.

"It is now." Mrs. Cane slides a piece of paper toward the front. Mia's birth certificate. Surprised Scooter kept his copy. "Christian had a lot going for him, and girls took advantage of that. You weren't the first person who claimed to be pregnant with his baby. You know that, don't you?"

"Are you going through all of this over Whitney's baby?"

97

"No, Whitney is capable of rearing a child. She has two parents in a stable home. You, on the other hand, do not."

Shana sits back in her chair, not saying a damn word. She must agree with them. I knew she wouldn't be on my side about this.

"Mrs. Cane brought up the fact that you're on the verge of losing your home on account of back bills." Dominique is now staring at Shana, but Shana ain't saying shit.

"We're working on it," I say. "I mean, we have a month before they actually start the eviction process. You haven't even given me time."

"We have to wait that long for our grandbaby to be on the street?" Mrs. Cane asks.

"She won't be on the street."

"How do you know that?" Mr. Cane asks.

"Because I know," I say through my teeth.

Dominique glances at a sheet inside her file. "If the grandparents of the child fear that the baby is in danger, it is within their legal right to go after custody of said child."

Mrs. Cane reaches out her hand to me. There's a gold ring on every other finger. "It won't be forever, B'onca. Just until you get on your feet again. You can come by and see her anytime you want. We won't keep her from you."

"We already have a nursery set up," Mr. Cane adds. "Baby food, diapers, clothes, toys, and day care in place. You can go back to being a little girl yourself."

"I haven't been a little girl in years."

I never got a chance to be small in the world. Grown before

sixth grade. When you're worrying about eating real food, playing with toy kitchens doesn't seem that appealing.

"B," Shana whispers in my ear. "Listen. Are you listening? Only having to worry about yourself can be a luxury. Finish summer school, go to cosmetology school if you want. Make mistakes. Be young."

But my baby. All that ain't worth it without her.

"What happens if I say no? If I don't turn over custody?"

"Then the Canes can and will file an official petition of custody," Dominique says.

"Think this through, B'onca. Lawyers cost money. We don't want to drag this to court," Mrs. Cane says.

"Give me a few months, please? You know I'm a good mother. You never fell on hard times when you were starting out? It's hard, but I know I can fix this."

The cracking of my voice must let Mrs. Cane know I'm serious. "Two months, B'onca. That's all, and if I hear anything about Mia being in trouble, I'll have you back here so fast."

I just need time. Time I'm going to use to get the bills paid, show Mia that I'll never abandon her.

I have sixty days.

Starting now.

PART 2

CHAPTER 13

"WE COULD BE doing a billion other things on a Saturday instead." Deja and I dodge honking horns and kids on bicycles as we make our way to Hilbert's information session. A few kids from our street follow. Word spread it'd be free swag and food: the best way to get a kid who might not have eaten since lunch the day before to come check out a college everyone knows they can't afford.

"Who you telling? Saturdays are the best days to work at Ms. Dubois, but Mrs. Crenshaw is gonna give me extra credit and I need that. Plus, I have to be on my best behavior, or the Canes are going to snatch Mia. Showing them that I'm trying to better myself will get them off my back." I adjust Mia in the sling across my chest. Her tears wet the fabric, and I know that cry. She's hungry. "We need to find a bathroom real quick. She'll cry her head off if she doesn't eat soon."

We find a bathroom in an old dusty building on the far side of campus. Deja guards the door. I know it's acceptable now for women to breastfeed in public, but folks already stare at me funny when they think I'm not looking.

"She takes a minute to latch on." I guide my nipple to her mouth like a spoon of peas. She bites down and I damn near scream.

"You know I can go to the store right now and get you a few cans of formula," Deja says. "Free ninety-nine."

"Nah, I'm okay. My body was made to do this. Right?"

Deja shrugs, and I keep trying to grin through the pain but it becomes unbearable. Tears threaten to fall. The one thing I'm supposed to be able to do, I can't.

Deja looks at me through the mirror. "Don't beat yourself up about it. She ain't even crying."

"Damn, it's like I can't give my baby nothing. No wonder the Canes want to take her from me."

"You give her plenty. You around, ain't you? That's more than some of these sorry mothers can say."

That makes me think of Ma and where she is. If she's safe. Would she be proud of me? All the things I want to tell her about life now. Mia's coos send me back to reality. She looks up at me with her big ole eyes and giggles a little.

"Ain't nothing funny, Doodlebug. Mommy nipples hurt."

"Words I never thought I'd hear you say." Dej snaps pics in the mirror. She catches one of me putting my boob back in my shirt.

"Don't post that," I warn.

"Trust me, I'm not trying to scare my followers."

She shows me her phone. Whitney's social name pops up. She hearted Deja's picture of Mia.

"She wants y'all to be friends, don't it?"

Mia rests on my shoulder as I try to burp her a little bit. "She thinks since Scooter died, we're supposed to be the ones to carry on his legacy. I truly would rather forget he existed."

That sounds harsh, but Scooter's death isn't something I can dwell on right now. You ask me, he has it better than me. An eternal rest is candy compared to my hell on Earth.

"It must be hard for her, though? Being pregnant and all."

I lift Mia to my face and sniff her diaper. She's good for now. "She ain't too fucked up about it. She posts every day about parties and shit. I've only been to one party since Mia was born."

It still blows my mind how much changes in a year. Last year I ain't even know nipples could chafe so badly or stretch marks could be over your whole body. That being an adult ain't that fun and growing up too fast is scary as hell. It's like a roller coaster you can't get off.

I wrap Mia up and then we're back outside with the crowd. The campus is huge. It's nestled between houses, but this place seems like its own little world. Deja actually getting into it too. She points at all the buildings on the map, and I point out all the tall statues and water fountains around campus. Mia must be fascinated because she doesn't cry at all. It's like we ain't even in the same neighborhood anymore.

"Aye, if you come here, we gotta check out all the frat parties." Deja nods to the houses across the street. GREEK ROW is what it's called on the map. "Trent might even come here too. You know what that mean."

"It means that we barely won't see each other like we do now. Boys not on my mind. How many times I got to say it?"

"Mm-hmm, that's what they all say."

Major booths are set up in the quad. The Fine Arts Department, English Department, and the Business Department. That one is for me.

"Welcome to Hilbert!" an enthusiastic student with a green Hilbert shirt shouts, and then lowers her voice when she sees Mia sleeping. "I'm sorry."

"Don't worry about it. She can sleep through anything." I kiss the top of her head. "Isn't that right, Doodlebug?"

"She has such gorgeous curls." She stands up to get a better look, and before I know it, Mia is wide awake. Guess she wanted to get her props.

"My name is B'onca Johnson, and I want to major in accounting."

"Our very own businesswoman." Deja tucks a braid behind my ear while flicking away invisible lint from my tank top. Dej swear she somebody mama.

"I'm Kara and I'm a senior here." Kara hands a folder to each of us. "Everyone who graduates from our program goes on to have a bright future. Accounting is a great option."

For some reason that word triggers me.

Options. You have options.

That's what the social worker with the bright eyes told me as I sat in the flimsy hospital chair under an unimpressive fluorescent light. *Pregnant. With child. Expecting.* She explained it fifty different ways, but I couldn't understand what was happening until

106

the word *abortion* left her lips. Then I thought of skinny Kimmy up the street. The one with two and a half kids, and she is my age. Did she know her options? If so, why did she choose that? From the outside looking in, she ain't doing too bad. Her kids always have new things, bellies full and hair combed. Nobody knows what goes on for real, though. When the babies are sleeping on a Friday night and your phone is blowing up, asking, *Are you coming out?* Because even though you're a mother, you're still a kid yourself. A child who had options, but those options never seemed feasible.

Deja skims through the folder. "Damn, people who graduate from here go on to work at places like FedEx and Amazon. You'll be making crazy money."

"Hilbert is slowly becoming a top-rated school for business," Kara explains. "We believe that with a little care, everyone can go on to achieve greatness."

I ask the question that I know can kill the butterflies that have settled in my stomach. Folks like me don't have options. "Do you have family housing?"

She looks over her shoulder and then back at me. "We do, but between us, it goes very quickly. Your best bet would be to put your five hundred deposit in immediately to hold your spot."

Five hundred dollars. That's more money than I can splurge right now. Every day it seems like there's new bills, new things to pay for with money that I don't have. I'm tired of not having shit, mane.

If it was just me, I wouldn't have to make all these decisions about my life. About the life of another. A year ago, I didn't think that the option to bring Mia into the world would kill anything else I'd ever want to do. That having her would cause me to have to make choices without thinking. Just doing, because it's all for her.

Everything is for her.

Even this.

What's left for me?

The quad is packed now. I can tell the college kids from the high schoolers. They seem free, as if college has made them move through the world with less baggage. In this academic bubble they don't have to deal with the things that happen outside these iron gates. The killings, the white men in suits.

"Hope to see you both on campus in the fall." Kara says bye to Mia and motions for the next people in line.

"College, dope." Deja pulls me along. We stop at each table collecting pens and bumper stickers, and a few folks even hand out shirts. This should be enough for me to prove to Mrs. Crenshaw that I came.

"We racked up." I hold up my knapsack of goodies. "I got enough pen and paper to last Cyn her whole school year."

"The table that was passing out the hoodies was really tryna draw people in. You know folks love free clothes around here," she says.

Two girls from our old history class wave at us. I think their names are Zora and Xandra. Deja waves back and we meet in the middle of the courtyard.

"B'onca, is this the baby?" Zora grabs Mia's finger and shakes her hand. "She's such a chunka-chunk. You must be feeding her good."

"Told you she is big for a five-month-old." Deja pinches Mia's jaw. Sometimes I wonder if Mia hates being treated like a doll or if she loves the attention.

"She eats thirty times a day, it seems like." Mia burps up milk and I dab the corner of her lips.

"Are y'all coming to Hilbert in the fall?" Xandra asks.

"B'onca might. You know she's always been the smart one."

"We're looking for a fourth suitemate. It'll be me, Zora, and Jewel. I don't know if you remember Jewel, but she's cool. If we find one more person, we can lock in—" Then she looks down at Mia and remembers. Her face goes red all over.

Zora tries to do damage control. "The family dorms are nice too."

But we all know that's a lie. It's basically a shelter for teen moms.

"Y'all should come to the café with us. We can have lunch together," Xandra says.

It's like Mia knows I'm about to have fun. She starts squirming and fussing. Any second now she's going to cut up.

"I should probably take her home. It's almost naptime, and y'all do not want to see her cranky."

Deja takes Mia from me. "Girl, go ahead. I'll watch the baby until you come back. You should get the full college experience. That includes the food."

I hand over Mia's diaper bag and give Deja detailed instructions. Five minutes later, Xandra, Zora, and I are off to the cafeteria. We talk about the boys in our life, grades, and our futures. Nothing about chapped nipples, breastfeeding, or naptimes.

For an hour, I'm not Mia's mama.

CHAPTER 14

THE SUN CREEPS into my room, doing more damage than the kids banging on the wall next door. Today I have an early shift at the beauty shop, which means I only have a few minutes with Mia before I leave. Today one of those mornings where I just want to cuddle in bed with her all day, but I know that isn't realistic. She needs me to go out and get it.

I roll over and reach for Mia, feeling around in the spot she's usually in. I know I should make her sleep in her crib, but our morning embraces are like coffee for me. Filling me up enough to get me through the day. Summer school kicking my ass. Between worrying about money and grades, something has to give. I reach out more, feeling nothing but sheets before opening my eyes. Mia not here. Thoughts start to creep in. Thoughts that make no sense, but I can't help but think the worst.

"Doodlebug?" I ask, as if she can answer me. She can, in her own way. With a clap or a giggle. A cry or even a smell. Something to let me not think the worst. Like the Canes coming to snatch her in the middle of the night or something. Our agreement off the table just because they want her, and when you have money you can just take, without thinking of the consequences, because money gets you out of anything.

"Mia?" I stretch across the bed to inspect the floor. She's not there either. I check underneath thrown sweaters and baby toys. Behind the bed and inside my closet. Nothing.

I grab my housecoat from the back of the door and tighten it. Shana must have taken her for an early walk, just to give me a break. I check my phone for a text message from her but there's nothing there.

"Shana, you got Mia? She's not in the bed." I walk down the stairs, stopping in the middle like a deer caught in the headlights. I mean, my body is straight frozen; even if I wanted to, I can't move.

The woman holding Mia, she looks like me. Rather, I look like her. Well, before, I looked like her. In the pictures where she posed with her hand on her hip in the front of our old apartment building. Her smile took up most of her face, like mine. Her child-birthing hips are no more, but the breasts still there. The smile is still there. Mia got it too.

"Mama?" The word sounds funny coming out of my mouth.

She floats around in Grandma's old rooster-decorated apron. Humming a hymn and fluffing biscuits like she a regular ole television mama. Mia on her hip like she's seen her before. Like before she was in my belly, she knew her or something. They twirl and laugh. Until she stops mid-twirl and looks up at me.

We both stare as if we're thinking of all the times when

greeting each other wasn't awkward but a regular thing. Mama props Mia on her right hip. That smile takes over her face. "You let go of that bed finally. I was going to come up there and check on you, but then I started on breakfast. Come on down. We have grits, eggs, bacon, and biscuits."

My stomach almost flips at the spread. We ain't had that much hot food for breakfast in forever. I want to run downstairs and take my plate. Let Mama feed me like she used to do. She always knew how to slice my biscuits and just how much jelly to put on them.

I check the clock by the front door. It's barely six.

I try to put one foot in front of the other but I'm still stuck.

"You gone let the food get cold." She crinkles her nose against Mia's. "Me and my grandbaby ready to eat. She's starting to cut a tooth, you know. I see it way in the back."

She acts like I ain't with my baby every damn day. I know she's getting her first tooth in. That's why I've been up all night with a teething baby, and she's been who knows where.

The real question is what does she know about her own children?

"What are *you* doing here?" The words come out with more fire than I want. She's still my mama. That's what everyone told me when she left and I wished death on her. When she missed my first period, my first boyfriend, and Grandma's funeral. But she ain't been my mama in a while. She gave up that title years ago, and the only reason I even still call her Mama is out of Southern respect. She did everything she could to strip herself of the title.

"Shana got in contact with me. Said y'all been having a hard time keeping up with the house payments and other things. I came to help."

"Shana knew where you were?" I ask. A surprise to me. Every time I asked about Mama and where she could be, Shana changed the conversation. She acted like she'd rather talk about the weather than about her.

"No, but I reached out recently. Honestly, I didn't expect to hear back from her." She looks down at Mia. "You know I got a good job now, bookkeeping at the shelter. I've been clean for seven months, going on eight. I've changed, B'onca."

There it is. Only a matter of time before she says the same shit she said last time. I ain't seen her in almost a year. I hoped she'd died. That'd be better for me: to grieve someone who's out of my life by death rather than by choice.

I grip the banister. "You think I'm falling for that again? You say you clean and then end up right where you left off. Gone."

"It's not like that this time." She pulls a red chip out of her back pocket. "See? Seven whole months. Raymond ain't around no more either. I kicked his ass to the curb."

Raymond her off-and-on boyfriend. The one that took more than he gave.

"Oh yeah? Where he at?" I ask.

She shrugs. "Last I heard, he was down in Louisiana with his first wife. He can ruin her life. He already swallowed up enough of me."

If you look at her long and hard, you can tell. The way she shakes sometimes, the tracks in her arms, her sunken eyes. In eighth grade, everyone knew my mama was a crackhead. She'd come to the principal's office in pissy sweatpants, demanding, "Let me see my baby." I'd run to her. Give her my lunch money in exchange for her leaving. One day she left and didn't come back for months. Came back clean and wanting to do better. Grandma let her. And then? She disappeared again.

It was a cycle until we got old enough to realize that Mama would never change.

"Well, I'm proud of you . . . if you're serious." I go to the bottom of the stairs and hold my arms out. "Let me get my baby, please."

She twirls again. "Mia, there's your mama. You want to go to your mama or stay with me?"

Mia rests her head on Mama's shoulder, ignoring me. I let my arms fall to my sides. It be your own baby sometime.

"Girl, I still can't believe you made me a grandma again." She fixes her hair in the microwave window. Pushes the matted dreads to one side. "I don't look like a grandma, now, do I?"

"No, Mama."

I don't look like nobody mama, either. Most of the time when I'm out with Mia, people think she is my little sister. Then they figure out that I'm her mama. Soon after that, the judgment starts. Sometimes I pretend—that we are sisters, that when I go home, I live a normal life—usually when I'm far away from Ridgecrest. Where people don't know my story. Sometimes I think Mia plays along with me. She doesn't cry or pull at my breast for a feeding, as if she knows that I'm not mature, that I'm nothing but a kid myself. She lets me be that for a few hours some days.

Mama sits at the kitchen table and bounces Mia on her knee. She feeds her grits and a little bit of the eggs.

"What's been new with you?" she asks, like she has only been gone a few weeks. I don't know how to talk to her. What do you say to a person that abandoned you during the most difficult time of your life?

I shrug. "Nothing. Being a mama, mostly. I'm trying to get back into doing hair. Honestly, I'm taking it one day at a time."

"You're still mad at me, aren't you?" She looks from Mia to me. "I just had to get myself together. I wanted to come when she was born, but I wasn't straight then. I didn't want her seeing me like that . . . didn't want you eyeing me like that. I'm straight now. You don't have to worry."

I'm straight. I'm clean. You can come live with me. The same lies.

"You said that last time, time before that. Your promises ain't no sturdier than an egg."

"You don't have to forgive me—I have a hard time forgiving myself—but I'm here now. I want to help. Get to know the woman you become and this baby. Cyn has gotten so big. Now I remember when she was born, wasn't bigger than a tadpole."

She wants to try to save me, like how she wanted someone to save her back then.

She can't, but she trying. That's all she ever do is try.

"Mia needs stability," I say while Mia babbles at her name. "And so does Cyn. They can't have people running in and out of their life. Shana and I are here every day with them. When we leave in the morning, they know we're coming home at night."

"I'm here," Mama says. "If you'll have me, that is. Shana says I can only stay if I get your blessing."

My eyes lift and meet hers, and as much as I hate to admit it, I want her, too.

There's a pull. I don't want to admit it, but that part of me that's stronger wants it badly. To fall into her arms and be a kid. To have a mama to tuck me in and tell me everything is going to be okay. To have that mama all my other friends got to have. It's too late to throw me sleepovers, to give me talks about boys, but maybe she can help me come into my own. Maybe she'll help me be a better mama to Mia. God knows I don't want to make the same mistakes. Mia may be a lot of me, but I don't want her to have my matching scars.

Mama's eyes blink; tears rush down. I cry with her. We stay like that for a minute. Even Mia is quiet. Then the memories start coming back. Back to Barbie bedsheets and kept secrets. Forts made from kitchen chairs and tea parties with Dixie cups. Play dates at the park and Mama-and-me lunches. To times when Raymond wasn't around, only me, Shana, and Mama, and that was enough. I was enough for her; the only drug she needed to keep her going was my voice. Back when I was her morning coffee.

"Don't leave me again."

"You gone have a hard time getting me away from this pretty baby," Mama says.

I open my eyes and swear I see a star.

CHAPTER 15

"YOU SURE YOU want to come to this park, Mama?" I ask. "I don't mind walking a little further to the nicer one. Mia needs to get the sun on her anyway."

The one near the courts isn't bad, but it's old. Weeds grow from the cracks. Nothing has been updated since the nineties, but the kids play on the metal slides anyway. Making something out of nothing. A skill around here.

"This is fine, right here." Ma lays Mia's bunny blanket on the asphalt. We set up the picnic spread Mama made this morning. It ain't a fancy charcuterie board, but it's the closet we're going to get. She gives Mia a Ritz cracker to mash on.

I gotta give Mama credit. We haven't been hungry since she got here. Between her food stamps and regular money, our bellies haven't growled none this week. Food is the way to the heart, and Mama trying her best to plant her flag there. Last night she made my favorite: oxtails, pinto beans, and cornbread. She makes it just like Grandma did. We even had a homemade dessert. Nothing freezer burnt.

"I heard Scooter's parents trying to take Mia from you. We won't let that happen, especially since I'm just getting to know her. The judge will see that she has a family that can take care of her now."

"The Canes got money, though. Long money. Who knows what they will and won't do," I say.

"Trust your mama, aight? I said they not taking her and I mean that."

Mama deads the subject, but it's always at the back of my mind. We're damn near halfway through the month, and I have nothing to show for it. The Canes not even taking Mia's favorite things because the stuff at their house is better. Would she even remember me? The way I sing to her at night and how I kiss her nose in the morning to wake her up. Eventually I'll be a foggy memory.

"Isis, is that you?" A tiny man whose clothes hang off him stops in front of us. He smells like he hasn't showered in weeks. I've seen enough drug addicts in my life to know he is one.

"Hey, Fred. What's good with you?" Mama spreads out the salami, crackers, and cheese and pours two Dixie cups of grape juice.

"Same ole, same ole. You know how it is. Don't tell me these your children?" He scratches at his neck and then his wrists. I pray that no skin flakes fall on our food.

"My daughter B'onca and my grandbaby Mia," Mama replies.

"Damn, I remember when you were pregnant with that one,"

he says like he's pondering how many years have gone by. "You look good, Isis. Real good."

"I'm clean now," she says proudly. "I want to be around to see my children grow up."

"That's smart of you, Isis. I'ma go see the people tomorrow. I'm tired of smoking up all my money."

The same lies that Mama used to say.

"You do that, Fred. There's more to life than dope." Mama puts a few crackers and cheese on a napkin and hands it to him. "You need to put something on your stomach."

He takes the food and asks, "You got a five I can hold until I see you again?"

Mama digs into her purse and gives him two dollars. Fred thanks her and disappears deeper into the park. When Mama used to do drugs, this park is where she'd go. I'd be playing jump rope and my mama three feet away getting high. Back then, I didn't know. I mean, I always figured she was a little tense.

But I thought all mamas were jumpy like that.

Hid marks that took up their arms during bath time.

All mamas had an Uncle Jimmy, Buster, and Avon that would come during the early morning and not leave until that next morning. Happier but eyes sunken in. They'd slide you money and small Now and Laters.

Wasn't until I was ten that I learned not all mamas were like this.

"One day soon, I'm going to get Mia a stroller. I know it's hard having to carry her everywhere," Ma says, and it goes in one ear and out the other. Her promises don't even stick anymore.

"I'm used to carrying her now," I say. "Besides, it's making me strong."

"Nobody in the world needs to be that strong," Mama says.

I lie back and lift Mia in the air. Her eyes widen each time she goes up. Then she hits me with her hands to do it again.

"Last time, silly girl." I blow raspberries on Mia's round belly.

Ma rubs her thumb on Mia's cheek. They have been inseparable this last week. "You're a good mother. You know that, B'onca? Even at your young age. Don't let nobody tell you any differently."

"No thanks to you," I mutter.

"Now, just go ahead and get everything off your chest," she responds. "You might as well, because walking around with all that animosity built up inside will rotten you."

I heave Mia up and down on my chest. Her brown eyes glow in the sun. "Did you even try? I know you were young and everything when you had us, but I'm young too, and I'm trying."

A kid's basketball rolls toward us, and Mama kicks it back. "When you were born, your grandma was younger. Stubborn. Hard to please. Emphatically Christian. Everything had to be perfect with her. My sister and I weren't given a choice in anything. Mama decided everything, and if we did stray, she found a way to pull us back in. Eventually I strayed far enough that she didn't even want to reel me in anymore."

"Don't try to blame your mistakes on Grandma," I say. "That's a cop-out. Grandma didn't force you to leave us. I remember all the times she'd try to get you back. We'd go out driving during

Christmas and she'd say it was to see the lights, but we knew it was to find you."

"Grandma forced me to have you and your sister." Mama's words aren't mean, but they still feel like a double-barrel shotgun pointed at my chest.

"Wow, thanks a lot, Ma." My face is dry, but inside, my heart is crying. "What any daughter wants to hear." I wrap Mia tighter around my body.

Mama never said I was unwanted before, but I could tell by the way she was always near but never close. Especially toward the end. When heroin, coke, and crack filled her arms. Leaving me with a shell of a mother, and no explanation.

"I'm trying to be honest with you." Ma stares at the side of my face because I can't force myself to look at her. I'm focused on the kids who double Dutch in front of us.

"Grandma told me I had a choice," I say.

"Maybe she saw how I turned out and didn't want to strike out three times," she says. "And what could I do? You couldn't get an abortion without your parent's signature, and if you could, there wasn't no way I'd know about it."

"Didn't having us make you want to be better?"

"It wasn't about y'all, B'onca," she says. "When you get older, you'll understand. Addiction doesn't care about nobody."

CHAPTER 16

"LET'S TALK BUSINESS," Shana says as she grabs Mia and puts her in the living room with Cyn. After dinner is always book time. Well, Cyn reads. Mia drools on the page, but Google says even the pictures will let her imagine more and quicker.

"Do I need to leave?" Deja asks, and I kick her enough to get her attention. If she leaves, I'm stuck here alone with Mama and Shana.

I'm the only one who hasn't gotten used to Mama being around yet.

Cyn geeked to have a grandma like other kids, Mia loves anyone that feeds her, and Shana only sees the paid bills that Mama took care of. I still can't find that love within me. All I see is abandonment and neglect each time I look at Mama. Two weeks don't erase almost two decades.

"No need," Mama says, returning to her seat. "I'm sure B'onca just gone tell you what we talked about anyway."

Mama never been a big fan of Deja. Even when we were

growing up, she always preferred Savannah. I think Deja reminds her too much of herself. Savannah is a safe friend, a person who never got herself in trouble, unlike Dej. Savannah someone who I could look up to. Even though we grew up together, Mama always knew Savannah was going to make it out of here.

Deja, not so much.

I guess Savannah and I followed in our mothers' footsteps. Ma and Ms. Howard still friends but they not as close as before. They had two different lives to live, and nobody wants to see their best friend mess up the way Mama did.

"With your check this week, Mama, we will be able to pay down the back utility, but it'll be the whole thing. That okay with you?" Shana asks.

Ma flinches and then smiles. "Of course. I'm here to help. Whatever we need to do to keep ourselves afloat."

"With my unemployment, we can at least put down a little on the back pay for rent. It won't be much, but they'll know we're trying to work with them."

Or they'll still swoop in and charge more rent. These folks don't care if you're trying. They'll take until we're left with nothing. Our pride is already our highest form of payment. Shana had to damn near beg the landlord for more time. He must not have any offers on the house, because he gave her an extension but added interest to what we already owe them.

"And I can ask Ms. Dubois to pick up more hours at the shop," I chime in. "I can manage thirty hours."

"You sure? I got this." Mama sets out the dessert bowls. Homemade baked banana pudding. Me and Shana's favorite.

I take a healthy scoop. "It's only a few more hours a week. I think I can handle it. I'll still basically be making minimum wage after paying all these bills."

"Minimum wage is better than nothing," Mama says in between bites. "Don't ever look down on an honest job."

The knock at the door causes Mia's head to pop up. Cyn runs to the door as if it's for her. It might be. People around the neighborhood always bring her and Mia toys, books, and hand-me-down clothes.

"I'll get it." Deja pretends to race Cyn. "It's Sir Trenton," she announces formally.

"Hello, everyone." Trent gives a short wave. "I didn't mean to interrupt your dinner."

"Now, that can't be little Trent." Mama shuffles toward him, plate of pudding in hand. We don't have the money to be offering to feed folks, but it ain't Southern not to offer. If you're raised right, you don't accept. "You've grown so much. Time waits for no one."

"What you doing around these parts, Trent?" I ask.

"My mama told me to bring by some leftovers for y'all. It's rice dressing." He holds out a blue-and-white casserole dish.

"Here, let's trade." Mama takes the dish, and Trent takes the plate of pudding. "Come sit down for a while. We're finishing up dinner, and then we're going to play some cards."

"I need some new competition," Cyn says. "I'm the Uno champion." She flexes her tiny arms and starts shuffling the cards in front of her.

"I really have to head home," he says. "I have some makeup work to do for summer school."

"Maybe you two can work on your homework together." Mama smirks as she passes me. "B'onca always says how she needs a tutor for English. Trent, you were so good in school. Your mama bragged on you all the time. Brought all your report cards to the church functions."

"That was when the work was easy. I don't know how good I'll be now. Math is kicking my a—" Cyn looks over her shoulder as he catches himself. "Behind."

"Math I'm good at," I say. "It's English and all that boring stuff we got to read from 1890. Don't nobody care about symbolism in the real world."

"I tell you what, if you teach me about ledgers and all that, I can teach you about *A Tale of Two Cities*," he says.

"Bet!" I walk him to the door. "See you at school tomorrow."

"I'm looking forward to it." Trent turns on his heel. I'm met with the eyes of three nosy-ass women.

"I don't know why y'all looking at me like that." I collect the dishes from the table. Tonight's my night to clean up. Which leaves me barely any time to study after getting Mia ready for bed.

"He's a nice boy, you know." Mama takes the pile from me, sets it in the sink. "Goes to church, from a decent family. Never heard about any real problems from him. He got caught up once or twice, but he's a good boy."

"I don't have time for boys," I say. "It's hard enough as it is."

"You're a beautiful girl, B'onca," Mama says. "You can't keep yourself locked in this house forever. Eventually you're going to meet someone, and you have to let them into that shut-off heart of yours."

I want to tell her that she's the reason that it's shut off. That loving ain't that easy when the fear of abandonment is always lurking. There's an electric fence around my heart, protecting it from any more break-ins. Besides, if anyone is looking for my love, they have to buy it. I learned early on, ain't nothing in this world free.

CHAPTER 17

OUR LITTLE HOUSE full of foldable chairs and chatty older people. The Davant Avenue Tenant Association has more people than I expected. Mama thought it'd be a good idea for us to host this meeting, but I don't think she was expecting this many people. I walk around with Mia on my hip and hand out flyers, a tentative agenda, and store-bought sugar cookies. A dip in our already diminishing budget, but you can't have guests and not feed them. That's tacky and triflin'.

I pray that our neighbors have the sense to not eat them all, but if they like us, struggling, who can blame them? I don't let free food go to waste. Every taste-testing stand at the grocery store must hear my stomach rumble, because they pretend they haven't seen me before each time I come back for another sample. The lunch ladies give me extra servings without me having to ask. Everyone must know what's happening in Ridgecrest.

Trent and Ms. Dubois knock before entering. They look too put-together to be here, but I guess this affects them as well.

Nobody wants to be the only Black face in a changing neighborhood.

Mia coos as Trent approaches us. "Girl, chill out. Acting thirsty," I whisper in her ear.

"Baby Mia in the flesh." He reaches out his arms for her. "May I?"

"Mmm, if she starts crying, don't get scared or she'll cry harder," I say.

"Nah, I'm the baby whisperer." First he tries to rock her, but Mia doesn't like that. Then he sits her on his chest to let her see everyone in the room. Her eyes scan the place, and she giggles when they land on Cyn. She's doing a dance in the corner to distract her.

"Don't get too comfortable with that baby." Ms. Dubois squeezes Trent's shoulder. "You have to give me at least ten years before I become a grandma."

"I'm just holding her, Ma, dang," Trent replies.

"Mm-hmm, that's how baby fever starts." Ms. Dubois goes over the basic flyer. None of us know how to work Canva, but we tried our best. "Are you still eating enough, B'onca?"

"Yes, ma'am. My mama is back. Things have been looking up for us."

Ms. Dubois glances at Mama and her lip curls like she smells something stink. "Your mama? Well, I guess. You know you always got a place at my dinner table whenever you need it. I'm still expecting you at your next shift, too. Ain't nothing like having your own money."

I nod as Trent hands Mia to me.

"Let's go get us a seat, son." Trent hooks his arm with his ma, and they sit all the way in the back as if they don't want to be seen.

Shana sneaks behind me. "Now, that's who should have been your daddy, Mia."

Maybe he could have been, in another dimension.

The one where movie-type things happen every day.

Shana lets in the last expected guests and peeks out the blinds before locking the door. A suspicious car came by earlier and hasn't moved yet, not even when the cops stopped and talked to the white driver. He been parked there, staring at our house like it's a turkey leg. We can't do anything about it either.

A TAKE BACK DAVANT AVENUE sign hangs inside over the front door. People cheer as they pass it. Others don't really know if they want it back. Some like the new parks and coffee shops, and that the potholes are filled.

Others don't think anything has changed.

"Why do we want this street anyway?" one of our church members, Mrs. Ernestine, says. She is one of those old ladies that keeps peppermints in her purse and shade in her heart. "There's no sun down here, and ain't nothing but troublemaking in that empty field across the street. Soon as somebody comes home, they gotta be looking over their shoulder. Wondering if this the day they gone get knocked over the head, or worse. They can have this place for all I care."

"Then why are you even here, Mrs. Ernestine?" I ask timidly.

Talking back to elders a no-no, but some things need to be questioned. Why she doesn't want to save the street she's lived in her whole life one of them. She got more memories of this place than anybody. All of them may not be fond ones, but they hers. The houses, the playgrounds, and the stores.

"I've been here the longest. That's why. In my opinion, if they can fix up the place, I don't see what's the harm. We have been begging them to do it all this time, and now that they have, we complaining about it. Black folks don't know what they want."

She raises her chin and crosses her legs as much as she can.

"They not trying to fix the neighborhood for us," I say. "If they were, they would have done it a long time ago. Those people out there"—I point toward the window—"are going to build all these things, and where does that leave us? Where we gone end up?"

This is our home. From the field to the streets. We gotta stand up for it, before white folk come in and change the whole thing. Tear down every piece of culture we ever bled into these streets. Change it into what they want it to be and then tell us we're not welcome here anymore.

"I'd rather have a garden than a bunch of weeds anyway."

Ain't no point in arguing with old people. When they mind made up about something, there's no changing it.

Shana calls the meeting to order. I place Mia in her rocker, setting it on fast since she sleeps best that way. Mama and I sit side by side in foldable metal chairs, next to Mrs. Thompson from next door and Ms. Howard, Savannah's mama.

"I'm so glad you're back and doing better, Isis. We've missed you around here," Ms. Howard says, sliding a plastic bag of baby clothes my way. "You should come by the house and bring Mia with you. I'd love to spend some time with her."

"Mia would like that. I been working a lot but I can make some time for next week."

"I don't mean to be rude . . ." Mrs. Thompson studies Mama's face, trying to place her name. She comes up short. "What even is your name?"

Mama stands up, smoothing down the miniskirt she rocks confidently. She really doesn't look like a grandma. Hell, barely a mama. "It's been a while since I've been around. You all may not remember me, but I'm Shana and B'onca's mama. My mother, Mae Johnson, used to live around here before she passed away."

People who know Mama ain't too thrilled. Gossip starts to spread, and they are right here in her face.

"Ain't she the one who stole the copper wiring from the church?" one voice in the back says.

"Mm-hmm, that surely is her. Got the nerve to show her face here. After all she put Mae through. God rest her soul."

"She doesn't bring anything but trouble."

Shana plays a gong sound from her phone, sending a shock through our ears. "All right. We're here to talk about what's going on in the neighborhood. Nobody gonna take care of this place like we do. All they gone do is tear it down, put in some condos, and call it some bougie-ass name. 'R. Crest' or something dumb like that. Make folks pay an arm and a leg to live here, push all the Black folk out."

"Seriously speaking, what are we going to do about the trash that hangs out in that empty field?" Mrs. Thompson asks. "All they do is smoke reefer and play music all hours of the night. Even on Sundays. It's disrespectful, and if they have no respect for God, ain't no respect for themselves or others." Heads shake again in agreement.

"Those kids ain't the reason we are here," I chime in. "If we don't save our neighborhood, we all gone end up in a crowded project building on the outskirts of town. Or some suburb that's forty minutes away so they can pretend people like us don't exist."

"Them your friends, ain't they?" an old man in the back asks. "I used to see you all the time hanging with them. Running up and down the street, even with your swollen-belly self."

The air knocks out of my lungs. Heads turn around and look at me, like they trying to find something. Trying to see if I've ever stolen something from them or flicked my joint at them. If I ever cursed at them or ran past them so fast, I knocked them down. I'd never do that, but I did watch my people do it. Does that make me just as guilty?

"They aren't my friends. Not anymore," I say, their eyes still piercing me. "I used to run around with them, but I don't anymore. I have a daughter now; I got someone to live for, and this is her home. Our neighborhood. We can point the blame at the field and all that, but the real criminals are the men knocking on our doors and scamming us out of our homes. Not some teenagers smoking weed."

"My sister is right," Shana says. "We are not here to discuss any of that."

"Well, there was a man slithering around the other day," our next-door neighbor starts. "He had a big fancy car and was walking around here taking pictures of folks' houses. Then he knocked on your door, but I guess you and B'onca weren't home, and he went away."

"You see what he look like?" Mama asks.

"Like they all look. Nice and unsuspecting. Smiling all in my face like I'm about to tell him what he wants to hear," she says. "He asked if I knew when they'd be back. I said no and shut the door in his face."

The room cheers. Giving her pats on the shoulder.

"Now that's what we all need to do. Slam the door in their face like they do us." I check on Mia and she is still resting. This ain't gotten to her yet. She doesn't know what none of this means, but she will one day.

"Call the police on them if you have to. We can't just wander around their neighborhoods; they can't come around here harassing us in ours," Mama says.

"Shana and I were thinking that we can raise money for a lawyer," I say. "You know, see what our rights are. He obviously can't be all our lawyers, but he can come here and explain our rights. He costs about two hundred dollars an hour."

"Now who gone be in charge of this money?" Mrs. Thompson asks.

"Shana and I," I say.

Mama grabs my hand and squeezes. "I am too. I'm here to stay now."

Mrs. Thompson shifts in her chair. "I don't know about that."

I'm tired of this old lady.

Someone in the front says, "Yes, no offense, but your mama doesn't have the cleanest record. How do you know we can trust you with our money?"

"You want to be in charge of the money, then?" I ask. "I don't care who is in charge as long as it gets taken care of."

"I'm no good at math," Mrs. Thompson says.

Ms. Howard defends me. "Well, then shut up and let the girls be in charge. Always starting things with people."

"Thank you." I almost cut my eyes at Mrs. Thompson, but I don't want them to roll on the floor.

"You just keep doing the right thing, sweetie," Ms. Howard says.

The papers in my hands stick together as I try to pass them out. Mama passes around the donation bucket. Dollar bills go in, and come out as people take change. One by one they leave. Taking their gossip right into the streets.

"This is more than enough for that lawyer." Mama counts the money and I look over every few minutes. Making sure she put back every cent. I don't want the neighbors making a fool of us.

Shana slips the money into the drawer and locks it with a small gold key.

CHAPTER 18

"I'M COMING." I close my textbook as the knock on the door gets louder. Mia stirs in my arms. She's running a fever, which means I have to miss class and work. Mrs. Crenshaw emailed me back my makeup work within five minutes of me clicking send. Ms. Dubois just told me to take care of myself. I don't think she's pressed that I'm flaking, just that I'm not within arm's reach of her.

If I'm there, she knows I'm eating.

If I'm there, she knows Mama doing right by me.

So far she is. Like today Shana and Mama went out to see the lawyer. Our fingers crossed for any good news. I googled about rent-control laws, but it might as well all have been in French. All stuff I don't understand, and who knows if it'll even apply to our situation.

I open the door mid-knock. A white man in a button-down and slacks stands in front of me. He looks familiar, but that ain't strange since men like him the norm now.

"Who are you?" I say behind the screen door. "And why are you knocking on my door like you the police? My daughter was taking a nap."

"My name is Kenneth Hines." He looks around me and into the house. I'm glad we haven't had time to clean yet. All he's getting an eye of is baby clothes and toys thrown all on the floor. "May I come in?"

"You must be trippin' if you think I'm going to let a stranger inside of my house. What do you want?"

He pulls a form out of his pants pocket and flattens it against his thigh. "Do you own this home?"

We don't, but he doesn't need to know that. "Why do you want to know?"

"I'm sure you've seen the 'We Pay in Cash' signs around the neighborhood. Those come from my company. We're looking to buy older houses, and this one caught my eye. It's one of the only brick ones on the block. Nice and sturdy."

The muscles in my jaw clench. "We aren't interested in selling."

"I forgot to mention that we really *do* pay cash. This house can easily be worth fifty thousand. Maybe even sixty. That would be a lump sum as well. No waiting for installments. We even offer direct deposit if that's easier for you."

Sixty thousand dollars. I can't even imagine having that in cash. The fact that that money can change my life and he can buy a house with it in cash right now ain't fair.

With sixty thousand dollars I could start college with no worries.

Mia could go to a day care that's not in someone's house.

Cyn could be in private school and not a public school with out-of-date textbooks.

Shana wouldn't have to apply for jobs where she has to stand up for twelve hours a day.

We'd be set. Not for life but for a while. Enough time to get on our feet at least. To not have anxiety about how we're going to eat.

"Do you know anything about this community?" I ask. "Do you know that this neighborhood was integrated by Black folks coming back from Vietnam? A lot of them still live here, or at least they used to before people like you came offering promises. Scamming old people out of their houses. Your mama must be proud of the profession you chose for yourself."

Back when our neighborhoods were ours, Ms. Howard said they didn't have to worry about police presence because our uncles and brothers were the police. Then crack tore this neighborhood up. The bad times, but we survived, and we're going to survive this.

"I am aware of the history of this neighborhood. My parents used to live around here. I have roots too, you know." He opens up the paper in front of him. "The development going on in this neighborhood has made it quite valuable. It'll be smart to strike while the iron is hot. Who knows what's going to happen within the next few years? You're holding on to bricks and stones."

They only want our neighborhood for a season. Until something better comes along.

"This house isn't only bricks and stones," I say. "That may be what it is for you, but for me and my daughter, it's our home."

"The house has good bones." He cranes his neck further. "But from the looks of things, it needs renovations. Paint is peeling. The ceiling has water marks. Even your yard needs to be cared for."

I fill the crack with my body. "We're going to get that taken care of."

"Think of your daughter's future," he says. "If people like me don't come in and change the place, well . . ." He points at the abandoned field. "Is that really the type of neighborhood you want her growing up in? There's a farmers market coming in, better playgrounds, and even renovated apartments. With sixty thousand dollars, you could rent a nice one."

"Get off my damn property."

He places the envelope on the doormat. "Think about it. I'm sure you'll make the right decision."

CHAPTER 19

I DIDN'T TELL Ma and Shana what happened. Ain't no need to get them started. White Man's words are fruitless. He left a card with his name and personal cell phone number. I ripped it into pieces.

"Time to wake up, mama baby." Mia tries to roll from her side to her back, but her head humbles her. "We're getting you a big-girl stroller today. Your mama hip can't take no mo'." It only takes a few minutes to get her dressed and ready to go. I don't look like anything, but I put on a little mascara.

"It's going to be really nice, Mia. Like the ones the rich ladies have, with the cover to protect you from the cold and rain." She lies on her tummy, looking up at the yellow sponge on television. "I'm sorry I wasn't able to get it before. This parenting thing doesn't come with a handbook."

Mia coos, and I pretend she understands. I like to have these talks now, so she isn't messed up in the future. I know she's going to have a million questions that I won't be prepared to answer.

"Mama just gotta get the rest of the money that I saved from the pizza shop."

Joe gave me the runaround about my last check until forever. Yesterday it finally came in the mail. I cashed it right away. You would have thought I'd won the lottery instead of only four hundred dollars, but that combined with the little I have saved up from the beauty shop and the two hundred dollars Scooter left, it's enough to get Mia a stroller and something extra.

I stand on my tippy-toes, fingertips barely touching the top shelf in my closet.

There's nothing but lint and dead bugs. It has to be here; I didn't hide it anywhere else. An empty coffee container filled with every dollar bill I ever saved. Filled with money for Mia's stroller, the light bill, and a hundred on the rent.

Gone.

I feel again, this time for the tiny silk bag that has Grandma's necklace in it. *Please be here.*

My heart beats regularly again when I feel it. I check the inside to make sure, and yeah, there it is. Right where I left it. The only thing of value that I have to pass down to Mia.

My money is still gone, though.

Think. Think. Think. Maybe I moved it and forgot, but where? I drop to my knees and reach underneath the bed, head pressed to the rail.

Nothing.

I throw out dresser drawers; clothes fly and land in every corner of the room.

Nothing.

I know I didn't move it. I know someone who would. The stars dim again. I prop Mia on my hip and fly down the stairs.

"Where is she?" The bass in my voice starts the baby to crying. She reaches her hand out for Shana. Staring at me like I'm a stranger.

"Who are you yelling at? It can't be me."

"Shana, this is important. Where is Mama at?"

My thoughts race to all the places she can be and with my six hundred dollars. The park, the Gel Hall—which is a den for drug addicts—halfway to fucking Timbuktu. Wherever she is, she is high as hell by now.

"She left early this morning. I think around six. She had an AA meeting to go to." Shana takes Mia from my hands, gives her a taste of the grits in her bowl.

"Wasn't no damn AA meeting." I whip my hand across the coffee cup that's sat on the counter; black liquid spills out the sides. "She's a fucking liar."

"Now, girl, you got one more time. What's your problem? Acting like you've lost your mind."

I shake the empty can in the air, the strength of my anger crushing it until the label is unrecognizable. "She took all of my money! Every dime. At least she had the decency to leave Grandma's necklace."

"Money? Who took your money?"

"Mama!"

The words like bile. We were becoming a family again, working like a well-oiled machine to make sure everything came into place for us, but Mama eyes forever stained with red, her soul

141

darkened by the poison she put into her veins. Her taking off proves drugs matter more than her daughters and her grand-daughters.

I look at Mia, and I could never. Never see her in this much pain and not notice. If I did, I can't even fathom walking away.

Shana shakes her head. "Naw, she wouldn't do that." Shana always tries to see Mama through her five-year-old eyes and not the twenty-five-year-old ones. "She wouldn't do that, B'onca."

"She would. Touching that money for the lawyer probably triggered something in her. Thank God that we spent that before she could get her hands on it."

Stealing money Mama MO. She got so good at it, you start to question your own sanity. She stole it, and I know it.

Shana knows it too, but she doesn't wanna be the same fool twice.

There aren't that many places in town Mama can be. If she's still in town, that is. The park is quiet, except for the old heads play-ing checkers. Rubbing their hands together before moving the pieces. They watch this place from sunup to sundown. Know more about your business than you do.

"You seen this woman?" I swipe different pictures of Mama.

Most shake their heads. The old head with the Kangol hat and boot-cut sweatpants lean back on his hands. "Show me her again."

He makes faces as we go through the pictures. "That's Mae's girl, ain't she?"

"Yes, have you seen her?"

"You look like you can be Mae's girl too, but you are too young for that."

"I'm her granddaughter, and this is my mama. I'm looking for her." It's getting foggier. By the time he answers, it'll be impossible to play chess or find cracked-out mothers.

"Don't nobody be in this park this early unless they on that stuff." The second older man knocks down a king, taking the place of the winner.

"She's been clean, but I think she may have fallen off the wagon."

An understatement. She has never been on the wagon. I ain't want to admit it. Didn't want to say what my eyes saw. Mama cycles between not doing anything and doing too much. Her good days quickly become bad. Infecting everyone around her.

"You might want to check toward the end of the park," he says. "They've made a fort of some kind. Gonna burn themselves up in there—made of nothing but recycled boxes. Be careful. I know she's your mama, but them drugs. You don't know what they can do."

I nod and tighten my jacket, brushing against branches that stick out and stepping over discarded needles. The smell. Damn that smell. The first time it ever filled my nose, I wasn't nothing but five. People say you can't remember things like that, that young, but I do. It smelled like Sunday mornings when Grandma

143

would make us scrub the floors really good, but there wasn't no cleaning going on.

Locked doors. Cartoons on television. Don't come back here, B'onca!

"Ma?" I cover my nose with the edge of my sleeve. "Mama, you here?"

Thin people crawl out of a tent, pulling at the clothes that fall off their bodies like melting ice cream. Twitching and clawing. Someone's mama, daddy, auntie, and uncle. The cause of someone's bad memories.

"That ain't what you said, motherfucker!" The voice stills me, planting me deeper into the wet soil. "Half or nothing. I swear I ain't never coming around you motherfuckers again."

"Mama," I whisper before taking a deep breath.

"B'onca." Mama smiles, teeth half showing. Hollow cheeks rising. "That's my baby, y'all. She came to see her mama. Your kids never come to see y'all."

It's the cafeteria all over again. This time, I can't give her money to leave. This time I'm on her turf. All the times I'd ask Grandma where Mama was, this was the answer. In a drug-filled tent.

I hold out my hand. "I just want my money, and we can forget the whole thing happened. You can stay out here and do what you gotta to do. Don't ever have to see us again. I just need my damn money."

"You know why I named you B'onca?" She staggers toward me, the smell becoming more distinct, like she's the main source. "It always reminded me of those fancy women on the hill." She stops in front of me, cupping my face in trembling hands. "I knew you were going to be something one day. Be more than me. I wanted to give you a name that matched."

I slap her hand off my cheek. "Fuck all that. I want my damn money, Isis, and I'm not leaving here without it."

"Your daughter doesn't seem to like you too much, Isis." The junkies light up and laugh as much they can before they start to choke from the smoke.

"I don't know what money you talking about," she says. "I ain't got no damn money, and if that's what you think about me, then why you even here? Get on somewhere. Embarrassing me in front of my friends."

Red. All I see is shades of red against the backdrop of cigarette lights and smoke. Red before she's on the ground beneath me, squirming. Red as I scratch at her eyes. Red as I hear, *Don't come in here, B'onca.* See empty Kroger bags and stolen clothes. Broken promises as I sat on the porch to wait for a car that never came. Red blood mixing with clear tears.

Junkies circle around. None even try to break it up. It isn't a fair fight in any way. Everyone is too high to know what's going on. Too caught up in their own drugs to worry about Isis.

"Kill me," Mama says right into my mouth. "Kill me. That's what I need. I'm never gonna be right until I'm in the ground."

"Naw, I ain't gone kill you," I say. "You're already dead where it counts."

PART 3

CHAPTER 20

"B'ONCA, I KNOW you are still grieving, but you got to pick up the pace, girl. There's hair all over the floor, and my clients ain't finna sue me if they slip." Ms. Dubois spins her chair around, giving her client a full view of her new twenty-seven piece.

"Sorry," I mumble as Kenya hands me the broom. Starting from the bottom sucks ass. All I do every day is get told what to do by people who are only a few years older than me. At least I had some sorta respect for Joe at the Pizza Junt, since the man was damn near retirement age, but here everyone went to school with me, and I can't help but think they act bitchy for a reason. They know me, and my situation. Know I can't say nothing out the side of my mouth or I get fired.

There ain't that many hood fairy godmothers who are going to give a chance like this, and I only have a few days left to show the Canes I'm doing better.

I take the broom and start from the back, working my way

through a row of different hairstyles. Kenya's doing a fade on a girl who just broke up with her man and needs a fresh start. Ms. Dubois got the First Lady of the church underneath the dryer—didn't even let me give her a wash—and Shay is waiting impatiently by the door for her last client of the day.

"This is why I charge a twenty-dollar late fee." Soon as Shay starts complaining, there's a beep by the door. Whitney's stomach introduces her. She's popped since I last saw her. Her skin is glowing; she looks like the pregnant women you see on Instagram whose bellies don't have nary a stretch mark and whose faces are beat for the gods.

"Before you start all that rah-rah mess, I technically have a minute left before I'm for real late," Whitney says. "You know how hard it is for a pregnant lady to get ready? My jeans don't even fit anymore. I had to go find some leggings unless you wanted to see all of my business."

"Please keep that to yourself." Ms. Dubois flipping through channels, trying to find something shop-friendly. She settles on BET.

"Hey, B'onca." Whitney doesn't hesitate to step and give me a hug, and not a fake side hug, but a real one. Belly to belly, like we are the best of friends or something. This girl really thinks we're grieving sister wives.

I play along. "How's the baby?"

"Oh my God. Lemme show you." She digs around in a large Telfar bag that spikes jealousy inside of me. No doubt a gift from Scooter. Then I look at her nails, studded with fake diamonds, and how her hair isn't even busted, yet she's getting it redone. The

Canes are right. The only thing we have in common is Scooter, but she got the better half of the deal. Her baby isn't going to want for anything, especially if she is still spending money like this.

Whitney finally finds what she was looking for. A 3D ultrasound, which I know cost at least four hundred dollars. I asked and then immediately accepted the regular one. The way Mia looked was a surprise to us all.

"She's almost the size of a coconut. The doctor said that if she keeps growing this fast, I'm going to end up with a big baby," Whitney says.

"I can see that. You're all belly." Ms. Dubois caresses Whitney's stomach.

"It's a little early to know the gender, isn't it?" I ask.

"Yes, but I'm manifesting a girl. That way Mia can have a little sister to teach the ropes to. They are going to have so much fun. Mia gonna hook up her hair, and my baby will teach her all about fashion, because you know I stay fly and so will she."

"Lord, you young girls just think babies are accessories. You'll see how *fly* you are when you up all night with a colicky baby." Here go First Lady with her rant, but she's not wrong. Whitney got a rude awakening coming if she thinks that's all raising daughters is, but for now it ain't no harm in her still dreaming. She'll have enough reality when the baby gets here.

"I know she isn't an accessory. I was just saying. Dang, old people suck the fun out of everything."

First Lady sits up like she's about to show Whitney better than she can tell her.

"Be respectful," Ms. Dubois warns. "B'onca, wash Whitney for Shay, please. Do it how I taught you. Three shampoo passes, then one condition."

"Yes, ma'am." I try to bite my tongue from being so excited. Washing hair is a nice break from sweeping it up. Whitney follows me to the shampoo room. It smells of peppermint, thanks to the diffuser that sits at the entrance. Ms. Dubois says her salon is an experience that keeps people wanting to come back.

Whitney sits in the chair in front of me. Her sandy hair is almost mid-back length. Them prenatal vitamins hooking her up. "You don't even need your hair done yet. Your silk press is still in good condition."

She leans back as I adjust the temperature of the water. "I know, but it's something to get me out of the house and my mind off Scooter."

"Oh yeah, Mia is that for me. She won't allow me to be sad."

"Can I tell you something?"

"I mean. If you want to," I reply.

"Sometimes I wonder if I can love this baby."

I accidentally shoot water in her eyes.

"My bad." I clean her up and then we're back to pass one. "What you mean? You seem like you love her a lot already. I mean, you're getting 3D ultrasounds and everything."

"Mama made me do that. She's forcing me to be excited, but it's hard to pretend all the time. Mama thinks that having this baby will keep the checks coming, but I don't know if the Canes are going to fuck with me like that, and I can't do what Scooter and I used to do anymore. It's risky being the only girl in the gang. The guys would take advantage of the situation."

Damn, money tight for Whitney, too. You'd never know from the outside looking in. People will do anything to keep up with the Joneses, not knowing that the Joneses are down bad themselves.

"Used to do?"

"Don't play dumb. I know you used to do it too. I mean, you hung around Trent *and* Scooter."

"I did nothing but sit in the car. Besides, Trent never told me what he did and I never asked."

"A.k.a. you were the lookout. I got tired of doing that. Plus, he gave more if I actually went in with him. Scooter was cheap, low-key."

"Did you ever go out alone?"

"All the time. Scooter would get mad, but I ain't have time to be waiting on him to make moves. Especially when I found out I was pregnant. I did one last order to hold me over."

I stop massaging her head. Before I can stop myself, I ask her, "Would you teach me?"

The smirk on her face comes and goes just as quickly. "Don't you make money working here? I know this isn't a volunteer gig."

"It's barely enough to survive, and we have all these back bills. I like this job, but I need money now. Real money. The Canes are going to take Mia if I can't support her."

"They want to take Mia? I always knew they were weirdos. Trying to take someone else's baby."

"Big weirdos. It'll only be once, and then I'm done. I just need enough to get me on my feet."

"I said that once upon a time too," she says. "There's a party this weekend. I'll text you the address. A lot of people are looking to buy. You get the orders, but you have to cut me in. Fifty-fifty. I can't run as fast as I used to."

"How much can I make?"

"Three thousand minimum. Unless you get caught or something." She chuckles and I cringe. Three thousand in one night. A month and I wouldn't have to worry about bills for at least six months. Quick money ain't always good money, but these bills aren't going anywhere. If I do nothing, then we'll be on the streets or in a homeless shelter, never knowing who lurks in the shadows.

I can't go back to that life.

CHAPTER 21

> Guess who's coming home for a visit this weekend!

Savannah's text makes me drop Mia's baby spoon, full of mashed sweet potatoes, mid-airplane. Mia think's we're playing and starts splattering the sweet potatoes everywhere.

Shit. Shit. Shit.

Normally I'd be excited to see my girl, but this weekend is *the* weekend. Whitney and I already got our plan set into place. I can't tell Savannah I'm at a party and didn't invite her. She'll get suspicious, *real* suspicious. Start asking thousands of questions until I have no choice but to break down and tell her. She should try to be a lawyer or something instead of a journalist.

Savannah doesn't get it. She knows the type of people I'm involved with and what Scooter did for a living, but she's always been a "don't ask, don't tell" type of person. That changed when Mia came into the world. She made me promise I'd pick better friends. Make better choices than them. It's hard to keep those types of promises, though. Hard to be a good person when everybody is leaning on you. When you're everything to everybody but nothing to yourself.

"Thanks for doing my hair, girl." Savannah smooths her tribal braids down while taking a million selfies. "It's hard to find a good braider where I am. My girl Tasha usually does it, but she's interning this summer."

"You're welcome," I say. "Don't forget to tag me in the pictures. I'm trying to get some more business rolling in."

Between school hours and Mia hours I'm only scheduled for ten hours with Ms. Dubois next week and not my usual thirty. Fifteen times ten equals us still in the poorhouse.

Mama stealing my money really set me back. Her leaving in general set us back. There're no more hot meals in the morning or extra fruit snacks from the grocery store. No more bills we don't have to think about. It's all on me and Shana again.

Savannah and I pass blowout bars, hot-yoga studios, and five different coffee shops with stupid names. Each within walking distance of the other. COMING SOON posters everywhere, for places no one asked for.

Tomorrow, new business owners are hosting a job fair for the community. TWELVE DOLLARS AN HOUR written in big bold letters everywhere. The future of Ridgecrest: a few dollars above minimum wage and we are supposed to bust our ass for that. Stand up on our feet all day for that? Twelve dollars ain't gone keep a roof over our heads.

"The neighborhood has changed so much." Savannah looks at the new buildings that line downtown. Gray square buildings tucked between vacant lots and boarded-up houses. They slapped paint on the projects, renamed them, and are now renting them for $1,200 a pop. Rats included. "Hasn't even been a full year since I left, either."

"It'd be amazing if it wasn't so sad," I reply.

"You can apply here." Savannah snatches a coffee-shop ad down. "'At Rose's, we're family.' Part-time and full-time hours. Benefits and everything if you become full-time. Then you and Mia wouldn't have to go to the health center."

"They won't give anybody full-time hours because then they'd have to give out health benefits. If they do, three months down the line they'll change their tune. 'Sorry, Ms. Johnson, we have to cut your hours back.'"

"On the bright side, that's three months to save." Savannah loves looking on the bright side of things. Gets on my nerves, high-key.

"All right, I'll fill it out. You happy?" She cheeses so big her eyes disappear. I fold the flyer into three before slipping it in my bag.

"Come by the house tomorrow. Grandma got Mia some clothes and toys."

"Your granny needs to stop. She's already given us too much, and we can never repay her."

Savannah grandma was a teacher, and her grandpa served in

Vietnam. They own their home, unlike most folks around here. Her granny favorite story is how it wasn't a hood when they bought the house. How the trees lined up just right, when the city cared about the folks in our neighborhood. How everything was cool before crack shook the neighborhood like an earthquake, leaving a line down the middle. She says she'll never forget the smell, or the image of motherless kids running into the street.

"Girl, we family. You don't pay back family. Besides, she got these little booties that I'm dying to see my niece in."

We follow the graffiti until we get to the top of the hill. It's instantly ten degrees warmer up here, like the sun gets here first and leaves last. As we get closer, the bass gets louder. Kids sit out on the lawn, smoke pulling from their lips to the air. Beer cans take the place of flamingo decorations. "Hide me, I need to change," I say.

Savannah holds up her jacket in front of me. "I don't know why you didn't do this at home. You being hella extra."

"You know Shana be trying to lock me in the house. Her mind wanders when I'm not home."

"She don't gotta worry, right?"

"Right." The lie rolls off my lips and to my feet. What Savannah don't know won't hurt her. I take off my Hilbert University sweatshirt and squeeze out of my skintight jeans, replacing them with a gold shimmery dress that puts Beyoncé to shame. Flip-flops change to clear stripper heels, and the nude gloss slathered on my full lips is overpowered by a red lipstick from the beauty supply store.

I check myself in my phone camera.

Not bad for a girl on a budget.

To get customers, I have to look the part. Men are the biggest clientele, and fortunately for me, they are visual creatures, lacking substance everywhere else.

"This better be fun," Savannah says to me as she taps on the door to the house and then lets herself in. The cluttered room is cloudy with smoke. I could get a contact high if I breathe deeply enough.

There isn't any space to hear yourself think. You have no choice but to touch shoulders with the person next to you. Women in dresses that move along the color spectrum from cream to soft pinks to different shades of red sit on the one leather couch that's pushed back to make room for a place to dance. Their tattooed hands are wrapped around wine-cooler bottles and fat blunts. No one coughs as they pass the drug around in a formulated rotation. Women in ombré Afros, multicolored weaves, and brightly dyed wigs float around the room. We grab two red plastic cups from the counter.

"Damn, took you long enough." Dej voice rings out from the dimly lit hallway adjoining the living room. She told me I was dumb for trusting Whitney but perked up when I told her we could clear three thousand dollars tonight. I just needed her to do one thing: keep Savannah distracted.

"I had to get Savannah," I say. "She takes forever to get ready now, since she is a college girl."

"Could have spent a little longer getting ready, if you ask me." Dej's judgy voice pops out, and it's always noticeable.

"Didn't know you were still hanging with losers."

"Savannah, don't start with me." Deja shakes the ice in her drink, shooting every curse word at her with her facial expression. I step between them. Last thing I need is them fighting and ruining everything.

"Dang, I can't ever have y'all in the same room because this happens. Both of y'all are Mia's godmothers, which means you need to learn how to get along."

"I ain't got time for the petty shit. I'm in college now," Savannah says.

"You literally mention that every two seconds. Nobody cares about your funky college. Didn't they kick your Black ass to the curb?" Deja asks.

"Stop! Damn." I feel like I'm their mama.

"Man, whatever. Can we get a minute? I need to talk to B *privately.*"

"Unless B'onca wants me to leave, I'm staying right here," Savannah says.

I turn my head halfway. "It's cool, Savannah. Go have fun. I'll link up with you later."

Savannah sits her cup down. "I'll be back in five. Not a minute later." She sucks her teeth before making her way to a group of senior girls on the other side of the room.

"You got your own timid bodyguard. That's dope." Dej takes a big pull from her blunt and holds it between her middle fingers. "Want to hit this?"

"We came here to sell. Not get fucked up, Deja," I say.

Deja coughs after inhaling too long. "That's why I need you.

You keep me in check." She passes the blunt to some random walking by. "Take this."

"Now, here's the plan." I pull her near the dark wall. Our eyes gaze out at the folks who can't see us unless they strain their eyes. "You see them boys toward the back?" I move Deja's head softly to the left. "Those big fish. I mean, rolling in money. I'll get them first. They'll put in orders with no questions asked."

"What if questions are asked? How do you know they ain't gone snitch?" Deja asks.

"They're cool. I've been knowing them most of my life," I say. "You keeping Savannah occupied, right?"

She nods. "My homeboy gone keep her moving the entire night."

I remind Deja: "Remember, we are going fifty-fifty on my half."

Deja slices the smoke that lingers in the air. "Right down the middle."

"This is the only time. I just got to get us on our feet; then I'm going to get myself together. Pick up more hours at the shop," I tell her.

"Whatever you say, girl." Deja slips around me, disappearing into the strobing lights. Savannah takes her place.

Hector from third period comes over, doing a salsa move. "Do you wanna dance?" He moves around Savannah as she spins, trying to keep up with him.

"Gone, get your dance on. I'll be cool over here," I say.

"You sure?" she asks.

Hector grabs Savannah's hand, moving his hips from side to side to the music playing.

"Go, have fun. I'm going to just have a drink and chill. You know this gone be my only baby-free night for a minute," I tell Savannah.

They move to the middle of the floor, doing the merengue. Hector winks at me, giving me a thumbs-up, while Savannah moves her hips to the music.

Five minutes pass before someone comes by. Suddenly I'm tweaking, I mean hands straight shaking, but I can't show them that. I glue my arms to my sides and fake it till I make it.

"I hear you're the girl tonight." Sean from science class taps my shoulder. "Didn't think that you were in the game."

"This isn't a game. It's my life," I say. "Now, what you want, and yes I have CashApp and Venmo." Scooter hated electronic payments. When he was teaching me about his process, he said those were the easiest way to get caught, since people can trace, but for me this easier to hide from anyway. After what happened with Mama, I don't want to risk my money being stolen again.

"A sweatsuit, and my girl needs a new purse." He slips his phone out, types in my code. We wait for the completion text before I shoo him away. "Nice doing business, Sean. I'll be in touch."

"I think I like you better than Whitney. You're way nicer."

He eye-fucks me, moving his green lasers from my breasts to my legs. I play the part. "Don't forget to tell your friends."

"Don't worry, baby. They already making their way over here." Sean takes off.

Whitney texts me each order she gets. One by one, I dance with different shades and sizes of guys. The transaction perfected by the fourth time. A dance, then the sale, and if I'm lucky, they won't let their hands linger too long. Cash slips between cleavage, fingertips, and pockets.

"What you got for me?" A peppermint breath lingers in my ear. Sweat pools in the middle of my bra, soaking the dollar bills.

"What you want?" I say, not meeting the glance that stares upside my head.

"You." He gets closer, his breath burning the side of my face.

"I have access to the Nike store, Michael Kors, Victoria's Secret, get something for your girl." I face him; his eyes are low and red. "Seems like you got too lit tonight."

"I'm good, love. I don't even have a girl. You bold being here . . . doing this."

"You gone snitch on me or something?" I ask Peppermint Breath Guy.

"Not if you give me a little kiss. That may give me amnesia."

"No, thank you. I'm here to serve, that's all."

Peppermint Breath grabs me, fingers pressing into my forearm. No one can see me, but I can see everyone at the party.

"Get the fuck off me." I lever myself up, trying to let go of his grip. "Yo, get off me. I'm not even playing right now."

"Neither am I."

His knee pushes against my thigh, pinning me to the wall. The money . . . what if he takes the money? Then this would all be for no reason. He leans forward, breathing heavy in my ear. The mixture of peppermint and rum almost makes me vomit.

There are two people nearby. I'm praying that they get that feeling of someone staring and look my way, saving me from this trap.

"Now, let's start over," Peppermint Breath whispers. "What you got for me?"

"He bothering you, sis?" Whitney walks up hand in hand with Scooter's old best friend, Jermaine. He pulls her close; his free hand rests on her now-swollen belly. She already got a new man. Damn, she moves fast as hell. Shit, maybe that isn't even Scooter's baby for real. That's why the Canes are coming after mine.

Jermaine's watching as Peppermint Breath lets his knee fall, unpinning me. "Yes!" I jerk, falling backward, the wall catching me. "He won't tell me what he wants."

"You good, man? What you need?" They dap up. Jermaine holds him just a second longer, whispering something I can't hear over the bass of the music.

"I'm good, bruh. Didn't mean any harm." Peppermint Breath nods to me, walking over to the couch of kids passing a blunt back and forth.

"Thank you," I say to Jermaine. He waves me off like it's no big deal.

"You good? You need anything?" Whitney shakes a baggie, holding one lone pill in her palm. "Might take the edge off."

The pill stares at me. It'd take the pain away, bring more than what was left with it. Mia curled up in bed right now, waiting for me to get home. She's never truly asleep until I'm next to her.

"I'm good. I'm about to dip. The baby waiting for me," I say.

"Aw, give Mia a kiss from me and her sister," Whitney says before they slither to a padlocked door in the back. Jermaine knocks three times with the flat side of his hand, and a tall man with a blond low cut opens the door. That must be where the real money is.

I follow and imitate Jermaine's knock, and the door flings open. The tall man hovers over me, his bare chest inches away from my forehead. The faint smell of Black & Milds and musk flows from the room.

"You can't come back here," he says, and begins to shut the door.

My heel stops the door from closing. "Jermaine said I could come."

He looks over his shoulder and shouts, "Aye, Jermaine, Scooter other baby mama at the door. You want her in?"

"Tell her we'll be out soon," he shouts. The tall guy doesn't wait two seconds before pushing my foot away. I walk back to my post at the door, checking the time on the clock.

Before twelve a.m. I meet my quota, selling more than I expected. Some old-school song playing, and everyone turning up in the middle of the front-room floor, dancing a hole in the stale brown carpet. I grab a drink from the makeshift bar in the kitchen. If I want to salvage this night, I can't be sober. I toss back a shot of Hennessy, hacking up most of it into the kitchen sink. I stopped drinking months ago to breastfeed Mia.

"You think I'm boo boo the damn fool, don't you?" Savannah's voice pierces the music.

"You talking to me?" I ask her.

"You been floating around here, in and out. You think I'm crazy. Why you even bring me here? You think I'm that stupid that I wouldn't figure out what you doing?"

There is no point in lying. Savannah got the gift of discernment. She knows. "I needed an alibi if anything went left. Plus, you needed a party. You've been mad uptight lately," I tell her.

"An alibi? That's all I am to you. You used me," Savannah yells at me.

"It's not even like that." I step forward and Savannah moves away from me, bumping into a partygoer behind her.

"I won't watch you fuck up your life. I'll snitch before I do that."

That makes me freeze. "I'm doing all this to keep Mia. You know that. Nobody gone take her away from me or me away from her. I'd die before that happens. Trust me, you don't want me as an enemy, Savannah."

"You're a damn joke, B'onca, and it ain't even funny anymore." She pushes through the crowd. It takes her a minute to find the door. The night air rushes in before it closes behind her.

I lean against the kitchen counter, folding my arms across my chest.

"What you need, sis?" Whitney comes out of the shadows.

"I want in with whatever's going on behind the door!"

"That's big-boy stuff. Even I don't mess with it. You ain't ready for all that."

"I'm more ready than I'll ever be," I say.

"How much you make today?" Whitney asks.

I look away, taking in the dying-down crowd.

"Girl, nobody wants a cut of your money. How much you get?" Whitney repeats.

"Three thousand if everything goes right," I say.

She smacks my shoulder with each syllable. "That's what I'm talking about!"

"You going to get Jermaine to cut me in or what?" I ask her.

Three thousand today, but I can make more. I know I can, and with less work. If I get behind that door, that's real money. Money that can last longer than a few months. That'll keep food in our stomachs and the air on when the heat waves come.

I don't know if this is addiction or survival, but I do know that whatever feeling it is, it's growing inside of me.

Whitney rubs her stomach in small circles. "I'll see what I can do, but if I let you in, remember: it ain't as easy to get out."

"Aight." I pull on my hoodie, covering the revealing parts of me. "I'm going to roll. I'll catch you later."

Going home, I feel sick. I shoot a text to Deja; she sends a picture back of her dancing. Which means she's staying longer.

Everyone now booed up anywhere they can make space. Women sit on the counters as their men stand between their legs, kissing their ears and necks. I have to interrupt a couple who's pinned against the exit door, tongues shoved down each other's throats. I hold my head with my hands as the cold air hits my face. The walk home takes twice as long this time.

Savannah sits on her granny's stoop across the street. She

waited for me to get home. She can't be that mad at me. I wave at her; she gets up and turns the porch light off. Our friendship will be remembered not by all the time we spent building a bond, but by the moment that it ended.

I throw up by the side of the house.

CHAPTER 22

"HI! WELCOME TO Jackson Street Market," an *I don't want to be here* voice says from the intercom. The cash-register station is empty. Only a few people look at the clothes on the racks. I pull up the list on my phone and memorize the order. Then remember the drill Scooter used to tell his people. *In and out. Don't make eye contact with anyone, and watch your surroundings. Pretend you're just like everyone else. Walk this store like you belong.*

That's what you have to tell yourself when you're used to being profiled. I can't count how many times I've been in the store to spend my hard-earned money and yet I still felt like a criminal. Eyes on me as soon as I stepped inside. Too many *do you need anything*s. An excuse for the clerks to breathe down my neck. Sometimes I felt like I should just put a piece of jewelry in my pocket. Run out with a rack of clothes. If they saw me as a criminal anyway, maybe that's what I should be.

A girl about my age stands between racks with her mother. They laugh together and pick up pieces of clothing, pressing them against their body. I stand next to them, doing the same, but it's not as authentic. You can't fake that kind of happiness. Sometimes I wonder how things would be if I had that type of relationship with my mama. If she didn't leave when I needed her the most. As I get older and grow into my motherhood, there are parts of Mama that remind me of myself. There are days where I beg God, or whoever listens, to never let me choose Mama's type of life over Mia.

Then there's always something that pulls you into this.

Mama leaving? Check.

Teen motherhood? Check.

White men in suits? Check.

Trouble comes in threes. Don't know how much more of these troubles I can put up with. Mama was younger than me when she had Shana. A few years later, she got caught up in the streets. Here I am, following in her footsteps. According to Google, that is called a generational trauma. It's kind of embedded in my DNA for me to be this way.

"That'll look nice on you, baby," the older woman says from the mirror. Her eyes trace the tracksuit in my hand. "It's a nice color. Complements the gold flecks in your eyes real well."

She's getting too good of a look at me. Nobody needs to be able to identify me if something goes wrong.

"Thanks." I lower my head and move through the clothing racks. My shopping tote is filled with two tracksuits, a pair of Nikes, and some jeans that cost more than some folks' car note.

I wait for the mother and daughter to check out. Listen closely to the total amount of their stuff. Three hundred dollars and forty-two cents. She doesn't hesitate to swipe her card, and her daughter doesn't waste time grabbing the bag. I wonder what she does to be able to spend three months' worth of groceries on clothes. What would I need to do to live like that?

The door is clear. A straight run to and from. Pretend you belong, B'onca. Walk to the door like you got it like that. Like what you're about to buy is chump change to you.

"Ma'am." The clerk's got a little attitude in her voice. I ignore it, picking up my pace.

"Ma'am!" This time, the clerk runs from behind the counter. I take off faster. The beeping sound of the alarm gets softer as I get further. The bridge. I hold on to the payments in my bag for dear life. People don't pay for half orders. I run until I can see the field. The sun just set, which means people are starting to come outside. People I need to dodge until I have they order. I have about five more to fulfill, but after all that running, I need a break. This baby fat slowing me down.

"I got your order right here." I hold out my bag for Jacob to see. His street name is Fat, even though he is the size of a tadpole. Nicknames always don't match in the hood. "Before I give you this, I need the other half of my money," I say.

"Damn, you don't trust a nigga?" He reaches into his pocket and pulls out a roll of bills. He counts and re-counts, trying to show off. "You know I'm good for it. I ain't never cheated Scooter before. You know that," Jacob tells me.

I shrug, looking over my shoulder. "You the only one out here?"

We exchange products. The money is like honey in my hands.

"For now. You should stick around. I told everyone you're boosting, and they want to put in orders."

"Nah, I'm good. I made everything I needed today. Don't tell anybody else. You know how word spreads around here. I'm going to get the rest of my orders done and then chill."

He laughs and pulls out his bankroll again. "How long will that money last you?"

"If I budget, at least a month or two. We got some back bills to pay," I tell him.

"You know how bills work right? They keep on coming," Jacob says.

"I'll see you later, man," I say, tucking the money deeper into my bra.

"You know where we at if you need more," Jacob says. "No need to be ashamed. We all know what it's like out here."

I nod, tighten my jacket, and head toward home.

The doughnut light pops on just as I make it to the building. Something I can control for once: my craving for something sweet. I'm not too far from home, but you never know what might have happened or who might have been watching. I check again, pressing against the soft spot in my bra.

I stop and get doughnuts and must eat at least three before I even step foot in the house. It felt good to just ask for what I wanted without having to think of all the things I needed. Even let the cashier keep the change. She probably needs it more than me right now.

"Mama! Can I have one?" Cyn attacks the bag. Digging deep for the last jelly-filled doughnut.

"After dinner, Cyn." Shana stands over the stove, giving Mia a taste of what she's cooking up. Veggie chili. I can tell by the aroma in the air. Her favorite low-cost meal. Beans ain't nothing but sixty cent a can, and then some on-sale veggies. We're eating good for at least three days.

"Where you been, B'onca?" Shana checks the clock on her phone. It's only nine o'clock, but to Shana that may as well be a big four a.m. staring back at her.

"The library." I take Mia from her arms. She's learned how to kick her feet out now and won't stop. "There's this study group that meets there. Don't bother making me a plate. They had pizza." The lie makes my stomach turn in anticipation, but I'd rather Cyn have an extra serving.

"You got a goofy look on your face." Shana glances at me. "Why, I hear on the street that you done took Scooter spot. You boosting now, huh?"

Fuck these big-mouth-ass people.

"I ain't got no reason to lie." I balance Mia on my knee. She looks between us like she knows the energy is off. Her giggles fill the room as if she wants to glue us together with them.

"If you doing that shit, I'll take Mia to the Canes myself," Shana says. "You know I will. When it was just you riding around with Scooter, it was different, but now you got that baby. She's getting bigger every day and knows more than you give her credit for."

Back when I first had Mia, I treated her like a baby doll. When she cried, I'd cry and pass her off to Shana, who could quiet her in five minutes. When she was sweet and silent, I could hold her for hours. Getting lost in her eyes. I just did what the nurse told me to do to keep her alive. Now she's a real human.

"You don't have to tell me I have a baby now," I say. "She's my whole life. I'll do anything to make sure she's safe and healthy and with *me*. Anything."

Everyone says go slow. Take your time. You don't have to get to the finish line so soon. They don't know there ain't no finish line for me. I won't run through a big ribbon at the end. My life is a never-ending race of surviving. Death might be my only way out of this. At least Mia will know what I did wasn't in vain. That I did it for her.

"Dammit, you better act like it, then." Shana comes closer, her steps slow. "Running the street. How is that going to keep her healthy? I told you to let me deal with the grown-up things. You stay in a child's place. I know Mama leaving put us in a bind, but I got this. I always take care of things."

"I don't know if you noticed, but I ain't been a child in a while." I can't remember a recent time when I wasn't worrying about something. When I wasn't trying to keep a roof over my head or some type of money in my pocket. When you ain't got nothing and taste the fruit of money, it's hard to go back. When your seed is watching, it's even harder.

"In this house, you're still a child," Shana says.

"You can't pay all these bills by yourself," I tell her. "I've seen the ones you've tried to hide. We can't let them people out there put us out of our house. We can't let the Canes take Mia from us."

If I cry, I give in to her theory that I'm a child.

"You have to have some faith that God will see us through this," Shana tells me.

"God helps those who help themselves. I'm not waiting around for his divine intervention. I got to get it myself," I say.

CHAPTER 23

"YOU CRAZY, GIRL." Deja sucks the side of her strawberry-crunch-cake ice cream. Some daytime talk show is on. A weird person, doing weird things. Which celebrity, deemed problematic on social media this month, keeping us so distracted that we both skipped school today.

Grief my excuse. Cramps are Deja's. Mrs. Crenshaw understands mine. She threatens Deja with not getting her diploma.

Mia lies across my lap. She weighs like fifteen pounds now. I maneuver and reach for the bag of chips. If Mia wakes up, then it's over. Skip day turns into us watching *SpongeBob* or *CoComelon* on repeat. "It's a good plan. In and out, remember?"

"In and out a store is different from in and out your dead baby daddy house."

In my opinion it'll be easier. Nobody would expect it. I'm supposed to be grieving. Sad. If someone sees me, they'll think I'm getting something of Mia's or wanting to be close to him again.

When all I want is what I'm owed. I had to give everyone back their deposit money since someone was going around spreading my business to Shana. The little I already made will be gone by next week. If I don't do this, then we back to square one, and I didn't start this to not finish it. I have a month before the Canes make good on their promise. Thirty days to prove that I can be a good mother and provide.

Deja shoves a handful of Cheetos in her mouth. Her salty-and-sweet cravings are out of control. "I'm sure whoever he rolled with got that money by now. Unless they think loyalty applies after the grave. Which I doubt, because we all in the poorhouse."

"Not necessarily. He had a secret hiding place. He thought I was asleep one time, but I saw it. Deja, it's so much, mane. Think of it as my back child support," I say.

"I still think you are crazy as hell," Deja responds.

"I only need you to be lookout. You don't have to touch any-thing, and we can split the profit. Fifty-fifty, like last time."

Deja brushes Cheeto dust to the floor, but the broom is on standby 'cause her mama doesn't play that. "You keep it. It's money for Mia."

I tilt my head. "You sure?"

"Uh-huh. I still have enough from last time. Use this to get on your feet for real. All this illegal stuff can't last forever. Especially with Mia. Maybe use the money to go to school, get your cosme-tology license, and buy a shop or something. Be your own boss."

My own shop. Something to call my own. To keep me out of this for a while. I'll forever be grateful for Ms. Dubois giving me a job, but that's not real money. She'd understand, too. Before their come-up, Trent was out hustling like me. Trying to make something out of nothing.

I need consistent money. Life-changing money. I need to one day send Mia to college without getting the government involved. Feed her without food stamps and WIC. House her without Section 8.

A dream.

Mia starts to stretch and yawn. In a minute it'll be feeding time. Breastfeeding still doesn't come easy to me, but I'm not stopping until I get it down pat. Mia grabs for Deja. Like she's trying to be my wing-baby. "Even Mia wants her money. You see?"

"Don't bring my godbaby into your sins," Deja says. "What's the plan, then? You not just going to roll up in there. Matter fact, you don't know who's in that house. How are you going to get inside?"

I dig around to the bottom of Mia's baby bag. "Technically, I have a key. He gave it to me a little before I found out about Mia. Hopefully it still works."

"And if it doesn't?"

"I'm not against busting a window."

"Crazy."

"Stop calling me that. I'm a mother who's trying to provide for her kid."

Deja pulls out a piece of paper and draws a messed-up sketch of Scooter's house.

"Aight, now you get to the house. Let's say the key works. What you gone do? Just run up in there?"

She draws a stick figure with hair all over its head.

"Is that supposed to be me?" I ask.

"Mm-hmm, you know you look like you stuck your finger in a socket these days." Deja draws a group of people in front of the house. "Now, how do you expect to get past all these people?"

"I don't get how seeing fake-ass people do fake-ass crimes is going to help us," I say.

We've been cooped up in Deja's cramped bedroom for a good eight hours. Watching every robbery movie that she could find on Netflix. I stopped paying attention during movie two when she suggested that I get harnesses and break in through the sky-light windows, true action-movie style. I'm not a stunt double, and we damn sure don't have money for all these gadgets.

I grab the remote and turn the television off right as some white woman is about to set off the police alarm. "I don't know why you think we have to do all this."

Deja checks a message on her phone screen. "Over where Scooter lives is where all the snitches done moved in. You walk in the front door and somebody sees you, no telling what they might do. Fingers are probably ready to dial 911."

"I forgot. I don't know why he decided to move over there to this watered-down-ass area. Always talking about how he wanted better but never extended that to his daughter."

I look at Ridgecrest, and I see home. All Scooter saw was a place to profit off of.

I sit up a bit. A straightened back means you're serious. That's the only thing I got from these movies. "Do you think I need a mask? Just in case."

Deja sits on the arm of the couch. "If you want. I can get a ski mask, nobody gonna blink twice at those."

"That'll work." I open my note app and write down a list of necessities.

Masks.

Getaway car.

Clothes.

"Your brother still fixing up the car?" I ask.

She nods. "I mean, it's a hooptie. Doesn't have any air or anything, and there's always this musty smell in it."

"We just need to get from point A to point B," I say.

We brainstorm between action movies, Megan Thee Stallion EPs, and snack breaks. In three hours we have a plan. Or the outline of a plan. We have a time limit of five minutes. Five minutes to get everything we need and get out. This time, I'm not taking Nike sets or small electronics to resell to people in school. Money. Cold hard cash. The solution to every problem I've ever had. All mine within a blink. It doesn't seem real. It may not be real. Because with each outline of the plan, what can go wrong fills me with dread. The car breaking down as we try to get away. Dead on the pavement from gunshot wounds, having Shana identify my shot-up body.

Mia growing up without a *daddy* or a *mama*.

What will we do if we get caught? We have all these grown-up problems but we aren't real adults. Just teenagers trying to figure out the right thing to do.

You're not a bad person, B.

I have to tell myself that every morning, noon, and night. I'm a good person in a bad situation. This ain't my fault. None of this my fault. I didn't ask to be born into this fucked-up world.

CHAPTER 24

I DON'T KNOW where I'll be next year—hell, even an hour from now.

Right now I'm parked across the street from Scooter's house with Deja. Mia is at home sleeping. Shana thinks I'm at some grief-counseling place. When I'm really about to do a crime that I ain't so sure about. No options for folks like me. Only decisions made by people you don't ever see. The white men in suits, the social workers who stop by once a month, and the neighbors who hear the hunger pangs but keep their eyes low so you don't notice theirs, either.

I go over the plan one more time. "Five minutes. If I'm not out in five that means something went wrong. You leave. Don't wait around. You're eighteen now. There's no more juvie for you."

"I can't leave you, mane," Deja responds.

"It's cool. I know what I'm getting myself into," I say.

The people who used to hang outside of Scooter's house have

been replaced with candles that still burn on his front porch. The teddy-bear pile has grown bigger. *RIP* is written on the sidewalk in yellow chalk.

"Everyone loved him," I say. "I loved him the most, once upon a time, but I don't think he ever loved me back. Not really."

"It's okay to cry, B. You haven't since everything happened because you try to play tough like nothing hurts you, but it's okay to admit this did."

I look at the ceiling and count the slashes in Deja's brother's old-ass Crown Vic. Tears still won't fall. "I'm good."

Deja sucks her teeth. "Whatever you say."

I stuff my hair in a large black cap. "I'm finna head in."

"Be careful and don't be greedy."

"It's a foolproof plan." That's what I tell myself each time doubt creeps in. Nothing can go wrong; we've played it out too many times. People think crime would never happen over here. Then there's us, two girls ready to shake up the bubble that they live in. I don't really feel bad about it. I mean, rich people shake up my life every day. Got the power to change everything I know with a signature in a checkbook. Now it's me with the power, and I may be drunk on it.

The old woman across the street puts out her cigarette and goes back into her house. It's time. Ten thousand in ten minutes. It'd take me a year to save that working with Ms. Dubois. Probably even longer, thanks to Uncle Sam.

Deja's leg shakes the car. "You sure you want to do this?"

I'm not a hundred percent. Nothing is ever a hundred percent.

The only thing I'm sure of is that my money is gone. My mama is gone. Mia daddy is gone. My house might be next, and normal jobs only pay $7.25.

"No, but it's too late to turn back now."

I exit the car, which is hidden close enough to the house but far away that no one notices it. I straighten my back and push my head up. All fear out of the window. Mia deserves better, and I won't stop until she has it. Until we have something that's in our name. Until the Canes aren't trying to snatch her from me.

Doodlebug, forgive me for what I'm about to do.

I hide in the shadows, seeing the others, but they can't see me.

My hands tremble as I try to unlock the door. Please, please work. Scooter ain't one to ever take precautions. The door sticks, and I push.

Five minutes. In and out. Just a little more.

I give a big push that's met with the blaring sound of Scooter's alarm system.

Fuck. I forgot the code. Didn't think it would be on, honestly. Who'd want to protect a dead person's things?

Four minutes.

I look toward the car. I should run to safety before the cops come, but I didn't come all this way to give up now.

Scooter's bedroom door is right ahead of me. Ten thousand dollars waits for me. I sprint toward the room, tripping on turned-over Yeezys and PS5 controllers. His bedroom still looks the same. A California king bed that I never wanted to get out of. The seventy-five-inch mounted television with every streaming service you could think of.

His hiding spot glistens in the back. Tucked behind the washing machine in the master bathroom. I knock against the floor, checking for the hollow spot. The blaring of the alarm is still going strong. There's no sound of police cars yet.

"Come on. I know it's here." I tap with my knuckles harder, trying my best to hear. One more knock and the floorboard rises.

Three minutes to collect as much as I can. To leave before the police can come flying down the street. I stuff my duffel bag with everything my hand touches. Each stack weighs down my shoulder.

Two minutes.

I zip the bag and take one last look at his room. A picture of newborn Mia sits next to his bed. A lonely bag of pills spills over next to it.

I take the back door this time, throw the duffel bag over the fence. I land on my knees next to it. The wind almost knocked out of me, but I keep moving while shooting a text to Deja.

> Alarm went off. Meet me around the corner.
> Next to the park.

> On the way!

I wait at the corner for Deja. My foot taps the pavement. She drives like a bat out of hell any other time.

A young guy catches my attention. His eyes roam over mine, and to my hand. Shit! My sleeve, the tiny red heart tattoo that dances around my wrist. A sign that I was here. As he gets closer, I notice the waves, and the familiar hoodie.

Trent.

Deja swerves around the corner, leaving a streak in the street. She smashes the horn, and I jump inside the car. Trent's eyes are to the ground now, as if he's trying to forget he ever saw me. There are tons of people with heart tattoos. That's what I tell myself as we drive away with one minute left.

Deja cracks the window; the humid air hits up, filling us with relief. Adrenaline pumps through my body faster, making my body limp in the passenger seat. Scooter is behind me, and our future is in front.

Deja lights up a joint.

"Put that out," I scold. "I need a clear head."

"It's a celebration," Deja says.

"Turn the music up," I say.

"Money Trees" by Kendrick Lamar blasts on the radio. The bass beats against us, rattling the car underneath our feet. We bump our heads, turn to look at each other, and smile. This is my social security.

We sing along to the rap song, taking turns with the ad libs. I relax in the seat as I think of all the things that this money will bring.

"Mia's going to have a good birthday this year," I say. "The Canes are going to be so impressed, they'll forget all about taking her from me. They'll see I can take care of my baby."

Our celebration ends with a whooping sound and flashing blue lights in the rearview mirror.

CHAPTER 25

"FUCK, MAN!" DEJA shouts. She's slowing down as the police get closer. I've never been in this position before. *Foolproof.* We are the fools, thinking we could pull this off perfectly.

"Where you think they going to take us, huh?" I peek at the rearview mirror. My nails dig in between the seat cushions. "Especially you. Real jail is worse, and that's saying something."

The dragging. Pulling. The inhumane treatment when you're in jail.

I dig harder into the cushions, looking at the side mirror. The police car right on our bumper. If we were to stop, they'd crash right into us.

Deja leans forward. "I'm with whatever you're with, but think about this, B'onca. You look more guilty if you run."

It ain't about looking guilty. Black folk are always guilty without a fair trial. Even though this time it'd be accurate. If they were to look under the back seat and see all that money. We're fucked.

"B'onca, you gotta make a decision." The disadvantage of being the leader. Everything rests in my hands.

Think. Think. Think. There's a turn coming up. If Deja makes it, there's a good chance they won't catch us. That we can take a shortcut and be over the Mississippi border within ten minutes.

Deja lingers her fingertips on mine. "B'onca." I look out the corner of my eyes. "You're shaking. We can't outrun them, not in this car. It's already overheating and we're barely going over fifty miles."

I loosen my grip on the door handle. Let life come back into my fingers before giving Deja the signal to pull over. The bright lights flicker behind us, and two cops get out.

"We didn't realize they were behind us. Apologize and act innocent," I say.

Deja doesn't say anything. I keep both hands visible. No sudden movements, or this may end badly for both of us.

The two officers separate. One stands near the passenger side, and the other one peers down to get a better look into the car. One's white, with balding brown hair. The other Black, with dreads that reach his shoulder. They don't look threatening, but they never do until you're on the seven o'clock news.

The Black cop examines the car. "Took you a while to pull over."

"I'm sorry, sir," Deja says with her best innocent impression. "We didn't realize you were behind us."

Only speak when spoken to. Cops aren't your friends no matter how many times they come to your neighborhood to play ball. If it came down to it, they'd shoot first and ask questions later.

The white officer looks deeper into the car and smirks. "License and registration, please."

A simple instruction that feels like a death sentence. The glove box is a complicated maze. Not too fast and not too slow. Don't make any sudden movements. Always tell the officer what you're doing even if it's obvious. The talk.

I got the talk before I learned about where babies come from. The police talk. What to do if you see one. Normal childhood things criminalized. Not being able to play with water guns outside because to the cops you're never a child.

"I'm going to reach with my left hand to get to the glove box."

Deja stays straight. Back pressed hard against the leather seats. This isn't the first time for either of us, but it's the first time in a while. The sweating and heart beating. Not being able to catch your breath.

The police officer nods toward the box.

I hand the papers and my license to Dej.

"You ran a stop sign back there," he says. "You could really hurt someone, you know."

The car fills with an unsaid sigh of relief. The outside air from the rolled-down windows starts to smell sweeter.

"We're sorry." Sweet and simple. No explanations to keep us here longer than need be.

He pats the top of the car. "Hold tight."

We both breathe a sigh of relief as they walk away.

"Your record clean, right? Nothing they can pull up?" I look over at Dej.

She nods. "I got everything sponged a few months ago."

"Good, good." I tap the glove compartment as the Black officer comes back to the car.

"I'm going to let y'all go tonight, but in the future, be more careful, all right?" he says, handing Deja back the documents.

"Yes, sir. Thank you," she says.

He nods and goes back to his car, turning off the blinding lights. I blink, trying to turn my eyesight back to normal. Blue dots float in front of me.

"Damn" all I can say.

CHAPTER 26

"I'M SORRY AGAIN that I had to bring the baby." Mia snores softly in her new stroller. After trying for hours to find a babysitter, I gave up. It was either bring her or cancel. I have to find out how much Trent knows, if he knows anything at all.

"I told you, that's fine. Trent loves the kids." He bends down and strokes her cheek. People pass us, smiling at the scene. They must think we're a family of three on a night out. I can't lie—it's nice to be seen as a family and not a single mother. When people assume you fit into what society thinks you should be, they treat you better.

Trent takes the stroller from me, pushing Mia in front of him. We pass one of them fancy restaurants that's been popping up. Cloth napkins and candlelight just to eat barbecue. The best barbecue joints are the ones where you can see the cooks behind plastic barriers chopping up your food. Not the ones that expect you to eat your ribs with a fork and knife and not your hands. I ain't want to assimilate Trent back into the street culture yet.

From his looks now, these are the type of places he used to. Plus, he paid for it. I wouldn't ever put my Black dollar back into these vulture businesses.

"That over there is Jackson's Pit." My nose follows me to the smell of fried chicken and chitlins. "It's new but one of the best soul-food spots around here. If you go in, ask for my discount."

"Oh, you got it like that?" he says. "Then why didn't we go there instead of this bougie barbecue place?"

"I thought you'd enjoy this type of place more."

He slaps his hand in the middle of his chest. "Ouch."

Mia giggles at the gesture.

"Have you heard about the store robbery?" I pull at my sleeve. Making sure the tattoo is covered.

"Which one?" he asks. "Seems like every day a place is getting hit. There was actually a robbery nearby the other day."

I chew on the inside of my gums. "That's crazy. Where about?"

"A few houses over. I was taking a walk and heard some alarms going off. I chalked it up to ignorant teenagers with nothing else to do. My next-door neighbor kind of shaken up about it. Said he was getting some cameras."

"Damn, he must not be from around here."

"Barely anyone from my street is," he says. "Seems like I see a new face every day, and they look at me like *I'm* the stranger."

Trent continues to push Mia. I wait for him to say he knows it was me. He never does. I let the anxiety wash away. Maybe he was scared himself and didn't get a good look.

"You see that place over there?" He points to the building that stood with every riot that came through Memphis. The oldest place here, with the most history. "That business has been in my family for generations, and we don't serve anything bougie."

"I never put together the people who run Dubois House was your kinfolk."

"Mm-hmm, started by my great-great-great-granddaddy, back when they were trying to pay up some money for slavery. He took his bit and built this place right on the strip. Now, legend has it that if you are there late enough, you can see him roaming around. That's why I get my food to go."

"You ain't scared of no ghost, are you? I mean, the living are scarier."

"I ain't trying to find out," Trent says as we stroll further down the street. Owners come out of their doors one by one, locking up for the night. Black faces smile at us as they double-check the locks. The divide is noticeable on the street. On one sidewalk it's Drunk Henry and them, sitting out, cooling and playing dice. They been there since before we were thought of, keeping an eye on the block. Always taking care of the kids if we need it.

"How's that pretty girl of yours?" Drunk Henry shouts.

"She's doing fine. Getting bigger every day."

"Let me know if you need anything, now," he says before turning back to his game. And I know he doesn't mean it like that. He doesn't mean money. He means support, love, and community. That's what folks around here give, and it's damn sure worth more than a dollar sometimes.

"This street is nicknamed Magic," Trent says. "Because most

of the shops are owned by Black folk. That's why they aren't ever damaged during protests. You good to your community, and they'll be good to you."

"I never knew that," I say. "I guess I'm never down here long enough to know. My part of downtown is cut off at MLK Avenue. Well, it used to be before people started coming in and pushing us even further out."

"We gone be all right. They can't have our hood," Trent declares.

"It ain't exactly your hood anymore," I say.

"I'm here for good. I don't plan on going anywhere." Trent connects his pinky with mine, pulling me along the street. He stops us at a metal bench on the curb. A new addition to our changing neighborhood. We sit and take in the neighbors. Their dogs and their coffees even though it's too damn late for caffeine. The way they don't acknowledge us at all, even though they walk right past. Some look down at Mia and then up at our young faces. Pity sweeps theirs as if they want to take her for themselves.

I'm determined to give her the best life I can.

CHAPTER 27

"CYN, DON'T TOUCH that." She skips past the utility poles that are covered with advertisements of missing people. Yard sales. WE BUY HOUSES IN CASH signs.

Me, Cyn, and Mia are on a family outing to the park. The one far out. It seemed morbid to go to the park where Scooter died. Today is the coolest day of the summer, and everyone is outside while the sun is up. The smell of barbecue and water-slides. Watermelons and ice-cream trucks. Dance competitions and hand-clapping games.

Cyn runs into the middle of the crowd and blends right in. She looks at me for permission to get wet underneath the sprin-klers. I give her the go-ahead. Shana gone be mad, but Cyn a baby. She deserves to have some fun. We try to shield her from things. She knows we have trouble with money, but she doesn't know how deep. She knows she can't have things the other little girls have, but she doesn't understand why.

Neither of us has the heart to burst her bubble of innocence. Wish we could have held on to ours a little longer.

"Nice stroller," a voice says beside me. She's an older mother. Well, I guess compared to me, everyone is an older mother. I learned that quickly when I went to my first Mommy-and-me class. "You know the bottom part there turns into storage, so you don't have to carry the baby bag on your shoulder. It saved me a lot of aches."

The white lady points at the bottom of Mia's stroller. Then she takes over. "Here, let me show you." She flips the compartment out and I feel mad dumb.

"Wow, I guess I should have read the instructions." I situate Mia on her blanket, spreading out all her favorite toys. She grabs at everything in sight, trying to figure out how the world works.

"I had one of those strollers with this one. She had it until she was at least three. Saved my life," she says.

"That's why I got it. I wanted something nice that she could grow in." Anything to make me feel better. To ease my guilt about what I've done. Not only to myself but now my daughter.

"You did good." The white lady walks to the wooden bench and pats the spot next to her. "Sit. It seems our girls have taken a liking to each other."

Mia plays next to the little blond child. Well, her definition of playing, which is slobbering on everything.

"She's a social butterfly. Always finding someone to get friendly with," I say.

"She's a cutie-pie," she says. "She's yours? I don't want to assume, but you two look alike. You have the exact same eyes."

"She's all mine," I say. "Most folks say she looks like her daddy, but I don't see it."

"That one is my spitting image, but the other two are their father's all the way," the white lady says. "Where does she go to day care? I'm trying to get Bethany into one a few blocks away, but the waiting list is so long she'll be five before any spots open up." I hate when people are all in my business, but she doesn't seem harmful. It's a regular conversation between two moms.

"Mia goes to an in-home day care, but the owner is out of town, so she's closed for the next three days," I tell her.

"You're a good mom. Missing work and all, I'm assuming."

I ain't got much choice. Shana has a packed schedule this week. She got a quick job down at a warehouse, and lucky for us, it's peak season, which means she's working sixteen-hour days. Between the back rent and all the other bills, we're barely getting by. I can only give Shana enough not to get kicked out. If I give her too much at once, she'll get suspicious, start asking questions. I played off the stroller and said that the Canes came to their senses and offered me money.

"I wish there was another way," I say. "I need the money, you know?"

"If you're interested, Bethany's day care is hiring. If you're hired, you can get free childcare. I can put in a good word for you," the white lady says.

"You'd do that for me? I mean, I don't really know you like that." Only one hit until I get a straight job. That's what I told myself. Free day care and a check. I could do worse.

"I just moved into the neighborhood. Right off Franklin

Avenue. I'm the owner of the new coffee shop on the corner," the white lady says.

Figures. That coffee shop ain't so cute to me. That coffee shop raised my rent. That coffee shop is the reason that I got to steal to make ends meet. Why Shana got to stand up on her feet all day.

"Nah, that's okay. I mean, I don't have any experience with kids other than Mia and my niece. Besides, I already have a job," I say.

She reaches over and lifts Bethany into her lap. "Oh, okay! Well, if you ever change your mind, just reach out to Just Like Home Learning Center and tell them that Clara recommended you."

I reach for Mia and wrap up her toys. "Will do. Thanks again."

Clara makes Bethany wave goodbye. I give a smirk as I push the stroller through the iron gates. I call for Cyn and she comes running. Her braids are a frizzy mess now.

The buzzing on my hip stops before we get halfway down the street.

Deja: Lay low. The cops are around your house.

CHAPTER 28

Can I come over?

The three dots appear and reappear three times before nothing.

Stupid of me to think Trent would reply after all this time. I haven't replied to any of the texts he sent checking on me and Mia.

I'm sure he knows I'm the one he saw that night. He should have heard it from me, but I didn't have the guts to bring it up when we went out to eat.

People talk. I hear it every day. The only reason they don't know for sure that it was me is because of the timing.

She wouldn't steal from him, not at a time like this.

Look at her—she's grieving too.

Whoever saw her must need glasses or something.

But then when I walk past people, they stare at me. As if

they are trying to see if there's something different about my outfits, hair, or body. I'm not stupid. That money tucked away until it's the right time to spend it. Until we can no longer stand the hunger.

Trent still hasn't texted back as I push Mia as far away from the block as we can go. Cyn keeps up beside me. She's always happy not to be cooped up in the house.

Going to Deja house is out. As soon as I push the gates open, Savannah's mama would be calling Shana to tell her where I am.

We walk until I no longer see the wall at the end of our street. Until the air gets a little cooler.

Trent doesn't owe me anything. He isn't Mia's father. Could have been, but ain't no point in reliving a past that was never meant to be. He did what he had to do to get out, and that meant snitching on the people he vowed to protect. He's bold for being here, and that makes me attracted to him. A bee to a honeysuckle. I'm not meant to be protected. I'm strong. I'm Black. I'm a woman. I'm not meant to be saved. I'm supposed to bear these burdens alone. Walk with my head high with Mia on my hip because she didn't ask to be here. She didn't ask to be created when I barely knew what life was. She didn't ask for parents who didn't know the first thing about sex, and damn sure not babies. All she did was be born. Born into the same world that I was.

The buzz on my hip sets off the racing in my heart.

Trent: I'll be home in about 10 minutes. Where are you? I'll come pick you up.

I'll meet you at your place.

I'm only a few minutes away. The extra steps won't kill me.

"TeTe, it's raining." Cyn lifts her face up and allows the drops to drench her. That child loves the water. Too bad none of us know how to swim.

Rain in the South, no matter how little, is cause for everyone to retreat home. To sit on their porches and allow God to do his work. Or heavy enough for old folks to disconnect their electronics and reflect. Mia's asleep in her bunny coat that Shana got her before she was even here. I take a deep breath and the first step. Each step gets easier as the wind picks up, spitting hard raindrops in my face. I make sure Mia's safe from the rain and march forward.

"We're almost there, y'all. A few more houses." Mia stirs underneath her blanket. Grabbing at her face, and then upward toward my boobs. It's been a minute since she last ate. Cyn jiggles her stuffed animal in her face. The greatest way to distract her, at least until we get to Trent's house.

Light crackles behind the tall oak trees that line Trent's yard. He's pulling into his driveway at the same time we are.

Cyn stops at the end of the driveway. "Whose house is this?"

"A friend," I say.

"A boyfriend?" For a nine-year-old she's so damn nosy.

I respond, "No, now come on before you catch a cold. I don't want to hear your mama's mouth."

Trent takes out brown bags from the trunk of his car. He

drops them at his feet when he recognizes our faces. "B'onca, you should have let me pick you all up." He takes off his jacket and wraps it around Cyn and then grabs Mia's stroller from my hands like it's the most natural thing in the world.

"You didn't need to be around my neighborhood." I rotate my arm, trying to navigate the feeling back into my hands. I was gripping the handle harder than I thought. "You know you have beef with everyone in the neighborhood."

"I'm not worried about that." He points toward the clear-glass front door. "If anyone wants smoke, they know where to find me."

Cyn leads the way to the house as if she lives here. Trent opens it up and she sprints inside.

"Don't track water everywhere, Cyn!" I yell.

"Don't worry. I'll get her some fresh clothes."

I pull off my soaked flip-flops at the door. "Are your folks still on vacation?"

"Yep, they won't be back until Thursday." He goes to the room closest to the front door and comes out with two oversized T-shirts. "They're my dad's, but he won't miss them."

After we get changed in the bathroom, he pulls out a long quilt.

"We only need to stay for a little while. Until the rain calms down." The hour hand on the clock above the mantel is perfectly placed on the six. Even though the cops are a new fixture on Franklin Avenue, they don't stay too late. They know they aren't welcome.

He makes a pallet of thick blankets on the floor for Mia and Cyn. Mia sprawls out around the pile of toys Ms. Dubois keeps for the kids. Cyn jumps in the middle, her shirt double-knotted to keep it from falling down.

"The toys are sterilized, don't worry."

"I'm not. This house is spotless—you can eat off the floor."

He walks toward the kitchen and comes back with a silver tray of hot drinks, then hands me a mug with dancing Santas on the side. He pauses, giving me a long stare upside my head. "You gone tell me what happened?"

I take a fast sip. The liquid burns the roof of my mouth. "Nothing happened. We said we were going to link up again and there's no time like the present."

Cyn gives me a look, like she knows it's bullshit.

"You been blowing me off all week."

"Like I said: life happens." I pick up the mug for another sip. He stops me before it reaches my lips.

"You call me out of the blue when it's damn near a tornado outside." He takes the mug from my hands and sets it down. "You are sure it's not about all those cops around the hood?"

I tilt my head. "How you know about that?"

Like I even have to ask. News spread like wildfire in the Crest. All that's needed is a person with a phone and a couple of Instagram followers.

He taps his phone. "I get citizen alerts in case something happens."

Or that.

"That doesn't have anything to do with me." Doodlebug gives me a reason to leave his glare. She reaches out to me and I touch her cheek.

"You sure?" He grabs my wrist and flips it over. My tatted wrist in between the both of us. "I'd been thinking where I saw that tattoo before. When it happened, that stuck in my mind. It wasn't on Instagram or anything. Then when I saw you at the rib spot, that's when I remembered . . . it was you."

"I don't know what you're talking about."

Keeping him close was a stupid idea. I was stupid for thinking he wasn't going to figure it out. Mia babbles and slobbers all over these folks' toys. All for her. No regrets. I won't regret taking care of my daughter.

"You brought this shit to my house." Trent drops my wrist. "You work for my mother. You don't think if you get caught, they'll start coming around here, asking questions?"

"You gone snitch on me like you did your boys?" I ask.

"If I hadn't, you know where I would have ended up. The same place you are going if you don't take a step back. You don't have to steal. There are so many other ways. This ain't even being judgmental. I've been where you are, and you know that."

Another lecture that I don't have time for.

"A thousand dollars a month," I say.

"What?"

"That's how much it costs to send her to a good day care. One that isn't off your mama's beauty shop. No offense." I fumble in Mia's baby bag and pull out different pharmacy receipts. "Two hundred for baby supplies weekly, and that's with cheap baby food. Sometimes I have to buy the cheap baby food just to have three dollars left for bus fare, and they never let me have a seat. No matter how pathetic I look."

"B'onca . . ."

Every price of everything I've bought over the past six months floats in my head. The medicine that meant no solid food for a week. The crib that meant my bed pushed against the wall of my room. The price of being a young mother is one that I didn't realize was so high.

"I did this for her. They raised the rent around my hood. People are moving in, and they aren't going to stay. They're going to take the culture, soak it up, and in a few years they're going to go back to where they came from."

"Mia needs a mother. She doesn't need organic food or expensive toys, but she needs *you*. You know what it's like to grow up without a mother. How can you do that to her?"

Trent won't use this against me. He doesn't know what a mother can do when her back is against the wall.

I place Mia on my hip. "You're going to snitch or what?"

Trent rests his head against the wall. "You know I'm not, but why my neighborhood? Why Scooter house?"

"It wasn't anything personal," I say. "I knew the layout, knew that no one would be there to stop me. That the people around here are in the house early. It was an easy lick."

"You act like you don't even care."

I shrug. "I'm not going to apologize for taking care of my family."

"I've known you my whole life. You are *not* that person."

"Maybe you don't know me as well as you thought you did."

I bundle Mia and Cyn up. The rain letting up a bit. This was a mistake. Another snipped thread in my web of crime. "I'll leave now. I don't want to upset you anymore."

"I'm not upset." Trent helps Cyn pack away the toys. "More so disappointed."

Those words gut me in the chest. I pause to catch my breath again before tying Cyn's shoes. "I'll let you know when we get home."

He stops the door from slamming. "B'onca. Be more careful. Mia doesn't need to see you behind bars."

Even if I do get caught, I won't ever let Shana bring Mia to see me behind bars. To her, I'll only be a smiling picture on a mantel. That's the greatest thing I can be to my daughter.

CHAPTER 29

"WHAT ARE THESE?" Shana holds up a pair of gray-and-white Jordans. The only luxury I allowed myself. There was a news clip going around of folks stampeding inside of the Wolf Mall to buy them. Wolf Mall is on the "good side" of town, and you already know what color folks they showed on the screen. Now, I don't think it takes all that for some shoes, but some folks that's all they got. The only luxury thing they might be able to pay for out of their own pockets. That don't make them animals. In fact, it makes them more human.

"Hold your head back." The client in the chair trying to get a look at what's caused Shana's voice to go from mousy to mad as hell. I already had to beg Shana in the first place to let me braid her hair in the house. Even Shana couldn't turn down the $350 that I'm charging.

"You like them? I just got them. I think they'll be cute with some biker shorts and a tank." I grip the front of my client's hairline a little too tight. She jerks, shooting me a look.

"I told you to hold your head back," I say. She wanna be nosy so bad. To go out and tell everyone that B'onca got chewed out for buying shoes. Then the rumors start. *Oh, B'onca can't afford this and that. Oh, B'onca really did steal from her dead baby daddy house, y'all.*

Shana comes closer, dangling the shoes by their strings. "I don't care nothing about what they gone look like and with what. How much did these shoes cost?"

"They like two hundred and fifty dollars since they just came out a few days ago," my client says for me. "If you would have waited a few more weeks, you could have gotten them for cheaper. I hope you didn't go to the mall for them either. You can order them online and they come right to your front door."

"Two hundred and fifty dollars! For shoes?" Shana drops them and I cringe. The only pair of sneakers I've bought myself in years and they may already be scuffed. I don't dare pick them up, though. I let them lie there in front of my client. I'm sure she already storing information to tell folks at the courts.

"How'd you get the money?"

"Ms. Dubois has been giving me more responsibility at the shop." Which isn't a whole lie. It's part of the truth. I've picked up more hours to explain away the paid utilities, and extra packs of meat and fruit snacks from the store. Two hundred and fifty for shoes may not be that easy of an explanation.

"Looks to me you been working the same hours."

"I don't tell you everything. I didn't want you on my ass about overworking and neglecting summer school." The lies keep coming up like vile-tasting vomit. One lie leads to the other, and before I know it, I'm swimming in it. I have an answer for every question, and there's no hesitation. Shana seems to be satisfied by them all.

"I'll take these back upstairs," she says. "Keep them out of the middle of the floor next time. I almost broke my ankle." She mumbles about cleaning, and the smell of burnt hair, before her voice fades upstairs.

"If you ever start boosting again, you have a clientele."

"That was a one-time thing," I say, more to myself than to Aniya, who's focused on the who's-the-father storyline on the television. "It was a way out of a no-way thing. Something for now. Until I do something better for myself."

She nods as much as she can. "I feel you, girl. I don't know what I'd do if I had a baby who needed things all the time. One day you're going to be a real adult, and that shit doesn't fly when you're twenty-five, so you might as well do it now. When people still think you're just a dumb kid."

For a moment I allow myself to see the future. To picture Mia hugged on my side with myself dressed in a cap and gown. To a FOR SALE sign on an actual salon and not this cramped kitchen. A degree that hangs right as you walk in to remind people that I'm legit. Dreams that one day the girl from the past will no longer exist.

"You looking at college applications again?" Deja taps my left shoulder before sliding into the booth across from me. She's munching on cheese fries. A cafeteria specialty, since it's only two cheap ingredients and the kids love it.

"The cosmetology school is having an open house tonight and I'm going." Every time I go to the website there's something new to ooh and aah at. A portal of testimonials about life after graduation, how easy it is to apply, and the level of education you can receive. All the victories of people who look like me, with their smiles painted on. They make it seem attainable. They must be actors.

"I got a better backup plan." Deja leans toward me; the sounds of rowdy teens and metal trays drown her out. "One more hit."

"You're tripping." I don't look up from the faces on the screen. "You couldn't have spent all that money already. It's impossible." We each took home a good amount at that party. More than enough for Deja and then some. Some folks don't see that kind of money until a relative dies or they hit it big at the casino.

"You'd be surprised. After paying my mama's medical bills I had to treat myself." She lays her ring-decorated finger in front of me. That's when I look up. Her ears are adorned in white gold, with a mouth to match.

"You spent your money on a grill and now you want us to go back out less than two weeks later. Especially after folks still looking for who hit Scooter house." Deja tripping and hard. If she wants money, then *she* has to be the one to make things shake.

"I spent a good portion on my car, too. You should hear the new sound system; it's booming." Deja imitates an explosion.

"I have most of my money left. Going back out is stupid and greedy. You don't think the cops aren't already on the lookout for us? Plus, I can't be doing this no more. I'm the only parent Mia has."

Each morning I watch the news, holding my breath. Waiting for my face to pop across the screen with a wanted sign underneath. So far that day hasn't come, but I still haven't exhaled.

"You right." Deja pulls her hand back into her lap. "I'm sorry. You about to have a future. Can't be partaking in hood-rat activities anymore."

"Deja, you are *not* a hood rat. You have dreams and goals too. Sometimes they just hard to see in the beginning."

"Mrs. Crenshaw did tell me about a community college and how it's free when you're below a certain income level. I'll see what they talking about."

"I'll come with you. I know it's hard to turn your life around, but we can do it. We *have* to do it."

CHAPTER 30

"I DON'T KNOW what my essay should be about." Mrs. Crenshaw looks up from her stack of papers. She's grading our last test of summer school, and based on her groans we didn't do too well. I studied between feedings and colicky cries. If I got a C, I'd take it. You only need a high school diploma to get into beauty school anyway.

"You can talk about anything. This assignment is to show me you can write cohesively. That's a big chunk of your final grade. Maybe it can be about Mia and how you overcame those obstacles."

I don't know if *overcame* is the right word.

"I love the baby, but I'm tired of talking about her." To anyone else, that may sound harsh, but Mrs. Crenshaw gets it; she was a teen mom herself. She knows what it takes to break loose of those stereotypes. Eventually you aren't only a teen mother, but it seems the stigma always follows her, no matter how many accomplishments cover her home walls.

Shaking off my past is going to be like cutting iron chains with safety scissors.

"You can talk about your advocacy work." She hands me my test personally. A 76—two points away from being a D.

I raise an eyebrow, making a mental note to study over every missed question. "Advocacy?"

"You're always telling me about the meeting you and Shana ran for the neighborhood. That's being an advocate."

"I guess I never saw it that way."

The bell rings, marking the end of the first lunch and the beginning of the second.

"If you need help, you know where to find me." Mrs. Crenshaw waves me away as her third class of the day starts to make their way in.

I follow the other kids into the cafeteria. Today's Taco Tuesday, but not authentic tacos. Hard shells with greasy old burger meat. The smell makes my stomach do turns. I find a booth, pop in my earbuds, and pull out the school-issued laptop.

The school counselor sent me an email about due dates for scholarship applications.

The list long. There seems to be free money for everything. Singing, dancing, band, and academics. Each criteria lists talents I never seemed to master. I sound like a wounded cat, have two left feet, and C's may get degrees, but they don't get scholarships. My grades fell way off after I got pregnant with Mia. I went from making straight A's to barely bringing home a 2.3 GPA. The only scholarship that I have a shot at getting is the need-based one. A five-hundred-word essay about why I believe I deserve the ten thousand dollars they give out. I have to explain why my hunger pains are sharper than others'. Why my life is more horrible than my neighbors'. When in reality, it's all the same. Who's to decide whose pain is worth more? Why is there a price on it in the first place?

I save that one for later and start on my final paper.

Mrs. Crenshaw walks up to me; I take one earbud out and almost smile. Until I see the men behind her. Two cops, whose faces tell me they are not here for career day.

"B'onca, they just want to talk." She frowns, apologizing with her eyes. I'm not mad at her. I know she didn't have a choice. I knew this moment would eventually come. Chickens always come home to roost, as Grandma used to say.

"What do you want to talk about?" I ask, noticing the crowd of students. Teachers try to direct traffic out of the cafeteria, but the drifters take extra steps to clear their trays. Trying to hear what B'onca Johnson has gotten herself into this time.

"Come with us, please." They come closer, keeping their hands near their belts, which contain the one thing I'm afraid of.

Mrs. Crenshaw nods and I pack up my things. Officer number 2565 pulls out the metal cuffs from the holster. "You have the right to remain silent. Anything you say . . ."

The room begins to spin. *Mia. Shana. Cyn.* Mrs. Crenshaw follows along next to me. She says she already called Shana and she'll be waiting for me at the station. Mia staying with Savannah and her family until Shana gets back. Mrs. Crenshaw rubs my shoulder, assuring me everything will be all right. It must be a misunderstanding. I don't have the spirit to tell her that it isn't. This is my karma. Own up to the consequences of your actions.

Police officer number two bends my head and secures me into the police car. Faces are in every window. Watching the scene that takes place. A few students disobey school orders and come outside. They whisper behind their hands to their friends, shaking their heads at me. Whitney's eyes find mine from the second-floor window. She waves a small goodbye as the police car flashes the lights once and drives away.

The guards check for weapons, take my mugshot, fingerprint me, and then I get my one phone call. Since Shana is already on her way, I don't waste my call on her. I dial the only other number I knew by heart.

"Hello," Savannah says on the other end.

"Savannah. It's me." She doesn't respond. I can feel the eyes of the guard on my back. "I know you're disappointed in me. Talk to me, please."

"I ain't got nothing to say to you. You just couldn't do right," she says. "You know where I am right now? I'm taking care of your daughter because her mother couldn't be bothered to think about her."

I place my mouth as close as possible to the unsanitized wall phone. "All I do is think about Mia. She's been my entire life from the day I found out she was growing inside of me."

Savannah scoffs. "If that was true, you'd be here right now.

She wouldn't have to go to bed tonight not knowing the next time she'll see her mama."

"Tell her that I'll be home," I say. "Tell her it's only for the night."

False promises. Just like my mama used to make me. She'd be here for this, that, and the third. Never showing up for either until it was too late for me to be sad about it anymore.

"Unlike you, I don't lie." Before I can respond to Savannah, the dial tone comes. I slam the phone down, notifying the guard I'm ready to be taken back.

"Your lawyer is here," the guard says between the metal bars. He guides me into a small gray room. There's one barred window that gives us a hint of light. It's only been a few hours, but I already miss the warmth of sunlight.

"B'onca Johnson," he says matter-of-factly, flipping through the folder in front of him. He isn't a public defender, I can tell by his suit and cuff links. You don't think about cuff links when you're underpaid.

I don't respond. I let him judge me from the papers that are in front of him. It's a step up from people who don't even have a screenshot of my life.

"Shoplifting. They have some solid evidence on you. Shoddy camera shots from a store surveillance camera." He closes the folder and moves it to the side. Finally seeing the true B'onca and not the one that lives in files and pictures.

"What happens next?"

"Sit tight, and hopefully we will have you out of here by tomorrow morning at the latest. I'm sure you know how this all works."

CHAPTER 31

I'M GIVEN A thin white sheet and a deflated pillow. I spend the entire night jumping in and out of sleep. It's either too cold or too hot, like the guards are playing with the thermostat. I sit up and stare at nothing.

The girl across from me flicks her nose ring and sighs. "You got a man?" She shifts, crosses her legs, and looks toward me.

I ignore her. Ain't nobody in here to make friends.

She stares at me hard as hell like she is taking apart the dip of my nose, the curve of my lips, and the darkness of my eyes and then putting them back together again. "I know you."

She doesn't know a thing about me.

"You Scooter baby mama." Hate that title. It's either Scooter baby mama or Mia mama. I was a whole person before them, and had a whole personality. Dreams and aspirations. All that flew out the window when I became those titles. All of them titles, none of them my name.

"How you get into here?" She looks around the room in disgust.

"Same reason you are here." I try my best to end this conversation. It's almost morning. I can tell by the birds that chirp outside the small, barred window.

"Damn, you ain't gotta have an attitude. I'm just trying to make the time go by." She turns straight on her cot. "If you ain't notice, we the only ones in here."

This time I turn to her and take apart her face. "Cassie? From up the street?"

She turns her legs toward me again, shaking her head. "Yeah, girl, that's me. We ain't seen each other in forever."

Cassie that girl, at least she used to be. Always had the flyest fits, hair stayed done each week, she never had her hand out. She's what I used to aspire to be.

"Scooter always bragged about you. I'm sorry for your loss, by the way. How are you holding up?"

"I barely am," I say quietly.

"Damn, I'm sorry to hear that." She leans in closer. "How you end up in here?"

"Stealing, but after this time I'm done. My baby needs me."

"I tell myself that same thing. My baby boy is almost three now. I've tried to go straight so many times, but it never sticks. I got busted for lifting down at that little boutique on Third, but it was a bogus charge. They don't even have six hundred dollars' worth of stuff in there. They trying to get me sent to juvie. This time, I might not have any more chances."

"I wouldn't wish juvie on anyone." Everyone in there got a point to prove. Being the toughest in a place that's just gone beat it out of you.

She shrugs. "It'll only be for six months. My man, he's a freshman at Hilbert. He says he gone hook me up at all the college parties when this shit over with. College kids pay *soooo* much for the stuff we boost. If that was me, I'd be stashing my refund check instead of spending it up in a week."

"Oh," I reply dryly. "How long you been together?"

"Almost six months. He is supposed to be here too, but he's hiding. Can't come if you can't find him."

I want to put her on game. How that dude is going to find another one of her in those six months. How when she comes home, everything is going to be different. But ain't no point in that. Cassie got to fall out of love on her own.

I scratch at my sleeve. "After this, I'm done. For real."

"Mm-hmm," she says like she knows I'm lying. "That ain't a choice for people like us. Can't go from making licks to working a real job."

"You don't want better for your son?"

"I want my son to have shoes and food."

"I want my daughter to have a mama," I say.

"I mean, me too, but what I'm supposed to do? What I'm supposed to say when they ask have I ever been arrested? All the jobs that pay more than minimum wage ask."

"You tell them the truth," I say. "You're young. Nobody expects you to be perfect."

"They expect things, though. Things I can't give 'cause I have a baby. Then I expect things they can't give, and I need them 'cause I got a baby."

"He has *you*," I say. "A six-month stint in juvie can instantly change everything."

"I can't take advice from someone who is in the same cage as I am."

And although it hurts, she's right. I lean back against the cold brick wall and fall into some sleep until my name is called with a force that makes me jump up.

"B'onca Johnson. You've made bail."

Cassie eyes me as I damn near run to the opening of the cell.

"Wait," she hollers. "Take my number. Guard, can you write it down for her?"

Surprisingly, he does, and Cassie gestures for me to come over.

Cassie whispers in my ear. "If you ever need a job, hit me up."

My eyes roll over the number before I crumple the paper in my hand.

CHAPTER 32

WITHIN A BLINK of an eye, I'm in Shana's old Buick, breathing in fresh air. The colors of my future are murky, and all hopes of college are left behind in that five-foot-five holding cell.

The ride home is silent for the most part. Shana playing her oldies, the ones that make you want to dance, but this ain't a happy occasion. Sometimes she starts to snap her fingers, then stops. Sometimes she looks over to me, and I see her out of the corner of my eye. She opens her mouth to speak, but only a sigh escapes. Shana moved heaven and earth to pay for a real attorney. I want to ask her where she got the money, but I'm not bold enough for the words to leave my lips. It isn't the money I took. That money is tucked away. Somewhere no one can find it until it's time. If there will ever be the right time.

"What did the Canes say?" I ask.

"That they'll see us in court."

I prayed the whole night that they hadn't come for Mia. That they'd at least have the decency to let me say goodbye to her. If

she leaves, I have to tell her sorry. That sometimes even mamas make mistakes.

"Shana." I hold my breath for a response that never comes. "Can I make a stop?"

She lets out a small snort and then a louder one. Until she's having a fit of laughter. "The nerve of you to be asking me for favors. After all this hell you done put me through."

"I just need to see a friend," I say. "He only lives ten minutes away from us. It's important."

I haven't heard from Trent since going to his house, but I'm sure he's already heard about what happened. The whole neighborhood must know by now. *B'onca in trouble again. That girl always keeping up mess.* Everything I'm used to hearing. Usually as a whisper behind my back, smirks as I pass, but this time they are probably screaming it in Shana's ear. The problem child, like her mama. Not one sweet bone in her body, like her grandma.

"If it's Trent you want to see, he's at the house already." She makes a sharp left.

"He's at the house?" I ask. "What's going on there?"

"It was going to be a surprise, planned way before you tried to be Robin Hood. Ms. Dubois throwing a fundraising party. We had to move it up but everyone still came. Got food, music, and games for the babies. She even knows this program where folks help low-income people pay back rent. We are next in line. You'd know that if you *just* asked me."

Shana pulls up along the graffitied wall. Little kids play hopscotch and jump in the bouncy house that's inflated in front of the yard. The big kids throw paint at the concrete wall, adding life to the dead-end street. There's a sign in front of our house made of an old T-Mobile sign: FISH FRY AROUND BACK $15. The Blackest of traditions. Nothing couldn't be solved with a fish fry. Not even a delinquent like me.

"Fifteen dollars for a fish plate?" I ask.

"The girls are asking for extra." Shana turns off the engine and finally looks at me. Her eyes are barely open. Lack of sleep because of me. "To get you a good lawyer. For your mess and for Mia."

"You don't have to do that, Shana." She probably couldn't even come up with the words to ask for help. *Help my jailbird sister* met with tons of *God bless her heart,* which is Southern for "that's a damn shame."

"They want to help us." She points at the three women who sit in white lawn chairs. One flours fish, and another takes a bucketful around back. "No matter how much this neighbor-hood changes, we got to carve out our sense of normalcy."

"Do they know what I did? Or did you tell them something different?" I dodge Shana's eyes and look at the sign. "I know you're ashamed of me."

"If I was ashamed of you, I wouldn't have brought you into my house, around my daughter, loved you, and loved your child like my own child. Now, that doesn't sound like shame to me."

"Guilt, then."

"Because you're my sister." She nods to the door. "And those people in there love you like you're their own. Everybody in there has made mistakes. I've made more than I care to count. I never wanted you to be grown-up at your age. I wanted you to be a child, to live your life. That's why I never told you about the money problems. You'd just worry yourself. Mama never gave me a choice. I wanted better for you."

"I'm sorry. That I fucked up again," I say.

"You had the right idea, just the wrong execution. We going to be all right." She pats the top of my hand. "We got family."

Aunt Nora taps the passenger-side window. I roll it down and she sticks her head in. "Y'all come on in here. Everyone's waiting to present you with the money."

Shana lets my hand go. "We're coming, TeTe. Can you get the pies out the trunk?"

"You're looking well, B'onca, considering." Aunt Nora smiles just enough to barely form one smile line. She pats the trunk of the car and Shana pops it open.

"Don't mind her. She a little butt-hurt because she had to chip in for your lawyer."

"Shana," I groan. The last thing I need is to be on a repayment plan with Aunt Nora. She's worse than a loan shark.

"Don't worry about it." She reaches over to open my door. "Go inside and find your friend. I'll be right in."

Ms. Dubois opens the screen door for me. The frown on her face says everything she doesn't, but she pulls me into a hug anyway. She squeezes me tight. A sob catches in my throat. I wipe my eyes before she pulls away.

"I fucked up, Ms. Dubois. The Canes are going to take my baby from me. I did all this for her and I'm going to end up losing her."

"You are seventeen. If you didn't fuck up from time to time,

I'd look at you funny," she says. "If you needed a higher wage, you should have just asked me, honey."

"You'd already given me so much. Asking for more seemed greedy."

She squeezes my hand. "Come to the shop on Monday. Twenty-five an hour and I'm going to enroll you into somebody's school. The streets aren't going to eat you up."

"You for real? I still got my job after all this?"

"Yes, I am. Ain't nobody in that shop that ain't made a mistake, including me. The thing about mistakes is that you recognize them and try to do better the next day. I'll see you on Monday, okay?"

"Yes, ma'am." She gives me one more comforting auntie hug before going outside.

"Look who it is, Doodlebug," Deja says.

Mia sleeps inside of Deja's arms. Savannah stands beside her.

"She's been asking for you all day." Deja walks a pace behind Savannah. "Well, I think that's what she's been saying. You might have a baby genius on your hands either way."

She's gotten bigger even though it's only been a day.

"I've missed you, li'l mama." I nuzzle my nose into her neck. Taking in the baby smell.

I look up to Dej. She's in her barbecue attire, complete with cutoffs and brown sandals. She's second-in-command on the grill if my drunk uncle has one too many beers. "Thank y'all for taking care of Mia."

"We take our godmama title seriously, you know." Savannah bounces on her heels impatiently. "Where's my hug?"

We hug long and hard. "I'm not going to give you a lecture. Just know I'm here for you." She pulls us apart, stares over my face, and brings us together again.

"Savannah," I say softly into her shoulder.

"No matter what happens, I got Mia," she says, and I nod.

"Let me get back to this grill," Deja says. "Come out back when you say hey to everyone."

I put Mia in her crib and give hugs and daps to the neighbors who sit around with plates of fried fish and spaghetti on whatever surface they can find. I scan the room. Smiling and waving until I catch the eye that I want.

Outside, I mouth, and point toward the door blocked by nameless play cousins. We take the back door to the hangout spot.

"It's good to see you, B'onca," Trent says, rubbing his hand across the back of his neck. "I'm glad you're okay. Everyone's been working to come up with the money for your lawyer. He's my cousin, by the way. He says he's going to do everything he can to get you off. It's your first offense, so it shouldn't be too hard."

"I'm not feeling too good about it." I knew what it was when I did it. That it was a possibility I wouldn't see my baby for a while. That I'd be facing real time. A choice that I have to live with even if it breaks me to my core.

He places one hand on my shoulder. "Trust me, you're going to be fine."

I give a small smile even though I don't believe him. "I need a favor."

He doesn't hesitate. "Anything. Is it for Mia?"

"Kinda." I lean on the fence that faces the streets. "I want you to hide the money for me. Put it away until Shana needs it. She won't take it from me. She knows that Deja has dirty money and Savannah has no money."

His face goes blank.

"You're the only one she'll believe it came from. I don't want all of this to go to waste. I know it wasn't right doing what I did, but it's done now. Mia needs that money."

He steps closer, straightening his back. "I'll do it."

I suck in the thick humid air and let it out with one breath. "I'll never be able to repay you."

"Make sure Mia grows up well. Don't do no stupid shit anymore. Give her a good life with a mother who will be there for her. Even if it doesn't make sense to others, be there."

"You're a good guy, Trent," I say.

He smiles as we watch the children who do TikTok dances with extra flair. They drop the *ing*s and prolong their *man*s. Creating words and languages that only they can understand. Mia already has a piece of the Crest inside of her.

No matter what happens, she'll carry it in the way she walks and talks. That's what this neighborhood is. A family, even with outsiders moving in who want to tear us apart. Even if we go in different directions, we know who we are. The Ridgecrest family. Davant Avenue. Homes built by hand and trees planted by ancestors gone by. That carries with us.

And I'm going to fight to be here to see it.

ACKNOWLEDGMENTS

Like before, I may leave a few people out, but just know that if you have supported *Sun Keep Rising* in any way over the last three years, I appreciate you.

Phoebe—I'm forever grateful that you've given me the opportunity to share my voice with the world. Thank you, Molly, for holding my hand as I walked through the dreaded first draft stage and for our multiple brainstorming sessions.

Mercedes—thank you for helping me form this story and for giving me the courage to tell it.

Most of all, I want to thank every person who will relate to this story in some way, shape, or form.

Your stories will forever be valid.

MATTERIO HAWKINS

KRISTEN R. LEE is a native of Memphis, Tennessee, and the celebrated author of *Required Reading for the Disenfranchised Freshman,* which *Publishers Weekly* called "a timely, quickly paced look at the trauma Black students often face in white institutions" and *Kirkus Reviews* lauded as "moving and authentic." Kristen wrote *Sun Keep Rising* for teenage mothers—including those in her own family—because she knows their stories are more than cold statistics and filled with a beauty that deserves to be seen.

Kristen has worked as a mentor for foster youth and interned in a school setting, where she counseled middle-school-aged children. Writing stories that reflect often-unheard voices is what she strives to do.

KRISTENLEEBOOKS.COM

The Garden Is Doing Fine

The Garden Is Doing Fine

CAROL FARLEY

Illustrated by Lynn Sweat

Atheneum   1975   New York

Library of Congress
Cataloging in Publication Data

Farley, Carol J   The garden is doing fine.
SUMMARY: Corrie refuses to believe that her father
is dying until she realizes that no matter what happens,
a part of him will always live in her.
[1. Death—Fiction] I. Sweat, Lynn. II. Title.
PZ7.F233Ga   [Fic]   75-9516
ISBN 0-689-30475-7

To my sisters,
Eva Hartung and Sally Thompson,
because the three of us shared
the love of a father who was
much like Joseph Sheldon

The Garden Is
Doing Fine

Corrie Sheldon hurried along beside her mother on the way to the hospital in the early evening darkness of a Michigan November. The tiredness she felt seemed to radiate from her in all directions, and she imagined that her fatigue was like a huge antenna that surrounded her and made her keenly aware of everything that was happening.

There were the sounds of the waves of Lake Michigan, for instance, as they beat against the nearby shore. Corrie felt she could hear each single wave, and although she knew that the force that churned the lake was simply wind, she visualized a huge hand hovering over the waters, stirring and swirling the waves with its fingers. She felt the sharp wind whip against her thin body, too, and the skin on her hands and face grew tight, like the taut coverings of thickening ice spreading over the occasional puddles they were passing. From the distance came the drone of the foghorn.

"It's below freezing," her mother said, bending further into the wind. "I'm glad you got that coat today, Corrie."

Corrie hunched her shoulders inside her billowing garment. It was an ugly coat, she thought, a drab, dull, old-woman coat that nearly flapped against the top of her bobbysocks in the sudden gusts of cold air. It had been given to her by a neighbor who no longer needed it. Even though lots of people had been giving clothing to the Sheldons lately, Corrie still couldn't get used to the idea. She wished she could be like her two brothers—they thought all the shabby outfits were just like new.

"I guess it'll be warm enough, Momma," she said. "But it's too big."

"That makes it all the better, then. It'll last that much longer now."

Corrie frowned in the darkness. Angrily she reached up and yanked the ends of her scarf tighter. Of course her mother would say that—she always thought that clothing that was too large would somehow last that much longer. It was one of her crazy ideas about economy. She liked dark colors, too, because they didn't show the dirt so fast. Corrie wondered whether her mother had ever wanted to buy pretty things, bright things, good things that really fit. Now, in the reflection of a passing car, she saw that the only bright color her mother wore was the yellow neck scarf she had thrown around her head. It was her father's scarf, Corrie realized. Her father always wore colors like that. But he had worn only hospital things for a long time now, it seemed. A long, long time.

They turned onto Lincoln Avenue, and the wind whipped Corrie's coat tight against her body. It must look like a blanket hanging on a clothespole, she thought. And why does it have to be brown? It must make me look even more mousy than I already look. Why can't my hair be blond or red or black instead of this plain old brown? Why can't I— She stopped her thought before she finished it. She didn't dare think about herself anymore. It was selfish to do that, she had decided—selfish and immature. After all, she wasn't a little girl anymore. Life wasn't as easy as once she had thought.

She remembered with a twinge of envy the way her thoughts once had been. Once she had thought that life was like the sky, unending and everlasting, there for everyone, free for anyone who wanted it, waiting there for you and everyone you loved. You never had to worry about anything as simple as life itself. But now she knew that she had been mistaken. Life was really a fragile thing, a special thing, a gift that could easily be snatched away, and it wasn't free at all. You had to pay for it, keep paying for it, and everyone who loved you had to pay for it, too. First you paid with money, and then you paid with worry, and then there was fear, fear and fatigue.

One . . . two . . . three . . . four . . . five . . . scuff.
One . . . two . . . three . . . four . . . five . . . scuff.

Corrie heard her mother's footsteps, and she looked over at the worn, familiar face. All those things she had been thinking about were mirrored there for all the world to see. There was worry, fear, fatigue. They had been etched there after the third operation, and daily they seemed to grow worse.

5

How could she ever have taken time to think about a dumb thing like a coat? Corrie moved slower, matching her long strides to her mother's short, hurried steps. Her mother was short and stout, and now she was nearly out of breath.

"This hill!" she said. "Sometimes, you know, I think this hill grows higher every night."

"It's the wind," Corrie told her. "It's just the wind making it harder to walk, Momma."

"That's it. That's it, all right."

Corrie turned back to her thoughts. What had she been when she first left the house? A sponge? An antenna? It didn't matter. She had been playing the game suggested by her drama teacher. "Sharpen your senses," Miss Doner had told her. "Feel everything around yourself, notice everything there is." Corrie had decided that she would play the game often. It might keep her from thinking about her father's terrible illness.

She sniffed the wind. There was the fragrance of baked goods. Soon they would pass by Jorgy's Bake Shop. Corrie closed her eyes, and she could see the window there in her mind. It was full of cardboard cookies frosted with pink icing, and artificial cakes with tiny brides and grooms. There was a sign in the window too: BUY WAR BONDS. The Jorgys didn't talk about the war anymore, though. Their only son had been killed in France. Mentally Corrie went inside the store. In her mind she saw the gum ball machine. It was usually broken. Alan and Arthur were always putting pennies in it, and then Mrs. Jorgy would have to come from the back of the store and get their money back for them. She sat in the kitchen and read movie magazines all day long.

She needed to read about movie stars, Corrie guessed, because she was so homely herself. Her eyes were crossed, and she had three chins. But she had a funny laugh, and she was kind. She gave away almost as much as she sold. She had just brought some doughnuts to the Sheldons the day before, in fact. Corrie had found the bag on the porch.

Lots of people were bringing food lately, Corrie realized. Almost every day she would find a strange casserole sitting on the table in the screened-in porch. Neighbors would write their names on tapes and stick them on the bottoms of their bowls, and then they would come and get their dishes later. Corrie was always careful of those bowls. Their own cookware wasn't nearly so nice.

It was queer how so many people were doings things for them lately. How long had they been doing that? Corrie counted the weeks on her fingers. Her hands were stuffed into fists inside her coat pockets, and now she moved her fingers as she thought about the weeks.

. . . the war ended in August . . . in September Daddy got worse . . . he went to the hospital the day after my birthday in October . . . and now it's—

"It's not even seven o'clock and the sky's been pitch black for hours," Mrs. Sheldon said. She shook her head. Her dark hair was wound in a bun on the back of her neck.

"Nineteen forty-five is nearly over," Corrie said. The wind tossed her words away. She bent her head and tried to remember what her thoughts had been before her mother had just spoken.

She realized that she had been thinking about her father's illness again. Even though she played games with herself, she still always seemed to end up thinking about his illness. Did her mother do that, too? Did the nurses and the doctors?

One . . . two . . . three . . . four . . . five . . . scuff.
One . . . two . . . three . . . four . . . five . . . scuff.

Corrie listened to the familiar clicking of her mother's shoes, and she seized on the sound. It was good to find something so unchanging, so predictable, in a world that changed every day. Mrs. Sheldon had always walked that way, making that peculiar scuffing noise after five normal steps. When she was smaller, Corrie had marveled at it. "How come you make that funny noise after you take five plain steps, Momma?" she remembered asking.

"Why, I don't do no such thing, child," her mother had told her. "No such thing." And then her steps had been measured and precise, embarrassed and careful, and there was only the sound of sensible, solid clicking. But soon the two had begun to talk of other things, and the woman had forgotten the question, and then Corrie had heard the secret life of the shoes reveal itself again: *One . . . two . . .*

8

three . . . four . . . five . . . scuff. The sturdy shoes
with the run-down heels had an existence all their
own, a life that was unknown even to their owner.
Only Corrie knew about it, and she kept the secret
quiet in her mind.

One . . . two . . . three . . . four . . . five . . . scuff.
One . . . two . . . three . . . four . . . five . . . scuff.

"You look tired, Corrie," Mrs. Sheldon said.

They were passing under a streetlight now, and
Corrie turned to look at her mother again. "I'm all
right," she said. "But you look tired yourself,
Momma. You look all worn out."

Mrs. Sheldon's small shoes clicked against the sidewalk. They were passing over Lincoln Bridge now,
and the sound was different, almost hollow. "We had
a busy day today at the shop."

"And then all this walking back and forth you do
every night," Corrie said. "You—"

"Oh, fiddle, it's good for me. I need to lose a little
weight." Mrs. Sheldon laughed, and Corrie realized
that her mother always gave that strange laugh when
she talked about her weight. "But you! You're like
a stringbean, Corrie. You should have stayed home
tonight with Alan and Arthur."

"No," Corrie said quickly. "I wanted to come."

"But your homework! Don't—"

"I did it. I did it all after school today."

"But didn't you have play practice after school
today, Corrie?"

Corrie blinked and willed her voice to be even.

9

"Oh, I gave that up, Momma. I guess I didn't want to be in that play after all."

Mrs. Sheldon slowed her steps. "But you did! You did want to be in that play, Corrie! This is your first chance at a high-school play—you've wanted to do this even since kindergarten. I know you have!"

"It's all right," Corrie said. Her throat ached as she said the words because the play had meant so much to her. And she would have been the star! She, just a lowly freshman, had won the part over three active seniors! But today she had told Miss Doner that she couldn't do the role. How could she practice for a school play when her father was so ill?

"You've missed so much this fall," Mrs. Sheldon said. "It's a shame."

Corrie's heart-shaped face tightened, but she said nothing. Suddenly she became conscious of the moaning of the foghorn again. The sound of it was like the remembrance of her father's illness blaring out in her mind all the time. The thoughts about the school play, the secondhand coat, the sharpened senses, the shoes—they were like a fog swirling through her brain, a mist that came and went; but the fact of her father's illness was there all the time, droning out its mournful message in the middle of her brain.

She shrugged her shoulders and tried to peer ahead. No lights from the hospital were yet visible in the darkness. She used to look forward to that first sight of the huge building. There would always be shadows at the windows, shadows of eager patients staring out the windows, looking to see the visitors climbing up the hill. Corrie remembered how her father had stood at those windows the first weeks too, and he would wave and make signs with his hands. But he wouldn't be there tonight. Of course he couldn't be there tonight.

"Maybe he'll know us this evening," Mrs. Sheldon said.

Corrie tightened her fists. "Maybe he will." She was conscious even as she spoke that the two of them were repeating their lines like two actresses in a play. They had spoken the same words to each other for nearly three weeks now, as they walked the twelve blocks to Pointer Hospital. And as though it were a drama with action, too, Corrie knew all the movements. She saw her mother shift her worn purse to her other arm, and then she began to speak her lines again.

"He's bound to be getting better, Corrie. All that medicine! Why, it's bound to do the trick sooner or later. I think this last operation was all he needed." Her steps quickened, and she spoke faster. "He's just weak, that's all. That's why he's the way he is lately. It's just that he's weak. He's bound to be. Why, anybody would be weak after three operations in less than two years. Anybody would be."

"Yes," Corrie said. "That's right, Momma." In the distance the foghorn droned. The wind was stronger, and Corrie shivered inside her ugly coat.

She knew that her mother must be shivering, too. The sensible black coat that Mrs. Sheldon wore was over eight years old. If only they had the money to— Corrie stopped the thought. It was selfish to think such things. They didn't have the money and that was the end of it.

Mrs. Sheldon clicked her heel and took a deep breath. "Now about the garden, Corrie—"

"No," Corrie said. "No." She bit her lip and made a jerking motion with her shoulders. They moved heavily under the padded coat. She clenched her fists and suddenly added new words to their play. "I can't lie about the garden, Momma. It's dead."

"Don't tell Daddy that!" Mrs. Sheldon seized Corrie's arm. Corrie felt sudden pain wrench to her elbow. It was strange to be held like that—she hadn't known that her mother had that much strength in her fingers.

"Momma!" Corrie jerked her arm away. "Of course I'd never say that to Daddy! Of course I wouldn't! I wouldn't hurt Daddy for the world, Momma, you ought to know that. You ought to know that."

Mrs. Sheldon dropped her arm. She shook her head and took the handle of her purse into both hands and twisted it as she spoke. "I'm sorry, Corrie. I don't know what got into me. I'm as jumpy as a cat. Don't pay any attention to me, child. I know you wouldn't hurt Daddy. I know that, Corrie. Of course I do."

One . . . two . . . three . . . four . . . five . . . scuff.
One . . . two . . . three . . . four . . . five . . . scuff.

In silence they walked faster. Tree branches over their heads moaned. A newspaper came flying by, tossed and torn by the gusty wind. The lights strung across Lincoln Avenue were waving back and forth, as though they were dancing to silent music. Corrie looked at them, and she thought about her father's garden. She had always heard invisible, nearly silent music in the garden, too. The tomato plants had danced to its rhythm. It happened every year.

For her father planted a garden every spring, and he tended it every summer. He never missed a year, Corrie remembered, not even, not even this last one, when he had been so weak from his terrible illness. Of course everybody had helped; she had, and her brothers, Alan and Arthur, and her mother, when she wasn't working at the tent shop. Sandra, her best friend, had come over and helped lots of times. And then there had been old Lewie, their funny next-door neighbor. They had all worked during the hot days this summer, helping her father in the garden. He hadn't felt well—he had been thin and pale and his body had hung on his bones like a loose, rumpled suit—but he had planted his garden all right, and his laughter had echoed over the tomato plants. The summer had passed and he had thrived and grown strong and no one had guessed what the autumn would bring.

One . . . two . . . three . . . four . . . five . . . scuff.

13

One . . . two . . . three . . . four . . . five . . . scuff.

Corrie heard her mother take a deep breath. Then Mrs. Sheldon spoke. "But you know, Corrie, it would be awfully easy for you to say it. All you'd have to say is that the garden is doing fine."

"*You* can say it, Momma. You always say it anyway."

"But he wants you to say it."

"He doesn't even know me," Corrie said. Then she swallowed loudly. This was the first time she had spoken the words flat out like that, and now she cringed as she realized what she had done. Would saying the words make them all the more true? Quickly she raised her voice. "What I mean is, he hasn't known me lately, Momma. But maybe he'll know me tonight."

"Yes, maybe he will." Mrs. Sheldon's voice grew quieter. "And if he should ask about the garden, why, why, couldn't you—"

"No." Corrie shook her head and looked down at her moving feet. "I couldn't do it, Momma. I just couldn't. It would be lying, Momma." She clenched her fists inside her pockets, and she felt her nails dig into her skin. The pain gladdened her. It was good to express on the outside exactly what she felt on the inside, and so she dug her nails in deeper.

This small agony called forth a larger one. She felt the pain of memory slice through her. It was a saber, a sword like the ones she had seen on posters all during the war. It started in the pit of her stomach and pierced upward, jabbing at her throat. She swallowed frantically, trying to blot out the words, the pictures, the thoughts that her brain hurled in front of her.

They were on the playground at recess, more than a year ago, she and Sandra, and three other eighth-grade girls. They didn't play anymore, of course, but they were standing there talking and giggling and glancing from the corners of their eyes at the boys. It was October, just a week before Corrie's birthday.

There had been a moment when no one was speaking. Then Elaine Moore had reached up, pushed her stringy hair from her face, snapped her gum, and spoken. "I hear your dad has cancer," she said to Corrie.

Someone gasped. Corrie felt the playground sway. "He had an operation," she said, looking down. "Just an operation." The playground had been covered with gravel, she noticed. Each little stone seemed perfectly round, and someone had lost the stub of a pencil. "He had a tumor," she said. "It was like that other tumor he had."

"He's going to be just fine," Sandra said loudly. She tossed her head and her red hair flashed in the sunlight. "I don't know where you get your stupid ideas, Elaine. Of all the stupid ideas! Mr. Sheldon just had a tumor. He's going to be fine, just fine."

"But my mother said that—"

"Oh, your mother's moustache!" Sandra grabbed Corrie's arm. "Come on, Corrie, let's get out of here. Who wants to talk to dumb old Elaine?"

Stunned, Corrie had stumbled after her best

friend. Cancer—the very word had a ring of horror about it. Of course Elaine was wrong. She never knew what she was talking about anyway. She and her mother were the worst gossips in town. But her mother did volunteer work at the hospital sometimes. Did she know something that—

"Corrie! For goodness sake, Corrie, get in—get in out of the wind!"

Corrie was flung from her thoughts. They had reached the hospital now, and her mother was holding open the lobby door. They had walked all that time, and Corrie hadn't even noticed anything. Would she never get her senses sharpened? Would she never be able to control her own thoughts? Quickly she stepped inside, where she was immediately engulfed in the odor and heat of the hospital. She felt her face grow tight, and she tried to steel herself against the sorrow that was mounting, growing in her stomach. Nervously she began to smooth down her straight bangs.

Mrs. Sheldon was taking off her husband's scarf. She seemed embarrassed by its brightness, its gaiety. She folded it into a tight square and tucked it inside her purse. Then she turned to Corrie. "That wind! Why it must be—" She stopped as her eyes stared at the far lobby wall. "The posters! They've taken down the posters!"

Corrie followed her gaze and saw that the walls were bare. Just the night before they had still been covered with old war posters, but now there were

16

only smudges where once the posters had shouted out their slogans. Only the portrait of the hospital founder still hung on the wall. He stared down angrily, as though annoyed at being interrupted in his lofty thoughts.

Mrs. Sheldon was straightening the front of her dress. She always kept a handkerchief down deep within her neckline. "Well now," she said. "I guess we'd best get going. Take your scarf off, child, and let's go upstairs. Daddy will be waiting."

Corrie followed her mother to the stairway. Her father would be on the third floor, where he'd been now for six weeks. But would he be awake and waiting? Corrie bit her lip and wondered, and she hurried faster up the stairs.

They saw a nurse shut the door to Mr. Sheldon's ward and start down the hall to her desk. It was Mary Lutz, one of their favorites. Some of the nurses were brusque, busy, abrupt. But Mary Lutz had always talked to them, maybe because they had known her before they met her at the hospital. They saw her in church sometimes and Corrie knew she went to movies with the high school's only bachelor teacher. Sandra had said she saw them just last week, in fact.

"How is he?" Mrs. Sheldon called, hurrying so fast that her heels clicked wildly on the hospital floor.

Miss Lutz turned, smiling. When she saw who had spoken, her face did that trick again that Corrie had suddenly begun to notice. All the nurses did it now, and so did the doctors. It was grotesque, but it was fascinating. In the beginning, when she had first noticed it, Corrie had tried to do it, too. At home, in front of a mirror, she had practiced and practiced. But she had never been able to manage it. She couldn't decide what muscles to use, and her face always remained rigid. She finally decided that they had all learned to do it in medical school.

Now she watched Miss Lutz do the amazing feat again. Her whole face divided in two. Suddenly there was a top face and a bottom face, and they did two entirely different things. The top half got all tight and creased around the forehead and wrinkled around the eyes, and the bottom half got all slack and fell into a smile, limp and dangling.

"Why, he's asleep," she said in a high, tight voice. "I've just given him a shot."

"Morphine?" Corrie's mother was clutching her purse upward, the way she held her hymn book when they occasionally went to church.

"Why, yes," Miss Lutz answered, and her face divided again.

"Oh." Corrie heard the disappointment in her mother's voice. "Well, at least he'll be getting some rest now. He's been so restless lately. Don't you think it's rest that Joseph needs?"

Corrie dug her nails into the palms of her hands. Morphine didn't give her father a rest—it knocked him out, eradicated him, erased the tiny part of him that was still sweetly hers.

She blinked back sudden tears, and she bit the inside of her cheeks. What's the matter with you? she asked herself. Isn't it better that he be asleep than in pain? Do you want him lying in pain and asking about the garden?

"Go ahead," Miss Lutz said. "Go inside." The bottom half of her face smiled. The sign on the ward door said NO ONE UNDER AGE FOURTEEN ADMITTED, but the nurses had never mentioned this rule to the Sheldons. They all knew the whole family by this

19

time, and Alan and Arthur had visited once a week.

Corrie turned and opened the ward door. She caught her breath, hugged it close inside her lungs to help cushion the pain that she knew would tear at her throat when she went inside.

Her father lay flat in the first bed, his skin even paler than the white of the sheets. He was lying quietly tonight, breathing lightly. The tubes running from his body were hidden beneath the blanket. The ward had a strong aroma of alcohol, of camphor.

Mrs. Sheldon hurried to pull the long white drapes that hid each bed. The bed next to Mr. Sheldon was empty, but Mrs. Sheldon pulled the drape anyway, and the corner became private. The walls were painted a pale yellow. On the nightstand there was a large potted plant. Mrs. Sheldon watered it from the drinking glass as she spoke to her husband. "We're here, Joseph."

It was only since her father's sickness that her mother said "Joseph." Always before she had simply called him "Joe."

"I think he looks better tonight," Mrs. Sheldon was saying, as she dragged a chair nearer to the bed. "Don't you think he looks better, Corrie? More color or something?"

Corrie took off her coat. "Yes," she said. "Yes." She crossed to the other chair, near the curtain, and sat down. She looked at her father from the foot of the bed where she sat and marveled at how motionless he was, how fragile he seemed, how thin and pale.

All her life he had been so huge, so loud, so all-powerful. He could crank up their car and make the motor roar, he could laugh so loud the walls in the kitchen would echo. He could shovel coal into the furnace faster than greased lightning. But now he was a paper doll, a shallow bulge beneath thin blankets. Corrie folded her hands and stared at her fingers.

"Oh, I feel sure that this last operation did the trick," Mrs. Sheldon said. "He only needs to get a good rest, that's what. Don't you think so, Corrie? A good rest can do wonders."

More visitors clomped through the ward door. Corrie watched their feet beneath the curtain. They lowered their voices as they passed, then raised them louder as they moved on down the aisle.

"Joseph?" Mrs. Sheldon leaned over the bed. "Can you hear me, Joseph?"

The man made no movement. Corrie squeezed her fingers together so violently that the knuckles became white and the fingertips flushed bright red. She stared at them, and the sight made her remember her father's magic. He could do anything with his hands and fingers. Anything. He could even make them come alive, each finger seeming to have a life of its own.

"Look, Corrie, look," he'd said a hundred times as she'd been growing up. And when she'd looked at him, she had seen that all of his fingers were covered with little paper hats, and his fingertips were painted with faces. Fascinated, she would stare at the little people, and they would bow and nod and shake their heads.

His hands became whole animals when he made shadows on the livingroom wall directly in front of a flashlight. Snakes and rabbits and tigers raced across the living room on nights when darkness came early. Her father was like God—he created life and death.

"I'll get the flashlight," she would say, when he had finished eating in the evenings.

"Let your father rest," her mother would always put in. "He's worked hard all day at the plant. Let him rest and read the newspaper."

"Oh, she's only young once," Mr. Sheldon would say, and he'd clear the table for the flashlight. "Just watch this one, Corrie," he'd call, and suddenly a giraffe would spring into view.

"You're as bad as the kids," Mrs. Sheldon would tell him, but her voice would sound pleased. "You're just a big overgrown kid, Joe Sheldon."

Mr. Sheldon had been huge in those days. Years later, when Corrie was bigger, she'd discovered with a sudden stab of astonishment that her dad was only five feet eight; he was shorter, in fact, than most of his friends. But in her mind he was still huge, the way he had been when she was small. He was tall and strong and healthy, with curly black hair and even white teeth.

He brushed them with ashes. Right from the stove in their kitchen, right from the remains of their paper burnings. They didn't burn newspapers, of course, after the war started because that would have been a terrible waste; but in the early days they did, and these were the ashes her father liked best. Corrie would gasp every time he'd fish out a handful of the gray-black substance.

"They get teeth whiter than snow," he'd say.

"But doesn't it taste awful, Daddy? Doesn't it taste awful?"

Mr. Sheldon would laugh. "If you want something good, then sometimes you have to put up with a little something bad in order to get it."

He was wise, Corrie knew that. He knew everything there was to know. Far more than her teachers ever could know. There had been another shock, years later, when she'd discovered that he had only gone through the second grade in school. That knowledge had pierced her, had forced the air from her body and soaked her palms with sweat. But then she didn't care. She'd swallowed the pain and shame, and she'd finally decided that her father's wisdom was greater than anything a school could have given him anyway.

She was telling herself that now, as Mrs. Sheldon bent over the bedside table. "You know what, Corrie?" the woman said. "I think Daddy read that magazine we brought in last night. It's been moved. Do you see that? It's been moved all right."

Corrie nodded. Her mother's voice had a quickness about it—an urgency—a pitch that pleaded for agreement. Corrie's smaller brother, Alan, used that same tone when he wanted reassurance about God, about Santa Claus, about cocoons that might hatch into butterflies in the shoe box in his bedroom.

"He always liked to read," Mrs. Sheldon said. "I thought he might go blind he read so much."

Again Corrie nodded. But she knew, of course, that her father had not read that magazine. It had been weeks—maybe months—since he'd been able to keep his mind clear enough for things like that. At first it had been the terrible pain. And then the drugs. Before, long before his sickness, though, he'd read everything he laid his eyes on. And he shared the best of it with everyone around him.

"Listen to this," he'd say, and he'd read aloud from the daily newspaper. His voice was deep and pleasant, rumbly, and he could read words—any words—and make them sound as good as verses from the Bible.

Mrs. Sheldon would hum and nod and continue to do the dishes. The boys would keep on building bridges or drawing airplanes. Their dog, Brandy, would scurry her feet in sleep, dreaming visions of forest chases. Only Corrie would listen, lost in the wonder of the things she heard.

She loved to watch her father's face as he read. It transformed black print into human emotions, a mirror reflecting things unseen.

. . . A child had fallen into a well—only heroic

24

measures could save her . . . A young sailor, on three days leave, had hitchhiked all the way to Alabama to marry his sweetheart before going overseas . . . Neighbors in a nearby town were collecting money to buy a pony for a boy with infantile paralysis . . .

Mr. Sheldon always read things like this. The war was raging in the Pacific, in Africa, in Europe. The economy of the country was going crazy. Criminals were making fortunes in the black market. People were being robbed and murdered. Men were predicting that the horror of the war would cause the whole world to collapse. Corrie knew these things because she heard them all in school. But Mr. Sheldon read aloud about the girl who would soon be rescued and the boy who would soon have a pony. The kitchen was a refuge against the evils of the world. Mr. Sheldon blotted out the bad in people, he brought out the good. The people he read about were real, as real as the criminals who made headlines on the first pages. Realer, he said, because the things they did were good, and good was always much stronger than evil. Corrie listened to these things, and she knew that all his words were true.

The figure on the hospital bed groaned. Corrie darted from her chair, Mrs. Sheldon sprang to her feet. They stood on either side of the bed, peering down, barely breathing.

Mr. Sheldon opened his eyes. He stared up a moment, then frowned. His gaze moved to Mrs. Sheldon. He struggled to sit up.

"No, no, Joseph, you need rest," Mrs. Sheldon said. She put her hands on his chest. "Lay back down, now, Joseph, lay down."

"The garden—" the man said. "The garden—" His words were hard to understand, his eyes were blurred, his lips hardly moved.

"The garden is doing fine," Mrs. Sheldon said. "It's just fine, Joseph." She stared at Corrie, beckoning her closer.

Corrie's mouth went dry. Her stomach knotted, and she wavered on her feet. She looked down at her father. "We're all fine, Daddy," she said.

"The garden—" the man said. "The garden—" As he struggled, a tube running down the side of the bed wiggled against Corrie's leg. She jumped back, touched, burned.

"The garden is doing fine," Mrs. Sheldon said, louder now. "It's fine, Joseph, just fine. But you must rest now, dear. You need rest."

But the man struggled on. His pale, thin arms were pulling at the sheet as he tried to sit up. "The garden—the garden—"

"Now, now, Mr. Sheldon," Miss Lutz said suddenly. She'd come so quickly and quietly that Corrie was startled at the sound of her voice. "You must stay quiet, Mr. Sheldon," she went on. She patted his forehead. "Lie back down and sleep now."

Corrie saw her father drop his head back to the pillow. He closed his eyes. His face relaxed. He began breathing evenly again.

"It was just a dream," the nurse said. "He wasn't

really awake, you know. It was just a dream."

Mrs. Sheldon nodded. Her face was flushed now and moist. She fell back into her chair.

"Most of them do the same thing," the nurse said, not explaining who the "them" were. "It's the morphine, I guess." She sighed. "What a wonderful patient your husband has been! Not a single word of complaint! Can you imagine? The other girls and I, why we'd catch ourselves telling him *our* troubles. He seemed so understanding somehow, as though he really cared about all of us."

Corrie's fingernails were digging into her palms. She uncurled her fingers.

The nurse shook her head. "Never saw a man so interested in a garden, though. He must have loved it very much."

"He did," Corrie said aloud, moving back to her chair. Then she abruptly stopped. "I mean, he *does*."

Mrs. Sheldon eagerly nodded. "All growing things. My husband always has loved all growing things. That's how the two of us are alike, I guess. I love them, too."

Corrie looked down at her hands as she heard her mother's words. It wasn't true, of course—that her parents were alike. It wasn't true at all. Her mother believed it because her father allowed her to believe it. But really the two of them were entirely different. Their ideas on growing things, for instance, could never be the same. Her father loved them for their beauty—her mother loved them for their usefulness.

Corrie remembered the day she had become aware of this, and she marveled at how perfectly this one thing showed how different her parents were.

It had been early autumn, long before the sickness, centuries before the sickness, it seemed, and her father had wanted to go into the woods. For weeks he had talked about hunting, but he had no equipment—his guns had been sold to pay for the birth of the twins just a few months before.

"Why keep talking about hunting?" her mother had asked. "Wishing doesn't get you anywhere, Joe. You can wish in one hand and spit in the other, and just look which one fills up first."

"There's something special about hunting," Mr. Sheldon answered.

"But you never catch anything," Mrs. Sheldon said. "You've been out hunting every year for nearly twenty years, and you've never caught a thing."

Corrie's father had laughed. He was most handsome when he laughed, showing his white teeth, and the sound came up from deep inside his chest. "Oh, I don't know—seems to me that I caught a cold back in 1936."

"You!" Mrs. Sheldon waved her hand. "Go on with you, Joe Sheldon! You've always got a smart remark, now haven't you."

"Well, I think I'll just get off to the woods for a while," Corrie's dad had said. "I think I'll take Corrie out early tomorrow morning."

"But why?" Mrs. Sheldon was genuinely puzzled. "Why do a thing like that?"

"Might find some hickory nuts. We just might find some hickory nuts."

"Oh." Mrs. Sheldon nodded and smiled, and Corrie saw that now the plan made sense to her. "I'll pack a lunch for the two of you. I can save the nuts for cookies this winter."

And so they had gone to the woods, Corrie and her dad. Since they had left early, the sun was just beginning to rise over the tops of the trees when they walked into the forest. It made little circles of gold flicker on their faces under the hushed branches. There was a delicious smell, an aroma of damp earth and dry twigs, a mingling fragrance of fulfillment. Corrie tasted a needle from a pine tree, and it tasted better than candy. Her father wore a bright red coat, but she thought the red of the leaves was brighter. All around her the forest seemed to be alive and moving.

She walked along proudly, happy to be alone with her father, glad he had decided to take her with him. She wasn't afraid of anything when he was there, but her mother's warnings were haunting her mind, so she swallowed loudly and asked, "You think there might be any hunters out here, Daddy? Do you think we could get shot by mistake?"

Mr. Sheldon laughed. "You sound like your mother now, Corrie. No—no need to worry about a thing like that. There's never been a hunter here. I've hunted here for years and have never seen another hunter ever."

"You never caught anything, Momma said."

Corrie's father winked and whispered. "I never tried."

They walked slowly. Sometimes they crashed through underbrush that sent birds flocking to the sky. The sound of dry sticks snapping was beautiful —it was clear and clean, like the sound of music. And the crunch of the leaves was like poetry. It made a rhythm, Corrie thought, and she picked up great piles of them and tried to understand the words they whispered as they fluttered to the ground.

The pine needles were fingers clinging to their clothing, to their hair. A naked white trunk stood next to a green fir tree, and next to that was a fallen maple. Dozens of little trees were growing out from the decaying hulk—the fallen tree was a cradle for a wealth of new life. Corrie's father showed her these things. He told her that life always springs from death, and so there really was no death at all.

They ate their sandwiches near a pond and heard the scurry of the living things around them as they began preparations for the cold of the winter. A snake glided in front of them, sluggish already from the cold, but hurrying to hibernate. There was a hush, a lull, as Corrie chewed on her sandwich, and she had the marvelous warm feeling that the woods were protection, safety, and that in the forest she really was home.

Later in the day they saw a flock of geese heading south. They fed a squirrel bread crusts, and they studied the moss at the foot of huge trees. There were strange bumps in some leaves that Corrie found. Her father told her that they were insect homes, and when she opened them, tiny insects scurried out.

"Look how little they are!" Corrie cried. "They're such tiny little bugs, Daddy! Do you think they're surprised to see how big I am?"

Her father laughed. "They don't see you at all, Corrie. You're so big that you're just a blur to them."

"I am?" The idea astonished her. "They can't see me because I'm so *big*?"

"We can't any of us see things that are a lot smaller or a lot bigger than we are ourselves," her father told her. "We only see the things that are near to us in size."

"Is that why people can't see God?" she had asked.

Mr. Sheldon had looked down at her in amazement. In amazement and pride. Then his face broke into a huge smile, and his white teeth gleamed. "Well, you're quite a thinker, Corrie, do you know that? A real thinker!"

Corrie remembered how happy she'd been at his praise, how warm she'd felt when he ran his hand over the top of her head.

Later that day, tired and happy, they had started back for the car. Corrie was running along in front when she had a sudden thought. "Hey!" she called back to her father. "Hey, Daddy—guess what? We forgot to look for hickory nuts!"

Her father's face looked puzzled. "We forgot what, Corrie? What'd you say we forgot?"

And it was then that Corrie had suddenly known that what her father wanted in the woods that day had nothing to do with hickory nuts, had never had. What he wanted was something invisible, something that had no name and no substance. But her mother needed something solid. Everything in life had to be seen in order for it to exist, she thought; whereas her father seemed to know that everything good was invisible. And so, because he loved his wife, Corrie realized that he gave his invisible pleasures names so that she could share them too.

This difference in her parents had come as a shocking revelation to Corrie that day in the forest. But it led to understanding, and it left Corrie struck with the depth of her father's wisdom.

She remembered how she had turned that day and put her hand into her father's. "Hey, Daddy," she had said. "You know what? I love you."

She said it now, too. Sitting alone in the chair in the hospital at the foot of her father's bed, she said it again and again. But she said it silently. Her father couldn't hear her. And who else would ever really understand just how much she meant it?

When they started walking home from the hospital, it seemed that the wind was blowing even more fiercely. Tiny dry snowflakes were whirling in the icy coldness, and the naked tree branches groaned over their heads. The night was dark. Even the small diner on the corner was black and silent. Corrie felt the familiar questions whirling inside her thoughts: Why does this have to happen? happen to me? happen to Daddy? happen to us? She felt cold and puzzled and frightened.

One . . . two . . . three . . . four . . . five . . . scuff.
One . . . two . . . three . . . four . . . five . . . scuff.

Corrie concentrated on the sound of her mother's footsteps. By counting, she was almost able to blot out the thoughts of her father, the ache in her legs, the sting of the wind. Her hands were in her pockets, and her fists clenched and unclenched in the rhythm of her mother's steps.

"Corrie—" The woman's voice was hesitant, her words drifted with the wind. She caught them up again. "Corrie—do you think he looked any better tonight?"

Then, as though ashamed of sounding uncertain, Mrs. Sheldon grabbed Corrie's arm and walked faster. They were both hunched into the wind now, and the woman spoke rapidly, without waiting for any answers.

"I mean—don't you think he had a bit more color? Don't you think he'll be well again, Corrie? Don't you think so?"

Corrie felt her lungs harden with the quick intake of cold air.

"He *hates* being sick like this, I just know it," her mother continued, breathing quickly. "He doesn't like having other people do everything for him, doesn't like it at all. He's always wanted to make his own way, taking care of himself. And he's done it so far, too! He's paid all them hospital bills right along, all right, what with selling the car and the land by the lake. Why can't he be left in peace for a while? It's awful, this cancer, it's awful. What can God be thinking of to allow such a thing? What can he be thinking of?"

One . . . two . . . three . . . four . . . five . . . scuff.
One . . . two . . . three . . . four . . . five . . . scuff.

The footsteps became louder, angrier, it seemed. Mrs. Sheldon jammed her hands into her coat sleeves. Her gloves were lying on the table beside the hospital bed. Corrie suddenly remembered seeing them there as they left. They were patched and darned, and now her mother needed them, but she hadn't mentioned them. Her purse was bumping against Corrie's elbow.

Corrie walked quicker, trying to keep even with her mother. They were going downhill, but the back of her legs ached. She was panting now and marveling that her mother could hurry so fast after working so hard all day at the shop. How could she manage? There would be dishes to do when they got home. Lunches to pack for the next day's school.

"What did he ever do to deserve this?" her mother asked. "That's what I'd like to know. Oh, Corrie, when I think of *some* people who live their whole lives—long lives—hurting people and cheating and lying! Oh, when I think of them, it makes me get all sick inside. They live on and on while your father— who never hurt a fly in his life—while your father—" Her voice faded, and she moved faster.

Corrie was speechless. In all the months of her father's illness, she had never heard her mother talk like this—she had always assumed that her mother bore everything without complaint, without imagination. She had always appeared to accept the events of her life as calmly as she accepted the movements of the planets.

"Well, I'll tell you something. Just let me tell you something, Corrie. He *will* get well! He will! He'll fool them all, that's what he'll do. I don't care what everybody else says. The way they all hush their voices and hide their eyes when they see me. I don't care. They don't know everything. He'll get well— Daddy'll get well all right. I just know."

Corrie reached for her mother's arm. The outburst had weakened the dam that held her own thoughts silent. "But Momma—Momma—if you

36

really do think that Daddy will get well again, then why do you tell him that the garden is okay? It's dead, Momma, it's been dead for months. It's winter now, and it's even been covered with snow. Why keep telling Daddy that his garden is fine? If you really think he'll be well again, then you can't tell him that. When he's well, he'll see that you didn't tell the truth."

One . . . two . . . three . . . four . . . five . . . scuff.
One . . . two . . . three . . . four . . . five . . . scuff.

It was a long time before there was an answer. When it came, the voice behind it was tight, as if it had been forced through narrow walls. "Is that it, Corrie? Is that why you never answer him when he asks about the garden—because you think that your answer might have something to do with whether he gets well or not?"

Corrie dropped her hand, amazed that her mother might truly understand. "I guess so, Momma," she whispered. "It's silly, I guess, but that's why."

"Of course," her mother said. "Now I can see it, all right. Now I see." She caught a deep breath and didn't speak again, and the two of them grew colder and walked faster down the hill.

Can she really know? Corrie felt this question run up and down her body. How could anyone else truly understand the queer bargains she made with herself in her mind? It was like the dumb things she had done when she was little—crazy things that she had never even told Sandra about because she was afraid that even a best friend might not understand. Everyone else seemed too caught up in sensible things—too sure that sensible actions always brought sensible results. Corrie never believed that. She put unusual things together in her mind because she believed that she could make things happen by balancing events on an invisible teeter-totter inside her head. She would do one thing, and in return, she would get something she wanted.

She would go a whole day without stepping on any grass, for instance, and feel positive that because of her efforts, she would find a quarter. She would kick a rusty can all the way to school and be sure that she would get an *A* on a test because of it. She would search the sky for birds and know that if she saw a robin, Daryl Hanson would start to like her. He lived on the same block, but he was two years older than she was and he never even noticed her. She knew he probably never would, but she still made her quiet plans. They were foolish ideas—crazy even, maybe—but they were real to her; and sometimes they worked for her, and then she felt she had the power to connect these strange things together to make life turn out exactly the way she wanted it to.

And so now she had made a bargain with her father's sickness; if she never admitted that he might die, then he never would. How could she tell him that his garden was all right? That would be like admitting that he might die and never see for himself that his garden was gone, frozen, half covered with snow and leaves. No, she would never tell him that it was fine. She couldn't hurt him with the truth either, and so she must say nothing at all about the garden. She had to keep that invisible teeter-totter steady in her brain, balancing the events around her the way she wanted them balanced.

It's all like a game, she was thinking, a game without any rules. But we have to play the best we can, we have to play the game somehow.

One . . . two . . . three . . . four . . . five . . . scuff.
One . . . two . . . three . . . four . . . five . . . scuff.

The wind seemed to grow quieter now. The foghorn was silent, and the rush of Lake Michigan became a steady whisper. Far off in the west, Corrie saw the lighthouse flashing its slow signal. The traffic on the streets had disappeared. Mrs. Sheldon's shoes clicked against the hollow pavement of Lincoln Bridge.

Corrie looked out at the lapping water of the river, and she smiled. I wonder how the turtle is, she thought. The turtle! Just the idea of that summer day with her father and that turtle made the sorrow in her stomach melt away, made her questions disappear. She smelled the aroma of the water and remembered that hot afternoon just four months before. It had started in her father's garden. Everyone but Lewie had been there that day—her father, her mother, her brothers, Sandra, and herself. There had been the taste of tomatoes in the air, she remembered, even though no redness was yet visible on the bushy green plants. It had been twilight, that magic time of the day when the sun hung low in the west over Lake Michigan, and the shadows became long and important. Anything seemed possible at that time of the day to Corrie, anything. Twilight meant peace and hope. Mr. Sheldon had been watering the bean plants.

"We need a good rain," Mrs. Sheldon had said. She always made that comment, sometimes only a day after a rainstorm, for she had been a farm girl once and weather was important. It was her way of being friendly to people, her way of showing that she was ready for a chat.

"Oh, I don't mind getting out the hose," Mr. Sheldon had told her. He'd been home from the hospital for several months, but he still looked pale and weak. He was wearing loose pants held up by suspenders because he couldn't stand anything around his waist anymore. He held the nozzle of the hose near the yellow blossoms of the cucumber plants, and he made the spray spread out in a huge circle. In the bright afternoon sun, he could make rainbows, but now the sun was nearly gone.

"Squirt me again, Daddy," Arthur called. He was dancing around the yard in a pair of ragged blue jeans, cut off at the knees. Alan had a real bathing suit—it was a castoff from a neighbor. He was smaller, so he had everybody's castoffs, sometimes even his brother's.

Mr. Sheldon turned the hose. Arthur jumped and squealed. "Do me too, Daddy!" Alan shrieked. Then he ran when the water arched out at him. Brandy dashed after him, barking.

"That's enough now, boys," Mrs. Sheldon called. "We got to be thinking about bedtime."

"Naw, not yet, Mom," Arthur said. His words sounded funny since he had lost his front teeth. "It ain't time for bed yet. Right, Corrie? It ain't even getting dark yet."

"Isn't," Corrie said.

Arthur hadn't heard. He was hopping by his father now. "It ain't time for bed yet, right, Dad? Right?"

Mr. Sheldon was stooping near a tomato plant. "Take a look at this," he called.

"Oнннннннн!" Sandra, standing nearest to the plant, quickly jumped back to the sidewalk. Her red face grew pale. "It's a tomato worm! One of those awful tomato worms!"

Everyone stared at the fat green creature. It was crawling on a stem—half the leaves there had been gnawed away.

"Let's step on him!" Arthur shouted. "He's been eating our tomato plants!"

"Let me keep him in a fruit jar," Alan said.

Mr. Sheldon lifted the worm from the plant. It was a huge one, and its green was almost chartreuse. It curled itself into a tight ball. Corrie saw the wonder in her father's face as he watched it. He handed the worm to Alan. "Be sure to make plenty of air holes in the jar lid." He glanced at Arthur. "Every creature has to eat, son. He hasn't hurt the plant that much."

Mrs. Sheldon clacked her tongue. "Why, I never!" she declared. "The very idea, Joe! Why keep an ugly thing like that?" She shook her head as Alan ran to get a fruit jar. "It's the craziest thing I ever heard of, Joe Sheldon! What on earth good are they, I'd like to know, ugly things that they are! Why, they can ruin a garden if you get enough of them in it! They're awful! Awful!" She grumbled on and on, but Corrie knew that she was happy. She was nearly always happy on Sundays, when she didn't have to go to work in that dusty old tent shop. Mr. Peterson made her sad, she told Corrie. He was her boss, and he was the only other worker in the shop.

"Can you find another worm for me, Daddy?" Arthur was saying. "I guess I wouldn't step on him. I guess I'd keep him and feed him, Daddy."

Everyone examined the garden. It stretched out beside the gravel alley, running behind the houses, and simultaneously, it seemed, everyone noticed a large black circle slowly moving across the stones of the alley, near the wire fence.

"Why, look at that!" Mr. Sheldon turned off the nozzle and dropped the hose. He started through the alley gate. "Just look at that poor old fellow there! Don't let Brandy get out here!"

"Why? What's there?" Alan came running from the house. "What'd you find, Daddy?"

"It's a turtle!" Mr. Sheldon called. He stooped to pick up the huge black circle. "It's a big old, tired old turtle! Scared to death, he is."

Corrie saw the paws of the exhausted turtle wave feebly in the air, as her father lifted him. She hurried forward and held open the gate. The underside of the turtle's shell was dry and worn, she saw, grimy and dusty. His head and limbs were making frantic motions.

Arthur drew closer to stare. "He smells ickky!"

Mr. Sheldon shook his head. "Poor old fellow—he's tired, that's what. Probably half starved, too, from the looks of him. He must have been crawling for hours and hours, trying to get down to Lincoln River."

Mrs. Sheldon stepped back. "Well, I wouldn't touch that thing for all the tea in China! Goodness, Joe, put him down! He must weigh a ton!"

"He's one of the biggest I've ever seen around here," Mr. Sheldon said. "And one of the tiredest, too, I'll bet. Why, he must be nearly as old as I am!"

"I'll bet those darn Mitchum boys had him," Corrie said. "They keep all kinds of animals trapped in their back yard."

"And they all die, too," Sandra added. "They starve to death."

"They catch birds in rat traps and cut off their wings," Corrie said, feeling angrier as she talked. "They're terrible!"

"Well, this old fellow was too smart for the Mitchum boys," Mr. Sheldon told them. "He got

away." He held the turtle in both hands and turned him over slowly. "But he's nearly worn his shell away crawling over cement. He's been trying like the dickens to get back to that river."

"Well, put him down," Mrs. Sheldon repeated. "He's only a few blocks from the river now. Why, you couldn't *pay* me to touch that smelly creature!"

Mr. Sheldon frowned. "He'll die for sure if I put him down now. Why, he's practically dead right now, Verna. He could never crawl another two or three blocks. He could never make it to the river. And what about the traffic? No, I'll carry him down to the river myself."

"Carry him!" Mrs. Sheldon put her plump hands on her hips. "Joe Sheldon—are you crazy? You mean to tell me that you'd *carry* that smelly old thing all the way down to Lincoln River?"

Mr. Sheldon started walking toward the front. "That's what I'm going to do all right."

"But a man in your condition shouldn't even *walk* two blocks, let alone carry a heavy thing like that! No, Joseph, I can't allow it. Put the turtle down!"

Mr. Sheldon didn't answer. He straightened his thin body and started out the front gate. Mrs. Sheldon looked at Corrie and Sandra. Her face puckered with uncertainty. "Then, I'm coming too!" she called, starting after her husband. Corrie knew that her mother hadn't been near the river for years—she was afraid of snakes and quicksand—but she started after her husband anyway. "I'm coming too, Joe."

"Me too!" Arthur shouted. "I'm coming too!" Alan echoed. They spent half their waking hours playing by the swamp near the river, but they'd never seen their parents there before.

Corrie stared at Sandra. She was still caught up in the wonder of seeing her father win out over her robust mother. She grinned at Sandra, then they both turned and started running. "We're coming too! Want me to carry the turtle, Daddy?" Corrie called.

"No," her father answered. "I can manage him all right." Brandy, barking crazily, came dashing down the steps.

Corrie thought they made a grand parade walking down Lincoln Avenue in the twilight. Her father, carrying the exhausted turtle, led the way; her mother, walking beside him, was like the band.

"Joseph, Joseph! Think what you're doing! Remember your last operation. The doctor said you should be taking it easy. A turtle! For heaven's sake, why strain yourself over a worthless old turtle? People eat them, for goodness' sake. Be careful, Joseph, be careful. There's no need to rush, no need to hurry. Why, you couldn't get me to touch that awful thing with a ten-foot pole!"

The twins were running on the curb, their bare feet black from the soot of the nearby factories, and Brandy was running ahead now, her tail flying like a banner. There was a toot from a boat on the river, the touch of the wind on their faces, and the sound of their laughter and voices. Corrie felt happy and proud as she hurried along beside Sandra.

And then they had reached the river. They had lined up on the bridge and looked out over the water. Both Mr. Sheldon and Mrs. Sheldon were panting. Mr. Sheldon from the exertion of the walk and the burden he had carried, and Mrs. Sheldon from her weight and her constant conversation.

The turtle had obviously scented the odor of his home. Corrie saw him frantically wave his legs with renewed force. He stretched his neck out, reaching toward the water.

"Well," Mrs. Sheldon said, "I must say that he seems to know he's home all right. He's nearly crawling right out of his shell. Throw him out into the water, Joe."

But Mr. Sheldon was exhausted. The determination to reach his goal had kept him moving, but once his goal was reached, his energy was gone. Corrie saw that his face was white and his lips were blue. He was standing against the cement railing trying to catch his breath. Everyone could see that he would never be able to throw the turtle out away from the posts and debris directly under the bridge. Corrie felt a sudden panic. She cleared her throat, but before she could speak, her mother stepped forward.

"Or better yet, Joe, let me take the poor thing and throw him out there," she said. "Oh, I know you can do it yourself, Joe, but I want to do it." She took the struggling creature then, even though she had declared a dozen times that she'd never touch it, not even with a ten-foot pole, and she threw with all her might so that he'd fall into clear water, away from the rocks and tin cans near the bridge.

The turtle seemed to skim over the top of the river, like a skier on a lake, and then he sank from sight into the fresh blue water. Corrie caught her breath. In two or three seconds, she saw him pop up again, and he seemed to wave one flipper at the watchers on the bridge. Then he disappeared.

The six of them on the bridge drew closer together. Corrie felt united to the others by the aroma of the damp, the warmth of the sinking sun, and the sound of the lapping water. They all stood silent, and Corrie felt an unexplained sense of having done something fine. Then Mrs. Sheldon smiled.

"Well," she said. "I guess that was a nice thing to do after all. Did you see that turtle wave his arm at us? He came right back up out of the water a minute there as though he wanted to say, 'Thank you! Thank you!' "

Mr. Sheldon grinned. He had caught his breath now, and Corrie saw his eyes light with hidden laughter. "On the other hand," he said, "he might have been waving his arm and trying to yell, 'Help! Help! I don't know how to swim!' "

Mrs. Sheldon's mouth dropped open. Her plain face was loose with uncertainty, then she started to laugh, and Corrie thought she suddenly seemed beautiful. "Go on with you, Joe Sheldon! You're the limit, that's what you are. You're the limit!"

Everyone laughed then, and for a moment it seemed to Corrie that they were all caught up in a special place all their own, a bubble kind of thing, where everyone was happy and everyone was good, and they all shared a marvelous, exciting kind of love.

One . . . two . . . three . . . four . . . five . . . scuff.

One . . . two . . . three . . . four . . . five . . . scuff.

"Well, here we are, Corrie," Mrs Sheldon said. "And I see the boys left every light in the house on again. Goodness!"

Corrie shook her head and looked around—they were walking up the steps to their house. For a fleeting moment she marveled that she could have walked along without even knowing that she was walking, for she had been lost in the memory of the summer evening. But once she felt the cold again and the darkness and she sensed the fatigue of her mother, reality erased her wonder.

"Hurry up, Momma," she said. "I'll make you some coffee when we get inside." She reached out to open the door.

It was nine-thirty when they opened the kitchen door. The aroma and the warmth of the house blanketed Corrie. She stood for a moment on the threshold and happily breathed the fragrance of home.

"Good Heavens!" her mother cried. She hurried inside, her heels clicking on the worn linoleum. "Just look at the mess in here, Corrie! Just look! Oh, those boys, those boys! What'll we do with them, Corrie? They shouldn't have to go to Lewie's every night. She's nearly eighty, for goodness' sakes. And I hate to keep asking other neighbors to check on them. Everyone's done so much already. But look what happens when we leave those two here alone. Just look! They've turned this kitchen into a pigpen, that's what. A pigpen!"

Corrie smiled as her mother fluttered around the room. The kitchen wasn't really so bad, she thought, but she knew her mother was happiest when she could complain about something that she could immediately take care of herself. "Look at the brown sugar all over the counter!" she cried. She threw off her coat and clucked her tongue and began clearing the table.

Corrie hung up her coat, smoothed down her

bangs, then hurried into the twin's bedroom. Both boys were sound asleep with all their clothes on, flung across their beds like huge rag dolls. Brandy looked up from between their beds. She wagged her tail and softly whined.

"You knew it was us, didn't you, old girl," Corrie said. She knelt beside the dog and buried her face in Brandy's fur. "But you can't understand what's going on now, can you," she whispered. She rubbed her face on the warm fur and closed her eyes and allowed herself only a moment to recall the pain of giving up her part in the school play that day. But then she felt immediate guilt, for how could she feel sorry for herself when her father—when her father—

"Oh, I can't understand it all either," she whispered against the dog. "I can't understand it either."

> *Royal Pudding!*
> *Rich, rich, rich in flavor,*
> *Smooth, smooth, smooth as silk.*
> *More food energy*
> *Than sweet, fresh mi—*

Corrie flicked off the radio. She carefully covered Alan—he lay flat on his bed with his arms spread out; then she pulled the covers closer around Arthur, who curled himself into a tight ball when he slept. She petted Brandy once more, then turned out the light and hurried from the room.

"Did you want that coffee now, Momma?" she called.

Her mother was standing near the table. It was clean and clear, and Mrs. Sheldon looked pleased. "No, no, Corrie, I don't feel like any now. You'd best run on to bed. I can finish up out here. You look worn out, child, you look worn out. Your eyes are like two holes in a white blanket."

"But there's lunches to pack and—"

"I'll pack the lunches. Hurry along now—hop into bed."

Corrie sighed as she pulled on her pajamas. I should curl my hair, she thought, but I'm too tired. She caught a glimpse of herself in her dresser mirror. Her dark hair, usually bouncy and tight from her nightly pin curls, was straight and straggly. What if Daryl Hanson speaks to me tomorrow? she thought. It was a nightly fantasy she used to force herself into doing her hair. She made a face, sighed, and reached for her bobby pins.

The church on the corner was chiming ten o'clock as she finished with her hair. Her arms ached with tiredness. From the other room came the clatter of pots and pans, the spashing of water, and she suddenly realized how tired her mother must feel, too. She padded, barefoot, to the kitchen to say goodnight again.

She stood in the doorway and she saw that her mother hadn't heard her steps. She was standing quietly at the kitchen sink, leaning against it, her little plump body growing wetter from the splashing water, which seemed to be forgotten, for it was running wildly. Her hair was straggling out from the bun on the nape of her neck, and her head was bowed forward. She was staring at the wedding band she wore on her finger, turning her small hand slowly until the gold reflected the dim light of the kitchen. The woman turned her head and gazed at her ring a moment, then her face contorted and she caught her breath. She gave a deep sigh, and the sound seemed to Corrie so filled with loneliness and sorrow that it echoed in the room and bounced against the walls and hung darkly from the ceiling.

Corrie stood motionless a moment, frightened and silent, caught up in a flood of emotion she could barely understand. Everything in her mind paled to insignificance beside the darkness of her mother's grief. She hesitated in the shadows, then backed into the bedroom again, her goodnight left unspoken. Oh, why are people born, she thought, when life is so very awful? Won't it ever be good again? Won't I ever feel good again?

The sun was bright the next day. It woke her as it peered in through a tiny hole in her window shade. She opened her eyes to the song of birds and the smell of coffee, and suddenly she felt fine. The despair of the night before had vanished with the darkness.

She stretched out in her bed, hardly noticing the cracks in the wallpaper near the ceiling. Usually this sight was the first thing she saw, and she looked for it nearly every morning, ready for the pang that shabbiness always brought her. But today she merely glanced at it, and then she looked at the window. She saw the shadows of five or six sparrows hopping around the sill, twittering and scolding. Their noise made her happy—they sounded exactly like people, all talking at once, never listening, all busy rushing around doing a thousand things, important and exciting to them alone.

Corrie wiggled her toes. She felt fine. Strength went bouncing through her body. It felt good to see the sunshine after three long, bleak days. It beamed determinedly through the tiny hole in the shade and grew into a bright circle that reflected on the bedspread. Corrie wiggled her toes again, and when the cover moved, it seemed as though the circle was dancing. "I can make the sun move," she thought. "I can do anything—anything." The thoughts of the night before seemed a lifetime away now, and here in the gold of the day, the sorrow of the darkness seemed foolish and remote. Her father would be well again. He would! And she could be in another school play, and life would be the way it always had been before. On days like this, anything was possible! Daryl Hanson might even speak to her. Corrie lay in bed and smiled at all the glorious possibilities.

"Are you awake now?" Alan, the smaller but older twin, was peering around the bedroom door. He was missing one front tooth, and he wore ripped, buttonless pajamas. His slightly freckled face looked serious. "Momma said I wasn't to wake you. Are you awake, Corrie?"

Corrie laughed. "Well, even if I wasn't, I am now. But how come you're up so early? The alarm didn't even go off yet."

"I got up when Mom left for work. I ain't very tired today." Alan sat on the bed. His eyes were exactly like his father's—a perpetually changing shade of blue.

"You mustn't say 'ain't,' " Corrie told him. "It's not good grammar."

"We went to sleep real early last night," Alan said. "Arthur got scared while we was listening to the radio, so I said let's wait for Mom and Corrie in bed, and then we fell asleep, I guess. I just put my pajamas on now. I guess I fell asleep with my jeans on."

"You fell asleep with your radio on too, Alan. You're supposed to be more careful. Electricity costs money, you know, and we haven't got a whole lot."

"Well, Arthur, he—"

"I did not!" Arthur walked into the bedroom, still wearing the jeans he had been sleeping in. His eyes were like his mother's and Corrie's—a deep dark brown. He was missing two front teeth, and Corrie saw that he needed a haircut again. He glared at his brother. "You always say I do everything that happens around here, Alan Sheldon. But you ain't so hot yourself. You always blame me for everything that happens."

Corrie laughed. Arthur was always sure that people were saying bad things about him, always convinced that the cookie he received was smaller, the apple more sour, the banana more spotted. He was the hot-tempered one in the family—the first to pick a quarrel, but usually the first one to forget it, too.

"It wasn't me who was scared!" he shouted. "You're the fraidy cat, Alan!"

"I am not! You're the one who wanted to go over to Lewie's house when you thought you heard somebody at the window!"

"Well, how about you? When that guy got shot on the radio, you nearly hit the ceiling, you jumped so high. How about that?"

"I didn't do no such thing!"

"Oh, yes you did!"

"Liar, liar, pants on fire!"

"Okay, guys," Corrie said, throwing back her covers. It had made her feel good to hear her brothers argue the way they always did. For a few moments she had been able to think that nothing was changed at all, nothing was different, and her father was really not sick. "No wars before breakfast." She pulled a few bobby pins from her hair, and the corkscrew curls came tumbling down. "I'll take care of this mess later," she said. "Let's go eat breakfast."

Alan made a face. "Mom said we ain't got no milk, Corrie. We can't have cereal because she don't have money to buy more milk today."

"Well, today's payday," Corrie said. "Momma always gets paid on Friday, so she'll buy some and we'll have it tonight. We'll have peaches and toast for breakfast."

"Yuk!" Arthur shouted.

56

"Oh, peaches ain't so bad on toast with peanut butter," Alan said.

"*If* we got peanut butter," Arthur added.

Corrie went into the kitchen and saw that her mother had already set the table. There was an aroma of coffee, and the sun was streaming through the open door to the shed. Mrs. Sheldon had packed the lunches. They were on the counter in the tin boxes they used with their names written in red paint. Corrie remembered that her dad had painted them himself.

She stood near the sink and looking out the side window saw Mrs. Lewis out in her backyard feeding sparrows. Corrie knew that Lewie was terribly old, but she seemed almost young standing there in the rising sunlight. She was straight and tall and her lined face was still tan from all her hours in the garden. She had been there almost as much as the Sheldons had.

"I think you got a green thumb, Lewie," Mr. Sheldon had told her often. "Just look at how this garden is growing this year!"

"Pshaw!" Lewie would always make a face. She could never stand it when anyone said nice things about her. "It's you, Joe Sheldon—you're the one who makes these plants sit up and take notice. Just look at these tomatoes! They're bigger than grapefruit!"

"Take a few, Lewie. Take a whole bunch."

"I'll take exactly what I earned, thank you."

Lewie would shake her head. "Money's scarcer than hen's teeth this year, what with prices going crazy. I'm glad to have these things for canning."

"Heck, if you took what you earned, then the whole garden would be in your pantry," Mr. Sheldon told her. "You're handier than a pocket on a shirt. It's thanks to you that these things look so good this year."

"Maybe things grow good for Lewie because she's so awful old," Arthur said one time.

"How old are you, Lewie?" Alan asked.

"Old enough to know better," the old woman said. She bent and put another cucumber into her apron pocket. Then she stood up quickly and laughed her deep laugh. "But you know what? I'm still too young to want to quit!"

Corrie was thinking of that now as she watched Lewie in her yard. She looked spry and happy, and the birds seemed to know her. They were fluttering down from the huge evergreen tree that grew in the Sheldons' yard. Corrie knew that Lewie hardly had enough money to take care of her own needs, yet somehow she still managed to buy birdseed, too. It seemed painfully sad somehow, but also strangely beautiful. Corrie stood at the window and marveled at the simple beauty of the old woman feeding the birds while the bright morning sun rose up behind her.

"Look," Alan said, when they sat down to eat breakfast. "I can put a whole peach inside my mouth at once." He shoved his spoon in, and when the fruit was inside, Arthur reached over and started to tickle him. Alan began laughing, nearly choking on the huge peach.

The telephone rang. Still laughing, Corrie picked it up.

"Sandra!" she said. She'd spoken to Sandra only the day before, but that seemed like a long time ago. "What's going on?"

"Hi, Corrie," Sandra answered. "Listen, kid, the radio says it'll be warm today. Want to wear our twin sweaters? The ones we bought with our fruit-picking money?"

Corrie had a sudden thought of how fine it would be to go without wearing that horrid brown coat. "You mean you think we can go to school without wearing any coat at all today?"

"Sure! It's warm out, Corrie. It may be the last warm day of the whole year. Let's take advantage. It's a long, long time until May, you know."

Corrie leaned against the kitchen wall and had a mental picture of how Sandra would look as she spoke. She'd be nodding her head, her thick red hair flying. When Sandra talked on the telephone, she didn't worry about her protruding front teeth, she didn't have to always be putting her hand up to cover her mouth, and she always sounded happier. "Let's wear our broomstick skirts, too," she was saying. "And our saddle shoes."

"Okay. That sounds good, Sandra. That sounds

good. I might even polish my shoes if I get the kitchen done fast enough."

There was a moment's silence, then Sandra's voice grew quieter. "How's your dad, Corrie?"

Corrie saw the sunshine streaming in through the kitchen window. She put her mouth closer to the telephone. "I think he looked better last night," she said. "Mom and I thought he looked better."

"That's terrific! My mom and dad will sure be glad to hear that! Hey, did you tell your mom that you won't be in the school play now?"

"I told her last night."

"You don't sound as sad about it as you did yesterday."

"Well, there'll be other plays, won't there, Sandra? And I can always try out for another play."

"Sure—sure, you can. And besides, Daryl didn't get the leading part for the guys anyway. And you wanted to act with him."

Corrie laughed. "You know everything, don't you."

"You sure sound happy today."

"I think I've got spring fever."

"Hey, that's what I've got! Sure hope it's catching and all the teachers get it, too!"

"I have to run now, Sandra. I'll wear my sweater and broomstick skirt. See you when you get here."

Corrie hung up the telephone and began clearing the table. From the bedroom came the sound of the radio and the twins arguing over whose dirty socks were lying on the floor. "You can each pick one up!" she shouted. She swished the dishcloth across the counter tops, and they gleamed in the morning sunlight. She heard a scratching sound at the back door. "Brandy!" She hurried down the steps and opened the storm door. A fragrant aroma rushed inside, friendly, brisk, pleasant. Brandy jumped up, her pink tongue waggled. She gave a small yip of greeting.

"Hi there, Brandy," Corrie said. "Hi there, old girl."

The dog gave another yelp, a happy rumbly sound that rolled up from deep inside her throat. Corrie patted her head, then looked out at the sun-filled yard. The garden was lying far in the back, and now, from this distance, it seemed green again, and ready to grow in the sunshine.

Corrie patted Brandy's head again and smiled. She could smell the coffee and the fresh air and feel the warmth of the dog and hear the laughter of her brothers. Lewie was still busy in her backyard. She looked over at Corrie and waved. "There's no frost on the pumpkins today!" she shouted.

Corrie laughed and nodded. "It feels like spring, Lewie!" she called. Suddenly she felt overwhelmed with happiness and hope. Everything is going to turn out okay, she thought. Everything is going to be just fine!

Corrie felt grand as she hurried down the steps with Sandra. They each decided to just put the sweater on over their shoulders and button only one button, so the rest would dangle down their backs like a cape. They wore identical cotton broomstick skirts, made one hot August afternoon.

"Green looks good on you, Sandra," Corrie said. Casually she looked back and she saw her own sweater swish out behind her as she walked. She felt elegant. Her arms were cold, but the discomfort was worth it because she knew she looked so fine. "Don't you wish we had real capes, though? Long velvet ones?"

"Yeah." Sandra nodded. Then she made a face. "Course I guess I would look like a balloon in a real cape. I wish I was skinny like you."

"Capes look good on everybody, Sandra. Besides, you're not nearly as heavy as you think you are." She shifted her book and her lunch box to her other arm, and she tried to see across the street from the corner of her eye. Would Daryl be walking to school now, too? If only he would see her when she looked so fine!

"You're going to put your eyes out of joint doing

that," Sandra said. "They'll get stuck right in your skin." She flung her hand against her mouth and giggled.

Corrie felt her face flush. "I wasn't doing anything with my eyes."

"You were looking for Daryl. Don't you do the same thing every day? But he's already ahead of us. I saw him on my way to your house. He even spoke to me today, Corrie."

"Oh, Sandra! You saw him? What'd he say? What'd he say?"

Sandra rolled her green eyes. She waggled her pale red eyebrows. Her voice was hushed. "He was wearing a suit of silver armor today, Corrie, and when he saw me, he said, 'Oh, help me, Sandra! Help me! I'm head over heels in love with Corrie Sheldon, and I don't know what to do. Help me because I'm so weak with love that I think I'm going to faint!' "

"Oh, stop it!" Corrie said, laughing. "What'd he really say, Sandra?"

"I said good luck for the big game tonight, and he told me he was hurrying off to school early because the coach had a special plan for the team. They're meeting before school and at lunchtime, too, in the gym, getting set for that game in Stoker City."

"Gosh, I wish I could go to that game tonight, Sandra! The first game, and I guess I'll have to miss it!"

"Darn it, Corrie, I wish we could get a ride. Stoker City's only an hour away."

"It might as well be on the next planet."

"Well, I haven't given up yet. I'm going to ask everybody in school today if they have any room left in their cars. Maybe the two of us can still get to that game."

"Listen," Corrie said. "Why don't we eat our lunch in the gym today? Then, even if we don't get to the game tonight, at least we can see the team getting set for it."

Sandra laughed. "You mean maybe we can at least see Daryl Hanson getting set for it. Oh, don't look so cross-eyed, Corrie! I think he's cute, too. I don't blame you. Anyway, I think it might be good to eat in the gym. It can't smell as bad as that lunch room does! That place smells like rotten orange peelings!"

"Lots of kids eat oranges for lunch, Sandra."

"I suppose I should, too. But I like peanut butter sandwiches too much. Darn it, I wish peanut butter didn't have so many calories."

Corrie raised her right eyebrow. It was a trick she used when she wanted to look extra intelligent. She could change her voice, too, and now she pitched it in a shocked, condescending tone. "My goodness, Sandra! Peanut butter *doesn't* have calories when you eat it in a gymnasium. Didn't you know that?"

Sandra's round face drooped. "Huh?"

"Scientific studies have proved it," Corrie said. "Peanut butter atoms feel the vibrations of all the exertion of physical activity in a gymnasium, and it makes them alter their molecular structure, thereby losing most of their calorie content."

64

"My gosh! I never knew that!" Sandra peered at Corrie. "Are you kidding me? Are you kidding?"

"Would I kid you about a thing like this? Listen, I just read this report in biology class. Professor Haasenstoffer of Ferkle University just—" Corrie was all set to launch into more double-talk, but Sandra looked so intent, she had to laugh instead.

"Oh you!" Sandra shook her head. "Darn you, Corrie! You always sound so serious when you pull those tricks!"

"Well, you were kidding me about Daryl, weren't you?"

"Yeah, but you never fall for my stories. I can't act as good as you can."

"Well anyway," Corrie said. "Let's do eat our lunch in the gym today. That'll be fun."

Sandra was still shaking her head. "I can't get over how you can act the way you do," she said. "You know what, Corrie? I bet that one day you'll be a famous actress."

"What?" Corrie cried in her special British accent. "You want *another* autograph? You little people are so trying to us famous stars!" Giggling, she opened the school door.

At eleven-thirty she hurried down the hall to the gym. The morning had passed in a happy blur. She'd done well on a Latin test, and she had a $B+$ on an English assignment. She could hardly wait to tell Sandra the good news.

But no one was sitting in the ancient gym yet. A few sophomores were tossing a basketball, but Sandra wasn't watching. Corrie leaned against the doorway and let the feeling of the room sink into her being. She would "sharpen her senses" the way Miss Doner had suggested. She loved the smell, the look, the invisible touch of the huge old gym. The floor was worn and the wooden chairs were decrepit, but Corrie thought the room was grand. She could almost hear the roar of a crowd as she stared into the bleachers. She'd been to nearly every home game since she'd been in grade school. This would be her first season as a high school student, though. The idea made her feel grown up and wise. She crossed her arms, and looked into the gym, wondering where Daryl was.

"Hey, Corrie!" Sandra was running up the hall. Her mouth was full, but she was waving a sandwich and shouting, "Corrie! Guess what? Guess what!"

"You got an *A* on your math test!"

"Nope—something even better than that!" Sandra wiped her hand across her mouth. "I got us a ride to Stoker City tonight. Both of us!"

"You did? Really? You're not kidding?"

"No kidding, Corrie!" Sandra was so excited she was nearly hopping. "Rosmund Wolfe said her dad could take two more kids in their car!"

"Oh Sandra, that's great! I'll ask my mom after school if it's okay."

"But Rosmund has to know now, Corrie, because other kids need a ride, too."

"Now?" Corrie twisted a button on her sweater.

"Gosh, Sandra, I can't call my mom now. She's at work."

"Well can't you call her there?"

"She can't get calls at work. Mr. Peterson has a fit because he says he's got to keep the telephone line open for his customers. She can only get called in an emergency."

"Well, shoot," Sandra said, slumping. "Shoot."

"Unless—" Corrie felt a new hope. "Unless I ran down to the shop right now and asked her. I still have forty minutes, and I can eat this sandwich on the way."

"And I found out that the coach is only going to talk to the guys, so we wouldn't miss anything here anyway."

"We?"

"Well, sure, Corrie, I'll walk to the shop with you. I've already nearly eaten most of my sandwiches anyway. The walk might help me lose some weight."

"Of course it will!" Corrie said, guiding Sandra to the hall door. "Why, Professor Miffintick of Waxendiefer University says—"

"Beans!" Sandra said, laughing. "Come on, kid, let's get going."

It was even warmer outside now, although some clouds had started to cover the sunlight. Corrie walked down Main Street eating a cookie and feeling that the day was turning out to be just as fine as she had thought it would.

"I'm glad you're coming with me, Sandra," she

said, unwrapping a sandwich. "I don't like that Mr. Peterson very much."

"He's looked grouchy every time I've seen him."

"He *is* grouchy! I don't know how my mother stands to work for him. He acts like life is a disease."

"A disease!" Sandra nearly choked as she swallowed her last bite of apple.

"Yeah. I guess that's sort of a dumb way to say it. But I can't think how else to explain him. You try to stay away from a disease, right? It's something you try to avoid. Well, that's how Mr. Peterson does with everything in life. He lives upstairs over that dusty old shop of his. He never even leaves the building at night. He hardly knows anybody—he never goes anywhere."

"People say he's rich."

"Rich? What's rich, I'd like to know. Maybe he's got scads of money, but is that rich? *I* sure don't think so. My dad doesn't think so either. Mr. Peterson is lonely and grouchy, and nobody likes him. He pays my mother pretty good, so she works for him. But even my mother doesn't like him very much." Corrie finished her sandwich, balled up the waxed paper, and stuck it in her purse. "I don't know how my mother can stand to work there."

"What'd they make in that tent shop anyway?"

"Bathing suits," Corrie answered, grinning. "My mother says they make bathing suits for fat ladies like her."

Sandra laughed. "Your mother is always making

jokes about her weight."

"You do too, Sandra."

"Yeah, but I don't mean my jokes."

"Neither does my mother." Corrie jumped over a crack on the sidewalk. They were passing in front of the Lerner Hotel now. Old Mr. Waverly was sitting on the porch. She would never be as old as he was. Never, never, never!

"I hope she'll let you go tonight."

"Oh, I think she will. It's payday. She's always in a good mood on Fridays because she has some money then."

"Yeah, and you haven't been anywhere in ages. Almost every night you've been to that hospital."

Corrie stumbled. She felt her stomach tighten up inside, and her throat got all hard. "The hospital! My dad! Oh, Sandra, I almost forgot about my dad!" She kept on moving, but she no longer saw the sidewalk. Everything around her blurred. "I forgot!"

Sandra ran her hand across her mouth. "Forgot?"

Corrie started walking faster, twisting the button at the bottom of her sweater. "I mean I haven't hardly thought about him today. And I was making plans to go out to the basketball game tonight."

Sandra hurried along beside her. "Well isn't that all right, Corrie? I mean, what's wrong with that?"

Corrie shook her head. "It makes me feel awful, Sandra. To think that I got so excited about that game that I didn't even think about visiting my dad. It makes me feel awful!"

69

"But Corrie—you have to think about other things sometimes, too. You can't always be thinking about your dad."

"But I've been trying not to have selfish ideas. Can't you see that, Sandra? I was thinking that if I didn't think about the things I want to have, the things I want to do, then Daddy might get better faster."

"But that's crazy, Corrie. What you're thinking about can't make any difference to your dad's sickness."

"Oh, I *hate* this sickness!"

"I know you do. Everybody does, Corrie."

Corrie stopped at the traffic signal. The clouds had covered the sun now, and she shivered under her sweater. "You don't know what I mean, Sandra. You don't know what I mean. I have some awful thoughts."

The light turned green. They started across the street. Sandra cleared her throat.

"Well, tell me, then. Tell me what you think."

Corrie bit her bottom lip. "I guess I hate the sickness for all the wrong reasons. I mean, I should hate it for my father's sake, and I do. He's sick and he's helpless and he's miserable. And then there's my mother—I should hate it for her sake, too. She has to work in that awful tent shop, and she's so tired and worried all the time. We had to sell our car and that land by the lake that Grampa left us so that we could pay for all our bills."

70

"Well that sounds all right, Corrie. I mean, that's the way anyone would think."

"But that's not all!" Corrie stared straight ahead. "Don't you see, Sandra? I hate it sometimes for those reasons I just said. But most of all, most all of the time, I hate it because it's spoiling things for me!"

As Corrie said the last word, she felt tears flood her eyes. She was horrified that she had let the awful idea creep out. It had been crawling around inside her brain for weeks, but she had been too ashamed to give it real form, make it even more real by putting it into words. The idea seemed so selfish—so unfeeling and so selfish. But now she had spoken out the whole truth, and Sandra would see her for what she was. Sandra would be shocked and ashamed. Corrie looked at the buildings. They were passing Farrel's Restaurant. Nervously she glanced at Sandra.

"I'm sorry I said that. It was an awful thing to say. I'm sorry I said that, Sandra."

"I know what you mean, though. You didn't get to go to the football games like you wanted to. And now you're giving up the school play."

"But those things seem so dumb." She sensed that her voice sounded as miserable as she felt.

"But they're important too, Corrie." Sandra stared straight ahead, and now she spoke more quickly. "I know what you mean, all right. Oh, I know what you mean, Corrie. It's just like how I feel about my grampa. He visits for three months every summer.

I love him and all, I really do, but here's the thing. He gets my bedroom those three months, and I have to sleep in with my little sister. She drives me crazy. Her closet isn't big enough for both of us and sometimes she wets the bed." Sandra's freckled face was flushed. She walked more quickly.

"And the air in my room gets all funny, too. Grampa smokes cigars, and it makes my things smell awful for months and months, even after he's gone away to spend his time at Aunt Alice's. I hate it, Corrie. I love my grampa, but I hate so many things that happen when he comes that sometimes I wish he wouldn't come at all. He's old and helpless, Corrie, and that's an awful thing for me to say, but there it is."

Corrie felt lighter, suddenly freer. "I never knew you felt that way about your grampa, Sandra."

"Well, why should I ever say such things? They make me sound terrible, don't they? Selfish and awful?"

"But I think anyone would feel that way."

"And anyone would feel the way you do too, Corrie!"

"Maybe," Corrie answered. "Maybe they would. It's just that I've been so mixed up lately. I mean, I can't think why my dad has to be sick like this. What good is life if people who are good have to suffer the way he's been suffering?"

Sandra sighed. They walked across another street.

"Because my dad *is* good," Corrie went on.

"That's what gets me so mixed up. If he should die—" She quickly stopped herself, and breathlessly added, "Of course he *won't,* but just suppose he did—well, then all the good he ever did would die right there with him. Can you figure that out, Sandra? Can you?"

A car horn honked and brakes squealed. Two boys in an ancient car came cruising near the curb. Corrie saw that the driver was Lyle Dodd. Sandra had been talking about him for weeks. He leaned across his friend and shouted out the window. "Hey, Freshies! Are you two tired of walking?"

Sandra's face brightened. "Well, yes, Lyle. Sort of."

"Then *run* a while!" Lyle shouted, laughing. He gunned the motor, and the car went roaring down the street.

"Oh that Lyle!" Sandra's face was bright red. "He thinks he's so smart, now that he can drive!"

Corrie started to giggle. "Well, it was kind of funny, Sandra. What he said, I mean." She stared after the speeding car. "And you know what? He must like you a little bit, Sandra, or he wouldn't of done what he just did."

Sandra shook her head. "But I thought he meant he'd pick us up," she said ruefully. Then she started to grin. "Oh, I'll get back at him! You just watch. Gee, Corrie, do you think he'll be at the game tonight? Maybe his dad will let him drive to Stoker City."

"He sure gets to drive all over town."

"Oh, it'll be such fun tonight! Gosh, Corrie, your mom has just *got* to let you go to that game!"

"I think she will," Corrie said. Her glance fell to the sidewalk. She jumped over a crack. Step on a crack, you might break your mother's back. "I bet my mom will let me go, all right."

Sandra did a happy skip. "Oh, we'll have such fun! It's been ages since we really had fun together."

"Fun?" Corrie wiped the happiness from her face. She pinched her mouth together and raised her eyebrows. "My dear young woman, do you realize how many calories there are in fun?"

Sandra flung her hand to her mouth. "You're driving me crazy, Professor Hasen—Hosen—Whosenwhatever you are!"

Corrie wiggled her eyebrows and burst out with her German accent. "You forget with whom it is you speak? What a dumbkoff! I, Professor Bonkleport of Witzgerkeef University!"

Giggling, they hurried down the street.

Corrie and Sandra stood for a moment staring at the sign.

PETERSON'S
TENT AND AWNING SHOP

It hung over an unpainted wooden building in the poorer section of Pointer. The door to the shop had a broken window that had been haphazardly patched with black masking tape. The display case was filmed with dirt and dust.

"What a wreck this place is!" Sandra said.

"It didn't used to be so bad, I guess. My mom said that Mr. Peterson used to be in business with his son, but they had a big fight and the son left town."

"You'd think he'd try to clean it up a bit, wouldn't you?" Sandra gestured at the scattered papers, the broken pop bottles.

"I'd better hurry inside," Corrie said. "Lunch is nearly over." She put her hand on the door latch, then hesitated. "Would you rather wait out here, Sandra? I'll only take a minute to talk to my mother." She looked down at the sidewalk. "I'm afraid Mr. Peterson might have a fit if you come inside with me. Momma says he's always muttering about people tromping in and out to see her."

"Don't worry about me, kid." Sandra crossed her arms and leaned against the building. "I'd rather wait out here anyway."

Corrie willed herself not to see the gloom and the grime as she stepped inside the door. Darkness swooped down on her. There was the smell of dirt, decay, the feel of hopelessness.

"What'll you have?" Mr. Peterson came moving toward her. He was frowning and sighing.

"My mother," Corrie said. Her eyes were getting more accustomed to the darkness now. She saw the heaps of canvases that were waiting for repairs.

"Oh," the man said, peering down at her through his thick glasses. "I didn't recognize you there in the dark. Another of them darned bulbs burned out. Nothing's any good anymore. The whole world is going to the dogs, and there's nothing a body can do." He raised his voice. "Verna! Verna! Your girl wants to talk to you."

Corrie heard the whir of a sewing machine suddenly stop. She quietly followed Mr. Peterson.

"Corrie?" Her mother's voice came from the darkness. "Is that you, Corrie?"

Mrs. Sheldon sat at a huge machine in the corner of the workshop, hunched over a large canvas. There were no windows; a ceiling light flickered fitfully. A small table light sat near the sewing area. Mrs. Sheldon was the only worker—the other machines were covered with dust, with cobwebs.

"What are you doing out of school?" Mrs. Sheldon

76

jumped to her feet. The terror in her voice pierced the gloom. The light of the small lamp caught her face. It was pale, almost sickly white, and it was stricken with fear. "Is it your father, Corrie? Did the hospital call?"

"Oh Momma! No, no, it's nothing like that!" Corrie felt a stab of pain in her throat. "It's nothing like that, Momma, nothing like that!"

Mrs. Sheldon heaved out a long breath. She straightened her shoulders and rubbed her palms against the sides of her brown dress. Her voice was nearly normal. "What's the trouble, Corrie?"

"There isn't any trouble, Momma. It's just that I wanted to ask you something. Rosmund Wolfe's dad said he could take Sandra and me to the game tonight if I can go. Can I go?"

"The game?"

"Yes, Momma. It's our first basketball game. At Stoker City."

"Oh." Mrs. Sheldon wiped her palms against the sides of her dress again, and then nodded. "Why, I guess so, Corrie. That might be good for you, child. Mr. Wolfe's a good driver. Of course you can go."

"Oh, thank you, Momma! Thank you!"

"I'll be home early today, too, so you won't have to make dinner tonight. You'll have lots of time to get ready for the game." Mrs. Sheldon smiled. "You need a night out, child. You need to get out."

Corrie wanted to lean over the table and kiss her mother, but Mr. Peterson was glaring at them. She shifted her weight to her other foot. "But you think it's all right, Momma? Really all right? I won't get to see Daddy tonight."

"There's no need for you to go to the hospital every night," Mrs. Sheldon said. "Besides, Daddy would want to have you go to that first game. Then you can tell him all about it. Scoot now, Corrie—I have a lot to do before I go home today." She wiped her hands again and sat down. The whir of the sewing machine started up.

Mr. Peterson guided Corrie back through the gloom to the door. "It must be hard for you all," he said, "what with your Pa being sick the way he is."

"He's getting better," Corrie said.

"But I was thinking of the money. Them doctor bills of yours must be sky high. And your Pa was never too good at handling money, now, was he." Mr. Peterson shook his head.

Corrie felt her own palms flood with sweat.

"Well, maybe he's learned his lesson the hard way," Mr. Peterson went on. "Maybe once he's out of the hospital this time, he'll act more like a family man. Life's a serious business—people ought to realize that." He opened the door and Corrie stepped out into the light. The door rattled shut behind her.

"What'd she say? What'd she say?" Sandra cried.

"She said okay." Corrie started walking. Everything around her was hazy and unreal.

"Well, gosh, Corrie, you sure don't look very happy about it."

"I'm happy about *that,* all right. It's just that Mr. Peterson. He makes me feel all creepy and dirty."

"Oh, beans, Corrie. Why listen to anything that old jerk says?"

Corrie crossed the street. The light was red, but she didn't care. "He said something about my dad." Corrie forced himself to blurt out the rest of it. "He said that my dad didn't handle money very well."

For a moment Sandra said nothing. Then she shrugged her shoulders. "So what if he said that?"

"So what!" Corrie stumbled on the sidewalk.

"Sure. I mean, what do you care if he thinks that?"

"Well, gosh, Sandra. It's just that—it's just that I thought everybody liked my dad. I thought everyone thought he was just perfect."

"Nearly everybody *does* like your dad. But nobody's perfect, Corrie. Nobody."

"Of course my mother always worries about how Daddy handles money, but it's okay for her to say it, because she loves him anyway."

"Oh, what the heck, Corrie! You can't go around worrying about the things that everybody says. Let's forget old grouchy Peterson. Let's think about tonight!"

The buildings around Corrie had gradually become real again. She saw that they were passing Farrel's Restaurant. The odor of hamburgers came drifting to the street. They were having a special in there today—eight hamburgers for a dollar.

"Maybe Lyle will be there," Sandra was saying.

"And of course Daryl will. Gosh, Corrie, it—"

"Hey you guys! Corrie! Sandra! Wait up!"

Sandra turned around. Her rosy face puckered. "Oh shoot, it's dumb old Elaine Moore!"

Corrie sighed. Elaine Moore! She was all they needed to make a lousy noon hour complete. Of course she had long ago forgiven Elaine for that afternoon on the playground. But she still didn't like her very much. In lots of ways she pitied her. Elaine tried so hard to be liked by everyone that no one liked her at all. She always said the wrong things, it seemed, always did the wrong things, too.

"Isn't this a great day!" She came bounding up now in a skirt that was too short, in bobby socks that bagged, and in a sweater that was slightly dirty. She was panting and brushing back her tangled blond hair. Elaine never set her hair like the other girls did every night; she never suffered with bobby pins or those hand metal curlers. She just let her hair fly, and then she moaned to everybody that her hair was a mess. No matter what happened to her, though, Elaine always told everyone that it was not her fault. Corrie supposed it was this trait that annoyed her most of all. She liked people who felt they could make a difference in the things that happened, who felt their actions and their thoughts were truly important.

"I ain't got my Latin done again," Elaine said now, falling into step with them. "Them darn sisters of mine was so noisy at lunch that I couldn't think straight. Where you guys been?"

80

"We went downtown for a few minutes," Corrie said.

Elaine snapped her gum. "I like you kidses outfits. Wish I had a cardigan sweater."

"We bought these with money we made ourselves when we picked cherries last summer," Sandra said. "And we made the skirts ourselves. You could have done the same, Elaine."

Elaine shrugged. She looked eagerly at Corrie. "How's your dad? I lit a prayer candle for him when I was at church yesterday."

"A prayer candle?" Corrie stumbled on the sidewalk. "What's that?"

"It's what we got in our church. They're little prayer candles that you can buy. Father puts a blessing on the big candle, then you light the little candle off from it and you say a prayer and then it comes true."

Sandra's steps were slowing. "You prayed that Corrie's dad would get well?"

"Yup." Elaine nodded and snapped her gum again. "I got to thinking about him when I was at church, and so I did it."

"He did seem better last night," Corrie said.

"Well, that's why then," Elaine told her. "My prayer is coming true."

Corrie looked at Sandra. She was Methodist, Sandra was Baptist—and hadn't the two of them been praying for things all their lives? But their prayers hadn't been so easily answered. Hadn't they been praying since the fourth grade that Sandra's teeth would straighten out? But they were still the same. And at the hospital, when Corrie sat at the foot of the bed and prayed silently for her father, hadn't he looked just the same? Were Catholic prayers better somehow?

"It costs a whole dime," Elaine said loudly. "I was going to buy two candy bars with it. But if your dad feels better now, why I guess it was worth it."

"A dime!" Corrie felt anger flood her body. "Of *course* my dad is worth a dime!"

"Then why don't you go to my church and pray the way I did?" Elaine shaded her eyes and stared at a figure walking across the street. "Your dad might really get well fast if a whole bunch of us bought candles and said prayers."

"But I'm not Catholic," Corrie said. "Can I—"

"Oh, that's Morris Bates!" Elaine turned away. "I got to talk to him about math. See you guys later." She ran across the street, calling as she hurried.

"Poor Morris," Sandra said.

But Corrie couldn't think about poor Morris now. She was thinking of what Elaine had said. Could it be true? Would a candle lighted in the Catholic Church really help make her father well again? Corrie frowned. Maybe this whole thing had happened this way so that she would go to the Catholic church, she thought. Maybe God wanted her to go there and light a candle. She could go after school and still have lots of time to get ready for the game.

"Corrie? Are you listening? I said what time can you be at my house tonight?"

Corrie brushed away the question. "Listen, Sandra, maybe Elaine had a good idea! Maybe I *should* go to her church and say a prayer for Daddy. I could go right after school today!"

Sandra looked doubtful. "Gosh, Corrie, you're not a Catholic. Do you think you can do that?"

"Well, people who aren't Methodists come to my church all the time. Sure, I bet I can do that. The Catholic church must be like everybody else's church."

"I've always wondered what that church looked like on the inside," Sandra said. She ran her hand across her mouth. "Do you really think you'll go, Corrie?"

"Yes. I'm going for sure. I'll use the money I saved from lunch today to buy the candle."

"Gosh, Corrie, I still have my dime, too. Do you think I should go with you?"

"Oh, that'd be great, Sandra! Then we can both light candles and say a prayer for my dad. That'd be great!"

"And then we'll hurry home and get ready for the game," Sandra said. "Oh, Corrie, won't we have fun!"

Corrie shivered. Black clouds were covering the sun now, and a cold wind had started to blow. "Sure we'll have fun, Sandra. But hurry up—it's getting colder and colder. Come on, I'll race you back to the school!"

 "Do you think we should just walk right in?"

Corrie jumped at the sound of Sandra's question. She'd been staring at the door of the Catholic church wondering what to do. Her confidence had faded with the November sunlight, and now she felt as undecided as the weather. The warm sun had disappeared completely, the day was suddenly cold and dark. Both girls were shivering, even though they had put their sweaters on and completely buttoned them.

"It looks bigger here than I thought it would look," Sandra said, peering around. "Funny how when you pass this church from the sidewalk, the door doesn't look this big."

"Yeah." Corrie hesitated. The door was heavy and ancient, with carvings and peculiar symbols. It seemed to bear the imprints of a thousand fingers upon its tarnished brass handles.

"Do you think a Protestant ever went in here before?" Sandra asked. She giggled, and Corrie recalled that Sandra always got giggly and acted silly when she was nervous. Her face was so pale now that her freckles seemed to pop out of her skin. "Do you think if we knocked, a nun would open the door?"

A cold wind whipped Corrie's cotton skirt. She put her hand on the latch. "I guess we should just go in, Sandra. That's what you do at other churches." She only planned to open the door a crack, but the wind pushed against her as she pressed the latch, and she was propelled forward into the church. Sandra was shoved in behind her, and, as if by magic itself, they were both completely inside the Catholic church. The door slammed behind them.

Shivering and blinking, the two of them stared around the empty sanctuary. It loomed around them and above them and beyond them in frightening splendor. Stained-glass windows colored the meager light from the outside, and Corrie felt small and scared. Statues high on pedestals lined the walls; they stared down with frozen faces. Strange utensils and tapestries hung over the alter rail far to the front. A huge crucifix with an agonized Christ faced them, and high, high overhead beautiful paintings of Biblical characters stared down at them.

Corrie caught her breath and looked back at the crucifix again. For a moment it seemed to her that the face of Christ was like her father's. She shook her head, and the vision vanished. It was just a statue after all. She trembled as the hugeness of the church overwhelmed her. Her mission and her very self felt dwarfed by the glory everywhere. She was almost afraid to look to the center of the domed ceiling— God Himself might be looking down.

Sandra cleared her throat. The echo of the noise

dashed against the empty pews and went scurrying up and down the aisles. "It's sure big in here," she whispered.

Corrie nodded mutely. Frantically she was staring about, searching to remember the little she knew about Catholicism, trying to put together what she saw with what she knew. She had to be certain that they did everything properly. Everything had to be perfect. There was a pedestal nearby holding a large bowl of water.

"I think that's holy water," she told Sandra. "I think we're supposed to get our fingers in it and rub it on our foreheads."

Sandra crossed and put her hand inside the bowl. "It's cold," she whispered. Then, as Corrie drew closer, she giggled. "If it freezes in there, do you think the Catholics call it *pope*sicles?"

"Sandra!" Corrie hurriedly glanced around the empty church. Jokes seemed sacrilegious in a place like this. She knew Sandra always made stupid comments when she was nervous or afraid, but still, she wasn't sure that God knew that.

"I just remembered something," Sandra said. "It's Friday today, and we haven't eaten any meat. We both had peanut butter sandwiches for lunch."

"Yes, that's probably good," Corrie whispered. She stared at the front of the church. There, at the far right corner, she saw a few candles burning. "That must be what we want," she said quietly. "But I think we're supposed to kneel or something before we can walk up to the front of a Catholic Church."

Sandra ran her hand across her mouth. She awkwardly bent her knees. Corrie followed. Then they started forward, their shoes clanking on the uncarpeted side aisle.

"This is it all right," Corrie said, when they reached the corner. The two of them stared at the long table, arranged in tiers. Several large candles were lighted on the bottom row, and two very small candles had burned themselves out closer on the top of the tiers. There were two dimes on a white saucer beside the unused small candles.

"I guess you just put your dime in there and take a candle," Sandra said. "The big candles must be the ones that Elaine said the Fathers bless."

At that moment a small door opened at the side of the altar. "Do you need any help, children?" a priest asked.

"No. No, thank you," Corrie whispered. "We're just going to light a candle." She swallowed, then quickly added. "We both have dimes."

"May God hear your prayers," the priest said softly. The door silently closed.

Corrie's hand was shaking when she placed her dime in the dish. "Start praying," she whispered to Sandra, and Sandra's dime clinked against the others.

The tiny candle flickered into immediate flame when it touched the larger candle. Corrie put it beside the other small candles, clutched her hands together, pressed her lips tight, and started praying.

87

"Make Daddy well, make Daddy well, make Daddy well. Please God, make my father well again. Let him be happy about his garden again. Please let his garden grow again . . ." She repeated the words over and over in her mind as she stared at the light, and soon she was unable to separate her thoughts from the flickering flame. They all became one, and she was controlled by the tiny orange blaze dancing in front of her.

Anything seemed possible at that moment—she felt obsessed with the power surging from the light. It seared into her soul, and strength poured through her body. "Make Daddy well . . . Let his garden grow again . . ."

Then the flame fluttered out.

Corrie shook her head, still seeing, for a few instants, the image of the flame burning in her mind. All her life she had wondered about God—about how he looked and where he lived. Now she was almost sure that she had some answers. For a few brief moments she was certain that God was a brilliant light that lived all around her. She merely had to turn and look, and the outline of God would still be there. She felt warm and secure.

Then suddenly the image was gone and she saw the darkening church. Pain was rushing through her fingers. She had held her hands so tightly during her prayers that now her fingers throbbed. Sandra had started back down the aisle. Corrie turned, stumbling, and followed her back to the church entrance.

An old woman had entered while they had been praying. She stood now near the back, crossing herself and mumbling. Corrie quickly whirled around and crossed herself, too. The idea that God was everywhere, was obvious and waiting, disappeared. God was a finicky old man who had to be wooed by a hundred crazy things that meant nothing at all to Corrie.

Still, though, she had done everything she should have done. She was sure of that. Surely God understood that. Surely now he would answer her prayer.

When the two of them were outside again, they stood leaning against the huge door, gasping against the wind. It was getting dark now, and the taste of snow was in the air. Neither girl spoke. At that moment, still entangled in the hope and faith of a miracle, Corrie almost expected her father, fully restored to health and vigor, to come happily walking toward her. A figure, in fact, *was* coming up the walk.

But it was only Lynwood Clark. He ran the last few steps. "Hey! I thought it was you two guys! I didn't know you was Catholic."

Reality drove away the last shred of her vision. Corrie glanced at Sandra, and Sandra's face showed exactly what she herself was thinking. Lynwood Clark was a pest and a braggart. His only claim to fame was that he still lived after having been a blue baby at birth. Now, thirteen years later, he still talked about it proudly, as though his survival at that age had been something that he, alone, had accomplished.

"We're not Catholic," Corrie said. "I just went in there to pray." Anxiously she leaned forward. Lynwood, after all, was a Catholic and he might tell her something she should know. "Anyone can light a candle in there and say a prayer, can't they?"

The boy shrugged his skinny shoulders. His face was pointed and, occasionally it seemed to Corrie, still faintly blue. "Can't you pray in your own church?"

"Well of course she can," Sandra said. "But we wanted to light a candle."

"Oh, *that!*" Lynwood reached past the girls to the door handle. "My mom's always doing that, too. She's lighted candles for me to have a baby brother at least a hundred times. But it's never happened."

Corrie felt a huge emptiness erupt inside her stomach. "It never happened! Even after she paid dimes and lighted candles?"

"Nope." Lynwood pulled on the door. "And I bet she's lighted a thousand of them. Well, I'll see you two—I got to get inside and get my gramma. She's in there praying for the war to end."

"But the war did end," Sandra said. "It ended last summer."

"I know that, and you know that, but my gramma, she don't know that." Lynwood made a circular motion around his ear. "She got started praying that the war would end and now she can't quit."

Corrie grabbed his arm. "But those candle prayers—aren't they always supposed to come true? When you pay a dime for those candles, isn't God supposed to answer?"

"Well, Father says God does answer all them prayers. But he says that sometimes God answers 'no' to whatever it was you asked. So that's what happens. You always get an answer, but sometimes you might not like the answer you get."

Sandra leaned forward. "But don't *most* prayers come true?"

Lynwood yanked his arm away and glared at them. "How should I know? I don't know everything that goes on in this church. But I do know one prayer that came true all right. When I was born, my ma prayed that I'd be okay, and I am, ain't I?" He stuck out his tongue and ducked inside the church.

Sandra stared at the empty doorway. "I'm not so sure about that!" she called. Then she turned to Corrie and ran her hand across her mouth. "Oh, don't listen to him, Corrie. What does he know? Don't pay any attention to him. God's going to answer our prayer all right—God's going to answer it."

Corrie nodded. She felt cold and puzzled. Her hands were drenched in sweat, and she shivered in the cold wind. They slowly began walking east. A few lights flickered on in houses along the way. Corrie walked silently. In the distance, the foghorn began to bellow mournfully. Had all the good things she had felt during her prayers been just her imagination?

"It seemed funny to see Christ on the cross," Sandra said. "In my church the cross is bare."

Corrie turned to her. "You know something really funny? For a second in there I thought that the face of Christ looked just like my dad."

"Gosh!" Sandra said. They walked a few more steps in silence, then Corrie cleared her throat. "Sandra—remember Lynwood's gramma? Remember how he said she prayed about the war ending? Do you think God heard her prayers?"

"I guess he hears all prayers. That's what our preacher says."

"Then how can he separate the good prayers from the crazy ones? I mean, our prayer was a good one, but Lynwood's gramma's was crazy. The war is already over, Sandra. It's crazy to pray that the war will be over."

"He must know the difference between good prayers and crazy ones."

"Well, what about Lynwood's mother, then? Wasn't her prayer a good one?" Corrie grabbed at Sandra's arm. She could hear the pleading in her own voice and willed it not to be there, but it came out anyway. "Didn't it make you worry when you heard what Lynwood said?"

Sandra's footsteps grew louder and she walked faster. "Oh, that stupid Lynwood!" she said. "You shouldn't have listened to him, Corrie. What does he know about religion? What does he know about prayers? His father's a drunk. Everybody in town knows that. We shouldn't even be talking about him and his dumb family. We should be thinking about how it was with our own prayers."

"I felt good when my candle was burning," Corrie said. "I felt like our prayers might come true."

"Me too," Sandra told her. "I felt sort of like God was right there—right there sitting with us."

"Oh, I did too," Corrie cried. She was filled with new hope. It couldn't have been just her imagination if Sandra felt it too!

"And I been thinking," Sandra went on. "My aunt prayed and prayed for my uncle to come home from the war safe. She told us she lighted all kinds of candles. Everybody told her he was dead, but she kept on lighting candles anyway. And then when the war was done, why they found my uncle in a prison camp in Japan. So there you are. That prayer came true all right."

Corrie held her head higher. "And my father's a good person. Maybe that makes a difference. Lynwood's dad isn't. That could be why they never got that baby Mrs. Clark prayed for. Mr. Clark drinks all the time and gets fired from jobs, and he cheated on war rations and I don't know what all."

"Sure, that's it, I'll bet," Sandra said. "God can't go around answering every prayer from every person. He must just answer them for good people."

Walking close together now, there was a warm

glow in their mutual agreement. They giggled about the dumb things that Lynwood had done during their years of grade school, and they repeated that it was no wonder that God never listened to the prayers of his family. When they came to Sandra's corner, she stopped and started to giggle.

"Listen, kid, don't be mad, but just before my candle went out, I said one quick prayer that wasn't about your dad."

"What? What was it about, Sandra?"

Sandra giggled again. "I prayed that Daryl Hanson would start to like you."

Corrie felt her mouth drop open. "You nut!" she said, laughing. "You crazy nut!"

"Well I figured it wouldn't hurt anything, Corrie. Nothing else we've thought of has ever worked."

Corrie shook her head. "It would take a real miracle for that to happen. But anyway, thanks for trying. Listen, Sandra, I'll see you in a bit. I'll be at your house by six-thirty."

"Okay—see you then."

Corrie ran up the hill to her house, smiling at what Sandra had done. She felt happy about the game, too. But there was plenty that she would have to do at home first. The boys would be home from school by now, of course, and they probably would be fighting or eating bread covered with brown sugar. Both were strictly forbidden, but the two ignored rules when no one was around to enforce them. Maybe her mother wouldn't be home from work yet, and she'd have to start something for supper. Her mother'd want to hear all about the Catholic church, too.

Still half a block away, Corrie saw that her house looked dark. The sight filled her with sour fear, and she dashed up the steps as fast as her tired legs would carry her. Arthur and Alan always turned on the lights at the first sign of darkness. Something had to be terribly wrong—

She flung open the kitchen door. In the half darkness she saw a note lying on the table. It was written in her mother's frantic hand:

> Corrie—hospital called work—
> Daddy very bad—boys at Lewie's house.
> *Mom*

Corrie caught her breath. She threw the note on the floor and tore out the back door again. Not even stopping to seize a coat, she began running the twelve blocks to the hospital.

Corrie threw back the curtain near her father's bed. She hardly knew how she'd gotten to the hospital; hadn't felt the winter winds, hadn't seen the snow. She'd thought only of her father.

Mrs. Sheldon was leaning over him. The dark hues of her clothes made him appear even whiter. She stood up suddenly when the curtain moved. "Corrie! Corrie—what are you doing here?"

Still panting, Corrie stared at her father. He lay like a wax figure, flat on the bed, the sheets over his chest barely moving. Dark circles under his eyes were the only color on his face. He seemed much more frail than he had the day before. Another needle and a tube was attached to his right arm.

"The note!" Corrie panted. "How's Daddy? How's Daddy?"

Mrs. Sheldon took a step closer. "Mercy, child, I didn't mean for you to run all the way up here like this. You look frozen to death, Corrie. You should—"

"But, Momma! 'How's Daddy,' I said. 'How's Daddy?'"

"He's better now." Mrs. Sheldon bit her lip. She stared at the potted plant. "The doctor said his heart stopped—that's why they called me like they did." She took a deep breath. "He's had another shot."

Corrie began taking great gulps of air. Her father's heart had stopped! Maybe while she was in the middle of her prayers for him! Shudders ran over her body.

"Are you all right, child? Are you sick?"

"No, no, I'm all right, Momma." Still panting, Corrie lowered herself into the chair at the foot of the bed. It was only then that she felt the stabs of pain in her chest.

"You look scared to death," Mrs. Sheldon said, moving closer. "It's my fault, I guess, leaving you that note the way I did. It's just that I was almost out of my wits after I got that call. I flew home and got the boys settled at Lewie's house, and I only thought to scribble that note to you as I started out the door. I—" She stopped. "Oh Corrie! The basketball game! I forgot all about that! You were supposed to go to the basketball game with Sandra tonight!"

"It's okay," Corrie said. "I don't want to go. It's okay." She took another deep breath. "What made his heart do that? Stop, I mean. Is he really all right, Momma? Is he really going to be all right?"

Mrs. Sheldon blinked. She ran the palms of her hands against the sides of her brown dress. Corrie saw that her mother's eyes were red and watery. She jumped to her feet. "Is he all right, I said, Momma. Is he really going to be all right now?"

"Corrie—Corrie—" Mrs. Sheldon clenched her hands together and bit her bottom lip. She looked away, then she looked back again. "He's suffering so much, Corrie. You've got to think of that. He's suffering so much."

"I know that. Can't I see that, Momma? But he's going to be all right some day, isn't he? And then everything will be just like it used to be." She leaned forward. "That's what I prayed in the Catholic church today, Momma."

Mrs. Sheldon blinked again. "The Catholic church?"

"Sandra and I went there right after school. That's why I was kind of late getting home. We paid a dime for a candle, and we lighted it from a candle that the Fathers bless. So the prayer will come true, Momma. It'll come true!"

"I've prayed too, you know, Corrie."

"We all have, Momma. I know that. But this kind of prayer is special. Elaine Moore prayed yesterday that Daddy would be better, and didn't Daddy seem better to us last night?"

"Maybe we only thought he looked better, child." Mrs. Sheldon caught a deep breath. "Maybe we wanted so much for him to be better that we only dreamed he looked better." She lowered her head and smoothed down the already smooth bedspread. "But my goodness, Corrie, it sounds as though you've been running all day, child. Did you get anything to eat at home?"

Corrie shook her head.

Mrs. Sheldon looked at her watch. "And it's after

six o'clock. I'll ask the nurses if they can give me a glass of milk for you."

"It doesn't matter," Corrie said.

"Well, you need something, child. You look like a ghost." Mrs. Sheldon started for the door. She stopped at the curtain. "You might still be able to get to the game, Corrie. Would you like me to call Sandra and ask them to pick you up here?"

"No." Miserably Corrie shook her head. "I don't want to go to that dumb old game, Momma. I don't want to go. Call Sandra and tell her I don't want to go."

Mrs. Sheldon's face contorted into that same peculiar look that the nurses all had. "I'll go get you some milk, child," she said. Her footsteps went echoing down the corridor.

One . . . two . . . three . . . four . . . five . . . scuff.
One . . . two . . . three . . . four . . . five . . . scuff.

Corrie dropped back into her chair. She leaned forward, toward her father. His face was ravaged, like that face in the Catholic church. Could it be that pain made all human faces seem the same? "Daddy," she whispered. "Daddy?" But the figure remained motionless.

A door opened and more footsteps clanked past the curtain. Visitors were coming in. At one time her father had had lots of friends and visitors too, but now the hospital only allowed the family to come. He still got cards from dozens of people, though. A pile of them lay right now on the table beside his bed. People wrote cheery notes that he no longer was able to read. But they still sent them.

It was because he was so wonderful, Corrie thought, so kind and so funny to everyone he met. He always had a smile, a joke, a story for a friend. And everyone he met was his friend. He gave so much, too—his thoughts, his affection, his money.

Most of all he gave his money. That trait was the biggest reason for quarrels in the Sheldon household.

"Joe! You gave that man five dollars?" Mrs. Sheldon had moaned this a hundred times through the years. "You just up and gave a perfect stranger five dollars?" She would bite her bottom lip and wring her hands.

"Well, he needed it," Mr. Sheldon would tell her. "His wife's sick," or "His baby's due."

"But what about us?" Mrs. Sheldon would ask. "Don't we get sick? Don't we need a vacation? Didn't we just have a baby? Two of them! You know how hard things can get, Joe. Why not save the few extra dollars we have? We may need them for a rainy day. Why throw money away by giving it to strangers?"

"Oh, they'll pay me when they can," Mr. Sheldon always answered.

And pay they did. Corrie remembered envelopes arriving with all kinds of strange postmarks—cities far from Pointer, Michigan. Her mother would look amazed, but her father would merely laugh. He said that most people always tried to pay their debts. The envelopes usually carried money that someone had borrowed. Sometimes it was one dollar, sometimes it was five or ten. Mr. Sheldon was never sure how much he had lent or to whom. Sometimes he couldn't even remember giving money to people who were thanking him profusely for helping them when they needed it most.

"I declare!" Mrs. Sheldon often said. "The way you manage money, Joe! The way you manage! Why, you don't know your head from a hole in the ground when it comes to money. I don't know what you'd do without me, and that's a fact. You'd be in the poorhouse, that's what, the county poorhouse for sure. We may *still* end up there!"

But no such thing ever happened, Corrie thought. Not as long as Mr. Sheldon had his health, anyway. They got along fine, just fine, and they even managed to buy a car. It was gone now, of course, but they had used it for hospital bills, not for foolish handouts, as Mrs. Sheldon called her husband's generosity. Those years of giving money away hadn't been foolish anyway. Lots of times now when the family was desperate for money, men came knocking at their door with little bundles of dollar bills. They would stare at the porch and stammer that Joe had lent them money two or three years ago; then, red-faced, they'd press something into Corrie's hand. Only recently had she realized that perhaps much of it was a pretense—some of them didn't really owe any money to the Sheldons—they just wanted to help. Corrie felt almost sure of it. She wondered whether

her mother suspected the truth. It was hard to know what her mother thought.

But she had always known what her father thought. Just as he could never conceal his affection, he could never hide his despair. When he had worked at the defense plant during the first part of the war, he had often been miserable.

"I'm making weapons so that men can kill each other," he'd say.

"Well, if you didn't do it, someone else would," Mrs. Sheldon would tell him. "That's the way life is, Joe. That's just the way life is."

"But who says it has to be that way?"

One . . . two . . . three . . . four . . . five . . . scuff.
One . . . two . . . three . . . four . . . five . . . scuff.

Yes, Corrie thought, sitting in the hospital beside her motionless father. Who says life has got to be this way? Did you say it, God? Did you?

"Corrie! Corrie!" Mrs. Sheldon was standing near the curtain, holding a glass of milk. "Mercy, child!" she said. "You were a million miles away. Are you all right, Corrie? Are you all right?"

Corrie nodded. The sight of the milk made her realize her thirst, her hunger. She stood up and took the glass.

Mrs. Sheldon sat down beside the bed. "He hasn't moved, I see. Well, I guess we'll just wait a while longer and see how everything goes."

With two gulps Corrie swallowed the milk.

"Mercy!" Mrs. Sheldon said. "You must be starving, child!" She shook her head and looked at the blank curtain. "Sandra said to tell you she'll call tomorrow."

Corrie crossed and put the empty glass on the table. Her father was like a stranger, distant, unmovable, unreal. She went back to her chair.

Finally Mrs. Sheldon cleared her throat. "I guess we'd better head for home now, Corrie. There's nothing more we can do here. Get your coat."

"I didn't wear any coat."

"Didn't wear any?" Mrs. Sheldon put her hands on her hips. "Didn't wear any coat? But it's snowing!"

Corrie hadn't noticed. She looked at the floor and curled her toes in her scuffed tight shoes.

Mrs. Sheldon began to bustle about the cubicle. She picked up her scarf, her gloves, her purse. "Well, I never!" she said. "Corrie Sheldon, if you and your father aren't two chips off the same block! Both of you the same—off on a cloud somewhere dreaming. I don't know what you'd do without me, and that's a fact!" She took her ancient coat from a wall hook. "Now you put this on, Corrie."

"No," Corrie said. "I don't want to wear your coat, Momma. It's too big."

"Oh, fiddlesticks!" Mrs. Sheldon shook her head. "It's warm, isn't it? Goodness, child, it's nearly December. You'll freeze to death out there."

"No," Corrie said again. "I can't wear it, Momma. Besides, you need it yourself."

Mrs. Sheldon frowned. "Do you want pneumonia? Is that it? Mercy!" She began taking off her sweater. "All right, then, wear my sweater over your sweater. That'll help a little."

Once the sweaters were on, Corrie felt smothered. "I feel all stuffed up inside here," she said.

"You look stuffed up," Mrs. Sheldon told her. "Like a fat lady in the circus." She moved closer. "Just look at us. Why, the two of us could be twin fat ladies in a circus." She laughed, and Corrie began to giggle. "But you'll be warm, child, and that's the main thing."

Suddenly they stopped laughing. They stopped talking. They stared at each other. For the first time in over two weeks, they had been talking out loud in the tiny hospital corner, they had been laughing. Simultaneously, they both turned to look at the bed. Mr. Sheldon was still lying motionless.

"Well, we'll be back tomorrow, Joseph," Mrs. Sheldon said. She walked over and kissed his forehead. Corrie went after her, and kissed her father too, but he made no movement.

They paused in the hospital lobby and looked out into the night. The wind had died now, and in its wake had come the snow. Great white snowflakes were fluttering to the ground. In the beam of the streetlight, Corrie watched them fall, whirling in a noiseless ballet. The flakes were huge, she saw, and some melted before they reached the earth. Were they really all different? Corrie knew that books said each one was special and unique. It seemed impossible, though, there were so many of them falling from the sky. Yet anyone could see that they didn't act the same. Some seemed to reach out to each other, struggling to meet, and when they did, they clung together as they fell to the pavement. Others seemed to deliberately fling themselves away from the rest, and they fell alone.

Like people, Corrie thought. All different, but still the same. All heading for the same end, but each reaching it by a different manner. And when all the snowflakes reached the earth, what a beautiful thing it was! The whole land would be covered with a blanket of white, and all the hidden dirty things would disappear. Could it be that way with people, too? One snowflake couldn't possibly know that it would be part of something vast and beautiful at the end of its journey. Perhaps, if snowflakes thought, Corrie was thinking, perhaps they might think that the journey itself was all that mattered. Really, though, it was the result when the journeys were over that made something grand. People thought that only their life had meaning, that death was meaningless. Could it be that, like snowflakes, they were unaware of what the result really was? Could it be that . . .

"You should have worn your galoshes," Mrs. Sheldon said.

Corrie smiled. She had been lost on another of those "clouds" her mother said she went off on.

Corrie looked at the snow and saw the beauty, her mother looked at it and saw the wetness. That was all right, Corrie thought. The snow *was* wet. She reached over and kissed her mother on her plump cheek.

"What? What?" Mrs. Sheldon drew back. Then, half laughing, she shook her head. "Now why in the world did you do that, Corrie? Why'd you do a thing like that?"

"Oh, I just felt like it," Corrie said. She opened the lobby door. Her mother looked pleased and happy, and she bustled out into the snow first. "Oh, it isn't so cold out now, honey," she called back. "The wind has died down. You ought to be fine in those two sweaters now."

Corrie couldn't remember the last time her mother had used that word for her—honey. The sound of it was good. She took her mother's arm. "Sure, I'm fine. And what's the difference if we get our feet wet? Now our shoes will be clean."

They began walking down the hill. When they passed the small diner on the corner, Corrie heard the chimes of the hour ring out. Once she had seen the clock that was chiming now, when her father had taken her inside the diner a long time ago. It was a huge grandfather clock with a shiny brass face and a long golden pendulum. Corrie remembered how she had stared at it in amazed pleasure. It had seemed so strange to her that something so grand and beautiful could stand so proudly in the midst of so much common ugliness. Wraps from the customers had been strewn all around it: tattered old sweaters and dirty caps and gloves. A smudged, torn calendar hung on the wall beside it, and the rug right before it was garish, cheap, and worn.

Some people are like that too, Corrie thought. They can stand proud and grand in the middle of ugliness, too. They—

"Goodness!" Mrs. Sheldon clicked her tongue. She, too, had heard the chimes, but it wasn't the beauty of the clock that was stirring up her thoughts. "It's late," she went on, "it must be way past seven —way past suppertime. Why, you must be starving, Corrie, you must be half-starving!"

"I'll bet you haven't eaten either, Momma," Corrie said. "I bet you haven't eaten since lunch."

"Oh, that don't matter," Mrs. Sheldon told her. "I'm fat enough already. You're the skinny one."

Corrie laughed and looked up at the falling snow. She stuck out her tongue and felt the tiny flakes melt in her mouth. When they touched her face, they felt like tiny cold fingers. The night was close and friendly.

In the glow of the scattered streetlights, Corrie saw the river and the bridge just ahead of them. As always, when they reached this point on the way home, Corrie thought about the day her whole family had trudged down to the bridge with the turtle. Only five months had passed, but it seemed like a long, long time ago. Did anyone else remember that day the way she did? Keep it all treasured in memory like a precious jewel in a valuable safe? She could take out her memory whenever she needed it, and it was beautiful and precious and warm. Sandra often spoke about that day, but Corrie wondered whether anyone could really feel as strongly about it as she did. She looked out at the lights blinking along the river, and she remembered how determined her father had been that the turtle would be saved.

One . . . two . . . three . . . four . . . five . . . scuff.
One . . . two . . . three . . . four . . . five . . . scuff.

"I wonder how our friend is," Mrs. Sheldon said suddenly.

"Our friend?"

"The turtle," Mrs. Sheldon said. "I wonder how he is."

For a second Corrie lost the rhythm of their steps. Then she picked it up again. "You remember that day, Momma? You think of that day lots of times?"

"Well, of course I do! Mercy, child, we all were here with Daddy just last summer."

"Well, I know, but I thought—"

"You thought I forgot crazy nonsense like that? No, no, I don't forget any of those crazy things your father has done over the years." Mrs. Sheldon shook her head. "The way that man loves animals! The crazy things he's done to save them! Don't you think I know why he never gets anything in hunting season? That man couldn't step on an ant! Oh, Corrie, the crazy things that man has done!"

Corrie stumbled. Her mother didn't turn. She was staring straight ahead, walking with her arms tight to her sides, and she was speaking barely above a whisper. "I still think the things he does are crazy, mind you, but I love him for doing them. Sometimes, you know—sometimes we love someone exactly because he does do crazy things. Maybe we all wish we could do those kinds of things." She paused, then blurted, "But some of us can't, you know. Some of us just can't."

Her heels clicked on the pavement. "All this talk about the garden with your father—it's made me think of something, Corrie. I got to thinking tonight when I was sitting there beside him—I got to thinking that maybe people are like the things that grow in a garden. Some people, like me, why they're vegetables—useful, but solid and dull. Then other people, like Daddy, why they're flowers—frivolous, but grand and beautiful. You see, child, if you want to have a full garden, why you need both kinds of things. You need both kinds of people to have a full life, too."

Corrie stared at her mother. It seemed incredible that her sensible, unimaginative mother could ever have thought of such a thing. "You, Momma? You—a vegetable?"

Mrs. Sheldon laughed. "A radish, maybe, or a big fat turnip."

"Momma!"

"Well, then," said Mrs. Sheldon, "maybe a stalk

of celery. But don't you see how I've been thinking? People like your dad, why they're special because they make things seem more beautiful. They're like roses, maybe, or even like orchids."

The snowflakes were still falling on Corrie's face, but she didn't care about them now. She didn't brush them away as she stared at her mother. She had never talked this way before—what could it mean? What could it mean?

"You're like your dad," Mrs. Sheldon said, serious and slow. "Always thinking of crazy notions, up in the air somewhere with wild ideas about how good people are, how good life is. Why, you brightened up that whole tent shop today, Corrie! You've got all these crazy hopes and dreams. Maybe you're foolish, but you're like those flowers I just talked about, and you make things seem better than what they really are, maybe. Alan's like that, too. But Arthur— Arthur and me, why we're different. I guess we're both sort of like those vegetables I was talking about. We've got both feet right on the ground."

"Well, that's okay," Corrie said, because she couldn't think of anything else to say. Her chest felt full—the sweaters seemed light over the burden beneath them. "That's okay you're that way, Momma. We like you that way."

"But what I'm trying to say, Corrie, is that if your dad should die, why we'd still have our flowers in the family."

Corrie stopped, speechless. A car passed, and the

headlights flashed against the two of them. Mrs. Sheldon had stopped and was looking at her with hands outstretched. Corrie stared, her face tight.

"Corrie?" her mother said. "Corrie?"

"He's not going to die!" Corrie nearly shouted the words. "He's not!"

Mrs. Sheldon caught a deep breath. She brought her outstretched arms tight against her chest, and her voice trembled when she spoke. "Oh, honey. Oh, Corrie. You've got to be prepared for anything. Corrie. Can't you see that now? He's suffering so much, Corrie. He's suffering so."

"I won't be prepared for *that*," Corrie said, beginning to walk again. She walked faster and faster, until her mother, hurrying along beside her, had to pant in order to keep up. Soon they reached the street where they lived.

When Corrie opened the shed door, she smelled potato pancakes. A sudden surge of happiness shot through her. "Lewie's here!" she shouted back to her mother.

The old woman opened the kitchen door and peeked out into the dark shed. She was short and thin, with a mass of gray hair. Everything she wore seemed to be too large. Right now a pair of glasses was sliding down her nose and an apron was hanging nearly to the floor. She was carrying a spatula.

"Oh Lewie!" Corrie cried, laughing. "You've got Momma's apron on!"

"What's that?" Mrs. Sheldon was panting, hurrying up the steps. "What's going on in there, Corrie? What's going on?"

"What's going on? What's going on?" The little woman shook her spatula. "Well, whatd' you think's going on? I'm making your supper, that's what. It's suppertime, ain't it? Past suppertime. Way past. The boys ate a long time ago. Bottomless, that's what they are. They got hollow legs. Both of them. Ate eleven pancakes between them. At least they said they did. If you ask me, they slipped a few to the dog. They're in the back now with their noses buried in the radio. They listen to that radio too much, if you ask me, but then of course nobody ever asked me anything." Mrs. Lewis sniffed and tugged at her huge apron.

Corrie grinned as she listened and watched. Ever since she could remember, Mrs. Lewis had been special to her. She was like a gramma, but not like a gramma because, as Mrs. Sheldon often said, she had queer notions that grammas never had. At least they never admitted having them, anyway. Now she whirled to face Corrie.

"Were you out there without a coat?" she said. Her voice had always sounded to Corrie the way sandpaper looked. "You ain't got the good sense that God gave to a grasshopper. What a ninny! Wipe your feet and get in here before you get a death of cold!" She turned to Mrs. Sheldon and her tone didn't change. "You there—you leave them wet boots of yours out there in the shed."

Corrie nearly laughed out loud. Lewie bossed everyone around. Obediently Mrs. Sheldon leaned her boots up against Arthur's and Alan's. They stepped into the fragrant kitchen.

"It's a wonder that I found the stuff to cook with," the old lady said. "The way you got these cupboards set up, Verna!"

Mrs. Sheldon cleared her throat. "Well, I haven't been to the store lately, Lewie."

"I ain't talking about *food*. I been without that often enough to know how to make supper with nothing but a wish in one hand and a hope in the other. I'm talking about stuff. Like this silverware drawer. It's here on the right side of the sink. I looked all over God's creation for a spoon before I found one. Why don't you put things where they belong? Silverware goes on the left side of a sink."

"But I'm right-handed," Mrs. Sheldon said.

"Well, I'm left-handed," Mrs. Lewis declared. "Now then, quit all this chattering and sit down. I been here an hour waiting this supper for you. How's Joe?"

"Better now, but he's still not—"

"We got to be sensible," Mrs. Lewis interrupted. "There's only so much a body can stand." She turned and frowned at Corrie. "You! Ain't you sitting yet? You're slower than molasses in January. Sit down before I hang you up by your thumbs."

Corrie laughed. Her dad always said that Lewie's bark was worse than her bite.

Mrs. Lewis shook her spatula. "You and that Horace of mine would have made a good pair! He was slower than a snail, that man."

Corrie glanced at her mother. Horace Lewis was also known to the whole family, although no one had ever met him. He had disappeared long before. According to local gossip, he'd gone out in 1900 for a newspaper, and he'd never come back. "Just plain flew the coop," Mrs. Lewis would announce. "And he hardly sent a penny to me all these years. It wasn't easy there in the beginning when I had them two little boys, but we managed. Besides," she'd go on, "it was good riddance to bad rubbish, that's what

I say!" Then she'd toss her head and begin to recite his numerous faults. As the years went by, the faults grew and grew, until now Horace Lewis had attained the status of a legend in Pointer—he was the man with a million faults. But Corrie knew that Lewie still kept his picture in a gold frame on a table in her living room. Corrie had asked her about that once.

"That old picture?" she'd raged. "Why, I just keep that there to cover up a hole in the wood. *He's* the one who made the hole anyway. Him and his cigarettes! Why, it's a miracle that he never set his beard on fire! Might have been a blessing to the world if he had! Oh that man! The things I could tell you!"

Now she began to bang the frying pan on the stove burner. "The both of you look like drowned rats. Still snowing out, I guess."

"I didn't mean for you to go to all this bother," Mrs. Sheldon said, dropping into a chair. "You making dinner and all, I mean."

"This ain't dinner—it's supper. And I know what you meant for me to do, but I don't pay no mind to what other folks want. I brought a quart of milk over here and started grating. Besides, I knew you was as excited as a chicken without any head when you come running over with them boys this afternoon. I knew you was too worried to be thinking of food then. But now's a different story. I've lived long enough to know when you need food and when you don't." She put a large pancake on Mrs. Sheldon's plate. "Anyway, you left the house unlocked, so after dark I brought the boys over and started. Good thing I did—the both of you look worn to a frazzle. Potato pancakes will perk you up. Get busy eating now. Drink your coffee, Verna."

"Is that you, Mom? You home?" Arthur and Allan came running to the kitchen. "How's Daddy?"

Mrs. Sheldon stopped chewing. She took a long swallow of coffee. "Daddy's still very sick. Awfully sick." She cleared her throat. "But he sends his love to you."

Corrie looked down at the floor.

"When's he coming home?" Arthur asked.

"Will he be here for Christmas?" Alan pulled at his mother's dress. "Will Daddy be home for Christmas?"

"Lordy!" Mrs. Lewis clanked the frying pan. "Just listen to you two boys chattering in here like magpies while your poor old dog is freezing to death outside."

"Brandy!" Alan cried. "We left her in the backyard!" The two of them thundered across the kitchen, down the step, and out to fling open the back door. Cold, damp air rushed in, and chasing after it came the big red dog. She dashed to Corrie and began nuzzling her hand.

"Hi, old Brandy," Corrie murmured. "Hi, old girl."

"Get that dog to the basement!" Mrs. Lewis

shouted. "Just look at the mud she's brought in on your mother's clean linoleum!"

"Wipe her off, Arthur," Mrs. Sheldon said. "Take Brandy to the basement and clean her up. You go help him, Alan."

"Come on, girl, come on." Shouting and coaxing, the two boys managed to get the dog to the basement door. It slammed behind them, and the kitchen was suddenly silent. Mrs. Lewis heaved a sigh.

"That dog! She makes almost as much of a mess in a house as Horace used to make."

Mrs. Sheldon stirred her coffee. "She's missing Joseph, that's her trouble. She can't understand why he doesn't come home anymore."

"Them two stuck together like glue all right," Mrs. Lewis said. She turned back to the stove and reached for more pancake batter. "I used to watch them out my window. Up and down the street they went day after day. Why, two years ago, when you first got her, they went like greased lightning, they ran so fast. Then they started going slower and slower." The batter in the frying pan sizzled and Mrs. Lewis's harsh voice grew quieter. "The last time I saw them go by, they were almost crawling."

Mrs. Sheldon caught her breath. "It used to hurt him to walk very fast there at the end, Lewie."

"But ain't it funny that the dog knew that? She kept the same pace he did."

"Well, they're both going to be running again," Corrie said. "They'll both run again someday."

The two women stared at her, and suddenly something huge seemed to well up in the room. Corrie felt all her senses heightened as this invisible presence oozed all around her. She heard her brothers quarreling in the basement, the faucet dripping in the sink, the furnace blowing through the register, the pancakes puffing on the stove; she smelled her mother's perfume and she sniffed the aroma of the coffee; she saw the black writing on the calendar far away: BUY LIBERTY BONDS; and she heard, saw, felt, and almost tasted the turmoil of emotions boiling up inside the women.

Then Mrs. Lewis broke the silence, and the invisible hulk, whatever it was, shattered and disappeared. "Lordy! I nearly let them cakes burn to a crisp! Just look at these! Will you have another, Corrie?" She flipped the dark-brown pancakes on a plate. "Lordy! Whatever was I thinking of?"

Mrs. Sheldon stared at the wall and stirred her coffee faster. "Maybe you were remembering the first time Joseph knew we had Brandy," she said. "We'd been talking about Brandy, so that reminded me. *That's* a picture to remember!"

"Ain't that the truth." Mrs. Lewis turned off the burner, wiped her hands against her huge apron, and leaned against the stove. "That's the nearest picture of heaven I guess I'll see until I get there."

"*If* you get there," Mrs. Sheldon put in. Then both women laughed. Corrie laughed too, louder than she had meant to, but glad to let loose some of the feeling that was erupting inside of her. "You know what, Momma? I still can't believe you did what you did."

"Sometimes I can't believe it myself," Mrs. Sheldon answered. She heaved a happy sigh. "All that money! But I've never been sorry I did it. No sir, never. Not ever."

Corrie wasn't sorry either. Any time at all she could dig into her mind and bring back the picture of that marvelous Christmas Day, and then everything bad disappeared and she felt warm and happy.

It was the first of December, 1943. The war was raging all over the world, and Mr. Sheldon had just found out that he was to have his first operation.

"It'll have to be in Ann Arbor," he told Corrie. "Next month, I guess. They can't do surgery like I need here in Pointer. It'll be a month I'll have to stay there, maybe more."

Corrie had only been twelve then, skinny and shy and awkward. She'd twisted a piece of her hair. "But where will I go? What will happen to Arthur and Alan when you and Momma go to Ann Arbor?"

"You can stay with Mrs. Lewis. We've talked it over. She'll take all three of you."

"Oh," Corrie had answered. "Oh."

The two of them were walking down Main Street. It was a dark, gloomy winter day with the dirty remains of an old snowfall littering the sidewalk. Her father had suggested they walk to see the ice shanties on the river, but now she knew he only wanted to talk to her alone, for they had turned away from the river.

"Is it a bad operation?" Corrie asked.

Mr. Sheldon kicked at a clump of dirty ice. "Any operation can be bad, I guess. But that doesn't mean anything." They started across the street. Pointer's business section was just ahead. "It isn't so much what happens to you in your life that matters as it is what you *think* about what happens."

"Well, what do you think, Daddy? What do you think?"

They walked in silence. Mr. Sheldon's face was expressionless. Corrie heard him catch his breath once, but he stopped his thoughts before they became words. "Well," he said at last, "it's a bad time for this to happen. It's hard on your mother, you know."

"But will you be all right?"

Again Mr. Sheldon's face was a mask. "We'll see," he said.

And then they walked without speaking. Mr. Sheldon quickened his steps, almost as though he had forgotten Corrie. He had his hands in the pockets of his leather jacket. His forehead was creased with lines, and he sighed deeply. He had been that way often the past few weeks, Corrie remembered. She tried to think of the last time she had heard him laugh out loud. She stared ahead and in the distance she saw a figure waving. It was Murry Beckman, calling from the front of his magazine shop.

"Joe!" he was shouting. "Come on inside a minute here and take a look at what I got!"

Mr. Sheldon smiled. "It must be the pups! Murry told me that Meggie was ready to have her pups two or three weeks ago." He walked faster. "Come on, Corrie, let's go take a look."

The news shop smelled good—it was the aroma of paper and ink and peppermint. Corrie breathed it deeply and curled her toes in happiness. The Sheldons and Mr. Beckman were the only people in the store.

"Joe, just wait until you get a look at these," the little man said excitedly. He was leading them to the back rooms of his shop. "She's outdone herself this time, and that's a fact."

Corrie ran ahead. There, in the corner, she saw Meggie, the big Irish setter, nursing three fat balls of red fur.

"Oh Daddy! Look at them! Just look at them!" Corrie fell to her knees and leaned over the dogs. "Oh Daddy—could we have one? Could we? Could we?"

Mr. Sheldon stooped down beside her. He picked up the fattest puppy, a female. Her pink tongue came out, and she tried to wag her tail.

"She likes us, Daddy," Corrie said happily. "She likes us. Can't we have her?"

Mr. Beckman cleared his throat. He had his hands clasped behind his back, and he was surveying the family as though he had given birth to them himself. "There's only the three, but they're all perfect,

all perfect. And they ought to be ready for the holidays."

Mr. Sheldon stood. He laughed, and Corrie saw that all the worry lines were gone from his face. "She did you proud, Murry. They're fine pups. Fine."

Corrie was holding the little female. It felt warm and soft and cuddly. She put her face down and stared into the puppy's eyes. They blinked, and the pink tongue flicked out again. "Wouldn't you like to come home with me?" Corrie asked the dog. "Wouldn't you like to live at our house?"

"They'll be all ready to leave by Christmas," Mr. Beckman said again.

"But a dog like that—" Mr. Sheldon hopelessly gestured at the puppy, "Why, a dog like that must cost a king's ransom."

Mr. Beckman nodded. "That they do, Joe. I got to admit they cost a pretty penny. But they're worth it, worth it! They can make a man feel like a king! And I'll tell you what, Joe. You've done lots of good things for me over the years. I'll tell you what—if you want one of Meggie's pups for your family, why I'll let you have it for twenty-five dollars. I'd like to give it to you, but I got to pay the fees, you know."

Corrie nearly dropped the pup. Twenty-five dollars! It was a fortune—an impossible fortune. It was a whole month's rent!

Mr. Sheldon laughed and shook his head. "Can't do it, Murry. It's a good offer, all right, and I thank you. But I can't do it."

"Well, let me know if you change your mind," Mr. Beckman said. "A dog like one of these—why, you don't see them too often."

It was nearly dark when Corrie and her father started for home.

"I'll talk to your mother about it, then," Mr. Sheldon said after they'd walked a few blocks and Corrie hadn't been able to stop begging. "But don't get your hopes up too high, pumpkin. Don't get built up for a big letdown."

That night Corrie lay in bed and thought about how it would feel to own a dog like Meggie. She'd name her puppy Brandy, she decided, because her father had said that the puppy was colored the same shade as good brandy. The dog would walk to school with her and meet her when school was over. Sandra would be so surprised that the Sheldons had a beautiful dog like Brandy. Nobody except rich people could ever afford a dog like that. Everyone in town would be shocked, and they'd stare at Brandy when Corrie walked her, and they'd all wish they had a dog as beautiful and wonderful as that. Maybe Daryl Hanson would start hanging around even, so that he could be near Brandy, too. That would be nice, Corrie thought, that would be nice.

Corrie had been so caught up with her thoughts that night that it was a while before she realized how loud the voices had risen in the living room. Her bedroom was next to the wall there, but seldom did she ever hear noises. Now and then music from the radio floated through, but never before had she heard words. Now the sounds were growing louder, and the voices had become shouts. She realized with a shocking stab that her parents were quarreling.

"Twenty-five dollars for a dog? Are you crazy, Joe Sheldon? Are you crazy?"

"It's a good deal, Verna. The dog's worth a lot more than that."

"So's a Cadillac convertible, but we're not buying one. You got to be more sensible, Joe. We can't afford a dog like that. Twenty-five dollars is a fortune!"

"But it can be for the kids' Christmas."

"I've already taken care of that. They'll have pajamas and mittens. Don't you see, Joe? We'll be lucky if we have *food* for the children for Christmas."

"Oh, it's not that bad at all, Verna, not that bad at all."

"How do you know how bad it might get, though? How do either one of us know? This operation— God only knows how much money that will cost. We'll have to sell the car for sure."

"We can't get gas for it anyway. And you know we won't starve, Verna. We can always sell the land by the lake. And if worse comes to worse, you'll get my veteran's pension."

"Joe! Joe! I didn't mean things might get *that* bad!"

"Can't you see we got to get our minds on some-thing good for a change? The war's got us all feeling down. If we had a dog like that puppy, why, we'd get our minds on something that would make us all happy."

"But why that dog? The dog is so expensive, Joe."

"Sometimes a man needs something expensive," Mr. Sheldon said, his voice rising. "For once in his life, sometimes a man needs to have something grand and to hell with the expense!"

Mrs. Sheldon's voice rose higher than his. "But a man having a big operation like yours can't say to hell with anything! A man with a wife and three children."

Corrie felt a long silence. Then, only because she was straining so hard was she able to hear her father's answer, low, sad, dejected. "Maybe you're right, Verna. I guess you're right—it was a foolish idea."

"Oh Joe!" Now Mrs. Sheldon's voice had been strange—all cracked and shaky. "Oh, Joe, don't look like that. All folded up like that. You'll be all right after the operation, I know you will. I can't think why I say the things I say. It's just that I'm so nervous about money, Joe. We've got to watch every penny. But we can get a dog of some kind. A cheaper one. Maybe one from the city pound."

"No!" Her father's voice was louder than Corrie had ever heard it. "We won't get any dog at all!" Then he added something else, but Corrie couldn't hear it. The huge sobs she had been swallowing had blocked off all her hearing. She had put the pillow over her head and buried her face into it. When she

127

was quiet again, she heard only the sound of the radio.

Nobody mentioned the dog the next morning. At breakfast Mr. Sheldon glanced at Corrie, and she saw that he knew she had heard everything. Mrs. Sheldon talked too much and laughed too much and gave them each too much cereal. As if enough food would help anybody forget anything.

The days before Christmas dragged by. Corrie couldn't feel any of the twins' excitement. Presents didn't matter to her. Often she walked past Mr. Beckman's shop, but she never had the courage to go in. She tried not to even think about a fat red puppy named Brandy.

Christmas morning was cold. The furnace had gone out during the night, and the house was freezing. By the time Mr. Sheldon had it stoked and going again, the twins had ripped their few packages apart.

"Pajamas!" Arthur roared. "Pajamas and mittens from Santa?"

"But we needed them," Alan said.

"And what about these?" Mr. Sheldon called, coming from the basement. "Santa must have dropped a few things when he came up from the basement." He carried two airplanes for the boys and a bracelet for Corrie—packages that he had hidden in his toolbox.

Corrie had blinked back tears. Her bracelet had a picture of an Irish setter on it.

"We sure didn't get much," Arthur said, when all the gifts from relatives were opened, too.

"But we're all together," Mrs. Sheldon told him, "and that's the main thing. Think of all them poor people in Europe in the middle of this awful war. Oh, we're the lucky ones to be together like this. Don't you worry none about that. We got plenty to eat—that's the big thing."

She began bustling around the rooms, picking up wrapping paper and ribbon. She always saved the Christmas things to use on birthday gifts. Her eyes were sparkling, and her cheeks were pink. When everyone had dressed and the house was neat, she looked at her family. "There's one more present this year. It's the best one yet, and it's for everybody."

Before Corrie could open her mouth, her brothers were screaming. "Where? What? Where is it? What did you get us, Mom?"

Mrs. Sheldon laughed. "Be careful—you might burst with all that nosiness. It's over at Lewie's house."

"Who's it from?" Mr. Sheldon asked, fingering his new tie pin. It was a gift from Corrie—Mr. Sheldon wasn't wearing a tie, but he had pinned it to his shirt pocket. "Lewie wouldn't have enough money to buy us a Christmas present."

"It's from Santa Claus," Mrs. Sheldon said. "It's a special gift from Santa. We'll go to Lewie's to get it, and then we'll all come back here and have dinner at our house."

"Let's go now," Alan shouted.

"Quit shoving me!" Arthur shouted. "I'll go first!"

The Sheldons trooped out into the cold, and they ran to Mrs. Lewis' house without their coats or boots. Lewie, waiting at the front door, hurried them inside.

"You come for your gift, eh?" She pointed to a box. A fat red puppy was fast asleep, curled around a ragged blanket. "There she is. And you're welcome to her. That creature squealed half the night."

"Brandy!" Corrie clasped her hands. "Daddy! It's Brandy!"

"Well, I'll be darned. I'll be darned!" Mr. Sheldon fell to his knees beside the box. He picked up the sleeping puppy and laughed when the tiny mouth opened in a huge yawn. "Just look at her! Oh, what a beauty! What a beauty!"

"Homeliest thing I ever saw," Mrs. Lewis said.

"What? What's that you say?" Mr. Sheldon plopped the dog into Corrie's hands, and he jumped to his feet. "Homely? You say she's homely?" He grabbed the old woman's hands and began dancing her around in a circle. "She's beautiful! That's what she is—beautiful! And you're beautiful, too! And you—" He stopped and stared at his beaming wife. "But how'd you do it, Verna? How'd you ever get enough money to do a thing like this?"

Mrs. Sheldon was laughing. "Oh, I managed. Paid cash for her, too."

"Is she really ours?" Alan asked.

"Ours to keep?" Arthur was cuddling the puppy. "Oh, I love her—I just love this little puppy."

"All this fuss over a silly dog," Mrs. Lewis said. But she was grinning, and she looked happy too.

Late that night Corrie sat with her parents in the living room while the puppy slept in Mr. Sheldon's lap. Dinner was over, the twins were asleep, Mrs. Lewis had long gone home. Corrie was feeling so happy she felt warm all over. The puppy smelled good, like a forest after rain, and Mr. Sheldon was so proud his face was glowing.

Suddenly he sat forward. "Verna! Where's your engagement ring? You don't have your diamond ring on!"

Mrs. Sheldon nervously folded her hands. "Oh, heavens, who needs an engagement ring once a body is married? It's all foolishness, that's what I say, plain foolishness."

Mr. Sheldon thrust the startled dog into Corrie's lap. "You sold your ring to buy that dog," he said, rising and walking toward his wife. "That's what you did, now, didn't you? Why'd you go and do a blame fool thing like that?"

Mrs. Sheldon stood up too. She was little and plump, but now Corrie thought she looked tall and regal. "Sometimes a woman needs to do a blame fool thing like that," she said. "She needs to do something grand and to hell with the expense."

Mr. Sheldon had stopped. He stared at her a moment, then he threw back his head and laughed, his white teeth flashing in the lamplight. Mrs. Sheldon smiled, and then she began to laugh with him, and then Corrie burst into giggles. Brandy sat blinking her eyes, looking from one human to another.

"You are the darndest woman I ever saw!" Mr. Sheldon burst out. "Oh, how I love you! I wouldn't trade you for a million dollars! Do you hear me? No, not for a billion!"

C-R-A-S-H!

"We're back!" Alan shouted.

The basement door slammed and the three females in the kitchen jumped. The twins were up from the basement with the big wet dog.

"Brandy's all clean again," Alan said. "Me and Arthur gave her a bath. But she sure didn't like it much."

The dog shook herself, and water went shooting all over the kitchen.

"Lordy!" Mrs. Lewis shook her head. "If that ain't the cat's meow! I don't know which is worse—having Brandy all dirty or having her all clean!"

The telephone rang in the middle of the night. Corrie thought she remembered hearing it, thought she had heard a voice, too, but when she woke in the morning, she wasn't sure. She had been dreaming of her father—he was well again, and the two of them had been running in the forest with Brandy, they'd been praying in the Catholic church with Sandra, and they'd been rolling in the snow. Her dreams had been more real than the morning sunlight, and now she had to blink her eyes to decide what reality was.

"Corrie?" Alan slowly opened her bedroom door. "Are you still sleeping?"

"How can I be sleeping? Listen to that racket!" Corrie sat up in bed, yawned, and glanced at Alan. "What's going on? Brandy's barking her head off outside. What's Arthur shouting about?"

"They're out in back playing. It snowed all night, Corrie—there's snow everywhere today. It's good packing, Arthur says." Alan came closer to the bed. "Momma's gone."

"Gone? But where'd she go? She wasn't supposed to work today."

Alan held out his hand. "I found this note on the kitchen table."

Corrie's eyes raced over Mrs. Sheldon's spidery handwriting:

> Daddy very bad again. I'm at
> hospital. Stay home with
> boys, till I call.

Corrie felt her insides go all hollow. Her throat tightened, her stomach went empty.

"Is Daddy dead?" Alan leaned on the bed. His blue eyes were wide and frightened. "Is Daddy dead, Corrie?"

"Dead!" Corrie stared at her brother. "Why'd you say a thing like that? Why'd you ever think of such a thing?"

Alan bit his bottom lip. "The kids at school—some of them say that Daddy is dying."

"Ha! Those brats!" Corrie spit the words out. Suddenly she hated those invisible schoolmates of Alan's. "What do they know?" she shouted. "They're stupid, that's what. Just plain stupid!" She reached for Alan and pulled him into bed with her. His legs were cold, and his bones were sharp against her. "Dumb brats!"

Alan looked at the pillow. "But he's been gone so long."

"Because he's sick, that's what. He's sick in the hospital. You saw him there yourself just a few days ago. Remember when the nurses let you visit? He'll get better, though. He'll get better."

"But the kids at school say he's going to die."

"That's crazy!" Corrie pulled away from her brother. She stared down at him. "That's a crazy idea, and you just better get it out of your head." She jumped from her bed and flung back the covers. "You just get out of here, Alan Sheldon! You just get out of my bedroom with your crazy ideas!" Now she was half crying. She yanked Alan's arm, and he tumbled from her bed. "Don't you come back, you hear me? You just stay out of my room!" She pushed him out and slammed the door. A picture on the wall rattled, and then the room was silent.

Corrie wiped her nose with the back of her hand. She sank on to the bed and stared at the mirror. A stranger looked back. A girl who looked normal, looked like anybody else, solid flesh and skinny body. That girl wasn't Corrie Sheldon—she couldn't be—Corrie Sheldon was torn apart, pulled into a million pieces, and each of them was empty. How could feelings so powerful be so invisible? Corrie threw herself down and buried her face in the balled-up blanket.

The twins were listening to the radio when she finally left her bedroom. They pretended they didn't see her, and she pretended she didn't see them. But she sniffed when she walked into the kitchen. It was a mess. Someone had tried to make breakfast, and cereal was spilled all over. Arthur's wet coat and mittens were strewn across the floor. Brandy was lying near the floor register. Corrie sighed and reached for the broom.

The telephone rang. She dropped the broom and grabbed it.

"Hello! Hello! Oh. Oh, Sandra, it's you. Well, I thought it might be my mother. She's at the hospital. Daddy got worse in the night again, so she had to go up there. She's going to call—guess I'd better not hold up the line. Sure—sure, come on over, Sandra. See you—"

Alan and Arthur were both standing at the kitchen door when she hung up the telephone. "It was just Sandra," she told them.

"Oh, her!" Arthur said, and he hurried back to the radio. But Alan stood a moment longer. He stared up at Corrie and sucked air through his empty tooth space. "I'm sorry," he said at last. "I'm sorry for what I said back there in the bedroom."

Corrie ran her hand across his head—it was the same gesture her father always used. She still felt sick inside, but she couldn't be mad anymore. Why was it so hard to stay mad at people who were small and skinny? "It's okay," she said. "It's okay, Alan."

Within half an hour, Corrie had finished sweeping and was sitting at the table drinking coffee. She rarely ever drank it, but today she felt she had to. Somehow, starting the day without the aroma of coffee in the kitchen seemed sad and hopeless. Now, with the hot coffee in front of her, she felt more optimistic, more powerful. The warm fragrance made her think of her mother, plump and busy, and her father, eager and happy, and all the early mornings they had spent together in the warm kitchen reading the newspaper and laughing. The smell of the coffee made the day seem normal again and made the possibility of permanent change seem impossible. Things would soon be the way they used to be, Corrie thought. Of course they would . . . of course they would . . .

Suddenly she realized that someone was knocking on the door. It can't be Sandra, she thought fleetingly, Sandra always walks right in. "Come in," she shouted.

Cold air came dashing into the kitchen as Sandra opened and shut the storm door. Despite the brisk day, though, Sandra's face was pale. Her eyes were strange too: red, watery, shaded, silent. Usually she grinned and yelled, "Hi, kid," but today she awkwardly stared at the worn linoleum. She held out a covered dish. "Hi, Corrie. My mom sent this casserole for all of you." Still looking down at the floor, she shifted from one foot to the other.

Corrie rose from her chair. It was astonishing to see Sandra like that—so subdued, so uncomfortable. A sinking apprehension flung itself up inside her stomach. She felt as if a thick glass shield had suddenly arisen between herself and her very best friend, between herself and all of reality. She forced herself to answer normally, but she knew that her voice had that phony friendliness it always had when she spoke to people she didn't much like. "Oh, that's great, Sandra. Be sure to tell your mother thanks. She's a great cook."

She saw Sandra awkwardly shift her position again.

She was wearing blue jeans that were rolled up to the knees. Her hair, in pin curls, was covered by a brightly flowered scarf. It made her face seem mournful and colorless beneath its gaudy colors. "How you been, Corrie?" she asked, as though they had been parted for weeks or months.

"Okay," Corrie turned to put the casserole into the icebox. She noticed that her brothers had left an empty pickle jar sitting on the second shelf. While her face was still turned to the shelves, she spoke again. "Why don't you take off your coat? Sit down and talk a while."

Carefully Sandra hung her coat over the kitchen chair. Usually she simply tossed it somewhere, but now she adjusted it slowly, until it hung exactly right. She pulled out another chair and sat down. Corrie thought the scraping of the chair legs sounded as loud as a clap of thunder.

"Hi there, Brandy," Sandra said, leaning over the dog. "How ya been?" She busily patted the dog's head.

"I was just having some coffee," Corrie said, sitting down again. "Want some, Sandra?"

"No—no thanks. I don't really like coffee, Corrie."

"It's not bad if you put a lot of sugar in it."

Both of them stared at Corrie's coffee cup. The moments stretched out until Corrie thought the room had grown so tight that something surely would have to snap. If nothing else, the glass on the windows surely would break. The sound of the radio was distant, hazy, foolish.

Loudly Sandra cleared her throat. "Everybody missed you last night, Corrie."

Corrie stirred her coffee. "I heard on the radio that we won."

"Yeah, but it wasn't very exciting. We beat them by too much, I guess. It wasn't much fun."

"How'd Daryl do?"

"He was high-point man." Sandra hesitated, then blurted, "Know what, Corrie? He asked me where you were."

"He did? He really did?"

Sandra nodded. She looked at the clock on the wall. "I wish you could've come with me, Corrie. I wish you'd been there."

"I do, too."

A huge silence fell on the room again, and there was only the sound of the ticking clock. Brandy curled herself into a new position, and her toenails clicked on the floor. Corrie felt an urgent need to say something, say anything. "I just finished cleaning the kitchen."

Sandra nodded and patted the dog again. "Where's the twins?"

"Listening to the radio."

"My sister listens to the radio all Saturday morning, too." She sat up, folded her hands together on the table, and stared at the pattern her fingers made as she crossed them. Then she gulped. "How's your dad. Corrie?"

Corrie swallowed a mouthful of hot coffee. Tears sprang to her eyes, thrown there by the burning pain. "Mom didn't call me yet. She must not know anything yet."

"Guess our visit to the Catholic church yesterday didn't help much."

"Yesterday?" Corrie shook her head. Had it really only been yesterday? Was it only a day ago that she had been beseeching God, begging Him, crying out to Him not to forget her father? And now she, she herself, had forgotten the whole business. How could she expect God to remember her when she forgot even talking to Him? "It seems like we were there a long time ago," she said to Sandra weakly.

"Doesn't seem that way to me. I really caught heck for being so late getting home from school. My mom almost didn't let me go to the game last night."

Corrie stared down at the table. "No one was here when I got home. My mother was at the hospital, so I went up there, too. Daddy was awful bad."

"That's what your mother told me when she called last night. Did you stay up there all night?"

"No—he seemed better, so Mom and I came home. Lewie was here—she made potato pancakes." Corrie's voice faded. "But then in the night Daddy must have been bad again, because Momma was gone this morning."

There was a long silence, then Sandra spoke. "Did he know you when you were there last night?"

Corrie shook her head. "He hardly talks at all lately. Sometimes he asks about the garden."

"Gosh, Corrie, it's winter now."

"I know that, Sandra! But Daddy doesn't know it."

Sandra bent and patted Brandy's head. "I guess it must be awful to be as sick as he is. I remember how he was just before school started."

"You don't even know," Corrie whispered. "You can't even know how he looks now, Sandra. He's awful bad."

Sandra stared at the floor. "Do you think he might die?"

"No!" Corrie jumped from her chair. The back of her knees shoved against it and the pain felt good. "That's an *awful* thing to say!"

"Gosh, Corrie, I'm sorry." Sandra ran her hand across her mouth. "It's just that after your mom called me last night, my parents told me that—they said that— Oh, Corrie, it's just that some people's fathers do die, you know. Joyce's father died just last year."

"But there was a reason for Joyce's dad to die. He died in the war. But there isn't any reason for my dad to die."

"But does there have to be a reason? Does there have to be a reason for dying?"

"Well, sure. Sure there does!" Corrie walked to the sink and stared out at the naked branches bending in the cold wind. Her heart was thumping so wildly she could hear it. "There's a reason for everything, isn't there?"

Sandra shook her head. "I don't think so. I don't

even know why people are born—how can I know why they die?"

Corrie whirled around. "But my dad hasn't finished living yet! Isn't that a good enough reason for him not dying?"

"Who says he hasn't finished living?"

"Me!" Corrie shouted, leaning forward on to the table. Her hands were flat, and she could feel the oilcloth under every finger. "I say it." She stared at Sandra, and a long silence stretched between them, a taut string in a widening gulf.

Sandra swallowed loudly and looked away. "I do hope he gets better, Corrie. Really I do." She cleared her throat. "Hey, maybe I *will* try some of that coffee of yours, Corrie."

But they couldn't feel close anymore. Sandra had spoiled the umbrella of understanding that usually hovered over them. It was a frail thing, but sometimes it enabled them to nearly read each other's thoughts. Sometimes it even made Corrie feel that she *was* Sandra, that she could see the world through Sandra's eyes, feel the frustration of having protruding teeth and too much weight. But now the fragile thing was broken, and Corrie was positive that nobody could ever truly understand her thoughts, feel her sorrow, or know her anguish. Nobody could ever really understand anybody else.

Suddenly Sandra pushed back her chair. "Guess I'd better go home now."

"You haven't finished your coffee."

Sandra reached for her coat. "Guess I can't drink

it after all." She started for the door, then turned back. Her eyes were watery, and Corrie saw her chin tremble. "I'm awful sorry, Corrie."

"People keep saying that—" Corrie started, but the door slammed and Sandra was gone. Brandy looked up questioningly. She stood up, stretched, and whined.

"You want to go outside?" Corrie asked. She felt empty and shaken. "You want to go outside?" She put the coffee cups in the sink and then coaxed the dog through the back door. Doing something so routine made her feel strong again. "I'm going out back," she shouted to her brothers. "Be sure to call me if the telephone rings." She took her father's sweater from a hook in the shed and went down the stairs to the storm door. Brandy rushed outside as she slipped on her boots.

The snow was falling steadily. Inches of it covered the ground, and more was falling on the bare places where Arthur had been making angels. Corrie glanced at the footprints Brandy was leaving. They seemed so tiny for such a big dog. There was a faint smell of cigarette smoke on Mr. Sheldon's sweater. Corrie breathed deeply, then started back for the garden. It was nothing but barren, frozen ground now, but in her mind it became alive again, and the tomato plants were waving their leaves in the wind. She could see the rainbow her father could make in the arch of water from the hose, and she thought she heard him laugh. He was there, she felt him all around her.

"Cat got your tongue?"

Corrie jumped. Mrs. Lewis was standing beside her. The old lady was wrapped in a huge black coat, and her head was buried in a wool scarf. "I been talking to you for five minutes, and you've just stood there like a bump on a log. Ain't you freezing to death out here in that skimpy little sweater?"

"Oh, Lewie! It's you, Lewie!" Corrie shook herself. "Guess I was just dreaming. I didn't hear you."

"Ain't nothing wrong in dreaming, Corrie. But if you get pneumonia while doing it, then it ain't so smart."

"I'm okay. This is Daddy's sweater."

"I thought so." The old woman pushed at the handle of a shopping bag that was draped on her arm. "I was just on my way to the store when I saw all the snow. I got to thinking about all them snowmen your dad makes every year. How's he doing, Corrie?"

Corrie hugged her elbows. She turned to watch Brandy running around an evergreen tree. "He got awful bad in the night again, Lewie. Momma went up to the hospital. She's going to call when she finds out anything."

Mrs. Lewis pressed her lips together. Her lined face puckered. "Too bad. Too bad." Silently they stared at the empty garden. Corrie knew that they were separated by generations, but she felt the years meant nothing now. She heard Mrs. Lewis click her tongue. "How that man loved life!"

"He did!" Corrie whirled around and grabbed her arm. "That's why I keep saying he can't die, Lewie! Why, what would be the reason for living if people like my dad just simply died? Just died and disappeared forever?"

The old woman pulled her arm away. "Disappear? Be gone forever? Why what ails you, girl? Your dad will never disappear, never be gone forever!"

"But people keep telling me that he might die!"

Mrs. Lewis thrust her face directly in front of Corrie's. "*What* might die? That poor sick body in the hospital? Why, that ain't what's really Joe Sheldon! That ain't what we all love! Ain't you still young and healthy—ain't I changed because I knew your dad? Ain't your ma? Listen, Corrie, no death can take all *that* away! Disappear indeed! No sir! Death ain't strong enough to make Joe Sheldon disappear and be gone forever!"

Corrie blinked, pulled back, overcome by the force that was throbbing from the old woman.

"What's the matter with you, girl? Are you so dumb and blind that you can't see that it's love that keeps folks alive? Why, their bodies don't matter none at all. Don't you know my Horace?"

"Well, y-y-yes, I guess I do," Corrie stammered.

"Well, you ain't even seen him!" the old woman said. "But you know him because I made him alive for you. Because as long as I live, he'll live, because I love him!"

Corrie gasped. "You do?"

"Of course I do! Ain't I talking about him all the time? It's love that keeps us talking, and love that keeps folks alive no matter even if they're dead."

"Oh, but still, still, I don't want Daddy to die. I—"

"*You* don't?" The old woman shook her head, and her voice was softer. "You got to stop thinking of yourself, Corrie. You got to think about your poor dad."

"No!" Corrie shouted. "I won't think that he might die! I won't!" She glared at Mrs. Lewis, then she whirled around and ran for the house.

She lay on her bed crying for a long time. The sobs shook her body and left her trembling. Her pillow felt drenched, and she was coughing and shaking. Never before had she given in to such wild emotion. Her grief had always been polite—it had hidden behind occasional tears; but now it sprang to the surface, powerful, bitter, and noisy.

At last she was quiet. She sat up, became aware of the silence in the house, and felt a quick pang of guilt, of fear. She was responsible for Alan and Arthur, after all, yet she hadn't even thought of them.

"Alan?" she called. "Arthur?" It seemed to her that a hundred years had passed, but she saw by the clock that she had been in her room less than hour. "Arthur? Alan?" She hurried to the kitchen and peered out the side window.

They were in Lewie's backyard, trying to build a snowman. Lewie was there too, half tripping on her long scarf as she gathered snow together. Her empty shopping bag lay on the ground, and she was laughing in the falling snow.

"Oh Lewie!" Corrie said aloud, suddenly sick to think of how she had shouted just an hour before.

The woman was unbelievable—she was so old and her life had been so miserable, and yet she took such pleasure in simple things.

"It's true, that song, you know," her father had told her dozens of times. "Lewie found that out years ago. The best things in life *are* free."

Corrie remembered one time he had said it when the two of them had been walking out to Lake Michigan on the long cement break wall. It was just getting dark, and the beach was deserted. White fingers had reached up from the waves, lapping against the cement, glistening in the late twilight. The light from the foghorn at the end of the pier was flashing on and off, and a full moon was hanging low in the sky. There was the aroma and the feel of the lake all around them—damp, tangible, mysterious, wonderful.

"You take all of this," her father had said, gesturing all around. "It's all free—everything you can see or smell or hear right now is free. A poor man gets it the same as a rich man does."

"Are we poor, Daddy?" Corrie had asked.

"Not on your life!" he had answered, laughing and running his hand across her head. "I'm the richest guy I know. I've got your mother and three of the best crumb snatchers in the world, haven't I? It's people that I care about, Corrie. It's knowing and liking and loving people that makes me feel rich."

Corrie was thinking about that now as she stared

out the window at Lewie and her brothers. It was true all right. Money never had meant much to her father. Maybe Mr. Peterson had been right when he said that yesterday. Her dad didn't seem to handle money very well, because it meant almost nothing to him. But was that bad? Was it?

She pressed her hot forehead on the cold windowpane. All the snow was free, of course, and so was the snowman that was growing there in the yard. But it wasn't growing very fast. The boys were small and Lewie wasn't very strong. Arthur was taking a rest—he was wrestling on the snow with Brandy—but the old woman and Alan were still piling handfuls of snow together. No matter how hard they tried, though, Corrie knew they would never be able to make a snowman as grand as the ones her dad had made every year. She had to smile just thinking of the amazing creatures that had sprung up on their lawn every winter. Where were the pictures they had taken?

Corrie found the photo album beside her mother's bed. She sat there on the green spread and turned the pages. There they were—seventeen snowmen, one for every year of her parents' marriage. In the later ones she saw how fast the twins seemed to grow, as they were photographed proudly standing beside each snowman. She laughed at the early pictures of herself—in one she was just a baby propped up against the snowman's shovel. She wondered whether her mother had made the same comments with the first ones as she had made with the last.

"Heavens, Joe, you're worse than the kids! What a mess you make tramping in this kitchen all covered with snow. What in the world gets into you every winter—you're supposed to be a grown man. No, you're not going to use my vegetable strainer for a hat on that snowman. Think of the expense, Joe. And a cucumber for a nose? My goodness! What a waste of money! What a waste of food!"

But, somehow, despite his wife's objections, Mr. Sheldon had always had his way. Every year their yard sported a gigantic snowman, and he was usually dressed in marvelous fashion.

"You want my wool scarf for what?" Mrs. Sheldon would cry, or "What happened to those big dill pickles from the crock?" or "Where's the umbrella?"

Even she had to laugh at the results, though. The snowman might have a pumpkin head or pickles for ears or apple eyes, he might be wearing a wool scarf or an old tablecloth or a pair of long under-wear, he might be carrying a broom or a shopping bag or an umbrella—but he always was the grandest sight in Pointer, Michigan. Kids came from miles around just to stare.

Just like they came every Halloween. Hurriedly, she flipped the pages of the album until she came to their Halloween decorations. But the pictures were disappointing. They could never show the real excitement of those thrilling October nights.

"Is your dad going to do his thing this year?" kids would start asking Corrie the first of every October. And, of course, she always answered that yes, he was, because Halloween was always the same —Mr. Sheldon made a chamber of horrors for all the trick-or-treaters.

"Such a lot of folderol for just one night!" Mrs. Sheldon would declare. But her eyes would sparkle and she'd laugh as she hurried to help make preparations for the big display.

The house would be lighted only by a few candles hidden in jack-o'-lanterns, and Mr. Sheldon would play a record full of scary music. He would think of awful things for the kids to feel after they were blindfolded. There would be buckets of raw eyeballs (skinless grapes) and a bowl of angleworms (wet noodles) and a can of bats' livers (warm okra) and Frankenstein's brains (boiled tomatoes).

When that hurdle was passed, the trick-or-treaters would get a treat from a moaning mummy. It was a dummy wrapped in old sheets and put in a box that Mr. Sheldon had made. It would sit up when someone approached and hold up a bowl of treats. Mr. Sheldon sat behind the box, making eerie noises and pulling the string to make the figure sit up.

It was a grand spectacle and one that the children of Pointer talked about for weeks. The Sheldons gave out only a handful of popcorn, but their house was more popular than the mayor's, where they gave out candied apples and nickles.

"It's nice to be the most popular guy in town once a year," Mr. Sheldon would say.

"It's just a good thing that I give treats to the little ones before they see what's inside the house, though," Mrs. Sheldon would tell him. "You could scare a three-year-old to death."

"He never scared me," Arthur would answer. "Me neither," Alan always echoed.

"Nor me," Corrie said now, looking at a picture of her father petting a fawn in the state deer park. She bit her lip and wished that she and her mother had tried to make a good Halloween display for this year. At first Mr. Sheldon had asked about it from his hospital bed, but then he'd grown too ill to remember it anymore, and Halloween had been just another day.

Corrie blinked her eyes and flipped the pages of the album. A note fell out.

Gone fishing with the boys.
Be back in three or four days.
Joe

Corrie smiled as she looked at it, remembering the story behind it. Mr. Sheldon had written that note and put it on his pillow on the first morning of his honeymoon.

"Oh lordy! Oh lordy, when I saw that note!" Mrs. Sheldon had often told Corrie. "Why, when I saw that note and thought he had gone off with some friends of his and left me all alone, why I was fit to be tied! There I was, a scared little eighteen-year-old, and I married a fellow I scarcely knew. He dragged me off for a honeymoon in the woods miles from everywhere, and then I woke up and found that note!"

She'd always shake her head at that point and catch her breath. "I was ready to turn that man inside out and hang him up by his thumbs!" she'd declare. "And don't you think I couldn't have done it! I was a skinny little wiffit in them days, but I was madder than a hornet!"

"That's the truth," Mr. Sheldon always would add. "I did it for a joke, you know, just to see what would happen, and I was really just hiding in the other room watching her. Why, I'm telling you, I never saw anything like that. That girl read the note and her eyes shot out fire! She *flew* to the door! And she flung it open so hard the whole cabin shook!"

"Oh, go on with you, Joe Sheldon!" Mrs. Sheldon would put in.

"And then what happened?" Corrie would shout. "And then what happened?"

"Why, I started to laugh," Mr. Sheldon answered.

"And I started to cry," Mrs. Sheldon added.

"And I never tried a joke like that again," Mr. Sheldon finished.

But her mother had saved the note. Corrie looked at it now, and in her mind she could still hear her father's laugh.

There was a picture of him laughing on the next

153

page. She had taken it herself after the sixth-grade play. Mr. Sheldon had been the only father in the whole gymnasium. Corrie stared at it and remembered the excitement of that day. She remembered the argument that led up to it, too, and the hurt and joy that had churned inside her that afternoon.

"Take the day off work?" her mother had cried the evening Corrie had first mentioned the play to her parents. "Did you say you think you'll skip your shift at the plant, Joe?"

"Yup." Mr. Sheldon had nodded. "Corrie's in a play—isn't she the star? I'll take the day off so I can go to the school and watch her. She wants to be an actress when she grows up, doesn't she? I want to see her now before she gets all famous and forgets her mom and dad."

"Oh, Daddy!" Corrie had cried. "I'll never forget you—you ought to know that, Daddy."

Mrs. Sheldon was appalled. "But you'll lose a whole day's pay! You can't just up and take a whole day off work like that! And what about that foreman's job you been offered at the plant? You'll lose your chance to make more money, Joe!"

"Oh, to heck with it, Verna. I ain't that keen on taking that foreman's job. You got to keep getting after the men, then, and I just don't care for that. No, I'd rather do what I'm doing now, even if it ain't as much money. And I can take the day off easy. I've never seen my daughter in a school play, and I think I'd like to."

"But only mothers go to them meetings, Joe."

"Is there any rule against the fathers going, too?"

Mrs. Sheldon's face had puckered. "Well no, I guess not, Joe. I guess there's no rule that fathers can't go. But no fathers went there before. I been going for six years, and I never saw a man there before."

"Then I'll be the first one to do it."

Corrie had listened in amazed happiness. Her father at an afternoon mother's meeting? It seemed too good to be true. And how grand it was that he would see her in a play!

"But it isn't a very long play," she had felt obligated to warn him. "And some of the kids don't know their parts very well."

"It'll be fine," he told her. "Aren't you the star? We'll ask Lewie to come along with us."

"She'll be glad to come, I know," Mrs. Sheldon said. "But I'm worried about you, Joe. About your job at the plant. There's a war on, you know. Won't they be needing you at work?"

Mr. Sheldon had sighed. "There'll always be a war on, I'm afraid. They may always need men at defense plants." His face brightened. "But this may be the only time in history that Corrie will star in the sixth-grade play. I'm going to take the day off and go."

Corrie had acted her heart out that day. She had thrown her soul into every line of the comedy, and the audience had loved it. Her father, the only male there, had laughed and laughed, and Mrs. Lewis had laughed so hard that tears ran down her cheeks. It had been the best play any sixth-grade class in Pointer, Michigan, had ever put on. Maybe, Corrie thought, maybe it was the best play that anybody anywhere had ever put on.

Afterward, over grape juice and cookies, she saw how the mothers fluttered around her father. All except for a few who were clustered in little groups near the other side of the gym. Skinny Mrs. Andrews was talking to Mrs. Stanston, for instance. Corrie knew both of them because their husbands worked at the plant with her father. She was standing near the rolled-up volleyball net waiting for Sandra, when bits of their conversation came floating over to where she stood.

"—a surprise that he'd be here. My Irving went to work. Personally I think that's where a man *ought* to be."

"Well, what can you expect? He gave up that foreman's job, you know. Said he didn't want it. I call that—"

"You can call it whatever you want, but *I* call it foolishness!"

"If it was *my* husband, why, I'd—"

As Corrie stared at the photo album now, she remembered the hurt that had exploded inside her stomach that day. "But you don't understand!" she had wanted to shout. "It *isn't* foolishness! It *isn't!*" But she hadn't said that. She hadn't said anything.

She had stood quietly with wet palms and a dry mouth. Then Sandra had come dashing up. Her face had been flushed, and she still wore the clown suit she had used for the play.

"Oh, Corrie! Weren't we good? My mother said we were the best two in the play!" Happily she stood beside Corrie. "And I'm so glad your dad came. Don't you love to hear him laugh? Just look, Corrie, just look at all those women giggling around him."

Corrie had glanced over near the punchbowl where her father stood. Sandra was right. Lots of the mothers and the teachers were fluttering around him like teenagers.

"Look," Sandra cried. "Even Miss Newberg is laughing. Let's get over there closer so we can see if her face cracks. All the seventh-graders say that she's never laughed before." Giggling, Sandra moved closer to the group.

As she followed, Corrie had looked at her father and suddenly realized how very handsome he was, with his white even teeth and his dark wavy hair. He had a way of looking and listening to every person— man or woman—as though that person was the finest person in the world. That thought made Corrie feel proud and happy again. People were what mattered to her father—what did he care about a silly old job? He knew what was important to him. What other people thought was fine for themselves, but her dad had to live his life the way he felt best. Corrie smiled as she watched him, and she didn't mind at all that Mrs. Andrews and Mrs. Stanston were still whispering in the corner.

Mrs. Sheldon had also noticed her husband's popularity that afternoon. Corrie remembered how she had walked past the cookie plates without even looking at the refreshments. Later she told Corrie that she wished she had worn her black dress because it made her look slimmer.

"The way those women carried on with you, Joe!" she said as the four of them walked home. "Why, they acted like a bunch of giggling schoolgirls." She was walking fast and not looking at anyone else, and her feet were making that peculiar scuffing sound they always made.

"But you're the only woman I really care about," Mr. Sheldon said, putting his arm around her waist, trying to slow her down.

"Joe! Heavens! People can see!" Mrs. Sheldon blushed and brushed his arm away. But her steps became slower. She cleared her throat. "Guess I have to admit that those women did look fine, though. Do you know what I found out? I'm the fattest mother in the sixth-grade class. I don't think there was another mother there half as fat as me."

"That means there's twice as much of you to love," Mr. Sheldon told her.

"Goodness!" Mrs. Sheldon said, blushing again. But Corrie saw that she looked pleased.

"For the love of pete!" Mrs. Lewis declared. "I never heard anything like it. Why, flies could light on the words from that man's mouth, they come out so full of sugar."

"There's nothing wrong with a mouth full of sugar, Lewie," Mr. Sheldon told her. "It tastes mighty good, I can tell you. Besides, why shouldn't I be saying nice things? Why shouldn't I be happy? Ain't I the father of the star of the play we just saw? Ain't I?" He turned to Corrie and ran his hand over her head. "You were good, Corrie. You did me proud."

These words were echoing in Corrie's mind now as she stared at the photo album. She had made him proud then, and he had told her lots of times that she made him proud. But what about now? Now, when he was no longer able to speak? What would he think of her now? He hated to see people "mope," as he called it, and she'd been moping half the day. And what good was it doing anyone? Alan and Arthur had looked so forlorn all morning, and she'd probably scared them to death with her wild crying. Poor Sandra and Lewie had only tried to help, and look what she'd done. Would her father say that she had "done him proud" today? Corrie bit her lip. He'd be ashamed, she decided, that's what he'd be— ashamed. Life, as he saw it, was no good unless you were making someone happy.

Suddenly Corrie slammed the pages of the album together and jumped to her feet. In two seconds she was at the shed door. She flung it open.

"Hold on out there!" she yelled to Lewie and her

brothers, still working in the snow. "I'm getting my stuff on and then I'm coming out and I'm going to show you how to make a *real* snowman!"

When Mrs. Sheldon came from the hospital in the middle of the afternoon, she looked tired. Corrie saw that her eyes were red with fatigue and her face was lined and pale. Her hair straggled out from the bun on the nape of her neck, her dress was wrinkled.

"He's still awful bad," she whispered. Then she turned to Alan and Arthur. "How's my little men? Been listening to the radio?"

"Momma," Corrie said, "haven't you had any sleep at all?"

Mrs. Sheldon shook her head. She hurried to the coat closet just off the kitchen and began hanging up her wraps. The boys followed her.

"Did you see that big snowman we made?" Alan asked.

"It's not as big as the ones Daddy always makes, but maybe next time it will be," Arthur said. "We used that big straw hat you had hanging here in the closet. The one you always use for berry picking."

"That's fine," Mrs. Sheldon said, trying to smooth her hair into place. "That's fine, boys."

Arthur and Alan stared at her. Corrie stood in the archway, and she could see that her brothers were puzzled and a bit disappointed. It wasn't any fun when their mother didn't complain about the things they used for their snowmen.

"Have you eaten anything today, Momma?" she asked.

"No, no, I guess I haven't. To tell you the truth, I never thought of it. One of the nurses brought me some coffee once."

Corrie turned to her brothers. "You guys scram now. Momma and I want to talk awhile. Play in the bedroom." She took her mother's arm and guided her from the hallway. Suddenly she felt older, wiser, stronger than her mother.

"I can fix a little something for myself," Mrs. Sheldon said, when they were alone in the kitchen. "I can fix myself something to eat, honey."

Corrie ached when she saw how tired her mother looked. It was awful to see her robust mother look so dejected, so defeated. "I'll just scramble you some eggs, Momma. The boys and I ate lunch a long time ago. Here—here's some coffee—I've been keeping it hot for you."

"He's awful bad," Mrs. Sheldon said when everything was settled on the table. "Daddy's awful bad, Corrie." She ran her finger around the coffee cup, stared at the hot steam rising from it.

Corrie stared at the movement, watched the steam. "Did he talk at all?"

"Not really. He's on more morphine now. But even that can't stop all his pain anymore. He just mumbled a few times—about the garden again."

Corrie swallowed loudly. Then she dug her finger-nails into the palms of her fists. "Is he going to die, Momma?" Even as she spoke, she knew the answer, but still she had to ask.

Her mother was silent—caught motionless in fatigue, in grief. Then she leaned forward and blurted out her words. "Corrie—the doctor told me he didn't see how Daddy lived through the night. He can't figure out how Daddy has even managed to live this long."

Corrie caught her breath. "But—"

"We've been fooling ourselves—fooling ourselves! Daddy can't ever be well again, ever—and we've got to face up to it. It's too late, too late."

"But what about those operations? All those medicines?"

"Sometimes cancer can be stopped by operations —sometimes by medicines. But sometimes it just can't be stopped at all." Mrs. Sheldon's voice broke, and she covered her face with her hands. "Oh, Corrie —he's in such pain! He's suffering so much, Corrie!"

Corrie felt as though a gigantic hand had seized her around the neck. The hand was squeezing her throat so tight that tears sprang to her eyes. "Oh! Oh, Momma!"

Suddenly the woman flung her hands from her face. She pushed back her chair. "Well now," she said, "I'll get at them dishes."

Corrie jumped up. "But you hardly even touched your lunch, Momma."

163

"I'm not hungry. I'm sorry—I'm just not hungry." Mrs. Sheldon started toward the sink, then she stopped. She staggered, her face ashen. Then she stumbled and reached for the counter.

"Momma!" Corrie was at her mother's side in an instant. "Are you all right? You look so white, Momma!"

"I'm just a little dizzy, that's all." Her voice was shaking. "I guess I got up too fast."

Corrie felt a strange power surge through her as she stared at her mother's ravaged face. "You've got to get some sleep, that's what," she said firmly. "You've got to get some rest." Suddenly she knew that if she had to she could whisk the plump figure of her mother into her arms and carry her into the bedroom. Strength made her voice steady and even. "You've got to lie down for a while, Momma. You've got to get some rest."

"But the dishes—I—"

"Oh, for goodness sake, Momma, *I* can do the dishes."

"Can you? Can you manage all alone?" Mrs. Sheldon was staring at Corrie, poised at the end of her questions, and in the silence, Corrie saw that her mother was asking about more than dirty dishes.

"Yes," she said firmly. "I can do whatever I have to do now, Momma. Really I can. Go on now, get some rest. Lie down for a while."

After her mother had gone, Corrie stood at the sink and washed the few dishes. She felt almost numb, drained of all sorrow, the hulk of an empty machine. There was this to be done, and there was that to be done, and she went about doing them without even knowing, without thinking. She had strength, strength and power, only in her body— her brain seemed to have lifted itself far above the earth, and it had left instructions only for simple things. Her father was dying, there was little doubt of that now. A tiny place deep inside her soul had known it all the time, all the time, all the time.

Through the haze of her movements, she heard the radio playing loud and brassy. She ran to the living room, twirled it off. Her outraged brothers jumped to their feet.

"We're going for a walk," she said.

"But we were listening to a good program."

"I said that we are going for a walk."

"Our mittens are still wet from the snowman," Arthur said.

"Our coats are, too," Alan told her. "They're hanging in the basement, all drippy."

"Well, we'll get them, wet or not," Corrie told them. She stared down first at Alan, then at Arthur. She hadn't raised her voice, but her words were like whips. They left the room silently. "Momma needs the house quiet so she can sleep."

When they opened the storm door, Corrie saw that the snow was slowly melting. A warm wind was blowing in from Lake Michigan, and little rivers of water were flowing down the windows. Water was dripping from the roof, a light, wet mist was falling from the sky. Corrie stared and started thinking. Maybe the whole world was weeping for her father, maybe the whole world was crying.

The boys stared at their snowman. The button eyes had fallen a bit, and when Corrie looked at it, she thought the snowman looked as though he might be crying too.

She had to be alone! Corrie wished she could run so fast she could outrace her thoughts. Her stomach was churning, her mouth dry; there was a peculiar ringing in her ears. But there were her brothers, Alan still staring at the snowman, and Arthur tromping down the steps. She'd have to stay calm, stay sensible for their sakes.

"Dumb old snowman," Arthur said.

"It's okay if he melts," Alan told him. "Winter's just getting started. We'll make lots more." The three of them trudged down the sidewalk in the mist.

"Hey! Hey, kids!" Mrs. Lewis was standing on her front porch waving. "Come on over, why don't you? I just made some cookies!"

Before Corrie could refuse, Alan and Arthur had darted ahead. She waved and hurried after them.

"Mercy!" Mrs. Lewis said, as she herded them inside. "Your coats feel all wet and soggy."

"Corrie made us put on wet coats and go outside," Arthur declared. "We was listening to the radio, and she made us stop."

"And go out in wet coats," Alan added.

Mrs. Lewis raised her right eyebrow and glanced questioningly at Corrie.

"Momma needs to get some sleep," Corrie said. "She just got home from the hospital, and she hasn't slept at all." She looked down at the floor and squeezed her fists together. "I was thinking that a walk might make us feel better somehow."

"We don't want to go for no walk," Arthur said.

"And we wasn't making noise," Alan told her. "Hardly no noise, anyway."

"Pshaw!" Mrs. Lewis hung the two coats over the backs of her only two chairs. Then she dragged them closer to the oil burner. In the winter Mrs. Lewis always shut off the doors to the other rooms in her house and lived solely in the kitchen and the living room with all her necessities piled around the oil burner between the two areas. She did this, she always said, because "Them fellows that sell the oil are highway robbers!"

Now she clicked her tongue. "Don't I know how much noise you two wild animals can make? No noise indeed! You'll get a wart on your tongue telling whoppers like that. Corrie did right. Your ma needs some sleep."

Corrie kept her coat on. It was hot and close near the stove and the smell of wet wool was overpowering, but she didn't care.

"I caught you guys just in time," Mrs. Lewis said. "You can lick the bowl. After we finished that

167

snowman, I had a little nap, and when I woke up I was starving for some good homemade cookies. 'Course the batter always tastes better than the cookies, so I already licked the spoon and beaters. But you guys can finish up the bowl. Go ahead, fellas."

"Hey, it's warm out here in the kitchen," Arthur shouted.

" 'Course it is!" the old woman declared. "Ain't I got the oven on? You don't need to think that I ain't got money to pay for heat in the winter. I do. Besides, I *like* having all my stuff all comfy here together."

But Corrie was sure it wasn't comfort alone that inspired Lewie to spend her winters in just two rooms. The old woman was poor, dirt poor, her father always said. But no one ever said such a thing to Lewie's face. No one ever dared. Corrie stared at Lewie and wondered how she could be so strong, so sensible, so—so—happy.

She was straightening a pillow on the sofa now. "This davenport is better than a bed anyway," she said.

"Hey, this cookie dough is good!" Alan called.

"But he's trying to get more than me," Arthur shouted.

"You could eat faster if you didn't waste time talking," Mrs. Lewis shouted back. She lowered her voice and looked at Corrie. "Are you all right? You must be roasting in here, but you're shivering. Are you all right, child?"

Corrie nodded. "I guess I'm all right. I guess I am. Fixing that snowman today was good for me, I guess."

"You'll find out that doing the things that your dad taught you will always be good for you."

The two stood alone in silence, then Corrie said, "He's going to die, Lewie. He's going to die for sure."

"I know." The old woman shook her head, and the lines on her face grew deeper. "I've been afraid of this all along. I've been afraid of this."

"And there's nothing I can do," Corrie said, twisting her hands together. "Oh, Lewie, life is awful, awful! We get all caught up in sickness and war and death, and there's nothing we can do about it."

Mrs. Lewis cocked her head. Corrie saw the lines in her face get softer. "You may be right in some ways, child. Them big things like death and war and sickness—why, I guess we can't stop them. But there is something we can do about them, Corrie, and don't you ever forget it. You can decide how you want to act when them things hit you. You can figure that out for yourself."

Corrie leaned closer. "How you act?"

"How you feel, how you are. When something awful hits you, you can decide to moan and groan the rest of your life about how terrible everything is. Or you can say, 'Well that's an awful thing, no doubt about it, but I won't let it get the best of me. I'll keep looking for the good things in life even if the bad things knock me down now and then.' "

Corrie had a sudden picture of how Mr. Peterson looked, hobbling and mumbling in his dark tent shop. He's given up since his son left home, she thought; he's defeated and useless, and he makes everyone around him feel sad, too. What's the good in that? What's the good in that? She shook her head, and her glance fell on the pictures of Lewie's sons. They were her only children, and both of them had been killed in World War I. "Oh Lewie," she cried. "It just isn't fair!"

"Who told you life was supposed to be fair?" the old woman asked.

"But you've lost two sons and a husband, and some people never lose anybody."

Lewie clicked her tongue. "Child, child, don't you know this yet? It ain't what you lose that you got to think about—it's what you gain. I've gained a lot knowing the people I've known. You've gained a lot from your father, too, child."

Corrie felt so full of emotion she could barely breathe. As she looked at Lewie, she became aware of the tick of the alarm clock. Faintly, as though far, far away, she heard the sounds of her brothers' voices. She was trying to understand what Lewie was saying, but she smelled the cinnamon cookies, she saw the wetness of the coats. She frowned, angry and puzzled. How could ordinary things still be happening? How could she notice such crazy dumb things when her whole world was falling apart? She twisted the ends of her scarf. "I wish I could be alone somewhere."

Mrs. Lewis gestured toward the front door. "Why not go for a walk, then? That little rain out there ain't going to melt you. Leave the boys here and go off for a walk by yourself."

"But that's not fair. You've had Alan and Arthur most of the day. That's not fair to you."

"What's one man's meat is another man's poison. I like having them around, Corrie. They bring back memories. Happy ones."

"Oh Lewie! How can you stand it?"

"I don't take any guff from them brothers of yours."

"That's not what I mean! I mean—I mean—" She gestured helplessly to the pictures of the two soldiers, the picture of Horace Lewis, the cluttered crowded room.

"I know what you mean." The old woman's voice softened. "Listen, Corrie, anybody who's lived a full life has got troubles. Lots of them. But you got to take the bad with the good. Sometimes, you know, you got to have the bad so that you can *tell* the good when you finally get it."

Nervously Corrie pulled at the sleeve of her coat. "Daddy used to say something like that."

"Go for that walk, child," Lewie said.

Slowly, Corrie moved to the door. She reached for the knob. "Oh, Lewie, I—" Corrie stopped, the door half opened. She swallowed loudly, then started out into the rain. "I just wanted to say thank you, Lewie. Thanks!" The door slammed and she was standing alone on the porch.

The mist had become a light rain now, and the melted snow was beginning to gush into the gutters. The sky was gray. A few streetlights flickered on in the dusky afternoon, and far away, from the direction of the lake, the foghorn began to moan. Corrie started walking down the street.

How could it be that the streets seemed just the same even though her father would no longer be able to walk them? How could the earth continue to turn, the sun continue to function? It isn't fair, Corrie thought. It isn't fair that birth or death means so little.

Suddenly she saw a man hurrying up the sidewalk toward her, and her soul gave a quick leap. He looked so much like her father. He had that same bouncy rhythm to his steps, the same eager movement. But then he turned, and Corrie saw that he didn't look like her father at all, and she hated him with a fierce intensity because he was strong and healthy. She jammed her fists into her pockets and walked faster.

"Corrie?"

The voice came from behind. Corrie whirled around. "Daryl!"

"Hey, I thought that was you, Corrie. I'm just on my way to work. You going out somewhere?"

Corrie's hands were drenched with sweat. For years she had dreamed of accidentally meeting Daryl Hanson on the street. In her imagination she had been beautiful, dressed in chiffon and carrying flowers. There had been soft music playing, and the moon had been full. But now here she was in her horrid winter coat with a tear-stained face. The only music was the distant bellowing of the foghorn, and the sky was gray with the afternoon's feeble sun. "I'm just out walking," she said. "I thought I might walk to Lincoln Bridge."

Daryl fell into step beside her. He was so tall that Corrie almost felt short. She straightened her shoulders.

"I was talking to someone about your dad today. I guess he's pretty bad now."

Corrie clenched her fists. "Yes."

"I'm sorry. He's a great guy all right. Funny how I could always hear his voice cheering above everybody else at the basketball games."

"He liked to see you play."

They walked a few moments in silence. Then Daryl cleared his throat. "Now I see why you gave up the school play. I couldn't figure it out before, because you were the best one at tryouts last week."

Corrie felt her mouth drop open. "You think so?"

"Sure! Everybody thinks so."

Corrie was so astonished she was nearly speechless. Then her words came bursting out. "I was hoping that you were going to get a part too, Daryl."

"Naw—I can't act my way out of a paper bag. Basketball's my game. But you—gosh, Corrie, you even made the principal laugh when you tried out for that part in the play!"

"The principal!" Nervously Corrie smoothed down her bangs. "I didn't know so many people were watching."

"Yeah, lots of us saw you, Corrie. Everybody said you were really good." He stopped and turned to her, and Corrie saw that he had a streak of dirt on his face. His jacket was ripped, and his sleeves were too short. Why, he's not perfect either, she thought, and the idea made her feel fine.

He was kicking at a lump of melting snow. "It's funny—up until tryouts I didn't even know that you were in high school now. But listen, I got to turn here—I'm supposed to be at the gas station in ten minutes." He started to turn, then looked back. "I'll talk to you again soon. Okay?"

"Sure," Corrie said. "Sure."

She stood for a moment and watched him hurry up the street. Her chest felt so full of joy she wanted to jump, to run, to wave her arms about. But then she felt the rain on her face and remembered why she was walking. And she felt a terrible thud of guilt. How could she feel happy when her father lay dying? When all the things that made him so fine were dying there with him? She lowered her head and turned toward Lincoln Bridge.

When she reached the middle of the bridge, she

stood at the railing and stared down at the water. The rain and snow had run into the river, and the current was strong as it rushed toward Lake Michigan. She watched the water hurrying beneath her, and she remembered what her father had said when the two of them had been standing on the bridge there one day.

"Why, the water down there today is the very same water that's been on earth since the beginning of time," he said. "It changes form over the years all right, but it's still the same. The water here in Lincoln River—why it might be the very same water that was here when Abraham Lincoln himself was president."

Corrie had thought about that idea. It seemed true all right—water evaporated and became clouds, then it fell as rain or snow, ran down to the river, evaporated, and became . . . "I guess it might be the same water," she said. "But don't you think it seems sad, Daddy? I mean, the water is still here, but President Lincoln, the man, is gone."

"Now *that's* where you're wrong," her father had said. And he took her hand and walked her down the avenue. He stopped the next three people they met and asked them who Lincoln was.

"So there you are, Corrie," he said triumphantly as the third person walked away, puzzled but polite. "Every one of the three knew who Lincoln was. They didn't mention the river or the bridge or the street—they mentioned the *man*. So how can he be 'gone,' then, if he's still so real to everyone?"

Corrie had been confused then, but now she thought perhaps she was beginning to understand what he might have meant. Lewie had tried to tell her that same thing, but it was all so complicated. What was a person, then, if he could be dead yet still live on? And why was it that some people died and were remembered, whereas others died and were immediately forgotten?

Someone was walking on the other end of the bridge. Corrie huddled closer to the rails, not wanting to speak, not wanting to be seen. But just as the figure started to pass, it hesitated.

"Corrie? Corrie Sheldon?"

It was Mr. Beckman, carrying a huge black umbrella. He peered at her. "Is that you? Why, you're soaking wet!"

"It's okay."

Mr. Beckman caught his breath. "Your dad! Is he—"

"He's the same."

Mr. Beckman sighed and shook his head. "It's awful, that's what, awful. It just don't seem fair! A fellow like your dad—why, he—the things he'd done for me over the years! And always a joke, always a smile. I ain't never going to forget that man, never! Why he—" Suddenly he stopped, breathless. He made a quick movement and thrust his huge umbrella handle into Corrie's hand. "You take this!" he said loudly. "That's what you do. Now you just take this umbrella and keep it! Yes sir, I mean it! You keep that umbrella, you just keep it!" Still talking, Mr. Beckman backed away, turned, and nearly ran on down the street.

Corrie stared after him in amazement. An umbrella! What in the world did she want with that huge umbrella? She was already so wet, a little more rain wouldn't matter. Still, though, Mr. Beckman had acted so strange about it—as though it would be a gift to him, a favor to *him,* if she accepted what he was offering. Why had he done such a crazy thing?

She turned and looked at the water again. Daddy would laugh at me, she thought. He'd laugh if he could see me here standing all wet in the rain holding this big black umbrella. She leaned against the cement again, and nuzzled the umbrella stick next to her face. From far off in the mist came the bellow of the foghorn.

People are so peculiar, she thought, so unpredictable and peculiar. She remembered that she had told her father that very thought one time. They had been walking in the woods, and their voices had seemed hushed in the darkness of the forest. They had stopped to rest for a while—Mr. Sheldon had already had his first operation, and he tired quickly.

"Why, people aren't funny at all," he had said. "Not a bit. Once you learn *why* they do the things they do, then everything makes sense."

"Then what makes people do the things they do? Tell me that, Daddy, tell me that."

"Well, I'm not a great thinker," he said, sitting down on a fallen tree, "and I don't have the big words to make a little idea sound grand, but here's what I think . . ."

He gestured her to the other end of the tree trunk. Corrie remembered that a red cardinal had been calling from a treetop as she sat down and listened to her father.

"I think everyone does everything in order to get more love—they want to love themselves more, or they want others to love them more, or they want some kind of God to love them more. And sometimes, although not often, they do something simply because they love someone else as much as they love themselves."

"Love!" Corrie shook her head. "Oh, I don't think that could be right, Daddy. Lots of people kill each other—or steal—or hurt. How could they do those things because of love?"

"They do them for mixed-up ideas of love," her father said. "Some of them think that they can love themselves more if they get more money or more things or more power, and they think they have to destroy in order to get those things. See, what they're trying to do is get more self-love by taking rather than earning. But it doesn't work that way, you know, and they soon find it out. You got to earn all the love you get in life. You got to earn it somehow."

Corrie was watching the forest floor. Some ants were building a tunnel around two pieces of decaying bark. A blue flower was standing all alone in the midst of dying moss. Everywhere in the forest new life was springing from death.

"You take me," her father said. "I work every day in the defense plant, even though I hate that job. I do it because of love. I want to have my family love me, so I provide for them."

"Oh, Daddy! We'd love you even if you didn't make any money!"

"Ah," her father said, "but then I wouldn't love myself."

Corrie was silent a long while, seeing in her memory all the times she had watched her father at work. "And your garden?" she said at last. "That's where I think you work the hardest. Why do you do that?"

He laughed. "Because of love again. I can give food to people that I love, and I love myself more because I can make things grow. It makes me feel good to be able to make things grow."

He paused then, and he stared at the trees in front of them. He rested his elbows on his knees and lowered his voice. "You know, Corrie—it's a grand thing, almost a godlike thing, to see the seeds that you plant grow into something good and useful. It's a fine thing to think that they'll be living on even after you're dead and gone."

At the time Corrie had been speechless, struck mute by the depth of feeling her father had put into his words. She had simply stared at him, and the red cardinal's call had echoed in the stillness.

But now, standing in the rain on the bridge,

thinking of her father's life, remembering what Lewie had said, recalling the words of Sandra, of Daryl, of Mr. Beckman, she felt the stirring of a new idea, a strange new thought.

Suppose, she thought, suppose Daddy was talking about more than just a garden plot and vegetable seeds—suppose he was talking about people and ideas and dreams and hopes. His thoughts could be the seeds, and the garden could be all the people he knew, and he tried to plant all his dreams and hopes in everyone around him, and he just hoped that something good and useful would grow because of him, even after he had died.

The idea took Corrie's breath away—suddenly everything fell into place, and all the pieces seemed to fit. The people who lived on after they died were the ones who planted lots of seeds in everyone they knew while they lived. Evil people with mixed-up ideas of love planted evil seeds, and they were remembered because something ugly and horrid grew from them. Others lived on forever because good things were still growing from the seeds that they had planted.

Corrie felt as though she had been walking on a tightrope across a deep chasm, and she had just reached the other side safely. She took a deep breath. "I'm Daddy's garden!" she whispered with amazement. "He planted the seeds of his thoughts in me, and he hoped something good would grow!"

Something huge began welling up inside of her.

She turned and looked ahead. Far away, on the top of the hill, hospital lights were blinking on. The rain had stopped. She punched the umbrella button —it came fluttering down and collapsed on the stick. She thrust it under her arm and started running— running up the hill to the hospital.

Miss Lutz was sitting at her desk on the third floor. She looked up in amazement as Corrie, wet, breathless, excited, came rushing up the corridor.

"My dad—" she was panting. "Is he—"

"He's the same, Corrie. The same. But whatever are you doing? What's the matter, Corrie?"

"I've got to see my father, Miss Lutz. Can I see him now? Can I see him, please?"

"Well, it's against the— Oh, Corrie—he can't talk to you, honey. He's unconscious, you know."

"That doesn't matter. I only have to see him for a minute. I've got to tell him something."

Miss Lutz bit her lip. She stared at the water dripping from Corrie's umbrella. "He won't hear you, dear. He won't know what you're saying."

"Yes he will," Corrie said, nodding. "And it'll only take a minute. I only want to see him for a minute." She teetered back and forth in excitement —she could feel heat from her body radiate in all directions.

The woman reached out. "I'll hold your wet things out here," she said. "Go ahead in, dear, go ahead in."

Corrie opened the door and hurried into the

ward. She tiptoed behind the white curtain. There was her father, lying flat on the bed, motionless and pale. She moved nearer to his side, and she stared down at him with a love so great she had to swallow quickly to keep it all inside of her. What a marvelous man he is, she thought, how lucky I was to have him for a father. My whole life I'll remember the things he taught me. I'll share the things he taught me.

She leaned over him now, hearing his quiet breathing, and then she placed her cheek next to his, and she started to whisper in his ear.

"You don't have to worry anymore now, Daddy," she said. "It's okay now, and I understand. The garden is doing fine, Daddy. Your garden will always be fine."